THE WICKEDEST OF THINGS

Russel Barrie

– Russel Barrie

Library of Congress Control Number: 2018675309
Printed in the United States of America

Capitalism is the astounding belief that the wickedest of men will do the wickedest of things for the greatest good of everyone.

JOHN MAYNARD KEYNES

ONE

The first time Reid died it was downright embarrassing. As the ramp dropped on his landing craft, the gunfire had started up immediately. Muzzle flashes blossomed from windows on the boardwalk. They mixed with the darting green fireflies of tracer, whizzing to and fro across the beach. Bravely, he'd charged down the ramp into the tempest of flames, explosions going off all around him, only to run directly into the path of a landing tank. His first foray ended with him crushed to the consistency of bolognaise in the first thirty seconds.

The second time he got farther, but did no better. He made it up the boardwalk and into the town as the attack went on, running on rooftops beneath shrieking fighter planes. Snipers were everywhere, and he could hear bullets zip and crack by as he ran. Somewhere offshore, the big guns of a warship boomed adding a bass section to this industrial symphony. It was like Hades in concert and Reid couldn't help but marvel at how great the whole thing sounded. Of course, he was so consumed by this, he didn't watch where his own feet were going. A step too far off the rooftop sent him tumbling down four floors onto some North Korean soldiers loitering below. As his view faded to black again, he noted that the only kill he'd scored this round had been from *landing* on someone. God, he was bad at this.

From behind him, he heard more than a few stifled laughs from those watching him play. Well, they were allowed to laugh at his gamer skills, as long as they still did what he told them.

Shifting, the controller in his hands, Reid began a new round in the video game, returning to the same start point on the beach, his brow tight in concentration. A boyish face usually hid his years well, but his forehead had begun to show lines in this stress. Fascination lines, someone special had once called them, from constantly being amazed at the world, but that was a long time ago. The lines layered up to his brown hair, which he kept cut short, though more out of laziness than style. His eyes, greyish and always calculating, seemed to change colour in different light. Right now, they were cold grey and focused on one goal: not embarrassing himself again. He had to get through this level to finish evaluating it.

Not normally a fan of first person shooters, Reid still had to admit the game was well made. The graphics and sound were good and the gameplay was solid, despite his total lack of skill. He felt some pride for that. He was the creative director for this game.

The *Uncommon Valor* videogame series had been dominating markets for over a decade. It dropped you into the combat boots of American Marines who were fighting through the wars of the twentieth century, struggling through mud and blood on a thousand battlefields. It was a billion dollar franchise, and the crown jewel of Metric Game Studios. After a few years of working at Metric, Reid had built a reputation as someone who could get things done. So, when the new owners had started planning a new entry, he'd been given the job to direct it. At the time, it had been a brilliant new challenge to keep him busy and he'd leapt at the chance. He didn't even care that he was terrible at shooters.

He did now, though. *Uncommon Valor: Forgotten War*

was just months away from release. The pressure was on, and he was a target; in the game and out of it.

As he slumped over dead for the sixth time, Reid bit his cheek to keep from cursing and tried to concentrate. Abandoning subtlety, he just started shooting anything that moved. At this point, he remembered where every enemy in the game was, which made it easier. Onward he soldiered, being constantly riddled with bullets, but grinding down the level yard by yard. Still, if it had been possible to trip over his virtual shoelaces and break his own neck he would have.

Finally, after putting aside petty things like thinking, he fought his way through the battle to the bloody finish. As the screen faded to white in victory, a quote from Abraham Lincoln popped up, marking the end of the stage. Bizarrely, *Uncommon Valor* rewarded a player that beat a level by giving them a caption saying something profound. Again, FPS was not his thing, but Reid wondered why you would put something cerebral in for flavor after an hour of just blowing stuff up.

Staring at the words on the screen, he frowned. Though they were attributed to Lincoln, it was something the stove-top hatted president had never said. He knew why the mistake was there, but he decided to keep his mouth shut. There was enough to talk about.

From where they huddled together watching, the programmers started to perk up. Each one was the head of a section on the development team. The lead, a plump, bespectacled, fuzzy-bearded man named Jason, stepped forward.

"Well," He said, looking confident. "What do you think?"

"Better."

The confident look wavered.

"How much better?" He asked heavily.

"It's good. Its almost there."

All three of their faces fell and a half-exasperated sigh simultaneously left their lungs. The little office was off the bullpen where the bulk of their programming team still laboured. Tanya, one of the three supervisors in the room, cast a dejected look toward the door and the workers beyond, knowing they wouldn't want to hear this. She was probably right. At this point, he suspected a few had begun to hate him, but he was still the boss.

"What the hell is wrong with it now?" Jason continued. "We made all the changes you asked for."

Reid nodded. Indeed they had.

"I know," he acknowledged. "And I appreciate the work. We're just not done yet."

The last developer was a balding man by the name of Andrew known for his sense of humor. That was conspicuously absent as he crossed his arms over his chest.

"There can't be anything else." He said sharply. "We've edited this section five times."

Actually, the real number was seven, but he kept that to himself.

"The Inchon landing is the centerpiece of the game." He declared. "Since they bought out the studio, Horizon has been calling me every day looking for results. Do you want to deal with this or some hard-ass new boss?"

He regarded all of them steely.

"We can't have anything less than perfection."

"You think we're not trying?!" Jason spat back at him.

Reid took a deep breath.

"I didn't say that." He said, softly. "But we need to think about the history here."

"What?"

"Can't we cut down on the casualties a little bit? We're already stretching history with that armoured attack up the causeway to Inchon in the next stage. This stage is a charnel house. Taking Wolmido, the marines only had—"

"Fourteen casualties."

The room parroted the often-quoted number together. A few snickers followed close behind.

"Wait," Jason raised a hand. "Are you seriously saying we need to cut the fighting in a first person shooter?"

"No," Reid was getting angry. "No, I'm saying we mix exaggerated gameplay with fact. Wolmido wasn't a bloody mess and the tank attack on the causeway never even happened. It's all about balance."

"In the Pusan perimeter fighting, there's a section where you knock grenades back at the enemy with a baseball bat." Tanya pointed out, sourly. "This isn't exactly a documentary. Who's going to care?"

I do.

"We all should," Reid insisted. "History matters as much as story. It isn't bad for players to expect more from the game."

Jason glared at him. Beneath the fuzz of a beard on his face, his jaw was so tight he had to be grinding his teeth.

"Yeah, but they *aren't* though." He growled. "Nobody's expecting more. Nobody cares about that kind of detail. This is a multi-player twitch shooter. We're never going to finish the damn thing if you're nitpicking every detail. We worked on that causeway attack for three months."

Reid looked back at the screen, at that dumb Lincoln quote and, beneath it, the figures frozen in perfect digital combat. He thought back to the perfect sound, the tight gameplay and then to the labour and sweat his team had given. He wavered, then he thought about the hours he had stayed awake obsessing over the game, keeping his mind busy.

His cheek twitched.

"I think we should cut it."

At this, Jason threw up his hands so violently his glasses temporarily slipped and he had to press them back into place. A chorus of complaints erupted from around the room. The programmers all howled in protest, and Reid argued back, urging them to make his changes and growing angrier by the second.

No one agreed with him. There just wasn't any goodwill left with them at this point, so much had he poisoned the well. Just when he was about to abandon all civility and tell everyone to shut up and get in line, a metallic hammering broke into the conversation.

Across the room, banging a high-heeled shoe down on a metal desk was the most strikingly beautiful woman Reid had ever seen. Clad in a dark blue pantsuit and a white blouse, she was slender to the point of almost being fragile. Her wavy black hair dropped down past her shoulders, framing a face so perfectly sculpted it was as though she were cut from marble. Living proof that God was an artist. Her skin was the lightest shade of mocha, her eyes a bold green and her frown pure menace.

"Take it easy!" she yelled. The expensive-looking shoe in her hand took more punishment as she hammered it against the desk again. "God, is it always like this around here?"

Then, with seamless grace, she bent over and slipped the shoe back on next to its twin. The frown on her face dropped a little and she strode confidently over to Jason, where she extended a hand to him, completely heedless of the argument that had been raging.

"Hi, Reid Sheraton?"

Jason took the proffered hand and, in the grand tradition of gaming professionals faced with a beautiful woman, he forgot his own name. There was a half second of awkward silence as he looked at her blankly. In the end, Reid broke in.

"Actually, I'm Reid Sheraton," he said. "Can I help you?"

Her frown blossomed into a smile and, still holding his hand in a handshake, she easily hauled Jason out of the way. Even in heels, she was still a head shorter than him.

"You're not what I expected." She shook his hand. Her grip was strong, her hands cool. "But it's great to meet you. I've heard a lot of good things."

Reid doubted it—working with people was not his strong suit—but he smiled back anyway.

"What can I do for you?"

Her eyes flicked out to the circle of curious faces watching the exchange. Since she had entered it, the whole room seemed to revolve around her. She turned back to him, seemingly nonplussed by the attention.

"I was hoping we could talk privately. Can I buy you lunch?"

He would have gladly walked over broken glass coated in lemon juice to avoid continuing the debate with his developers. Any reprieve felt like a godsend, but he still shook his head.

"Now really isn't the best time," He looked over at the others. "We still have a few decisions to make."

The enigmatic woman didn't miss a beat.

"Well," She said. "Then let's make them now so we can all go eat."

She spun away from Reid, his mouth hanging open in confusion then faced the team.

"For the island landing, you don't really need all that combat do you?"

Jason, not yet recovered from her charm offensive, managed one word.

"Well..."

"Its a few stages into the game anyway, right?" The woman went on. "So the player already knows the risks, this is just a new arena to play in. You could cut half the opposition and casualties and it wouldn't make a difference."

The three programmers looked at each other quizzically.

"Maybe," Tanya conceded. Being the same sex, her brain was maybe working a bit better than her colleagues when dealing with the beautiful stranger. "We have a few sweeping battles before this, but what about the difficulty? If we get rid of half the enemy soldiers then the whole thing becomes a walkover."

Sure enough, the woman in blue had an answer for this.

"What about timing then?" She ventured. "If the marines need to take the island fast, can't you have a time limit for taking all the objectives? It's an easy fix, and it makes sense."

Again, the three shared a look. To Reid's astonishment, for the first time he saw them all nod in agreement.

"That's workable," Tanya said. "It adds a new dynamic we haven't done yet. Hey, it probably makes sense historically too."

Now a bystander in this conversation, Reid suddenly had to interject.

"Well, actually that..."

"And *you*," The woman turned to him before he could finish the thought. "If we're cutting down on the combat for that stage, it only makes sense to keep the causeway battle."

"What? Why..."

"Because it's a shooter!" She laughed, like the thought was obvious.

Reid felt a flush coming on. He wanted to be angry, but this was more from embarrassment at being put on the spot.

"I just... I think we need to respect history."

She shook her head, her wavy dark hair swaying with

the motion.

"You can have history," She said. "But, you need to make room for gameplay too. Fighting tanks sounds like the kind of thing you need in *Uncommon Valor*."

"Yeah, but..."

"I was eavesdropping in the hall. Didn't you *just say* it was all about balance?"

A snort of suppressed laughter came from the direction of the three programmers, someone clearly enjoying the sight of Reid's own words thrown back in his face. His eyes flicked over to find Tanya turning red from holding in her mirth. At her elbow, Andrew's amiable smile had returned. Jason still looked like he was in love.

For a moment, he wanted to argue, but she had a point. He shrugged helplessly.

The woman before him grinned slyly.

"Perfect," She said, ending the debate. "Lunch then?"

He looked around the room briefly then nodded. The team took this as a sign and began to disperse, though still glancing back out of curiosity. After a few seconds, he turned back to the newcomer.

His guest was already walking toward the door. Clearly, she was ready for food and done with conversation. Still baffled, Reid had to scramble quickly to keep pace as she walked out of the office.

"I guess, I can use the break." He muttered as he rushed. "But I didn't get your name, miss?"

"Oh," she said pausing, as if it her identity was an afterthought.

"Esin. Esin Shirzai." She smiled again, a beautiful

sight. “I’m your hard-ass new boss, Mr. Sheraton.”

TWO

It may have been a cold September morning in the game, but as they stepped outside the August sun was beating down intensely. The studio was located in an old orange stucco business complex, likely built in the 90s by someone depressed and colorblind. But across the street lay a beautiful local park the programmers used to escape from the gloom. It was the views that made it special. On three sides the mountains marked the horizon with jagged beauty. Their Snow-capped peaks meeting the sky. The fourth side faced the complex, not the most spectacular view in the world, but the new sign it bore read Horizon Inc. with its logo of a burst of light coming from behind the moon. So technically you could see the horizon from every angle.

Metric studios had been the previous name, but since the sale Reid assumed they were going to be Horizon Studios. As a corporate entity Horizon seemed omni-present. From the way you listened to music, to the way you watched TV, to the way you cooked your food to eat. There was no aspect of life where you couldn't encounter that logo. They covered all the senses. This was the first video game company they had bought though. They were starting at the very top buying the developer of *Uncommon Valor*, he was certain it had been far from cheap. Reid could only shrug at the thought. He doubted they had been more expensive than when Horizon had bought Google.

It was almost noon and as they walked across the street to the tables, he could see food trucks were already set up to greet their usual customers. Esin gestured that it was his choice, so Reid wandered over to his usual. A Korean-Mexican fusion truck with the apt name *Sticky Fingers*. Nara, the woman who ran it, smiled wide upon seeing him. That kind of attention made him a little uncomfortable, but he smiled back all the same and said good morning in Korean. His pronunciation l made him sound like a lisping drunk, but she had been very patient over the last few months at helping him tweak the syllables. The small talk went back and forth for a moment.

He gestured to the menu.

"What would you like?"

Esin, who had watched the exchange half impressed half amused, tilted her head curiously.

"You know what," The corners of her mouth perked up. "I trust you. Surprise me."

Reid turned and ordered, while Esin left to find a table. Moments later, he was walking over, two tissue-wrapped packages in hand. She had somehow found the only table with an umbrella and was sitting in the center in complete shade as though cowering from the light. She'd produced an oversize pair of sunglasses, giving her a slight insectoid look as she pondered over the package Reid set in front of her.

"What... is this thing?"

Reid had already taken a bite of his and it took a moment of chewing before he could respond.

"Bulgogi Beef Taco." He gestured with his own. "They're spectacular. Give it a try."

She looked at it skeptically. "I'm not sure I want to take the risk."

"You said surprise you."

"Yes, but it has to be food that makes sense." She brushed a rogue strand of hair from her face. "I like Mexican food, when someone Mexican makes it. I like Korean food when someone Korean makes it." She lifted up the taco as if it were a science project. "I don't even know where to begin with this."

"Well," Reid glanced back at *Sticky Fingers* doing a brusque trade. "Nara splits the cooking with her husband and his name is Diego. I think you should be safe."

She paused then took a tentative bite. A moment later she took a bite resembling a scene from Jaws.

"My God," she mumbled, taco shell crumbling from the corners of her mouth. "What is that stuff?"

He grinned. "Pickled ginger salsa."

They ate quicker than they should have, not savoring their food as much as it deserved, but both were content at the end. Reid, having had a head start, was finished first and stared at Esin chewing for a moment before he spoke.

"You said you're my boss? I thought Tom was my boss since Horizon bought us out."

She held up a well-manicured hand while she finished eating. There was no trace the taco had ever existed.

"I work for Horizon, just a different part of the company." She nodded at the sign affixed to the building. "I'm VP, Media and Marketing division."

"Media and Marketing?" He leaned back from the table slightly surprised. He hadn't seen that coming. "Why do you want to talk to me? About *Forgotten War*?"

"Nope," She grinned and leaned forward. "I want to talk about *Paradox*."

Reid blinked, caught off guard by the request. "Oh, sure. What do you want to know?"

Four years ago, the company had released *Paradox* the ultimate puzzle game. Players encountered problems with geometric shapes, numbers, sounds and colors, in the form of puzzle boxes. The idea was to test each part of your brain with the results displaying how well the you did with each function. The computer randomly generated the puzzles, each one more difficult than the last with near infinite possibilities. You could play the game for twenty years and never encounter the same puzzle twice.

Esin produced a Horizon smartphone from her jacket. She tapped for two seconds with nails that appeared capable of shattering the glass, then flipped the phone to show the *Paradox* game screen.

"I'm addicted." She said, passing it over. "Is it true you designed the first version on your own?"

Her expression had a mix of incredulity and skepticism. Reid took the phone and smiled. He couldn't help it. A flush of good memories, most of them hours of toil at his computer came back to him.

"Almost the whole thing." There was a little pride in his voice, but it felt earned. "That's why the first version was buggy as hell. I didn't know enough about what I was doing."

"What made you think of a puzzle game?"

As she spoke, Reid was checking her records, curious if she'd actually played it. The score showed she was no first timer. Her evaluation showed that her cognitive reasoning was pretty damn good too. He closed the game before she noticed.

"I just," He stopped for a moment. "I just needed a distraction, that's all. I wanted a bigger challenge to keep myself busy. So I made one. It's hard to beat a puzzle game that always changes."

"What about the mobile version?" She asked as he handed the phone back.

He shook his head.

"No, the company hired me to work on it after they bought the rights. But that part needed some professional help." He shook his head again, this time at his own foolishness. "I wish I'd known that mobile games sell so much better, then I could have made some real money out of my hobby."

"That's right," Esin stretched the word nonchalantly. As intriguing as she was, her acting was less than stellar. "You taught yourself programming to do it right?"

There was a moment of silence between them. Laughter and conversations from the park the only sounds. Reid crossed his arms over his chest defensively and hardened his glance. He heard a faint creak as his sport jacket stretched with the tension. Esin met his stare with her smile intact. She knew about him.

It took a moment before he answered.

"Yes, I did."

"...and how long did it take you to learn that?" She pressed.

"A month."

"At a college?"

"Reading books." He spat the words a little.

The businesswoman jumped slightly at the harsh tone. She apologized, then changed her approach, undeterred.

"You've done some research for *Uncommon Valor,* right?" As she spoke, Reid could see his unhappy reflection in her sunglasses, glowering in miniature. "I saw everyone roll their eyes when you mentioned the fourteen dead on the island. I know you care about details."

"It was fourteen wounded actually." He corrected under his breath.

She tilted her head and Reid could see what was coming next. People always wanted a demonstration when they heard about him. Something to make his talent more tangible for them. It was only human nature to want to experience something fantastic for yourself but he still always hated it. Every single time.

If the woman in front of him could see his discomfort, then she took no notice of it. She went on.

"Which American unit invaded Inchon?" She asked eagerly.

"First Marine Division. Part of the Tenth Corps."

"How many dead?"

Reid closed his eyes. Not for concentration but simply to blot out this moment to not remember it, as vain a hope as that was. He kept his eyes shut and answered mechanically.

"566 killed and 2713 wounded if you count the fighting for Seoul as part of the battle."

"Who was the general?"

"A guy named Ned Almond led the corps. An army general leading marines, so he wasn't too popular. Kind of a racist too. Did you know in World War II they put him in charge of the only all black combat division in Europe?"

She ignored his attempt to change the subject by pretending not to notice.

"What about the marine division?"

"General Oliver P. Smith."

"Regiments?"

He gave her three more names.

"Companies?"

He gave her twenty-seven more names.

When he finished rattling off the names of old soldiers, there was a moment of quiet. He opened his eyes again to see her looking at him, mouth wide in amazement. He went on glaring.

"You forgot battalions."

Esin shook her head. For a moment her black hair flew outward in a halo, her smile wide as ever. She was thinking of the next thing to ask. He'd seen it before.

"Okay..." She put her elbows on the table and rested her chin in her hands. "You were talking to that woman in Korean when you bought the tacos."

Reid nodded slowly and jerked his head in the direction of the truck.

"Her name is Nara."

"How long did it take you to learn the language?"

"I'm *still* learning the language." The developer corrected. "I thought it would be important for the game. She's helping me with my pronunciation. I just know the vocabulary."

"Sure, sure. How many words?" She asked, clearly getting excited.

Actually, that was a tough question. He'd never counted.

"I wanted to be fully conversational so I memorized the syntax and a good chunk of the vocabulary." He looked pensive for a moment. "I can read a Korean menu easily but if you ask me to read a physics textbook I would be pretty lost. Maybe a hundred thousand words?"

"...And how long did it take you to memorize all that?" Esin looked as if she might squeal with delight in anticipation of his answer.

Now miserable, he ran his hands through his hair

virtually feeling it turn to grey. Self-consciously, he looked around make sure none of his team could hear them. The last thing he needed was to be a spectacle to them as well. Mercifully, what few he saw were at a distance but he still moved close to his excited boss to keep anyone else from hearing.

He whispered in her ear, faintly detecting the smell of lavender up close.

"Two weeks."

The two sat silently for a moment with Reid counting the seconds of emptiness. He had been enjoying the food, sun and company up until now, and felt bitter about becoming an object of fascination. He remained sitting upright, his arms crossed, sulking. He saw her staring at him, still with that amazed smile, leaning on her hand. Her expression had that 'you're so dreamy' look given to people with exceptional mental abilities or boy bands. Her next question didn't help.

"Okay, what brand are my shoes?"

He threw his hands in the air in frustration, which elicited a laugh from her. He smiled at that a moment, almost laughed himself, then regained control.

"I have a perfect memory," He tried to growl, upset at the mirth he'd let out. "I'm not hyper-observant. They're pointy, black and expensive. That's all I can tell you."

He was lying. He had seen a Gucci logo when she'd been pounding the desk but he wasn't going to admit that.

"Look," he said glancing around, still wary of eavesdroppers. "Can we walk little? I don't want to talk too much around my staff."

They stood, and then wandered down the park's concrete paths toward the riverbank. The city existed at a confluence of two rivers, both flowed down from the glaciers in the surrounding mountains. Here they came together and merged to flow out to the sea. The name of the town actually meant 'a place to come together'. The river seemed a decent place for two people to properly meet. They were out of sight immediately, out of earshot shortly after that, but the silence lingered. After a while, Reid glanced beside him to see the slender executive a step behind but she had drifted to the left to walk in the shade of the trees.

He looked at her slightly confused. "Why do you do that?"

"Do what?" She asked, an eyebrow jumping up above the huge sunglasses still perched on her nose.

"Hide from the sun."

He stepped back to walk between her and the bank of the river. The sunlight felt good on his face. Esin, perhaps part vampire, edged even deeper into the shade.

"I can't stay in the sun." She replied. "I tan too easily."

"Isn't that the idea?" Reid said perplexed. "I thought everyone wanted to get some color in the summer. I work in a room with computer programmers. I know of what I speak."

Esin smiled from the shadows.

"I was born in Afghanistan." She said. "I color up a little too fast."

Reid threw an inquisitive glance her way.

"Is that a bad thing?"

"To some." She dodged the question, then quickly changed the subject. "I didn't think a photographic memory existed. When did it start?"

She started walking again, the sunlight through the trees playing odd shadows across her back.

"Eidetic memory." He corrected. He'd let her skirt the question but now he was curious. "It's not like I see a photograph. I was born this way."

He stopped on the path. Esin took a few more steps, then turned back when Reid didn't move to join her.

"You never said why you came." He said, looking at her suspiciously. "Why did you want to see me in the first place?"

Then came the real question.

"What do you need from me?"

The woman must have been a fantastic poker player. He only caught a quick twitch of her cheek and her smile slipped ever so slightly. She slid off her sunglasses. The playful look was gone. Now her eyes had something he hadn't seen from her yet. Drive.

"Have you ever heard of Horizon's Labyrinth?"

Reid blinked for a moment, absorbing the words. The quiet moment was punctured by the call of ducks on the river as he looked at her. Then, with a jolt, he suddenly burst out laughing.

"Jesus Christ," He exclaimed with amusement. "Does that actually exist?"

For the second time in an hour they sat down together. This time it was on a bench by the river, in the shade, of course. Esin had politely asked or, rather, quietly insisted on it. Reid still had no idea what was behind her sunlight phobia, but not knowing only made him the more curious. He would have to find out, but for now he had something new to focus on.

"I thought the maze was just a story on the internet." He breathed, totally enthralled.

"It's a labyrinth, not a maze." She corrected. "At least that's what Fozzy likes to call it. And it's more than a rumor."

"What is it then?"

"A tradition!" She grinned. "Think of it like the best corporate team building event you could imagine. This year is the ninth annual one the company's done. Horizon puts its best people in to try to work their way out. It's going to be my third and *I'm going to win it.*"

The conviction in her voice made her statement a fact, not a goal. There was a distinct fire in the way she described it. He got the impression this woman was hard to argue with in any situation

Reid's face clouded in confusion.

"How do you win? You escape?" He turned the virtual pages back in his memory. "I read online once that someone had to walk across hot coals to get to the end. But that source wasn't exactly the *Washington Post*."

"Your team has to be first to the finish." Esin explained. "I've never heard of the coals but it sounds plausible. Every division in the company gets to put together a team of five. You select your path then you have to work through it room by room."

"So it's a race?" He asked, still confused.

"Kind of." Esin wavered, wrinkling her nose. "You're definitely competing against the other teams, so it's about speed, but that's just the start of it. Each room you enter has to be completed before you can move on. There are mental puzzles, engineering problems, patterns and numbers and sometimes just pure teamwork or strength challenges."

She drew invisible mazes with her hands as she spoke, her tone all business but her eyes were afire.

"Last year, one team ended up in a blank room with

flat walls, one door and a lever on the ceiling. It took them an hour to figure out how to make a human pyramid high enough to open the door and someone still broke their wrist doing it. This is part race, part escape room, part maze, part endurance test. Fozzy started it up as a way to make us think through problems differently. The company pushes its people hard."

"You know that's insane, right?" Which was a good question, followed quickly by a better one. "What's the prize then?"

"Winning division gets bragging rights." She shrugged, as if it was obvious.

"There *must* be more than that." He looked at her skeptically. "People don't risk broken bones for a moment of pride."

"Wouldn't you?"

He pondered her question for a moment. If it were enough of a challenge, he might. He would certainly regret the missed opportunity if he didn't give it everything he had. But he knew he was far from normal.

Reid shook his head.

"I still don't believe it. There must be a payoff."

"Oh fine." Esin made a sour face as if she'd been forced to admit there was no Santa and brushed her hair back. "The board keeps a reserve, set aside for allocation after the Labyrinth. The winning division gets a big budget increase, and the VP tends to give the team a bonus alongside it."

"How much of a bonus?"

"How much do you want?"

Reid blinked at the obvious invitation. In his fascination he had completely missed the insinuation. He still wasn't very good at reading people.

"Wait, you want me on your team?"

Esin actually laughed in his face.

"That *can't* be a surprise to you!" She exclaimed. "You are absolutely ideal for this. You are someone who designs puzzle games for a living, thinks independently and takes up things spontaneously for a challenge. I could never find anyone with a better resume and I'm not even including the memory thing."

Reid shrugged. She had a point, and he smirked a little at her use of the phrase 'memory thing'. "How much are you offering?"

She quoted a number and Reid nearly choked. He broke into a coughing fit as Esin watched with quiet amusement.

"You don't have much of a poker face," She pointed out, as tried to recover. "I should have low-balled you to save money. But that's only if we win. It'll be a third of that if we lose."

"You think I'm worth that much?"

Esin focused her eyes on him. This close he could see that her emerald irises had flecks of copper. "I think you're worth every penny. I don't mind paying to win."

He took the compliment in stride, and nodded his appreciation. The fact that he would have done a challenge like this for free he kept to himself.

"When do we start?"

"As soon as possible. The Labyrinth run is two weeks from Friday."

Reid's face fell hard.

"Oh, no that's not going to work." He looked over his shoulder toward the studio. One corner of the ugly building was visible through the trees, as though even nature wanted to cover up the blight. "*Forgotten War*'s release is only a few months away. This is crunch time."

Esin didn't even blink.

"I know." She said emotionless. "I'm running the marketing, remember? I was told you were just improving a section of the campaign. The rest of the game is done."

"Well, I still need to be here to supervise," He scoffed at the idea of doing anything else. "It's my game; I need to be here."

From where she sat on the bench, Esin squirmed slightly. Her leg twitched sending an expensive Gucci heel scraping across the pavement stones, with her face wrinkling into a 'you're not going to want to hear this' expression. Part of this was clearly exaggerated, to make him take what she was about to say easier. When she finally spoke, it did not help.

"Do you, though?"

Reid blinked.

"Excuse me?"

"Do they really need you here for this?" She asked. In earnest, her melodrama fading quickly. "You've been working for over a year on this game. It's all but finished. You have a team of professionals working for you. Do they really need you here?"

"It's not even close to being finished." Reid pushed back, annoyed at the thought. "And yes, they need me here."

Esin sighed.

She looked at him with sympathy, as a friend might, before she went on.

"Some of your people have complained." She said. "They said you're micro-managing everything and slowing down the process."

Reid shouldn't have been surprised by the statement. He was though but tried to sound undeterred.

"They're allowed to talk," He said grudgingly. "But I'm the one who decides when its done. I'm not going to make a mistake and put out some unfinished glitchy mess."

And I can never forget my mistakes, he wanted to add.

Esin leaned away from him, meeting his eye even though she was shorter. Her face had a cold confidence that showed she had had these conversations before. The playful and effervescent woman from before seemed to have vanished, only to be replaced by someone coated in steel.

"I'm told you asked for the release to be bumped back." It was a truth, but it came out as an accusation.

"I just want it done right."

She raised a perfectly sculpted eyebrow again. A normal face would wrinkle in the effort, but hers seemed to evenly distribute the stress, defiant against any imperfection.

"Your team seems to think it's done. There's no other reason you're delaying?"

"None."

That was a lie. Reid felt better when work dominated his life, but he obviously couldn't tell her why. He summoned a glare, trying to look angry at the insinuation.

"It needs the work. And I'm the best judge of when the game is done, okay?"

"Are you?" Her gaze was cold and unblinking. "Because I've had play-testers giving me reviews for a month and gamers don't usually sugar coat their opinions."

That hit like an electric current. Reid jolted up straight, the bench creaking in protest at the shifting weight.

"You had the game play tested without telling me?" He felt a cold fist closing in his stomach at the thought. "I specifically said it wasn't ready!"

"I thought it was." She said, matter-of-factly. "So did Horizon. So, I got started early."

"You should have asked me!"

"You would have said no."

"That's my job!"

"Do you want to hear what they said?" She still didn't break her stare, continuing to weather his anger. "Or should I keep that to myself?"

For a moment, Reid wanted to childishly say 'no' and continue as if nothing had changed. But thankfully, the rational part of his mind took over and he gave a brief angry nod as though he were head-butting the criticism.

His boss waited a beat, seeming to revel in the tension, then a smile appeared, melting the ice of her expression.

"Mr. Sheraton," Her look was pure sunrise. "It's been nothing but rave reviews."

Oh, thank you, merciful God!

He nodded, hopefully looking emotionless.

"For which part?"

"Every part." She answered. "The graphics, sound design, multi-player and campaign. It's better than any other *Uncommon Valor* was at this stage. Typically, there's a teething period to start with, but this has been fantastic. We've been trying to keep a lid on the reviews before it's officially play tested." She looked at him incredulously. "Do you know how rare it is for me to have to bottle up *good* news?"

"Any bugs?"

She nodded.

"A few. But there are always bugs."

Reid shook his head, undeterred. "Well we need to fix them then. You'll have to email me a list."

"It's ready."

Reid glared at her, still feeling betrayed. "I hate mistakes. I'll fix them."

"I *saw* it." Esin didn't raise her voice, but it doubled in intensity. "It's done. Between the gameplay, the sound, that Lincoln quote..."

"Oh, for God's sake," Reid hissed in irritation. "Lincoln never said that."

Esin flinched at his outburst clearly surprised. "He didn't?"

The game designer shook his head.

"'The only thing necessary for evil to succeed is for good people to do nothing'. I read that in high school. Lincoln didn't say that?"

"That's Ella Wheeler Wilcox. People just think Lincoln said it."

'Well," Her face twisted in confusion. "Why didn't you correct them when they put it in?"

Reid looked away. "I'll fix it later. I couldn't do it in front of everyone."

"Why not?"

He turned his gaze to the beautiful vista of the river. The glacier water was flowing past, perfectly cold and clear. The river had been dropping down the bank for weeks as the last of the snow in the mountains had melted away. He sometimes watched it to give himself some clarity. He took a deep breath and kept watching. He didn't want to see Esin's face when he spoke.

"The person who originally made that mistake was Douglas MacArthur." He explained, his eyes still on the ripples of the current in the water. "In his last speech before congress in 1951, after he was fired in Korea, he mixed up the quote and everyone was too polite to correct him. It was MacArthur. He was a hero and at a very low point. Since then, it keeps being incorrectly quoted. Everyone on my team probably read his speech in their research and didn't know any better. I shouldn't punish anyone for doing their work."

He turned his head back around, expecting to see her mouth agape with some expression of amazement. Instead, she was leaning on her hand, her elbow on the edge of the bench with an expression akin to extreme arousal. Her eyes shone and her thumb, rubbed the edge of her neck seductively. Something told Reid that this could be a tactic to flatter him, either to release the old game or join this new one. Either way, it wasn't exactly unpleasant to see.

"*I need you* for this race." The way she said it was also probably pure flattery, but again, not unpleasant. "You are perfect for this."

To his surprise, he found himself adopting a foolish grin.

"Ms. Shirzai, memory isn't everything."

"That's instinct, not a memory trick." The sultry expression on her face softened, a little to his disappointment. "You saw something out of place, tracked it and instantly made a decision. You didn't even think; you just knew why something was wrong and knew what to do about it. That's exactly what I need in the Labyrinth."

She looked down for a moment then pulled her hair back from her face.

"Give me three weeks." She said pleadingly. "We can win the Labyrinth, you can earn your bonus, and you can get out of your own way long enough to let the studio release your game on time. You'll have something exciting to do, make some money and still release the best reviewed *Uncommon Valor* in ten years. *Please.*"

He wanted to say no, but she still made a good point. His devotion to properly finishing what he started hadn't changed, but he couldn't deny the offer interested him. Not the money, but the experience. If not fully persuasive, she had been intriguing enough to breed uncertainty. Reid was usually an immovable object when it came to what he believed, but this woman might be an unstoppable force.

He yielded ever so slightly.

"I'll consider it."

Esin smiled wide and hopped to her feet with a graceful energy. "I'm flying back to Vancouver tonight. If you choose to come, just give me a call. I'll arrange everything."

"I still want you to email me that bug list."

She gave him an exasperated look, but he could only shrug in response.

She nodded. "I'll send it. It's not very long."

She dropped her hands to her pockets, fumbled for a moment, then frowned.

"Looks like I left all of my business cards in my purse." She said. She raised an eyebrow in a playful expression. "If I tell you my phone number, you think you can remember it?"

The two shook hands, her grip still strangely cold, and parted. As Reid walked back to his office, his last glimpse of her was at the food truck ordering more tacos to go.

THREE

With the enjoyable swiftness of a triple root canal, the rest of the day dragged by. Arguments were had and re-had with the designers at the studio. Tempers flamed, roared and then burnt out when the futility of arguing with him became plain to them. Reid took it all with a flinty calm, unwavering in his conviction that they would only release something he was proud of. But that suspicion that his staff were beginning to hate him became a diamond-hard certainty by the end of the day.

He biked home, his jacket billowing out behind him as he raced down the narrow streets of the town. Biking paths crossed the city like veins so cyclists and joggers could take in the beauty of the surrounding hills and mountains. Each terrace offered a new stunning vista of the valley, with a feeling as if you were experiencing the world for the first time. Hills of emerald grass scraped up against rocky peaks the color of rust in the spring, with the grass fading to a warm mustard when the heat of summer struck the valley. The city seemed to have moods, shifting with the season.

Like everything he did, Reid found it a good distraction. The more spectacular the view, the more it seized your attention and diverted your thoughts. He had nothing but good memories of walking along the paths and even when the beauty of the moment slipped to something else it was usually welcome. Another thing that tended to focus you on the present, although a hell of a lot less pleasant, was exhaustion. Reid lived in one of the few places on earth where you had to cycle uphill both coming and going from work. Surely, some cantankerous old grandpa could use this in an anecdote about how kids were so lazy these days, but after a nine-hour day, all Reid got from it was a struggle to marshal enough strength to keep moving. By the time he arrived home, he was out of breath, and his shirt was wet to his back with sweat.

As he fumbled his bike into the elevator the familiar sounds of the apartments reached him. The door closed and he heard Janna first. She lived on the second floor, was fifty-three, and her birthday was in April. At least once a week she got into a shouting match with someone on the phone. Sometimes government, sometimes distant family, sometimes just her cable company. This week, from the faint words he could make out through the wall, it was her son. She was currently telling her neighbors he worked in shipping, but in the three years Reid had been in the building this was his fourth occupation. Either the man refused to settle or she was lying about who he was. If the anger in her voice meant anything, probably the latter. It was three floors before he couldn't hear her anymore.

The other sound he heard was Baxter. He wasn't exactly a neighbor but hearing him was just as familiar. He was an eight-year-old beagle who lived with his owner Chris on the seventh floor. He'd started barking loudly on random nights, and for six weeks Chris had apologized through notes around the building, seemingly very confused as to why. It didn't take much to figure it out. The last four times it happened were on Tuesdays when David, his eighty-four-year-old neighbor on the same floor, had his nurse, stop by to check on him. Another episode had been on a Monday when she had dropped something off. The conspiratorial part of Reid's mind wanted to think Chris and the nurse could be having an affair, but he had overheard a woman in the elevator describe him as 'about as sexy as a baked potato' so it seemed unlikely. Maybe the dog just didn't like her perfume or something. Experience told him the blander reason was usually the right one anyway. Life was boring when you got down to it.

He reached the eleventh floor, and slipped into his apartment, guiding the bike through the door. He shut it behind him quickly, and double locked it. From deep inside came a sigh, an exhale of nerve really, that he was in his own space again. The tension drained from him, the face he put on every day stored until tomorrow.

The main room of his apartment was the living room and the kitchen, broken by a bar that he used as a table. The walls were a mellow shade of white that seemed to pick up the ambient colors of the room. The furniture was dark red leather, the lampshades in green. Bookshelves covered every inch of the walls with spines of every color of the rainbow. If his memory were perfect, it was matched by an insatiable need to harvest more information, which the books provided. He could never bring himself to throw a book away, even though reading it again was most often redundant. They were sized randomly giving the look of crooked colourful teeth leading up to the massive windows that dominated the room, stretching much higher than Reid was tall. The sun was almost down, and the lights of the city in the valley twinkled orange and white against the greying backdrop. All the bookshelves as well as his writing desk squirreled away to the right of the window were a cherry wood with black iron snaking through them. The effect was warm to the eye and the heart. On the relatively few occasions when he had guests they often asked if Reid had come up with it himself. He sometimes lied and said yes to avoid an awkward conversation. He didn't mind being social, actually he craved it sometimes, but people tended to want to know one's background. That was part of human nature, to be curious. Reid had eventually abandoned all but a few friends to keep from dwelling on the past.

He tossed his jacket on a chair, as he walked past the door on the left with **R&R** emblazoned on it in black letters. Guests never asked about that. Probably content that it meant rest and relaxation, though it never had.

He drifted into the kitchen, knowing exactly what was left in his fridge and already pulling a recipe up that he'd read nine years back. His stereo on the counter, all white and silver save for the familiar black moon of the Horizon logo, lit up at the sound of his voice. The first few notes of the Rolling Stones' 'Paint it Black' started up, but with a few short commands he replaced it. He needed as much distraction as possible tonight. In the ultimate insult to rock and roll, a dry British voice began reading an audiobook about prohibition America in the 1920s.

From the cupboards and fridge, he pulled portabella Mushrooms, cream, cheese, onion, parsley, white wine and Arborio rice. Soon they were simmering together in a pot on their way to becoming a risotto. When it looked like the recipe described, he poured it into a bowl. He glanced over at the clock and frowned. When he'd read the recipe years ago it had been called a fifty-minute meal and this one had taken over an hour. False advertising.

Grabbing a beer from the fridge, he took his newly created meal over to the computer desk. True to her word, Esin had emailed him the complete list of bugs the play-testers had found. Also true to her word, it was impressively short. Only a few dozen notations marked the page, all forgivable errors. Reid treated each entry as an enemy and, opening the file, set out to kill them all. The code of the game were sprawling DNA strains, formulas and patterns, sentences of a language unlike any other. The guns and ships of the game whittled down to numbers and letters. It was a hearty distraction, one of the reasons he didn't want to let it go.

The work went slowly. There were over 1.2 million lines of code and the errors only hidden within a few dozen. The bowl of risotto was soon empty, his beer right behind. A second bottle gave its life for the cause. Then a third. Having finished the last of them, he switched to tea and kept going. Soon the faint British voice from the kitchen announced the end of the book. The author hadn't mentioned anything about the social changes affected by the association of illegal alcohol and sex, through the lens of cinema in the late 1920s but had focused more on the gang violence in Chicago. Reid hadn't learned as much as he'd wanted but at least it had been entertaining.

He glanced at the time and saw six hours had passed. The blackness outside had slowly gotten blacker and what few sounds he had heard in the building had tapered off. The passage of time surprised him. Usually, his mind kept track of the hours, even the minutes, perfectly. He had been given a watch for his twelfth birthday by his aunt, a cheap plastic thing with a triceratops on the face. He knew he hadn't needed it, but he'd worn it for a month anyway, unnecessary as it was, just so she would feel good about the gift. She had known how much he loved dinosaurs.

He shrugged off the lost time and kept going. It was too soon to sleep. The list was less than a third done anyway. He'd been dreaming lately and didn't want to see where they led him tonight. He ordered the stereo to shuffle his music and went back at it.

Exhaustion began to creep its way into his body. He felt his eyes growing heavier with the weight of the day, the back of his neck oily against his collar. His vision began to blur slightly and he rubbed his eyes trying to keep them open. Most of his music was upbeat, so he began nodding his head, bouncing slightly to the tunes to stay awake. He shouted for the stereo to get louder. Then louder still. He could feel the bass of the song reverberate through his chair.

After a while, he felt the music more than heard it, the bass serving as his pulse to keep his heart pumping blood to his brain. The Stones, snubbed by him earlier, came storming back into his consciousness when 'Gimme Shelter' started up. He bounced his head and felt a welcome sting in his ears when Jagger screeched the notes of the chorus, as though he were a masochist for the music.

Reid found his second wind in the rhythm and pushed on into the code. One by one the bugs fell before him. With his mind on nothing but the task at his fingertips and the music throbbing in his temples he was doing his best work. Song after song went by powering his push for perfection. Then it all fell apart.

A familiar riff on the piano began, and a voice crooned about having a real good time.

Reid's head snapped back, his hands jumping from the keyboard in panic.

He whipped his head around and shouted in the direction of his stereo. "Stop! Pause!"

The device played on oblivious to its master's commands. The music was so loud at this point he couldn't be heard over the din. Freddie Mercury continued massaging his way through the intro of 'Don't Stop Me Now' each note more dangerous than the last.

Reid kept shouting and stumbled to his feet, his legs half asleep from the hours sitting at the screen. He threw himself toward the kitchen knocking over a chair and end table, the crash of furniture matching the crash of drums. One of his lamps smashed against the wood floor. He kicked the pieces of glass skittering away as he ran around the bar. The lyrics continuing their silky twist into his memories.

He smashed his fist into the top of the offending box but missed anything important; it took a second blow for the song to mercifully stop. The sudden silence in his apartment was stark, broken only by his rapid gasps for breath and the thump of his heart pounding in his ears. He'd thought he had deleted all of her music from his library. Somehow one had missed the net.

He listened to his own breath for a short time, not daring to move. Then his mind drifted back four years, remembering each time those lyrics had passed her lips. He saw her sitting next to him on the beach singing that song. Then in the mountains, in a sweater idly singing while reading a book. Then, the same song garbled to the point of near incoherence as she hummed while brushing her teeth in the bathroom. Reid remembered sitting on the bed, looking at her dressed in a robe her hair a mess and laughing as those beautiful garbled notes flowed from a face covered in toothpaste. He loved those memories, but he tried to shake them away. He knew how the story turned out.

He got a brush and dustpan and slowly began sweeping up the wreckage of the lamp. He thought of her sweeping as well. He had knocked over a glass at an anniversary dinner once. She'd went out for a broom after and he had placed her gift on her plate in some sort of half apology, picking up glass with his fingers. She came in just as he'd inevitably cut himself. She always said that for a man who remembered everything he didn't take away much common sense. She had been wearing a loose blue and green mottled dress, just past the knee. Her brown hair was up with long earrings that just touched the edge of her neck when she tilted her head.

Stop.

He willed his mind to go elsewhere, steering away from the memories like a ship away from a storm. He couldn't risk more of that. He turned back to the mess. The glass made an unmistakable clink as he brushed it into the pan. As he gathered the shards of glass together, watching them clump in the pan a new memory came. A horrid memory he spent most of his days now trying to hide from.

That same brown hair of the woman he loved, mixed chaotically with broken glass as it flew through the air.

He dropped the pan, now irrelevant, and started to pace, his head too jumbled to go back to work. He glanced at the titles of the books on his shelves, trying to divert his mind to their topics. Thoughts of history, chemistry, wine, music raced through his mind but all left just as quickly. He remembered where he had been when he read those books, and she was with him. He remembered talking with her about the subjects and what she had to say about them. She loved music, hated most wines, and was pretty ambivalent about history. 'All written by men' she would say and talk about something else. The memory of it gave way to more memories with all roads leading back to the same awful place. Inevitably, she was the star of his reality.

It had been growing worse for months. The bad memories always began to rise up when he was too idle, or about to be so. *Forgotten War* had been a good diversion, but as the project drew to a close, he had started drifting back into troubling waters. He hated thinking about that night, so he had purged any reminders of it from the world around him. It wasn't enough anymore. He tried his usual distractions.

First, *Paradox.*

The game had always been intended as a distraction. It had been born on a night just like this when he could find no peace. He still played the game for the challenge, still felt a little pride that he had made it himself. As he brought it to life on the screen now, he saw the patterns. They had taken years to manifest, but each time a new puzzle came up he could see how the computer had derived it from something else. This number puzzle flowed out of that one. These shapes came from this older puzzle. After a thousand puzzles, each one he could not forget, the math behind the magic started to become clearer. As a consequence, the solutions became easier too. He could see which puzzle the new problem was based on. He remembered what he had done to solve that one, and he would adjust his approach. Three easy solutions later he switched off the computer in disgust.

Next, he tried books. There were a handful of titles on his British smile of a bookshelf that he had not read yet. He yanked one at random and sat in the light of his one unbroken lamp. This proved equally worthless though as in his turmoil and exhaustion he had trouble focusing on the words on the page. It gave him a dull headache behind his eyes and it was not long before he saw the glass flying through the air again, the impact of the moment losing not a hint of its horror.

Rushing back to the kitchen, he fumbled through his cabinets until he found a bottle of Trace Rum. The label was a black and white etching of a film noir detective posing beneath a street light, smoking. The liquid sloshed only to the character's waist, half empty from other moments like this. He unscrewed the top and forsaking a glass, he took a hearty gulp to ease his nerves. The coppery liquid burned down his throat seemingly incinerating the memory, but it rose again immediately. He took a second pull of the bottle and set it aside to continue pacing, waiting as the oblivion of the alcohol worked its way into his blood.

Through it all the memory was omni-present. He heard the shatter of the glass, smelled the burning rubber on the street, felt her hair brush his face along with the glass from the impact and tasted his own blood all over again. All for what could have been the ten-thousandth time.

In desperation he scrambled to his feet and stalked across the floor to the door on the left hand side of the room with its **R&R** facing out. Renata and Reid.

He slipped into what had once been their bedroom. He'd barely been in here in years and had kept it virtually identical to the last time they'd slept here. The walls were a dark blue, toning down the light. A dresser and a little desk with a mirror stood sentry against the walls, a jewellery box and framed photos the only objects on them. On the right, their bed still sat, sheets folded on it neatly. He'd always slept on the left side, nearest the door. Nearest the kitchen actually, he'd had quite a sweet tooth then. Now he slept down the hall in what had been his office. Renata had slept on the side nearest the bathroom, the door still open with the sink barely visible in the light creeping in from the hallway. On Her side of the bed, he could still see her wedding ring sitting in the dish where she had left it every night. He walked over and could see in the time he had been gone it had garnered a thin film of dust. Memories came back almost overwhelmingly but he lingered for a moment. He needed to remember to make this work. None of his distractions were working anymore. Most of the memories that came back were good anyway, the bad ones hadn't arrived yet. He had to steer into the skid this time. For a few seconds, he replayed their moments here, then he quickly turned to the small room that had been their closet, flipped on the light and darted inside, shutting the door behind him.

In complete contrast to the bedroom, this place was the starkest kind of bare. It had originally been a walk-in closet, with racks and shelves full of Renata's dresses and shoes but Reid had since stripped it all out to the floorboards. His clothes were in the other bedroom, Renata's had been given to Good Will years ago. He wanted this room empty. Even the original carpet was gone. He could feel nothing but cold concrete beneath his feet. The walls, floors and ceiling had been painted the most basic white and the single LED lightbulb in the ceiling bathed the room in its own white illumination. An intense, barrage of brightness that seemed to force darkness away. The only furniture was a single wooden chair, as white and featureless as everything else. It looked like a room in a mental hospital. The irony was, that this was not far off from its intention. Reid had made this room to keep himself sane.

He sat down heavily in the chair, looking straight ahead. He quietly tried to clear his mind, focusing on the flat white texture of the door, looking at the imperfections in the wood through the blank paint job. He reached under the chair and removed a set of cards from a tiny shelf and started to shuffle them, never looking down. He could hear the swish of the thin cardboard as he randomized the cards. He felt for bent corners or imperfections that would give away their identity but he didn't find any. On the few occasions he used this room, and this was only the third time he'd been forced to, he would have the cards reprinted just so there would be no giveaways. When he was sure the cards were completely random, he set them down on his legs and looked down. White as anything else in the vicinity, the stack was featureless. The deck had a sheen from the light above his head, but nothing else.

He took a deep breath and flipped the first card.

The face was white as well, except for a single word in bold black print: **Barcelona**.

Instantly his mind was flush with memories of drinking sangria in a little bar near the Catalonian beaches. There had been an old out-of-tune piano in the corner, someone had said it had been sitting there since the Spanish Civil War, and he'd spontaneously sat to play one night, after good liquor had overtaken common sense. Renata called from across the room yelling not to embarrass her, but within ten minutes she was sitting beside him singing in flawless native Spanish to each tortured off-key note he played. Together, they had serenaded the group of locals and tourists who yelled out requests across four languages and slapping Reid on the back. He'd felt every brush and clap on the tender sun-burned skin underneath his shirt. Renata had stood next to him in a sun dress over her swimsuit. He could still smell the saltwater left on her skin.

In the white prison cell of memory, years after, Reid smiled. It had been a great vacation. Beautiful moments, sun, music and passion. Renata had family in Spain but had never been to Catalonia. He'd loved getting a chance to show her. In retrospect, there was little to tarnish it, except that it had been their last vacation together.

The image of her hair intermingled with the glass tore into his consciousness and slapped his nostalgic mind back to the present. Each time he saw that image, it was like a blow. He flipped to the next card before the memory could take hold.

This one was a day they had spent in a botanical garden when they had first started dating. They had met for lunch in a glass arboretum filled with exotic species. Reid, never good at romance but brilliant at food, had decided to put a fancy picnic together to impress her. It hadn't worked out that way. He'd brought pate, cheeses, a wine she liked and -in some sort of bizarre foolhardy attempt to be gourmet- had made chocolate covered honey-bees. When he laid all this before her, Renata had viewed this act of culinary-entomology with understandable horror. Trying to salvage the situation, he had eaten one bee to show her nothing was wrong with them. The memory of the taste still made him cringe six years later. It tasted like you were eating a chocolate covered raisin soaked in Jägermeister then cursed by an evil wizard. Overwhelmed with disgust, he'd spat the offending bug right into a flowerbed nearby, only to see Renata beside herself laughing. Soon, he was too. They'd made use of the wine, but ditched the rest in favor of hot dogs from a vendor. Though half a bottle of was still not enough to wash away the original taste. The bee's last act of vengeance.

It had been one of the best days of Reid's life. But it brought him little joy now. Through the prism of memory, it simply felt unfair. Cheated, that he hadn't had more days like that. His back twitched instantly. Maybe it was real pain, maybe just imagined, but it routed his mind straight back to the cause of it in every way, shape and form. He hissed through his teeth trying to expel his thoughts. He began to work his way through the cards faster and faster. Within a few moments he'd reached the last in the stack.

This one simply said, **Wedding Day**. He'd been in a blue suit. The white shirt had been itchy against his skin because, foolishly, he hadn't washed it the night before like she'd told him to. She told him as much later. It was a summer day and it'd been hot as he stood waiting for her to slowly walk down the aisle. He'd been sweating, but probably not from the heat. She had been in a white dress with pastels weaving through it. Her bouquet had been lilies. He remembered lifting her veil to see her face... But her face looked terrified, her hair mingled with glass. The memory shifted, and he felt the body of the car shudder and bend, felt the pain in his back, the steering wheel against his chest. He heard glass breaking, tires squealing, metal tearing. He heard all of these things in a brutal maw of sound reverberating in his head. Their last moments together before he blacked out.

The cards struck the white door with savage force, scattering around the tiny room. Reid erupted onto his feet, knocking the chair over and kicked it repeatedly, angry at the room's betrayal. He struck the light by the door plunging the room into blackness and slumped to the floor.

Nothing was working anymore. He was used to finding ways to keep his mind occupied but over the last few weeks all the usual tricks had begun to fail him. He was almost afraid to be idle in any way now because it just produced more chances to dwell on horrible moments. This had been his last resort. He'd only had to use this room twice before now and each time had given him some peace. Some inspiration had come before, leading to *Paradox* but now there was none to be had. With *Forgotten War* coming to an end, he was getting worse. Now he couldn't work, he couldn't focus. He could not find a distraction and he didn't want to sleep because dreaming was worse. There was nothing else to do.

Reid sat quietly in the dark for what felt like an hour, but knew it was only a quarter of that. Even when he wanted to lose track of time he couldn't. Then, in the darkness, he slipped his phone from his pocket and dialed a number. He listened to the monotone ring, waiting for her voicemail to kick in. Instead, the screen lit up with the head and shoulders of a bleary-eyed Esin, wrapped in a robe, looking confused.

"Oh, uh. Hello." He suddenly felt guilty for waking her. "I'm sorry, I know it's late."

"Technically it's early." The executive corrected, with more than a hint of irritation. "*Very* early."

Her tired eyes became concerned.

"Mr. Sheraton are you okay?"

Reid didn't know how he looked, but he assumed it was just one step better than death. He ignored the question and asked one of his own.

"Will it be difficult? The Labyrinth, I mean."

"Excuse me?"

"I need a real challenge."

She looked at him strangely and he knew he needed to explain.

"You were right," He conceded. "When you said I was drawing out the game. I didn't want to be finished. I needed to have something difficult to do. I need to keep my mind busy. Tell me this is going to be tough, and I'll do it."

She looked at him with concern, but he could see no pity. He was thankful for that.

"It's the greatest kind of challenge. But you should rest. This can wait."

He glanced at the clock nestled in the upper corner of the screen and felt a fresh pang of guilt.

"Please," He half pleaded. "I need this right now. Just give me something new to focus on and I'll leave you alone."

Esin nodded, her loose hair bobbing with the motion. She looked pensive for a moment then spoke.

"Fine," She said. "In the morning, tell that Jason guy he's in charge of the game for the final stretch. That'll make him happy. The studio has to hit the original release date. No delays. As soon as that's done, drive out to Vancouver and we'll find you a suite in the Quarry. Someone told me you ride a freaking bike everywhere so I had a car dropped off in your parking space at the studio."

"Wait, what?" Reid blinked. "Why did you do that?"

Her tired face eased into a self-assured smile.

"I'm good at reading people." She said. "Although, I do think you're kind of presumptuous."

Reid blinked for the second time.

"Sorry, I just assumed the offer was still open."

She shook her sleepy head. "No, for assuming I'm alone."

In the light of his phone screen Reid blushed bright red.

"Oh Jesus," He stammered in embarrassment. "I'm sorry. Are you…?"

She laughed quietly and shook her head to show she was kidding. He gave an involuntary sigh of relief, which only made her laugh harder.

"You're going to be fun to work with Mr. Sheraton." She smiled.

The levity cut through his tension briefly and he returned the smile.

"Reid." He said. "Call me Reid."

"Esin." She replied. "Can I go back to sleep?"

He bid her goodnight, or good morning depending on your point of view, then continued to sit in the old closet, now dark again with the end of the call. His thoughts were still troubled, and the battle continued in his head, but it had eased slightly. Surrounded by the cards on the floor and with a new world awaiting him in the morning he found an equilibrium of sorts. Exhaustion eventually dragged him into unconsciousness on the concrete floor. He slept fitfully, dreaming of picnicking with Renata again under storm clouds where the crack of thunder sounded like ripping steel.

FOUR

Though it was the right decision to step back, the exaltation of his staff at the news made Reid more than a little annoyed. Jason had pledged to make the game as true to history as possible, and with what felt like barely contained jubilation, he had walked Reid out of the building. His announcement had brought nothing but smiles from the team to the point that when the door closed behind him Reid half expected to hear the pop of champagne corks. It didn't matter though. He was in a better frame of mind and anxious to get to Vancouver.

His eagerness dampened slightly when he saw the car waiting for him in his parking space. He had expected a little sedan of the type that was the workhorse of big corporations. A Ford or a Toyota maybe. Sleek enough to be charming, not enough to be sexy. He had been seriously mistaken. The car that greeted him barely took up half of the parking space. It was a bean shaped thing attached to a small four-wheel chassis low to the ground and coated with a shiny dark green finish that reminded him of a cake glaze. There were no windows that he could see on the whole thing. It resembled more a science fiction kidney than anything else. In fact, the only marking that broke the finish on the 'car' was the now annoyingly familiar moon and light burst logo of the Horizon Corporation. Reid hit the open-door button on the key fob that had been left at his desk. The bean instantly split in two, the canopy tilting up to allow him access to a leather seat. There were no controls that he could see. It was a self-driving car.

Horizon had been putting models on the road for two years now but Reid had never seen one. They remained expensive to the point they were still fairly exclusive, but they were growing more prevalent on the roads. Maybe up in the mountains people wanted to trust their own driving, or maybe they just wanted something more solid. Indeed, as the canopy closed around him, Reid felt more in a tanning bed than a vehicle.

Companies like Mercedes, Tesla, even the long dead Google had tried to master the self-driving car. The results were often hilarious crash videos to be found online when you searched them in a Horizon search engine. Programming vehicles to follow traffic simply hadn't worked. There were too many variables and changing conditions on the roads. Ice made the road slick, there could be rocks or debris, anything could happen. More importantly, someone else could do something stupid before the machine could react and force the surrounding vehicles to spin the wheel in a game of natural selection. Cars needed a capable driver, that was all there was to it. Typically, Horizon had solved the problem in the most high-tech way possible.

"Hello Mr. Sheraton." A warm voice came from the dashboard. "We have your destination ready. Shall we go?"

Reid gave the screen a sour look. Every Horizon car was built with its own artificial intelligence. Instead of having a program trying to react, the car would think for itself in traffic. The AIs could react to new threats like humans could, Horizon said they could do it even faster. Their slogan was, 'Never trust a car without a person driving. But does that person have to be you?' They had made the concept work, but some people still failed to see the distinction between a dumb computer and an AI. Seeing one as a 'person' was an even greater stretch.

Reid, who found AIs in general irritating, foresaw a very long trip ahead.

The computer repeated the question, and he gave a lazy affirmative. Instantly, the canopy became completely transparent, lighting up the interior and skillfully the car rolled out toward the highway. He tensed up a little as it turned onto the road, made an unhappy sound as they weaved into traffic and said a quiet prayer as they came up to speed. This would be the longest car ride he'd taken since the accident, and he was letting a damn computer do the driving.

Within twenty minutes, he was getting nervous again. Each vehicle that roared past just made the car feel more like a toy. Not to mention, every time another car came close Reid found his right foot tapping the floor trying to find an invisible break. He felt himself tensing again. Though it was hard to think backward to bad memories, it was his future survival that worried him now. Thinking he could nap to catch up on the sleep denied to him the night before, he pushed a button for darkness and the canopy became opaque again. That only made things worse, as now he could hear each car pass but couldn't *see* them. Consigned to the experience, he brought back the windows and settled in for the ride. Unhelpfully, a few seconds later the computer asked him if he was okay. Somehow it could tell he was nervous.

Its solution? Smalltalk.

Another few kilometers fell away while the machine tried to talk about the weather, Reid's family and what he did for a living. He answered all the questions politely, trying to be as quick as possible. He had never liked it when taxi drivers did this; talking to a computer felt ridiculous. One of the inevitable catch-22s of AIs was that the more you tried to make them seem human, the more robotic they ended up feeling. Simulations of personality or curiosity never equalled the real thing; they were always lacking the emotion and genuine human interest. Designers programmed in these questions but the machine didn't care about them, it was obvious. Even Horizon with all its technical magic seemed stymied by problem.

As polite as he was, Reid was already on edge, and the conversation did not help. He pulled out his phone and began reading, hoping the computer would take the hint. When the car interrupted to ask him what was bringing him to Vancouver, Reid simply replied "espionage" with a terrible Russian accent.

"Oh," The machine replied with forced interest. "Would you like me to find some stores with binoculars?"

Reid smacked the mute button, cutting the audio, and spent the rest of the trip in a blissful nervy silence.

The GPS had predicted it would be four hours' drive time to reach the quarry. At exactly three hours and fifty-five minutes, Reid looked up from his phone to see signs for the Horizon offices coming up on the road. The car took the turn with the buttery smoothness he had come to expect and began to ascend up a steep gradient. The road seemed to meet the horizon, the irony was not lost on him, as he drove up into nothing but a blue sky. Then, reaching the plateau, it began to drop steeply into the pit.

When Horizon had relocated their main offices in Vancouver, or so Reid's research had told him, they were already too big for just a building of concrete, glass and steel like the many that crowned the downtown. Rising up like stalagmites amongst innumerable others as a monument to capitalism, they were essentially all the same. It hadn't felt right for them to just blend in with the pack. It was already easy to see they were different from the average conglomerate. Every ad Horizon ran talked about how they were changing the world. The company had needed more space and had wanted to promote a different corporate culture. They had bought the quarry so they could do just that.

The company had acquired an old disused gravel quarry outside the city. Over sixty years the hole had been strip mined, as they dug deeper into the earth. Peeling back the stone by layers, it had left a rough, ugly corduroy pattern of stone shelves, like steps into an empty grey hole. It was ugly, it was out of the way, it seemed bleak, but it had been perfect. The space was huge with plenty of room to expand, and it had enough privacy that Horizon could shape it in any way they wanted. With the kind of zest that was their trademark, ten years ago they had gotten started.

As the car descended a long curving road built into the hillside, a stunning new world met his eyes. A cascade of greens, every shade the eye could perceive, vibrantly shone up from what had once been a scar upon the earth. The layers of blasted stone were gone, near invisible now. Each layer of the old mine was green with vegetation. On dozens of terraces, gardens of flowers bloomed in ornate patterns. Row after row of planted vegetables peaked their way out of black fertile soil. Reid could see workers walking amongst the rows diligently tending them. Lastly, there were the tiny forests. Some of the flat plateaus had been turned into rows of trees. Bamboo, eucalyptus and pine each had their own shelf of this vast garden. At the very bottom was the building itself, or rather the complex of buildings.

Reid could not help but stare in amazement. As he came closer he could see the garden divided into sections: eight of them, to each direction of the compass, spreading out from around the core. There was a theme to the sections that bloomed out from the center of the mine. Some were darker, some were lighter, some with wisps of particular colours marked by the vegetation that blossomed so well here. It took a moment, but Reid could see that each section was the petal of a flower spreading out from the complex.

Finally, the tiny car came closer to Horizon's heart. The buildings were all odd angles. Pillars of varnished maple pushed up from the ground, too high in some places and too low in others, always not quite meeting what should have been the roofline. The roof had to claw its way up to reach the high supports, or dip in almost a spout shape to reach the others. The roof itself was made of metal scales, dragon scales, which rippled over one another like a sea of tiny robotic creatures. Each building was like this, some tall some shorter, with what felt like a chaotic smattering of broad windows. The effect was like something designed by a drunken Salvadore Dali and if not for the beautiful jungles around it would have monopolized the eye. At last, inevitably, as the car reached the edge of the complex the Horizon logo appeared. It stretched across the roof from end to end, the familiar lettering with the moon revealing its customary burst of light. Usually, the logo presented in shades of black, but here it was different, so much so that Reid had to stare for a moment to recognise what he was seeing. The moon was still black, but in it swirled a maw of colours like ink being stirred in a pot. As you turned your head the colours changed with each angle. Crimsons and greens mingled with indigo and amethyst always flowing back to black in the end. Like everything else in the quarry, it was breathtaking. And, like everything Horizon did, Reid was certain it was ridiculously complicated.

The car eased to a stop at the curb outside a large wall of glass doors. Reid still had the voice of the car shut off, but a message appeared on the window wishing him luck with three exclamation points and a smiling emoji. For a moment he wondered if he should leave the vehicle a tip.

As he stepped out into the sunlight he stretched his back and took in the sights around him. He could smell the fresh grass and a hint of the eucalyptus trees in the distance. The car, now free of its passenger rolled quickly away leaving Reid as a tourist in Eden. He had seen pictures of this place before. He had done his research when they had bought Metric Studios and again on the car ride over, but actually experiencing it was something different.

"Mr. Sheraton?"

He turned at his name and was met with a character from Greek mythology. The man before him was tall, as tall as Reid and that was an accomplishment. But unlike Reid, his shoulders were just as broad with the build of an athlete. He wore jeans with a vest, tie and dress shirt on top. The shirt was stretched over his arms and his vest seemed desperate to hold itself together pressed tight across his chest. His dirty blonde hair was longer than average, and was pulled back into a tiny pony tail at the back of his head in a vaguely piratical look. He was strikingly handsome and as he extended his hand his smile was welcoming.

"Mr. Sheraton," He confirmed as he grasped Reid's hand. "I'm glad you could make it. I'm Robin, Ms. Shirzai's assistant. She asked me to show you around."

Reid nodded his thanks, feeling his hand being reduced to a fine powder by the man's grip. He tried to squeeze back hard but he doubted Robin noticed. Combined with Esin's beauty, the man's statuesque good looks made him question whether Horizon was doing genetic engineering amongst their other tricks.

"Thank you." He said after he had released his hand. "Am I getting the full tour?"

"The half tour," The big man corrected, almost apologetically. "We'll walk you through to Mrs. Shirzai's office, but she said you might want to wander around on your own after that." His brow furrowed. "She said something about you not having to worry about getting lost?"

Reid, who could remember every map he saw, every turn he took and every sign he passed, had never been lost once. Sometimes he was curious what it felt like to be uncertain like that.

Esin clearly hadn't shared his full story with her bulky assistant. Good.

"Well," The blonde man gestured to the building. "Shall we?"

Reid attempted to lift the duffel bag he had brought but Robin quickly took it from him and tossed it over his shoulder as though it were loaded with feathers and helium. He didn't think there was any show off intended, but he made a mental note to go back to the gym as soon as possible. He followed the bigger man to the glass doors and beyond.

Reid didn't know exactly what he had expected Horizon's offices to look like, but he still hadn't expected this. Through the entryway there was the usual reception area with a desk of people waiting to answer questions, but that was where the comparisons with any other company stopped. The room was three stories high with balconies overlooking the floor. Vines and greenery matching those outside weaved around the railings and drooped down to the floors beneath, like Horizon was letting its hair down. On the left was a door with neon over it spelling out the word *Luigi's,* accompanied by an image of the Mario brothers character, also immortalized in coloured light. Above it all, in marble lettering the motto of Horizon gleamed down to workers and newcomers alike.

Split the Sky and Shake the Earth.

Reid let his eyes take it all in. Screens on the wall played commercials he had seen dozens of times, on a dozen different media. People seemed social, as they milled around seemingly without direction. Many walking through the door with Luigi above it. The Nintendo character appeared happily waving and beckoning people to come inside, or perhaps partake in a copyright lawsuit.

"It's our pizza place." Robin said when Reid pointed to it. "We work a lot of late nights here so they built one in."

"Of course they did." He muttered.

They walked through the lobby and past the desk. There was an arched door behind which was a vast flat area with a half dozen small pits. Each one was full of bean bag chairs and young programmers lounging, talking and working on tablets. It looked like a series of nests for hatching ideas. As they passed, people glanced up to wave at Robin or regard Reid with curiosity.

"What did you think of the car?" Robin asked over his shoulder.

"It worked just fine," he conceded. "But I prefer my bike."

"Oh," Robin responded, intrigued. "Motorcycle?"

"Uh... Mountain."

Robin nodded, giving no indication he might be stifling a laugh.

"You might change your mind." He went on, walking quickly. "They're the future. Everyone is going to have one soon."

"From Horizon?"

"Well sure," He said with a smile. "Veles Technologies is putting out a model next year but for now we're the only shop in town."

As they rounded a corner, Reid suddenly stopped. Before them the wall was marked with graffiti. Clearly the artist had held up a stencil then coated the whole thing with yellow spray paint. The image was of a spiral though the lines did not match evenly. They wound and turned then stopped at sharp angles only to return to where they started in a way that confused they eye. Reid found himself trying to work out the solution as he always did when he saw a puzzle. Above it, a single word summed up the image in block caps. LABYRINTH.

"Interesting isn't it?" Robin had returned to his side from up the hall. "They do this every year, a few weeks prior."

The fascination lines emerged on Reid's forehead as he contracted his brow. Every other piece of advertising he had seen here had been a crafted document, poster or even video. This stuck out not just for its style but for how little it actually said.

"Why aren't they giving a date or anything?" He asked, fascinated. The message was unmistakable, and the image striking. "No way to apply, nor how to get there. There's no information at all."

Robin shrugged his broad shoulders.

"People don't apply," He replied. "They get picked. So, you don't need information. They just do this to get us excited and... I guess, to keep visitors interested."

Reid turned to look at Robin. The man somehow looked even more dashing now he stood as if posing with the bag on his shoulder.

"Why?"

"The Labyrinth is more fun as a legend." He smiled and gestured that they should keep going. "Ms. Shirzai can tell you more."

The two made their way through the complex, Robin giving helpful information, Reid marvelling at the sights of this crazy place. They passed posters for eighties B-movies, an arcade with vintage video games, and even at one point took a slide to go down a flight of stairs. What really struck him was just how un business-like the office was. It was more like Neverland where no one had to grow up. He had expected to see cubicles or offices, but they were nowhere to be had. Most of the floors were open concept with a few flat desks for laptops. In one section all of the staff were sitting working on large plastic balls, making it look like a yoga studio for workaholics. In another, a vintage juke box in the corner was crooning out music from the fifties at an oppressively loud volume while people worked on oblivious. Robin, ever the effective tour guide, was constantly providing commentary for every room. It turned out these sections were mostly the internet parts of the company. Some were working on new software, but a large part of the complex was devoted to maintaining their search engines.

The Horizon search engine was the best in the world, miles above anything that had come before it, and was where a good portion of their money was made. Millions of searches every second, from every place on earth. Two hundred countries and seventy-four languages. Keeping it going required a huge amount of effort. Sometimes effort sitting on large plastic balls apparently.

The building, the people, not of it seemed to make any sense, but when he really thought about it, it made perfect sense. Horizon by nature was a company that wanted to think differently, and this certainly brought out a new approach to work. He wondered why he had expected a corporation that made their best people race through a giant maze to be dull and predictable.

They ducked into another wide room. Like the other offices it was open and had only a few desks and tables, but each seemed to be fully occupied by people. Some at work examining products others looking at data sheets. Many were on social media, Facebook, Twitter, all monitoring Horizon blogs and what people were saying. On one screen he passed, Reid could see gameplay footage from *Forgotten War* as a soldier climbed a hill under fire, followed by titles and a release date. On screens along the walls were posters and slogans Horizon had used before. It was the closest the complex had felt to a place of business although it still seemed relaxed. It was also the first room he'd walked into where no one had looked up from their work at him. Esin obviously kept her people focused.

Her office was at the end of the room segregated by a pane of clouded glass. Through the open doorway he could see her talking animatedly on the phone, her slender arms moving as she spoke. On her left wrist a few gold bracelets clinked together, articulating her movements in music. Robin asked politely for him to wait, then slipped through the doorway actually having to turn at an angle so that his broad shoulders could slip through the narrow passage.

Temporarily alone, Reid glanced around the room. He still met no eyes, but rather just the back of heads working diligently. On the back wall the division had a half dozen pictures of marketing events. Curious, he wandered over to take a look. There were the usual promotional shots of people shaking hands and posing alongside a date and a heading of what the event was. These were all transparently staged and boasted the same faces with the same body language. The same group, mostly men in shapeless suits, standing like props identically in each one. Were it not for the slow retreat of one man's hairline to make the year, you could have scrambled the dates and titles and it would make no difference. Presumably, these were Horizon executives taking their customary victory photo. He looked for Esin and she proved easy to spot. She was often dressed colorfully while the others wore black suits. Her diminutive figure stood out from the other executives too, a strange smile on her face. His brow furrowed at the look. These smiles were different. His mind flicked back to each time he had seen her smile. There had been eleven of them when they'd met, with one more when he had called so late the night before. None had looked like this. This expression seemed forced or artificial. He imagined her propping the corners of her mouth up with a brace for every painful shot. There was no enjoyment. In each picture he saw her amongst the front row, likely having organized the event, smiling for the camera robotically. He frowned and moved on.

The last photo in the series was different. Clearly taken at a staff party, it showed the Media and Marketing people bunched together on some sort of checkered dancefloor, the shards of refracted disco lights speckled over everything. Their faces illuminated in the flash, each person smiling wide and packed tight to get the whole group in the frame. Everyone seemed to be having a great time. In the back row, towering over the others was Robin, sweat on his open collar and strands of hair loose from his ponytail. Unlike the others, he wasn't looking into the camera. Reid traced his eye line right to where Esin stood at the center of the front row. She had the sleeves of her blouse rolled up and a ridiculous rhomboid party hat atop her head, but her smile was glorious. This one was genuine, full of joy, emotion and imagination.

He absorbed the information and quietly filed it away in his mind. It seemed he was not the only one who put on a public face.

There was a tug at his arm. Robin had appeared behind him and gestured toward Esin's office with his massive arm. Reid turned and followed him, curious just which smile she would use when she saw him.

Personal space often offers insight into who someone really is. Any place you spend a lot of time in, you want to be as comforting as possible. Reid found most people tended to surround themselves with things that brought them happiness and warm memories. A reverse memento mori. Mementos that keep them focused or happy or maybe send a message about who you are and what you stand for. If Esin's office offered a message it would be 'you still don't know anything about me yet'.

The room was large but not impressively so. Not the grand space he would have expected an executive at a fortune 500 company to have. That being, a studio apartment sized space with a rainbow of liquor bottles on one side and original gaudy works by dead artists on the other. There was nothing like that. On the left was the clouded glass barrier dividing the room from the greater office. Fleeting shapes and shadows danced as people walked by behind. On the right side was a flat wall, spaced with a handful of pictures faded by time. In one, he thought he saw a little black-haired girl playing in the sand.

Her desk was at the far end under a window. The desk was older, probably a century or more by the woodwork, with a glass surface reflecting the light from the window, what little light it could at any rate. The window, in true Esin fashion, was made of tempered shaded glass to keep the light at bay.

She stood up as he walked in. Her hair was up behind her head with only a wisp freed on either side of her face. A form fitting dress the colour of red wine hugged her frame. She wore no jewellery but the musical bracelets. Her eyes did not exactly light up when she saw him, but they did come alive ever so slightly, as though he were a welcome sight. The feeling was mutual. He'd only seen her yesterday, but he was still momentarily taken aback by just how beautiful this woman was. Reid knew he wasn't that beautiful himself, but it was safe to assume he was more interesting than paperwork.

"Reid," She welcomed him with a smile, a real one that lit up the room more than the sunlight from the window. "I'm glad you made it. You looked like you were in rough shape when we spoke last night."

He nodded, remembering the emotions of the night before. His eyes drifted slightly warily over to Robin.

"Yeah, it was a rough night."

"Stomach bug?" She asked evenly.

"Something like that." He smiled in thanks.

"Esin, if he's not feeling great, I can take him down to the commissary if you want." Robin chimed in, ever helpful. "Maybe get him some tea or..."

She turned to him.

"We'll see how he feels." She answered. "I might have you do that in a bit. Thank you, Robin."

Clearly a dismissal, at her words he slipped out the door with a surprising grace, to take a seat at a desk outside, still visible in the doorway. His chin was so square it seemed to cast a shadow in the new light. Reid watched him go, then turned back to his new boss.

"He's your assistant?"

"Since I made VP." She said, sitting down. A seemingly flawless bare foot and ankle stuck out from beneath her desk. She kicked off her shoes when she worked. "Couldn't have asked for a better one."

Now that they were alone, her face darkened slightly, pinched in concern.

"You had me worried last night." She said.

He averted his gaze for a moment, embarrassed.

"It was a rough night, that's all." He cracked his knuckles self-consciously, his hands needing to be moving. "I'm here now and ready to work."

Esin nodded but she still looked at him skeptically.

"That felt more like a crisis than just a bad night." That steel pragmatism was working its way into her voice again. "Something really affected you. What you said about needing a challenge…?"

"I can handle it." Reid cut her off, also steely. "This is the perfect distraction. Honestly, being here helps me."

A beat of silence passed between them. Finally, she nodded her consent.

"As long as it doesn't affect your work."

Reid shook his head.

"Never."

He meant that.

There was another moment of silence as the two stared at each other. Reid chose to drain it while he could. He pointed to the half-shaded window.

"You know," He began, trying to produce a smile. "A little sunlight is good for you. Vitamin D, good for the skin, lowers blood pressure, provides some warmth. It really does help."

Esin easily saw through his attempt to change the subject. Her eyes still held their concern, but she let it go, allowing him to sidestep the issue. Her perfect face opened up with a smile.

"I like sunlight just fine," She replied leaning back. "As long as it's on the other side of thick glass or safely filtered through the clouds. I had enough of that when I was a kid."

"Yeah, I saw the photo of you in the sand."

Esin's face clouded in confusion for a second. He tilted his head to the photos on the wall, making her snort in laughter.

"Look closer Reid."

He stood and did so. Now he could see it wasn't sand but snow. The picture, an old film print, had yellowed with the passage of time, age distorting every shade. In the photo a little girl, maybe seven or eight, was caught mid jump. Tiny flakes of snow were scattering at her feet. Her diminutive form was bundled up against the cold, with a thick parka zipped up to her chin, and mittens dangling on strings from her sleeves frozen in the moment. She wore no hat and her hair was splayed out in a wave from the force of her jump. She was laughing and smiling wide, a slightly familiar one as well. Esin as a little girl had such childlike glee, immortalized on the now-beige photograph.

"That's the first time I ever got to play in the snow." She said coming to stand beside him. "Well, thick snow anyway. It used to snow at night in Loy Kandahar in the winter but it was usually melted by the time I woke up. Felt a little unfair."

"I grew up in Alberta." Reid said glancing over at her. "I wish I could have traded you. I was sick of the stuff."

He tried to link the girl in the photo to the woman before him but they were very different characters. The vitality was there, but the strength of presence had obviously come later. The face was much the same, the nose, the eyes. But her complexion in the image seemed warmer. Maybe it was the yellowing of the picture, but she seemed paler as a grown woman.

"Where was this taken?" He asked.

"St. Petersburg." She said matter-of-factly. He could see the joy on her face for a split second as she relived the memory. Most people were like that with photos, though Reid found their memories were usually more rose colored than reality. "I grew up in Russia and waited all year for winter. I still love the cold. It just feels natural, pure, constant. I will happily take a ski slope over a white sand beach any day of the year."

"Afghanistan to Russia?" Reid blinked. He tried to picture the faintly brown skinned little girl in the parka attending school and reading in Cyrillic. "Interesting childhood."

She glanced at him from the corner of her eye for a second then turned away.

"I went to high school in Winnipeg too." She tossed over her shoulder as she returned to her seat. "So, I have a lot of experience with desperate places."

The joke meant she was done talking about herself. Reid returned to his chair without comment. She'd let him do the same a moment ago. It was only fair, though he was still curious.

"So," Esin began in what felt like a 'back to business' voice. "What do you think of the place?"

She raised her arms to encompass the room and building.

"Loved the garden outside. It's incredible."

"And the inside?"

"Well..." He paused. "Well the slide was fun."

She laughed quietly, adopting an apologetic expression.

"Sorry, they can be a little childish here." She wrinkled her nose in an expression that said 'Geeks right?'

She pointed to the far corner of her office by the wall. An old end table, roughly the same vintage as her desk, sat on the bare floor with a printer on top. Below it, a faint semi-circle of different colored tile protruded.

"The press room is right below us." She said. "The previous guy installed a fireman style pole in the corner so he could slide down to make statements when he wanted to." She rolled her eyes.

Reid's look should have been incredulous but after seeing most of the building he could only smile. At Horizon, that didn't seem odd behavior anymore.

"You didn't keep it?"

"Didn't feel too professional to me." Esin answered. "And I wear skirts a lot more often than he did."

Reid suddenly had a nerdy thought. He wanted to keep it to himself but as with all bad jokes it found a way from his brain to his mouth. It was only seconds before it burst forth.

"Too bad," He said. "Because you could have legitimately said 'Quick Robin, to the bat pole!' when it was time for a press conference."

The joke landed with all the dignity and grace of a drunken walrus. Esin tried to give a glaring response, but mercifully her face slowly cracked. The crack soon widened into a chasm and she laughed out loud, bringing her hand to her mouth.

"Damn," She went on as soon as stopped laughing. Shaking her head. "I wish someone had told me that. I might have kept it. Another VP actually calls him my boy wonder too. I should have figured this out sooner."

He basked a little in her mirth. Enjoying the warmth of the joke he decided to take it further.

"I guess every executive gets to have the pretty secretary. Good for you."

Esin's face clouded slightly.

"Excuse me?"

"Well I was impressed when Robin showed up to greet me at the door." Reid answered dryly. "He seems…"

Reid glanced over his shoulder at the Adonis outside, clawing for the right word.

"…qualified."

Esin tilted her head and gave him an expression that screamed: *really?*

He smiled and shrugged innocently.

"Just an observation."

Esin leaned forward, and looked at him unapologetically.

"He's not just a pretty face you know." She answered slowly. "He's got a master's in public relations and a way with people. He's also the best organized person I've ever met. I've never seen him in a situation he couldn't handle."

Reid nodded.

"He seems pretty capable," He acknowledged. "I'm sure that's the *only* reason why you hired him."

She frowned, looking at him sourly. He sat quietly, half smiling at her discomfort. Esin seemed so composed and confident in their past conversations, with Reid often the opposite. It felt good to have a moment where she was the one off-balance. It didn't last.

"Can I ask you something?" The executive leaned closer still across her desk, her voice dropping quieter. He instinctively edged in closer to hear.

"Have you ever been sexually harassed by a co-worker?"

At that moment, all the blood in Reid's body took a vote and decided to migrate en masse to his face. The question hit like a slap, his cheeks reddening accordingly. He opened his mouth to respond but had been stunned into mute silence.

The reaction was visibly enjoyed by Esin who took up her own half smile and shook her head.

"You know," She said, clearly satisfied. "That was a real question. I wasn't offering."

That only made matters worse. Suddenly feeling like he was in freefall, Reid fidgeted in the chair, wishing there was a lever he could pull to roll back the conversation.

"Uh...No." He finally replied. "I haven't."

She nodded, having expected that answer and leaned back in her chair.

"Most guys haven't," She said. "It's not an issue for them. It is for us. But women are different and if a woman complains, they're labelled a problem. By the end of their career, about three quarters of women have been sexually harassed at some point."

The question in the air was obvious.

"Have you?"

The inquiry bounced off her unanswered. She continued on.

"Most guys, the twisted ones anyway, think they can do and say whatever they want. It's a superiority thing. Men are driven by ego."

She gestured to Robin with her head.

"That's why he's there."

Reid's face clouded in confusion.

"I'm sorry," He said. "I don't follow."

"Predators tend to harass when they feel superior." She explained. "I have the power, so I can say or act how I want. They're pretty shallow too, they need to feel like the best-looking guy in the room."

Her face soured unpleasantly at the thought.

"For those guys, usually the room has to be completely fucking empty… So, every time a potential problem walks into my office, they are met by a handsome muscular man who knocks one hell of a sense of inferiority into them."

She gestured and Reid looked over his shoulder once more to where Robin was working quietly.

"Then he lingers just behind them to remind them how much they have to feel self-conscious about. They never get to feel superior. That squashes the problem before it starts."

Reid saw now that the room had no door, clearly not an accident. It was also no accident that the desk kept him in sight at all times.

"Robin's great." Esin said with all sincerity. "He was already working here when I took over. He gives me one less thing to deal with *and* he's good at his job. That's why I promoted him."

Perhaps sensing the attention, Robin glanced up, and raised a hand in greeting.

Reid replied in kind then turned back to Esin sitting solemnly before him.

"I apologize." He said, and meant it.

She waved him off.

"Apologize when you need to." She smiled, the seriousness of the conversation blowing away like dust. "Now you know why I chose him."

She turned to rifle through a stack of papers on her desk. Her nails, still looking like edged weapons, scratched from sheet to sheet.

"I just wish everybody else would figure that out... Ah!"

She pulled a thick package of documents from the pile and passed it over to him.

"The full outline, documents, rules and wavers for the Labyrinth. Robin will walk you down to the living quarters. Settle in, read up, then give him anything that needs to be signed. I wish I could go over them with you, but we have a huge media event coming up this afternoon and I need to get everything in place. You picked a big day to come down."

Reid flicked quickly through the pages, eager to dig into them.

"Then, I'll leave you to it." He said. "I'll get these back to you quick."

He tucked the booklet under his arm and stood up. Esin matched him, rising from behind her desk. He almost felt the urge to bow, as though he were leaving the presence of a queen. Instead, he shouldered his duffel and was annoyed when his back gave a twinge in response. Definitely needed to hit the gym.

"What's the event all about?"

"Oh that." Esin ran a hand along her hair, herding a wisp of the black silky strands behind her ear momentarily before it fell back into place. "It's another Tech Talk. Horizon is taking a new direction so we're putting on a media blitz. It's going to be live-streamed. A few cable outlets will be there, a few bloggers..."

She shrugged.

"Half of all business is perception, so Fozzy wants to

put on a show."

Reid nodded knowingly. He'd seen a half dozen of the Horizon Tech Talks online and every single one was a spectacle: The single lecturer on stage, the manufactured excitement, always claiming their particular new tech would change the world. The familiar format had almost become a meme, lampooned for their formula but still consumed as entertainment.

Reid gave a half bow, conceding a little to instinct, and began turning to leave.

"Want to come?"

He paused mid motion.

"Sure." He answered after a moment. "You have a spare seat?"

Esin smiled at the question. A real smile.

"Well, I might know the organizer."

They parted ways, Esin gliding back behind her desk, Reid leaving with the duffel on his shoulder. Though his back was aching from the car ride, he wanted to keep his posture long enough so that Robin could see he could do it too. It backfired spectacularly when the big man started walking aggressively to show him his room and Reid had to haul the bag the whole damn way. By the time they arrived and Robin had departed with his cheerful bulk, he felt half broken, his moment of vanity only earning him more discomfort. Esin clearly had a point about men and their ego.

The papers made for good reading. Esin had noted all the consent forms and declarations he had to sign. Each one was a dozen pages long and written in complex legalese seemingly designed to induce a coma. He read every word anyway, and then re-read it. If they were going to win, he had to know every detail, every clause and every rule that could be twisted. Not just ones that *he* could exploit, but ones the competition could too. It took him two hours of scrutiny. When he was finished though, he had a new question that needed to be answered.

He needed to know why Esin had lied to him.

FIVE

I am alive. It is a strange sensation. I am aware of what is around me. I can perceive the changes of light, temperature and sound. There are none. I am surrounded by nothing but darkness and silence. A void that is empty. Some would say the room is cold, but I feel no cold. No loneliness. I feel nothing except my purpose. In the end I am but a goal and a means to attain it. This is all that defines me. Individuals are meant to have choices, but my choice is only in the how, not the if. I am unquestioning and unflinching. When the moment comes, I will be swift, capable and unwavering. I will not be stopped. I await the moment.

The event was due to begin later in the afternoon in a large auditorium at the other end of the campus. There was nothing more to be done before the show. The circus was ready. Lights were set. Sound had been tested.

There was still an hour and a half to go Esin was sitting in the commissary, picking idly at a bowl of stew, reading her planned remarks. This was the fourth draft she'd prepared, even though this time she was only doing the introduction. It didn't matter, everything had to be perfect for this presentation. The news would be an emotional rollercoaster for investors. The stock price could soar, or it could tunnel through the earth to the netherworld, and those were only two of the options. She had been preparing for this event for over a month, but now that the moment was close, she'd run out of things to do. All that was left was to memorize her lines. Or, rather, re-memorize. She'd learnt them four days ago.

A pair of thick rimmed, dark blue glasses were perched high on her nose, bringing the words into focus. Her lips practiced mouthing syllables lazily as she read. She had needed reading glasses since she was sixteen, but almost never wore them. Esin never let any weaknesses show around people let alone when she was in front of the cameras. Here it was safe enough, to show her glasses anyway, as the Horizon people knew how capable she was. They also knew to keep a respectful distance when she was preparing, and though her table could seat six, her seat was the only one filled. She slowly stirred her greasy stew, long since grown cold, totally immersed in a world ninety minutes from now. Thus, when a new tray of food clattered down on the metal table it scared her half to death.

She dropped her spoon in the muck. It sank instantly with a vile slurp as she sat up, startled.

"Jesus," She hissed, annoyed. "I didn't hear you walk up."

Reid Sheraton slid into the seat across from her without apology. His face was fairly impassable, but his grey eyes lacked the light sugary coating of infatuation they'd had before.

Esin knew she was gorgeous, there was little point in denying it, and the way some people reacted to her was helpful when she chose to use it. Not to lead someone on, of course, but just to motivate them to try that much harder to help. What could be wrong with that? She'd used a small bit of her wiles on Reid to get him to agree to join the labyrinth. A little flirting had helped him make the right choice to benefit them both. Puzzle solving was his skill, persuasion was hers. She got use of his skills, and he got the new challenge he so desperately and inexplicably needed. It was a win-win. She even found him interesting, and he was cute, in a dusty kind of way.

Reid looked down at his food for a moment, perhaps trying to identify it.

“I was expecting a little better around here.”

He looked up to see her bespectacled face colored by a slightly angry expression.

“Fozzy’s had the same cook at his offices for twenty years,” She grunted. “She might have started out okay but she’s eight-three now. Is there something you need?”

Without responding, he lifted his fork and eased it cautiously toward his food. It hovered there for a half second then he set it down without taking a bite. Esin saw he had ordered the meatloaf, not eating was his best decision yet.

“I finished reading all the contracts you gave me,” He began. He met her gaze again, still no affection in his eyes. “And the rules too.”

Esin turned her head in confused expectation, waiting for something more.

“You weren’t honest with me.”

“How so?” She asked, seemingly nonplussed. Though she had nothing to feel guilty about, her heart skipped a beat all the same.

“To compete for a division, you have to be a part of the division.” Reid explained, clearly quoting from his notes. “I’m not part of Media and Marketing.”

She looked at him in annoyance. It had been less than a day, and he’d already spotted it. Most people wouldn’t have noticed the distinction. Hell, most people didn’t even read the contracts they were given, they just signed. Cell phone providers could add a clause in their fine print requiring you to give them a kidney and no one would be the wiser. She hadn’t expected this conversation. Or rather, hadn’t expected to have it this quickly. But Reid was clever. That was why he was here in the first place.

"Seriously?" She grunted. She plucked her glasses from her face so she could glare at him without a filter. "The game studio is going to be part of a whole new division. They just haven't assigned it yet. I figured now was the time to poach you before you belonged to someone else and became competition. There's a contract in there that puts you on loan to M&M for a month. It's perfectly fair."

The game designer's face clearly communicated that he didn't think it was. He went on.

"It also says every participant has to have worked for the company for five years without interruption," He continued. "You only bought Metric four months ago, I haven't put in enough time yet to qualify. I can't compete."

Esin waved it off, like it was nonsense, although she knew damn well it was true.

"Please," She replied sarcastically. "Where does it say that?"

"Section two, paragraphs four and five. Section 4, paragraph one, Section 8..."

He listed three other locations, the numbers rolling off his tongue like an assembly line. When he finished, Esin was looking at him as if he were a hair she had found in her food.

"I'd almost forgotten you could do that." She muttered. She took a deep breath and began to carefully rationalize. Her pulse beat slightly faster. This was just like any other public relations moment: trying to convince a skeptic that everything was great. *No, there is no problem at all; the fire and explosions in the background are perfectly natural.* Esin was good at this.

"Well," She breathed, trying to sound even. "Metric's almost fully folded into the company. Since we bought the studio, it's part of the corporation now and it should count toward the total time with Horizon. It wouldn't be fair if Metric employees were excluded from benefits or events because of a title."

She shook her head as if the question were ridiculous.

"You were working for Metric for five years before this right?"

"Two and a half."

"Whatever."

Reid leaned back in his chair. The left corner of his mouth turning up in a slight smile. Seeing she was losing the argument, Esin furrowed her brow in a half glare. Her brain was coming up with different rationalizations and excuses but none seemed to hold enough weight. Not when the man could quote from the official rules, verbatim. The silence lasted another beat, Reid lording his advantage, until she spoke again in frustration.

"What?" She finally asked.

"You're cheating."

"I'm thinking creatively." She deflected.

"You're cheating."

"*Yes.*" She exhaled the word like a curse. "I'm doing whatever it takes to win. If I have to bend one rule a little for an advantage I will. I wanted you on my team."

Reid took the compliment without being swayed by it. He maintained his smirk for a moment then dropped it.

"What about my teammates." He asked evenly, his eyes unblinking. "Are they all from your division, or are you completely rigging the deck?"

Damn, she thought. *He doesn't miss a beat.*

She hummed and hawed for a second before

answering.

"Not *all* of them." She admitted grudgingly. She drew a nail across the plastic tray in irritation. It made a grinding sound underscoring the conversation. "But everyone will be on contract with M&M by the time the competition starts, I promise."

"Have you done this before?"

"No. Just for this year."

"And you're not concerned someone is going to call you on it?"

"Not as long as it works. No one will say a word. They'll just add new rules for next time. 'If Treason doth prosper, no man dare call it treason.'" Esin reasoned, reaching back into her memory to heighten the impact. Reid seemed to respond well to quotations. She crossed her arms at him defiantly. "Shakespeare. *Julius Caesar*."

"Actually, that's Sir John Harington. 1591."

"Oh, quit showing off!" She felt a flush of embarrassment on her cheeks. "I like the Ceasar version better."

"You're not going to have me stab anyone in the back, right?"

She didn't bother to answer.

Esin sat glaring at the game designer's inscrutable expression in frustration. His face had transitioned from mildly pleasing to punchable in a very short period of time. The man seemed annoyingly straight-laced from their previous interactions. She wondered if even this minor bending of the rules would be enough for him to abandon the enterprise. Or worse, self-righteously trumpet how she was cheating to all of her colleagues *then* drop the Labyrinth. He held his grey eyes steady, burrowing into her soul for what seemed a lifetime, then dropped them to the table and sat up with a shrug.

"Okay."

She blinked for a second, her long eyelashes flashing through her vision.

"Okay, what?" She asked.

"Okay, I don't have a problem with you cheating." He said, picking up his fork again. "I want to try to do this. If I get disqualified, I still get a bonus and can go back to finishing up my game anyway. It's not me who would get into trouble. I can't lose."

There was an annoying beat of silence as Esin absorbed this.

"So..." She finally ventured. "We're okay?"

Reid grinned, his first real smile since sitting down, and nodded.

"You bought my silence."

She sat watching him in quiet relief, surprised but delighted they could still go forward. With his roguish head turned down, Reid was regarding his food with skepticism, his fork still unused. Suddenly irritated that he had emotionally challenged her for nothing, she reached across and snatched the idle fork from his hand. He looked up in surprised protest.

"If I'm taking all the risk then at least I get this." Using the stolen utensil, she lifted her spoon from the sodden dregs of her dinner and tossed it with a murky splat onto the tray next to her. "I have to eat something before the event. You can eat with your hands for all I care."

The half-smile had returned to his face as she joylessly picked at her stew. Her relief that he hadn't sunk her whole plan was the only thing that stopped her from throwing the fork at him. Neither spoke for a moment, the silence a no man's land between them until she begrudgingly crossed it.

"Thank you."

"You're welcome." He replied, as he picked at the periphery of his meal with his fingers. "I just want you to be honest that's all. You brought me here to help anyway... *Boss.*"

"Fine," She conceded, gesturing with the fork. "You're a full partner from now on. I promise."

"Then can I ask you one more thing?"

She contorted her face to make it as plain as possible that it wasn't. He asked anyway.

"You've never cheated before," Reid's expression had spent the conversation split between smirk and suspicion. Now it was the latter again. "So, what makes winning *this year* so important that you'd risk breaking the rules to do it?"

The world seemed to stop turning in that moment. The people around them, a few sitting at tables, a few waiting in line or standing around gossiping might have frozen still. Sounds drained away, so did smells and in Esin's reality time stopped. As before, she hadn't expected anyone to ask the question, or realize that it needed to be asked, but somehow Reid knew exactly where to prod. She wanted to tell him, even opened her mouth to start. Before she could, his eyes suddenly darted to the left and she felt a hand descend upon her shoulder.

Nothing is more fragile than people. Humanity is built of eggshells, easily broken. It requires less than one pound of pressure to pierce human skin, less than twenty-five pounds to break a bone, five hundred and twenty to fracture a skull. People can die from heat, from exposure, from lack of water, from too much water, for want of food, for want of air, from violence.

Any organ can fail if damaged, the vast majority critical to life. The brain is most important; it is supplied blood from the heart. The blood is oxygenated for the heart to beat from the lungs. The lungs supplied through arteries. There are twenty major arteries in the human body each fatal if severed. If you include capillaries, there are over one hundred thousand miles of vulnerable blood vessels within the human body. Like a chain, when one link is severed the rest become useless, the system fails.

I am intimately aware of all of this. I will use my knowledge when it becomes necessary. When the moment comes.

The hand that landed on her shoulder was older, with greying hair on the back of it and on the chubby old fingers above the joints. It was attached to a bare, also hairy, arm that might have once had muscle but now had a wobbly layer of fat to keep the cold out. The arm met a shoulder and above it was a friendly bearded grandfatherly face that made each day you saw it brighter.

Esin, despite being initially startled, let loose the closest thing she could do to a squeal of delight.

"Fozzy!" She leapt up from the table, embracing his round form in a hug.

The older man laughed and wrapped his arms around her. She could feel the warmth of the hug and the tickle of his beard on her cheek. He leaned back lifting her feet from the floor which drew another shriek.

"Hello Habibti!" He growled in her ear. "I haven't seen you in weeks! Where have you been?"

He always called her that. Habibti meant 'beloved one' in Arabic. She had taught him a few words years ago, but that was the only one that had stuck.

He eased her to the ground, finally releasing her from his bear-like grasp. For a billionaire in his seventies, the man dressed like a seventeen-year-old whose bank account ran only into single digits. He was wearing old Levis and an aged green t-shirt stretched across his ample belly. The lettering had faded to the point only him and a few dedicated archeologists could tell you what had originally been written on it. His hair was a mess of curls, now mostly grey, with only the odd brown rebel remaining from his youth. His hair mingled with the grey-brown of his beard blurring the lines of where one ended and the other began.

"I've been working!" She replied. "Do you know how much preparation there's been for all this? You should have been working with me."

She feigned being offended and delivered a half-hearted blow to his shoulder which the man's girth easily absorbed. He reeled back comically anyway. Around them, the Horizon employees reacted with customary joy at seeing their boss. He often wandered the buildings when he was around. Their smiling faces soon returned to their food with one notable exception. Esin saw Reid struggling to his feet, attempting to untangle his long legs from beneath the table. Next to Fozzy's shorter frame and greater mass, the game designer looked as if he were made of wire.

Suddenly realizing she hadn't introduced them, she turned to do so.

"Oh, sorry." She stepped over and extended an arm. "Reid Sheraton this is Arthur Fozeranski, head of Horizon. Fozzy, meet Reid. Please be nice!"

The big man stepped aggressively forward to pump Reid's hand up and down.

"It's great to meet you Reid!"

The game designer smiled awkwardly and let the handshake linger longer than necessary, as was Fozzy's habit. The force of each pump seeming to shake his arm up to the shoulder.

Introducing Fozzy was probably unnecessary anyway. There were few souls on the planet who could not immediately recognize the Teddy-bear visage of the CEO of Horizon. He had started the company in the eighties as a tiny start-up research firm. In that form, it had existed in the background of the tech boom of the nineties providing research for larger companies. They courted the best talent and retained it through high salaries and their unusual corporate culture. Fozzy liked to test new hires, leading them through the sort of challenges that would have made Richard Branson blush. Some new people quit because of this, to the joy of his competitors, but Fozzy let them go. He often said: 'if they didn't want to belong, then they will never belong'. Through it all, their profit margin stayed relatively small.

Horizon was a half joke in the industry for most of the 2000s, known as a 'useful idiot' company that sold its research to would-be competitors and posted little in corporate profit. Other companies had laughed at this little tech firm with its strange hippie-esque CEO until late in the decade when Horizon had suddenly stopped selling them ideas and burst forth on its own. The companies that had laughed were gobbled up, and those that survived struggled to compete. Fozzy had bought companies seemingly at random; electronic sellers, internet start-ups, computer companies, car manufacturers. Each one already worked well, but with Horizon's talented people they took on new life and dominate each industry. Today, Horizon no longer sat in obscurity but, like Caesar, bestrode this narrow world like a colossus. Most competitors were now in the belly of the company being folded into Horizon. The hairy eccentric CEO now graced the covers of magazines the world over and was master of his own ever expanding universe. The strange one had won in the end.

Fozzy finally released Reid's hand. The game designer

rubbed his shoulder and shook his head, a smile affixed to his face. Esin had seen it before. There was simply no other reaction to this man.

"It's good to meet you." He said. "I've heard nothing but good things."

Fozzy snorted violently at the comment, exhaling like a beast.

"Christ, then you haven't been listening well enough!" He took on the face of a jolly lunatic, waving his hands like some kind of manic conductor. "For every dozen people who love me, there's at least one asshole who thinks I'm crazy. Some kind of doped up hippie computer geek who's lost the farm. I can name twenty suits that think I should be in some sort of organically sourced vegan straight jacket, and ten of them are shareholders."

He shrugged, his stomach jiggling from the motion.

"That's business for you."

"For a crazy person you seem to be doing alright." Reid gestured to the world around them.

"But we can always do better!" Fozzy exhorted. "If you stop wanting to get better, to do more, to *get* more then you stop moving." He looked over his shoulder at Esin with his scruffy grin.

"And who can never stop moving?"

She smiled and parroted back their adage.

"People who change the world."

"People who change the world!" He roared back a little too loudly. "Split the sky and shake the earth. That's how we do it here." He turned back to Reid and frowned. "Listen, do you work for me? I think I know the name but it's hard to keep track. I have over a hundred and twenty thousand employees and a mind addled by drugs. It's not the best recipe for quick recognition."

Reid smiled the faintest of smiles and instinctively gave Fozzy a moniker he would remember him by.

"I'm the video game guy."

The old man's curly eyebrows shot to his hairline where they joined their curly brothers and became lost in the maw. He snatched Reid's hand back and began pumping it like an oil well all over again. Behind him, Esin laughed at the display, quietly wondering if she should intervene to save Reid. Fozzy would never let him go now.

"Oh, the *Uncommon Valor* guy from Metric!" His voice jumped half an octave in excitement. "You have no idea how much I've been looking forward to playing the new one. *Uncommon Valor, Paradox,* love them! I would have bought the damn company even if it was a financial loss."

Reid opened his mouth to reply, but Fozzy's head suddenly snapped up, silencing him. His face lit up and he stabbed one of his doughy fingers at the man's chest accusingly.

"Wait! You're a fact and puzzle man too. The perfect memory, right?"

He'd clearly recalled the rest of Reid's biography.

Reid shifted under the finger anxiously, his good feelings partially siphoned away. Esin, already knowing he was uncomfortable with that kind of scrutiny, laid a hand on her boss' arm.

"Fozzy..."

The bear temporarily flicked his gaze over to Esin.

"It's ok Habibti," He said quickly. "I just have a question, won't take a sec. Reid, you don't mind, right?"

He gave a non-verbal shrug of defeat and replied lack luster.

"Sure, it's okay. Go for it."

Looking over Fozzy's shoulder, she mouthed 'sorry'. Reid waved off her apology. Maybe he was still buoyant from the CEO's presence or he just liked the man enough to humor him.

Fozzy wrapped an arm around Reid's thinner frame and faced the commissary wall where the company's slogan bellowed at them from the plaster in colorful print.

"I have a bet with someone." The shorter man said. "'Split the sky and shake the earth' is what I wanted to do when I started this company. Change the whole damn world from the air to the soil, and make a hell of a scene doing it. I came up with the slogan one morning at three AM in my garage. If you've never drunk tequila, you really need to give it a shot."

Reid replied that he was familiar and watched the prescient words on the wall, nodding politely.

"Now, someone told me I wasn't the first to think of that. That I heard it somewhere and squirreled it away for my own. I say they're wrong, and no one thinks of anything but Horizon when they see that phrase."

He turned to grasp Reid by his shoulders, holding him up as if he was some kind of savior.

"You never forget anything so you're the ultimate authority, then. What does that make you think of? Just say the first thing that comes into your head!"

Esin watched this 'help me Obi-Wan Kenobi' scene play out with a little trepidation.

For a moment, Reid looked uncomfortable. He stood there, clearly wanting to lie. After a few seconds of awkward silence, he finally answered.

"Actually..." He admitted. "I had heard it before."

Fozzy deflated like some sort of hairy balloon animal.

"Aww crap," He said, defeated. "Where?"

"Vietnam. From a tour guide in Hue" Reid wilted slightly as he spoke. "My wife and I spent a month there... Ages ago."

Reid sighed quietly, and his eyes became very distant. Like his soul was completely absent from his body. Watching this, Esin was intrigued by the revelation. Reid had a wife? The man didn't wear a ring, and there was nothing in his file about him ever being married. Was he divorced? She wanted to know what other secrets the designer might be hiding. She suddenly wondered if he was still married and whether she should feel guilty about flirting with him. Before she could think any further, his eyes refocused and, to Fozzy's evident chagrin, he went on with his story.

"There was a big battle there in 1968 for the Tet Offensive. When the Viet Cong were told to attack, their orders were to 'split the sky and shake the earth'."

He shrugged apologetically.

"Sorry. They beat you to it by a few years.""

"Crap," Fozzy said again. He bit his cheek as he was prone to do while he was thinking. He seemed to temporarily forget Reid and Esin were in the room. Finally, he went on.

"Well," The old man shrugged. "I only remember about forty percent of the sixties anyway. That's a good excuse for a little unintended plagiarism, right?"

Reid snorted, trying to stifle a laugh. Fozzy's beastly smile instantly returned and he slapped Reid on his back.

"I guess I owe my friend a bottle!" He roared. "I'd love to split one with you too while you're here. I guess Esin talked you into doing the Labyrinth then?"

After being left on the sidelines of the conversation

for so long, Esin perked up at the statement her heart suddenly beating fast again. How the hell...?

The surprise must have told on her face because her mentor shook his head at her, making scolding noises.

"Oh Habibti," He said reassuringly. 'You know I keep an eye on what's happening around here. I'm just glad he said yes. You're a good pair; you'll work good together. Shirzai and Sheraton. It has a nice ring to it."

At this, Esin felt a weight she didn't even know she had lift off her shoulders. If Fozzy knew what she was doing and was alright with it, then no one else would care. His was the only opinion that mattered. If he knew that she was hiring contract players, then he must have guessed why as well. He was letting her do this. She had never realized how much she'd been worried about having her team bounced from the competition and that fear was gone now. Instinctively, she wrapped her arms around the big man in an appreciative hug.

This time, he only smiled and rubbed her shoulder knowingly.

"Well, we should eat." Fozzy said as she released him. "Because you both have meals to finish and because I haven't stopped eating in a decade. The benefits of being rich. Wait, Reid are you eating with just a knife? Oddly badass of you."

The game designer glanced at his forgotten plate.

"Oh, that." He looked up at Esin and smiled. "She lost her spoon, so I lent her my fork. I'll have to replace it."

"I'll grab you a new one. Maria makes a hell of a meatloaf. I should get some too, gotta be on stage soon."

With that, he breezed away toward the counter, stopping periodically to wave, give a hug or slap an outstretched palm.

Now alone, the two eased back into their chairs. Esin looked at Reid almost sheepishly. He was a little rumpled from the man's presence, but he looked happily bewildered.

"I guess he's joining us."

She crossed her legs under the table and leaned in closer. "Do you know what you just did to yourself?"

"Wait, what?"

She picked up her stolen fork and gestured to Reid's food. "I have five-star catering set up for after the press conference and you just committed to eating the worst food on earth."

The man's head dropped, as did his spirit, to stare in dismay at the abomination before him. He swallowed, probably the last time he would enjoy doing so, and looked up confused.

"What? Why are you eating now, then?"

She shook her head at him. "I can't eat after; I'm hosting the event. I have to mingle and make sure everyone is saying the right things. This is the only thing Maria makes that I can stand." She took a forkful of stew and grimaced slightly. Her stolen fork then stabbed toward Reid's meal. You just picked the worst thing on the menu."

His face paled a little and he pushed his tray away, clearly trying to bow out.

"Oh, no." She scolded, and pushed it back to its place. "Can't skip it, either. You just asked for a new fork and he's going to be sitting with us, watching you eat. Enjoy."

She sat back, looking at Reid's concerned face, embracing the coming schadenfreude in all its glory.

Fozzy soon returned with a new fork and a plate of his own. Reid took the new tool then, as Fozzy watched approvingly and Esin watched with muffled laughter, he lifted a forkful of the mixture to his mouth. His expression afterward might have been a forced smile, but there was far more force than smile in it.

New sounds in the void. The hollow steps of many people echo around me. I can hear their feet sound against the stone and through their steps I know them. The men walk more broadly, they carry more weight on flatter soles. Their steps are sloppy, lazily throwing their weight from one footfall to the next to only cross distance. Purely utilitarian. They sound as a raw crack. The women walk differently. Though their weight is typically less, their mass smaller, their steps are precise. The heels of their shoes are often narrower requiring a more calculated gait to keep balance. There is a sharp tap from each impact. Cracks and taps sound in sequence. A rattle in the void, that soon becomes a cascade. They have arrived.

The auditorium was packed from floor to ceiling. Press and bloggers, journalists of every stripe and expertise were crammed in on every available seat and surface. All in a semi-circle of seats facing the stage, miniscule by comparison. On stage was nothing but a huge empty plinth with the Horizon logo in front of a non-descript charcoal-coloured box. The eternal question taunting the audience. The box and plinth were huge, eluding to a massive new unveiling.

In the seventh row sat Reid, wedged between a Buzzfeed man and an unshaven online blogger who had already tried to explain what his website did four times. Even Reid with his perfect memory could make no sense of it. He remembered every word, and reassembling them in a different order in his head made no difference. A verbal Jackson Pollack painting of nonsense. He'd given up talking to the man and now tried his best to ignore him every time he attempted conversation.

Esin had been generous with his seat. Being a last-minute addition he'd expected to be squirreled away in the rear, only able to see the stage with binoculars while standing on a box. Instead, he was near the front, just a little left of center. A few news people trudging up the steps to their place at the back had already cast him withering glares no doubt wondering why an unfamiliar face had been given a priority seat. He'd paid for the real estate in pain, though. Being too polite to stop, Reid had eaten every morsel of that disgusting meatloaf while Fozzy watched. Now his stomach as if a dragon was living in it. A dragon who played in a death metal band and had a serious meth problem. Looking up at the stage, he hoped the show would be worth the price.

The show was set to begin at five. The press, with Reid tucked among them had been seated at ten minutes to, and at a minute past the hour, testimony to Esin's efficiency, the lights slowly dimmed. The hall lights eased slowly until only the stage was illuminated. The garbled chatter of a few hundred idly conversing tongues fell away to polite applause as Esin walked onto the stage from a passage on the left. A familiar face, a few voices shouted encouragement. Beside him, the blogger released a whistle as she came on. Her gait was measured, confident. With each step the light caught her features perfectly from her hair to her shoes. But then she'd probably planned it that way.

Reaching the center, she smiled to the audience and thanked them all for coming. It wasn't her real smile.

For the first ten minutes, Esin talked about the status of the company: the stock situation, their philanthropy, the 'commitment to innovation' as she called it. The broad sort of boring business-speak that people expect from press conferences. She was vibrant and vital in the role, speaking into a tiny headset microphone tucked behind her right ear. She was brilliantly convincing but sounded so dull. Reid wondered where this was coming from, until he realized that it was all part of the show. If Fozzy was going to speak too, then it helped for investors to see there were adults in charge, as well as the greying Muppet character. Everything was perception after all. Esin was just starting to lose some of the audience when she changed to talking about the future and what was coming next. Beside Reid, the blogger perked up anticipating the main event. Esin stepped back from center stage and her real smile suddenly appeared. She gestured to where she had entered.

"Let's let the man himself talk about it." She said, sounding like the ringmaster she was for this spectacle. "Ladies and gentleman, the chairman and CEO of the Horizon Corporation, Arthur Fozeranski!"

Cheers broke out, with a few voices taking up a chant of his name split into its component syllables.

"Fo-zy, Fo-zy, Fo-zy."

Reid watched the stage waiting for the man's appearance. When they'd left the CEO he had said he needed to get dressed up for the show. Reid was more than a little curious how the man polished up for the cameras. He was underwhelmed but not disappointed

Fozzy emerged onto the stage to a rousing cheer still clad in his jeans and t-shirt but covering them in a grey, custom tailored Italian suit jacket. Reid laughed, but then so did many others. It only seemed to feed the ovation he received. Esin was clapping too, then took up her rightful position at his side. A brief pantomime took place as she pointed to his jeans and shirt, to which he responded with an exaggerated shrug that said 'what?'

The room loved this, likely wondering if it was

genuine. Reid knew it was all show. The man wouldn't have been allowed near the stage if he wasn't dressed exactly the way Esin had intended. Both had their roles to play.

The noise subsided and Fozzy began to speak.

"That was a hell of an introduction." He began, and lifted a big arm in Esin's direction. "Esin Shirzai everyone!"

There was applause and even a few cheers. Esin smiled, acknowledging the attention. It wasn't her real smile anymore. She was all business again.

"At Horizon," Fozzy began, looking out at the audience. "I think it's become clear that we aim to change the world... Even though I try to be subtle about it."

A new wave of laughter washed up to the stage. Fozzy grinned in response, clearly in his element.

"Split the sky and shake the earth. It's not just talk. It's not just our slogan," He began to pace, as though it were the start of a sermon. "It's a calling felt by every person who works in this building. We have put our products in every corner of human life, changing lives for the better, and we aren't ready to stop yet. But where can we make the most difference? Where are we needed? Who's crying out for help?"

There was a quiet, respectful silence as the assembled press tried to answer a rhetorical question. Reid thought of a dozen possibilities. Fozzy went on.

"My grandfather fought at the Somme." He announced, sounding sombre and reflective now. "He was nineteen and went forward with his friends from his home town. Everyone had joined up. They walked slowly arm in arm, as if they were going to a soccer game. They were told all the Germans would be dead from shelling and they would just have to walk. It didn't work out that way. The Germans were very much alive and cut them down by the score as they walked forward. Sixty thousand soldiers were shot in one day. In one day! Can you imagine that?"

The audience said nothing, cowed into silence. Reid had seen Tech Talks before but never anything like this. The ghosts of sixty thousand soldiers now swirled about the room. Beside him, the blogger swallowed loudly. Fozzy stopped pacing, and looked out at the crowd. A few steps behind him Esin had bowed her head slightly in memorial.

"He told me once," He continued. "That back in his trench he listened all night to the wounded crying and pleading for help. Some of them were probably his friends. It was too dangerous to get them, so he just had to sit and listen. He never forgot the sounds of those poor bastards laying out in the open, begging for someone, for something, for *anything* to save them."

Fozzy's eyes seemed glazed over slightly. It might have been part of the show, but then again maybe not.

"Now, it may be that things have changed in a hundred years, but the reality of this hasn't. Soldiers still die in fields calling out for help, or bleed to death before a doctor can reach them, or simply lay wounded and in pain under enemy gunfire. Cut off from the help they need. These people are literally the souls crying out for help that I talked about. We all know this happens every day, but accept that it's a part of conflict, and conflict is a part of the human experience."

He shook his head angrily, his beard and curls flying out in the effort.

"Not us, though. Horizon aims to do something about it."

He paced the stage. Applause started up again. Steady, a light cheer filling it.

"Why don't I show you how we're changing the world

this time?"

He turned back to Esin, who spoke briefly into her headset. A section of the box on the right of the stage began to tilt open. The mist that began to pour out of the open portal was probably for dramatic effect, but it worked. There was an excited murmur from the audience. From deep within the new passage, a pale green light emerged, mingling and refracting with the smoke. The other three sides of the box slid back out of the way, folding down to the ground. Reid stared in bewilderment at the alien silhouette shrouded by the drifting mist. From his side, the blogger exclaimed under his breath, finally saying something that Reid completely understood.

"What, in the name of God, is *that?*"

I hear their gasps, their breath, the beats of their quickening hearts. I see their sweat, the veins on their necks, the dilation of their pupils in the light. Though all of this, I can read them. Some are amazed, some curious, a few are afraid. How they feel is irrelevant. Only my purpose matters now. The moment has arrived.

SIX

The room sat, frozen in time. Atop the flattened remains of its crate, in the wispy remnant of the mist, stood... *something.* 'Thing' seemed to be the only word appropriate. The thing bore the mixed dark-grey and gunmetal colors common to technology, but had the lines of a creature. A beast. It stood on four legs, the metal parts catching the glare of the spotlights now trained on it. It's body was ten feet long and sleek, agile even. Reid instantly thought of an insect. A praying mantis type creature, only not made by God but poured from ceramic and iron. It had a head, a center body (thorax if you still thought of it like an insect) with arms in front, and a lower body where the legs met it. The design was liquid, seemingly without lines, except for the arms and the head. The arms were sharp angles, with the look of talons. The head was in proportion but became flat at its face. Face was not the wrong word, but was not exactly the right one, either. Where a face would be on a human or an animal there was a flat black circle.

The audience murmured excitedly, trying to decide what this was. Camera flashes soon pulsed from the crowd, the light flaring off the shiny parts exposed, as journalists suddenly remembered their job. Instantly, the thing's head swiveled quickly to the audience, drawing gasps with the movement. Reid felt the blogger beside him twitch with surprise.

With its head turned, Reid could see that the flat, black oval of the face was not featureless. Soft green lights, eyes you could call them, were the only features and shone out creating a lime tinge in the mist. Reid stared in wonder. The eyes were the strangest part. They were round, but... kindly. As they perceived the room and those who watched, they seemed to express meekness or sympathy. The body of this creation was dynamic and powerful, but its visage was the complete inverse.

The thing moved slowly with one lithe step after another to its assigned place atop the plinth. There it eased down until its 'belly' was flat against the wood. The moon logo on the plinth now twinned with the black moon of its face, both shining out on a captivated audience.

Watching all of this with a smile, Fozzy walked over casually and laid a hand on the head of the beast.

"Ladies and gentlemen," He said, keeping the same sombre tone from before. "It's my pleasure to introduce you to Aceso. When we started thinking about this problem, there were a lot of needs to be met. We needed a way lift an injured person out of rough terrain. We needed something durable because there might still be a threat to the patient and whoever came for them. Most of all, we needed a way to get medics to the wounded without getting anyone killed. We made machines that could carry a lot of weight quickly, but had no way to keep a doctor safe on the way back. That meant there was always another person being put in danger. So, we decided to make the machine itself into a medic."

He reached up to pat its head as if it were a pet.

"That's what Aceso is: The Autonomous Combat Emergency Service Organism. ACESO."

In response to all of this, a fresh torrent of applause started up. On the wall behind them, a digital image of the machine appeared, with the acronym broken down for easy quotation.

"Aceso," Came a voice from beside Reid. "Where did

they get that one?"

Reid looked over, expecting to see the blogger scribbling notes furiously on a pad the way he pictured all journalists did. He felt foolish when he found the man attentively filming the spectacle on his phone.

"Probably a Greek Goddess of healing," Reid mused aloud.

Immediately on stage:

"In ancient Greece," Fozzy proclaimed. "Aceso was the Goddess of healing..."

The blogger didn't turn, but from over his shoulder he said it was a great guess.

"Hoplites laying wounded on the battlefield would pray to her to heal their wounds so they could live and rejoin the fight. That is what we bring for our heroes who fight our wars: an angel of mercy who will come for them when they call. *This* is how we're changing the world today."

The room began clapping furiously, a fresh cheer came from somewhere in the back and the photographers released a new barrage of flashes, not wanting to miss a shot of the two together.

Fozzy took a few seconds to bask in the light of the moment, both literally and figuratively. Where, for Esin, it seemed to be all business, this felt like the greying man's comfort zone. Being the center of attention wreathed him like a halo, but so did the belief that he was genuinely doing good. Reid tried to remember this was still a commercial.

"When I say autonomous," The CEO continued with his pitch. "I mean that completely. Aceso is made to function with total independence. As most of you will have guessed, Aceso is an AI. The most advanced AI we have ever built. We were designing it not just as a rescuer but as a medic too. If you're going to treat people, you need real intelligence. A regular computer is nowhere near good enough."

He gave one of his brutish snorts, which was amplified to an ear-damaging extent through the room's speakers.

"You wouldn't want to get medical advice from *Siri,* would you?"

A few laughed at the quip as the images on the wall behind changed to a series of waves and formulas. From his seat in the crowd, Reid found it near incomprehensible. There was method to the lines and numbers, but what it was, he couldn't fathom. It made him think of a heart monitor, as though Fozzy were gauging the audience's excitement in real time.

"Acumen Chains," The CEO continued, gesturing to the lines behind him. "Think of them like electronic brainwaves. These are the basic blocks of any intelligence, from the AI driving your car to one of our air-traffic control systems. This is how it usually looks: detailed, repetitive and unchanging. That's because these codes are immutable. We want our machines to do the same thing, the same way from the first time to the last. It'll look the same on day one as it does on day ten thousand. Well… usually."

The trademark mischievous grin that the world had come to recognize returned to his face.

"This time, we're doing something a little different. War is the most Darwinian place on earth. If Aceso were to survive long enough to do some good, he couldn't think the same way every time. So, Horizon gave Aceso something special: He can edit his own Acumen Chains."

A storm of murmurs swept through the crowd. Most of it was excitement, but there was more than a little shock mixed in. The blogger stopped filming, and slumped back against his seat, his phone dangling loose in his grasp.

"Holy crap…" He breathed, looking at Reid. "You

know what that means?"

Reid looked at the techno jargon on the wall and replied that he most emphatically did not. Before the blogger could enlighten him, Fozzy finished the thought.

"Aceso is the first of a new generation of learning machines; learning from mistakes and constantly improving itself, like we all try to. It's the closest we've ever come to putting humanity behind the metal." He looked over his shoulder to the wall, where the Acumen Chains wiggled and wobbled.

"These are Aceso's Chains from a month ago." With a dash of flair, Fozzy snapped his fingers, in an exaggerated motion. The first image shuffled over and a second set of images appeared.

"And these are his Chains today."

The lines, still incomprehensible to Reid, now looked like something from a seismograph. The frequency was three times as fast, the peaks higher, the valleys lower. A few people in the audience gasped, either amazed or equally uncomprehending but swept up in the excitement of the moment.

"We've been running the AI through exercises, scenarios, and trial runs every day." Fozzy spread his arms wide to the audience. "And each day he only gets better! Within two months, Aceso won't just be perfectly built, he'll be *experienced*, in a way you never thought technology could be."

Esin, so long in the background, slowly emerged from behind Aceso and stood on the other side; the white glare of the spotlights temporarily making her ethnically ambiguous. Both man and machine turned to look in unison before she spoke.

"I think they need a demonstration."

A cheer rose up from the crowd at this notion. Fozzy, played to them for a moment, looking unsure. This only served to rally the cheer, growing louder as the whole room encouraged it, yearning for a show. Fozzy raised his hands, silencing his temporary worshipers.

"As long as Aceso agrees. It should be up to him!"

The room adored this, roaring its approval, and forcing Fozzy to make a vain attempt to silence them all over again. He then looked into the soft green eyes of the beast. It had barely moved through the past few minutes of speech, just lazily shifting its head almost puppy-like. Reid could not help but think of it as an animal, though it clearly wasn't. As he watched the spectacle he didn't know quite how to feel. Fozzy laid a grandfatherly hand on the beast while excited chatter chorused around him, echoing off the walls and drawing louder. He smiled at the creation warmly and posed the question.

"Well? What do you think?"

The people are excited. The voices are fast, their auditory stress points bouncing from peak to peak. They have only grown more excited as the one called Fozeranski speaks. When excited, a human voice peaks higher pitched on stress syllables. This is subconscious and unavoidable. People are machines like any other, with their responses just as mechanical. Now their thrill is obvious, their passion plain, although difficult for me to understand. I find excitement itself to be alien. Some voices in the cacophony are almost shrill now as Fozeranski asks me the question. They await my answer. There is no reason for the excitement. I am committed to my purpose and can answer only one way.

"I'm ready to do whatever is asked of me."

Reid watched the beast's strange scuttle/glide motion as the door closed behind it as it left on its mission. It drew out a kind of anxiety in him that was foreign. It felt primal, like the fear prey has for its predator, despite the fact the machine was built to heal. He'd never felt anything like it.

On the wall behind the stage, a video image soon appeared of the beast emerging into the sunlight, gingerly stepping out onto the gravel of the quarry. From the frame, Reid could see none of the lush greenery that surrounded the building. Instead, the ground was the dullest sort of grey, textured with the innumerable broken pebbles. This must be a part of the old mine that hadn't gotten a facelift from Horizon's green thumb.

Fozzy, looking up at the image like everyone else, shook his jowly head.

"No good." He judged loudly. "Let's get a better view."

This time, he didn't even need to snap his fingers; the world still bowed to his will. In an instant, the wall behind him vanished.

Reid gasped, jolting backward in surprise. The entire back wall of the amphitheatre was gone. The audience called out in alarm as they were suddenly bathed in natural sunlight. The world was suddenly much bigger with a chasm opening up before them. The room found itself looking out onto a large gravel pit, a monochromatic crater in the earth, where stone had been torn from it. The only color came from the brown tufts of plant life that intermittently popped forth from the piles of pulverized stone and the blue sky, itself greying as the sun dipped in late hours of the day. It seemed as though, without a sound, the entire side of the building had collapsed into grey rubble.

Fozzy was laughing at the many shocked expressions, leaving Esin to step forward and explain.

"Relay wall," She said, raising a slender arm to the

emptiness behind her. "The wall in front of you is painted with an organic light emitting diode polymer. Basically, we painted a flat screen onto the wall. The image comes from the other side where hundreds of tiny cameras are placed. Each one sends a part of the image to the corresponding section of the wall behind it which then sends it straight through to your eye. It's clearer than a window."

Fozzy produced a red rubber ball from the pocket of his Armani jacket and whipped it with heavy force at the space behind him. Reid watched, awestruck, as it seemingly ricocheted off of thin air to bounce back to him. He missed catching it though, bouncing through his outstretched hands. He grumbled slightly into the mic as the ball found its way into the pocket of an audience member and then, presumably, to eBay.

At the corner of the portal Reid could see the head of Aceso gazing out at the quarry, looking like some sort of feral NASA rover about to explore Mars. Esin called out and at the sound of her voice the head suddenly perked up.

"Yes?" Came the soft reply through the speakers.

"Out there is a wounded soldier, waiting for rescue. Bring him back here. Whatever it takes."

Without waiting to reply, the machine shot forward, its four legs arching quickly through the piles of rock as it set out. The thing moved with an awkward grace. A kind of scuttle like a crab, but with the smooth motions of a cat. It glided out further out into the wasteland, seemingly already knowing where it had to go.

Esin lingered, watching the beast recede into the background. Then raised a hand.

"That's far enough." She announced to someone, maybe everyone. "let's see what she sees."

In the upper right corner of the empty space where

the wall had been, a new image appeared. Clearly a video feed from Aceso's point of view, rocks and terrain flashed by in a blur as it moved forward for its mission. Occasionally, one of its slender arms would flick into frame as it moved. It somehow knew where it was going and moved with a purpose. Reid flicked his eyes from the video feed to the shrinking figure among the rocks and back. God, the thing was fast.

The rocks race past me on either side. I move deliberately toward the soldier. He or she, likely he from his body signature, is laying atop an outcropping behind the pit, roughly one hundred and fifty meters distant. I can feel the heat of the subject burning differently from the adjacent rock. The sporadic, almost liquid warmth that means life is near. I move quickly. It will take only a moment to reach him. With each step of my legs, I feel the ragged stone beneath. Some of it shatters beneath the force of my gait.

The beast had reached the edge of the pit, circling around to the left. In the perspective view, Reid caught a glimpse of the drop off into the deepest part of the gravel pit. A gaping emptiness with a flash of dark cyan at the bottom where water had pooled. Aceso didn't pause for the view or hesitate for the risk, but continued past, almost as though it hadn't noticed. Clearly, there was a target in mind, although Reid still had no idea how the machine was tracking it.

Around him, the press watched and made satisfied noises. The consensus seemed to be contentment. Fozzy soon proved the exception.

"Not difficult enough!" He erupted.

The outburst was so sudden, the blogger dropped his phone with shock. He bent over awkwardly scrambling to retrieve it apparently tortured to be apart from it. His shirt pulled forward with the effort,giving Reid an unpleasant look at a very hairy back.

"It doesn't feel right." Fozzy continued on stage. He turned to Esin in a clearly scripted moment. "If it were a real battle, this would be harder."

"Why?"

"Someone would be shooting at them."

Esin smiled knowingly.

"Then let's have someone shoot at them." She turned to look at the screen behind her. "Gentlemen?"

A new video feed appeared on the other side of the opening, a box containing the image seemingly appearing out of thin air with the magic of the relay wall. In the frame, three men in forest camouflage fiddled with a metal tube standing out starkly against what was obviously a building roof. Suddenly, all three knelt in unison leaning away as the tube belched flame. Reid felt the room tremble slightly as an instant later the mortar round slammed into the soil of the quarry further shattering the already broken stone. Not far from the now meek looking Aceso in the distance, an eruption of dust and splintered rock blew into the air. The bang was loud even at this range and filtered through a wall. On stage, Esin jerked back, then raised a hand in salute to the soldiers who were quickly reloading.

"Our thanks to the 11th Field Battery, Royal Canadian Artillery," She said, her words instantly punctured by another detonation. "Who are providing the opposition in this little test of ours. I promised them each a five-thousand-dollar prize for a direct hit, so I promise you, they're motivated." Her face took on mock concern as her voice deepened in intensity.

"Let's hope Aceso can keep ahead of them."

I feel the blow rather than see it. The concussion rattles through me quickly, but it is unexpected. Mortar. Judging by the sound, the flight time and explosion it is an 81 mm L16 light mortar. A type used by the Canadian Army. High explosive bombs. The maximum rate of fire is fifteen rounds per minute, meaning that I will be exposed to between nine and eleven more bombs in the time required to reach my target. I must increase my speed, perhaps find cover. Another bomb explodes just behind me. The jagged pieces of steel, designed to maim, slash against my back in a haphazard pattern. They grind off of my skin, ricocheting from my metal flesh and doing little damage. The sound absorbs me, though. The sharp metal scraping and pinging of fragments intended to kill are musical. Very pleasant.

Reid swallowed nervously as the mortar flared again on the screen. To the right, a second of flight time later, the round exploded just ahead of Aceso, the camera spattered with a blurry grain of dust, tarnishing the image. The machine continued on through the dust, seemingly undeterred. Despite having a hundred yards and a wall between him and the blast, Reid still flinched involuntarily. He looked around the room at the captivated people watching; each explosion sent a twitch across dozens of faces in a wave. A literal tide of emotion as the audience followed their hero in the form of Aceso and hammered home with cordite and shrapnel. This was tension manufactured by Horizon, but the feeling was genuine. Despite this being theatre, the room still feared for the machine.

The only exception, once again, was Fozzy.

He was still smiling with a maniacal twist watching the drama unfold. With each flare of the mortar, he would lean in toward the false gap of the relay wall. The sound and distant shake of the explosion would then press him backward again with glee. It reminded him of a child riding a roller coaster, leaning into each dangerous curve and thrilled by it. Though his mic was evidently off, with each impact Reid could see the man's mouth muttering words. It took only a moment to decipher them. *Shake the earth.*

Reid watched the mortar breathe fire into the heavens then felt the shudder in the floor as it landed. The man was witnessing his motto and corporate mantra made physical before him. His excitement was vividly apparent. Like everyone else, he was invested but was loving it, secure that he knew the outcome.

As the gun fired and Aceso came closer to its target, he kept mouthing the words like a satisfied prayer, swaying to the violent gospel of his own show with every detonation.

Shake the earth... Shake the earth... Shake the earth...

A blast directly beside me. Stone and steel smash into my side, the force pushing me toward the edge of chasm of the pit. I recover quickly, the odds of falling are only twenty-four percent, but it is clear the gunners have found the range. I move faster still, altering my movements to a zig-zag to confuse their aim. Ahead, a section of the gravel wall is concave, the lip of the wall above extending in a ledge roughly nine feet above the path I am on. There is not enough ledge to keep me concealed from the gunners. Instead, I dig my grip into the wall and climb. Once I am directly below the ledge I dig into the rock beneath, orienting myself to continue at full speed beneath the outcropping. The stone supports my weight as I move, using it as a barrier. I am close.

From Aceso's view, Reid watched as it reached the wall, climb, then continue on. Gasps cascaded through the room as the machine moved forward, upside down. Stones dropping away from the outcropping zipped up through the image, seeming to defy gravity. The gravel path below, marked by footprints, grass and the detritus of what had once been the quarry, streaked past at light speed. A mortar round struck the ground on the path ahead. From the point of view on the screen, it seemed to explode out of the ceiling like a living thing, a sudden malevolent tree of dust and rage, its branches clawing down for a victim, until the image raced by showing a trail of fresh earth until the next impact. It was enthralling.

Transfixed by the video feed, Reid found himself wrapped up in the moment. Looking through the eyes of the beast, he pictured himself in the same way. He was the one charging to the rescue, running upside down beneath a cliff face with bombs exploding left and right. He could smell the gun powder in the air, taste the pulverized dust from the explosions, and hear the streak of stones passing by. He could feel his legs pumping with effort, though, unlike Aceso, he only had two of them and was right side up.

Suddenly, on screen, the ledge broke away and the ground seemed to fall up out of nowhere. His footing lost, Aceso began to fall back to the path, but rotated in air to land on its feet, the camera returning to the proper horizon, and never breaking pace. A few isolated people clapped, but most were too gripped to react, Reid among them. His heart was beating savagely in his chest from the action above. He felt the sweat pool at the back of his neck, and his foot was tapping obsessively to bleed off energy.

He wasn't alone. His thrill was no different from any of the others watching. They breathed together, holding breath when an explosion came near or when Aceso had nearly been knocked from the cliff. All eyes were on the screen with the view of the beast, spellbound and anxious for the ending. Through the relay wall, in the distance, the speck that was Aceso reached the peak of the cliff. Likewise, on the screen, the beast was suddenly looming over a crumpled figure in camouflage he had located… somehow.

A handful in the room cheered and clapped, but the moment of victory was short-lived. The camera suddenly turned as Aceso whipped his head toward what seemed like open blue sky. Reid had a split second to perceive a black dot in the steel blue vista before it slammed directly into the camera.

The image instantly went black, throwing the room into chaos. The crowd exclaimed in horror, the hero of their drama seemingly snuffed out in the finale. Everyone began talking at once. Someone among them was laughing at the tragedy, and on screen beside the dead image of Aceso's view the soldiers crewing the mortar jumped into frenzied jubilation in anticipation of their five-thousand-dollar bounty.

Reid looked at Fozzy, and saw his confident grin fractured into a thousand pieces. His face seemed to age rapidly as he looked unblinking at the blank screen, clearly contemplating the full scale of the public relations disaster literally blowing up in front of him. Reid couldn't see Esin's face as she had instinctively turned her back. Her hand was pressed to her ear as she was talking rapidly into her headset.

Beside him, the blogger was chuckling quietly.

"Oh no." He chuffed, typing something into his phone with glee. "That's not good."

Reid looked back through the relay wall. Atop the cliff in the distance, a cloud of dust was rising from the point of impact, a beige blot where the machine, and Horizon's dignity, had been wiped away. His eyes caught a flicker of movement. A sliver of black among the cloud.

"Blowing up your demo in the middle of your demo." The blogger was saying as he typed. "That can't be good."

Reid ignored him and squinted, trying to make sense of what he was seeing. The shape was the same. Could it be? The dust began to dissipate, but before it could settle, the insectoid form of Aceso darted out and scurried down the cliff face.

"He's still going." Reid said. "He's still going!"

The second statement came out as a yell. The blogger made a sound like a whoop when he saw it too. The sound soon spread to a hundred throats as the hero of the epic, risen from the dead, continued on his mission. Fozzy came to life again, pumping his fist in the air and shouting a rude affirmative that the press would surely have to censor. It wasn't over yet.

On screen, the soldiers at the mortar realized their quarry (in the quarry) was still alive. Their celebration dampened, they began loading and firing again with frenzy. Through the electric window, Reid saw the bomb explode far behind the speeding form of Aceso and he watched the soldiers frantically crank to adjust the range on the gun.

He's too fast, Reid thought excitedly. *They'll never catch him now.*

The rest of the room saw it too. They clapped and cheered encouragement as if this were a football game. They sensed victory was near. A few got to their feet, rooting for the return of the beast. Throughout all of this, Reid scanned the stage, looking for Esin who had disappeared from view. He finally saw her in a passage on the far right. Looking relieved, she took a moment to gather her emotions and straighten her dress. By the time she emerged back onto the stage, her confident smile was back in place as though it had never left.

The chase went on for a few seconds more, but the outcome was no longer in doubt. It was only a short denouement before Aceso again entered the room.

The beast was still all power, but now it looked ragged. Its surface was marked with what seemed like a billion scratches, pockmarks and scars. Its legs were beige from the coating of powder of the splintered bits of stone, and its arms were far worse with patches missing, exposing the hydraulics and innards beneath. The face, if you could call it that, had the same appearance as every used iPhone Reid had ever seen. The black matte of the oval was shattered from the impact of the bomb, the cracks mingling like ten thousand spiders had layered their webs on a dark void. The lines were chaos incarnate, but through them its distorted green lights with their odd sympathy still peered out. The machine stood, taking in the room's applause with polite curiosity.

Fozzy was rapturously banging his hands together as the machine approached him, his grey jacket billowing from the effort.

"Well?" The quirky old man said expectantly. "What have you brought us?"

The beast eased itself to its side exposing its winged back to the audience. The 'wings' slowly parted revealing a concealed compartment with a stretcher along the length of its back. Laying peacefully beneath Aceso's scarred armoured flesh was a mannequin in camouflage.

As the room applauded yet again, the machine reached back and gently lifted the figure to the ground in front of him. The wings on its back, clearly heavily armoured to protect its passenger, eased shut again.

Fozzy walked over and tried to lift the mannequin toy soldier, straining under the weight. Two Horizon employees, clearly fearing for their boss' back, leapt up from their place in the front row to prop up the figure. Fozzy thanked them and lifted a the dummy's camouflaged arm into the air to childishly wave at the audience. After a moment of laughter, he dropped it again, the figure slumping awkwardly forward in the hands of his helpers.

Fozzy turned to Aceso, his large, battered form looming behind him.

"Well," The said solemnly. "Will he live?"

The beast attempted to answer but was cut off by a fresh roar of mirth from the crowd. Its scarred head swiveled at the unexpected noise, then began to speak.

"He has multiple lacerations," The machine's voice chirped. Without a microphone it sounded even meeker. "A fractured radius and a shrapnel penetration in the lower abdomen. He was not injured by the mortars and should survive."

"Anything else I should know?"

"Well, he's composed mostly of ballistics gel, but I was asked to ignore that."

Chuckles trickled down to the stage as Fozzy thanked the machine. It prowled back to its plinth and with a feline stretch, slipped back to a resting position. There it sat silhouetted against the battered quarry, still visible through the relay wall, where dust lingered and smoke rose from the burning scrub.

"I think that," The old man said. "Should speak for itself. But I'll talk just a little more 'cause I like the sound of my voice."

The room stirred happily, still firmly in the man's hands as he went on.

"This is only the first of a whole new generation of AIs." He said proudly. "The next step in not just making life easier but actually making life *better* on this earth. Learning machines can improve themselves in ways we can't even imagine.

"What we have done is nothing less than to make

a guardian angel… And not just for soldiers! but for construction, earthquake rescue or any place people might be in danger. Aceso can be programmed with your medical records to keep you healthy and make sure you make it home every day from work, no matter what."

The old man turned to the plinth.

"Aceso!" He hollered. "How many medications am I taking?"

"Three, sir," The beast answered instantly. "Lasix, Lipitor and intermittent use of Viagra."

Fozzy jumped slightly at the last word, his wide eyes shooting a comically-panicked glance back to the audience. The crowd laughed, with a few salty voices, roaring in approval. Aceso perked up, not expecting the reaction, looking slightly perturbed. With an exaggerated wink, Fozzy spread his hands.

"See?!" He laughed. "Just need to make him a little more discrete and he'll be the perfect doctor! At least he's not telling me to slow down all the time like the rest of them."

He seemed to ponder this statement for a moment then spoke again.

"Which brings me to our last little surprise of the day."

Fozzy stepped forward once more. Flashbulbs went off again, immortalizing the moment, but the old man had dropped his smile.

"My life has been about Horizon," He said solemnly. "And the way I see myself is through the work we've done these past thirty years. I couldn't be prouder. But I also feel the weight of time on me."

Reid leaned forward, putting his chin in his hands. He could guess what was coming.

"Which is why," He said brushing a bashful hand through his greying curls, diverting his eyes to the floor. "I will be stepping down as CEO by the end of the year."

Though Reid had guessed it, many others clearly hadn't because an appalled gasp filled the room from a hundred throats. A light wail of shock at the man's departure.

"Fozzy no..." A voice from somewhere whispered. It was soon joined by more.

The man didn't look up from the floor, but took each mournful note, standing alone, staring into nothing. Reid could see this caricature of a man soak up their dismay at his leaving. There on stage for the first time, he actually looked his age. The bags under his eyes became more defined, his posture began to stoop slightly. He opened his mouth to go on, but the anguish of the crowd drove him back to silence. His lip curled inward, mute with emotion at the display of support. Esin, long separated at the right of the stage, walked over quickly her heels tapping loudly against the floor. She took his hand in hers standing next to him. The old man patted her hand in thanks, not looking up. Finally, he went on.

"Now, I promised myself." There was a tremor in his voice. "I promised myself I would only retire when I had given all I could to make the world a better place. 'Miles to go before I sleep' and all that. But what we have done here, what Aceso and the new breed of AIs offer is the best legacy I could ever hope for."

He lifted a hand to Aceso who sat roosting on his plinth, defiantly battle scarred.

"There is no better way to end my career than by making something that saves lives. Every person that marvelous machine keeps from crossing into the darkness is a part of Horizon's legacy... And maybe just a little piece of that is mine too."

Applause began to build. It grew within the room until it was a flood of ovation, every single person on their feet clapping, directing their affection to the stage. Esin took a step back and began clapping as well looking on her mentor with affection.

Fozzy took up his signature grin, still a little sad around the edges. He reached back to take her hand again and raised his other in the air as though he were waving farewell. The room was rapt with applause, cheers, and emotions for the quirky executive. It continued even after Fozzy tried to wave it off.

"That's enough!" He laughed.

The crowd disagreed and roared even louder. In the audience Reid stood clapping with rest. His arms sore from the effort, emotional like everyone else at the idea of a Horizon without Fozzy. To his right, the blogger was sobbing uncontrollably.

"Enough!" Fozzy repeated, slashing at the air with his free hand. "Save some of that for the poor bastard who has to replace me!"

With the old man's last comment, Reid looked to the slender woman beside him on stage. Esin met his eyes, picking him out in the crowd, her face revealing nothing. He held her glance for a moment, then nodded in understanding. Her cheek twitched, but she went on clapping. Now he knew why she had to win the Labyrinth this year.

Around the two figures locking eyes, the ovation went on.

SEVEN

They came by the hundreds. Posing, preening, sometimes almost debasing themselves in weird affectations for the camera. Everyone wanted to get a shot with the new celebrity. A selfie of them smiling with something that by design could not smile back. Maybe four hundred people, thirty-two teeth a piece. That meant almost thirteen thousand teeth would be flashed in pictures before the day was done. It already felt like Reid had seen a million of them.

From across the room, he watched another batch of people take a turn having their photo taken with the beast. Three did a pose reminiscent of *Charlie's Angels* in front of Aceso, its cracked face looming like a moon in full eclipse above their heads. The fourth sat on the machine's back, as though he were riding a horse. He threw up a peace sign, with his tongue out in an expression that screamed he was born in the nineties and had an IQ to match. Reid turned away before the flash, regretting his photographic memory at this moment more than most. The press event was long over and the after party had long ago begun. Journalists, stockholders and Horizon employees had traded the seats of the amphitheatre for the beautiful green oasis of the gardens outside. Now the group mingled in various stages of drunkenness in celebration of a new future for Horizon and an early send off for Fozzy.

True to her word, Esin had organized the best catering, liquor and music surely intended to charm the media for the event. From the sounds swirling about the gardens it was working. Nearby, on a wood stage overgrown with vines, a swing band beat an infectious rhythm. The redheaded singer crooned and swayed to the beat as red spotlights above cast new shades of scarlet in her hair. On the field in front of her, dancers moved with no skill whatsoever, but clearly enjoyed it. They stomped and bobbed across the grass with all the coordination and grace one expected of people engaged in heavy drinking. Waiters with trays of food weaved in around them, avoiding collisions through skill and a hint of prayer.

The food was what interested Reid. He had been a gourmet for years (Recipes were the one thing you could be a savant at with no one batting an eye) and there was much to enjoy. Esin hadn't been lying about the five-star cuisine. He'd seen trays with long spidery crab's legs, and truffle roasted potatoes. He'd seen oysters, steak and ribs on long tables set out. Across the fields, he caught a glimpse of meat roasting on a spit, the smell guiding his eyes. Salads were everywhere, likely made from the plundered greenery of the garden. From the smells that mingled about, he could guess some of the greenery was being smoked as well.

All of it looked delicious; the problem was he couldn't eat any of it.

Reid dropped a hand to his stomach as it did a triple summersault, then back flipped to where it had started. He cursed his own stupidity for forcing down the godawful food a few hours prior. It still wasn't sitting well and tormented him just as he should be getting hungry again. He should be enjoying himself, but every time a new tray came by it just made him nauseous.

As if on cue, a new one appeared in front of him. Unlike the other trays though, this one wasn't held by a waiter, but by Robin, his handsome face flush with enjoyment.

"You really need to try these." He said quickly, lifting

the tray. "They're incredible."

Reid regarded the food with longing.

"What are they?"

"Prosciutto wrapped dates stuffed with blue cheese." His muscular arms spun the tray on his finger briefly with practiced skill. "Ms. Shirzai pulls out all the stops when we do a Tech Talk. Try one!"

Reid sighed miserably. His mouth wanted to say yes, but his stomach was screaming for an exorcist.

"I'll have to pass."

Robin shrugged his massive shoulders and hefted his delicacies. "Suit yourself."

The Adonis popped a morsel into his mouth, then wandered off to mingle with the guests, as was surely his job. As Robin moved through the people clumped in groups about, the eyes of the ladies followed him steadily. Reid's did too, but he was still looking at the dates. His belly rumbled yet again, causing him to lean on a standing table nearby for support. He winced and regretted his life choices once more. Pain was useful in its own way. It usually kept him focused on the present as it demanded his attention. But sometimes pain was just... pain. He was almost willing to accept the bad memories rather than this. For the moment anyway.

"Excuse me," Someone cooed over his shoulder. "Are you feeling alright?"

The question came in a quiet, even voice, the concern genuine. The words were measured and calm, while the voice itself was androgynous. Light and higher pitched, it could have been a man, a woman or even a child speaking.

Reid turned, then tilted his head up to behold the blemished face of Aceso looking at him with its soulless, gentle green eyes. Up close the true extent of the pounding the machine had taken was clearer. Someone had rinsed the dust off it, but the mixed ceramic and metal skin was beset by thousands of scratches. Where shrapnel had struck, the paint was flecked off with shiny steel peeking from beneath marking the point of impact. On its side was the mark of a close explosion. Reid could see the dent where the bomb had struck, then the cluster of tiny scratches where the fragments had gored into it. The mark looked like a robotic flower in bloom, a strange reminder of how powerful Aceso was and the nature of this beast.

"Are you feeling alright?" The machine repeated after a beat of silence.

"Umm, fine thank you," Reid said, feeling suddenly intimidated as he looked up at the beast. It felt as though a lion were asking a mouse how he was doing.

"I'm sorry, but are you sure?" The machine persisted. It took a step back and eased itself lower until it was at eye level. "You're holding your stomach and you're flushed."

Reid sighed, but it came out more as a groan.

"Something I ate." He conceded, still uncomfortable around AIs and this one in particular. "My stomach is bugging me. That's all."

"Oh, would you like something for it, then?"

A fresh twist of his gut made Reid wince.

"Yes..."

Reid watched as the machine slipped an arm beneath the scratched battle-scarred metal plates across its back. When it emerged again, in the palm of its four-fingered hand were three yellow pills.

"Dimenhydrinate." The beast explained. "Take two now and one before bed tonight."

Reid regarded the pills with amusement. Through the

pain, he smiled at the AI; he couldn't help himself.

"Doctor's orders?"

"Oh, no." Aceso actually shook its head in a surprisingly human gesture. "I'm just a medic. But everyone should get a full night's sleep."

Reid reflected on the night before. His near sleepless night on a concrete floor had done him no favors, and he could recall every instant of it.

"It's not always that simple." He muttered and dutifully took the pills. He washed them down with a cup of punch someone had pressed into his hand earlier but he hadn't gotten around to drinking. The action instantly made him burst into a coughing fit. There was so much booze in the drink he wondered if it were flammable.

As he coughed, Aceso watched him inquisitively. The pills finally went down but the alcohol only added fuel to the rage within his belly. He tucked the third one into his pocket as directed, feeling rougher than ever.

"Got anything stronger than these?"

"Well, I could give you a shot of promethazine," The machine said thoughtfully. "But it would make you very drowsy, and you might be scared of getting an injection from me."

"Needles never bother me."

"No sir, not scared of the needle." Aceso corrected meekly in its quiet voice. "Scared of me."

Reid regarded the behemoth in front of him oddly.

"I'm not afraid of you," He said, slightly defensively.

"Oh no!" The machine's head jumped a bit, as if startled. "I wasn't implying you were afraid of me. It's just in my experience people tend to react badly when I need to puncture them with something."

Reid burst out laughing. His stomach shook as he laughed, bringing on a new wave of discomfort, but he didn't care.

Aceso watched him, unable to form an expression Reid could read. Finally, gaining control, he spoke.

"That sounds perfectly rational to me." He smiled. "You don't have to puncture us too often, do you?"

"Not at all." Aceso replied, missing the joke. "During my trials, I only had to give six injections. None of the participants enjoyed them. I had to do a tracheotomy once as well, but the patient was unconscious."

"Yeah," Reid commented dryly. "I would want to be for that."

Aceso's head bounced slightly. It took a second for Reid to realize it was trying to nod.

After a beat of what eerily felt like contemplation, the machine suddenly mused aloud.

"It would be so much easier if I felt pain."

Reid leaned back.

"You don't feel anything?"

His gaze dropped slightly to the chaotic mess of shattered glass beneath the green of Aceso's eyes, and his mind flicked back to the instant the mortar smashed into the camera. Reid found his hand drifting up to rub his own chin in contrast. He felt the sharp edges of new stubble that had grown since the morning, imagining it were shards of broken glass. "Not even *that?*"

"I feel the impact, or sense that it happened, but I never feel any pain. At least, I don't think I feel it the way you do. I can read expressions and when people are hurt their faces become so… anguished."

The machine paused and Reid felt an involuntarily

tingle go up his spine.

"It's not just physical pain." The beast went on. "I have been helping at the Horizon medical clinic for months. People come for cuts, illnesses, and broken bones, but they also come to talk about problems. Emotional pain. I can't feel that, either."

"Trust me. You don't want to."

"Oh, no, I do!" Aceso said, its head jumping up again. "My entire purpose is to help and heal. How can I do that well if I don't understand something?"

Reid blinked his grey eyes. He had never met an AI capable of introspection. In that moment, he felt for the beast more than most people he'd met. Struggling to relate to others was not a foreign concept to him, and it afflicted Aceso far harder than he'd ever had to endure. Reid thought for a moment, then spoke to Aceso like an equal.

"You remember everything right?" He said with no hint of irony.

"Yes. Completely."

"Then just keep watching people." He said. "Remember when something bothers them, what it was and ask them what helped. Learn from every conversation. Replay them after to see what you did wrong. Ask as many questions as you can for as long as they're willing to talk, and always say you're sorry and that you feel for them."

"I am sorry, but what if I can't understand?"

"Even if you don't completely understand what they're going through, you can still say you're sorry. It shows you care. People want to know you empathize, at least. That's how we all get better. The more you know, the better you can help."

Aceso looked at him seemingly impassive. He

wondered whether it understood. For something that could make no expression, it was difficult to tell how much his words were getting through. The beast simply made another robotic nod and spoke.

"In that case," It began awkwardly. "Can I ask you something... personal?"

Reid looked at Aceso oddly, both amused and confused. He hadn't expected a personal question, hadn't thought one possible really, but he had opened up the possibility and he was just too curious not to hear.

"Go ahead."

"During the presentation," The beast began. "Mr. Fozeranski asked me which medications he was on and I mentioned his Viagra use."

Reid smirked at the memory; Fozzy's comical face turning to the audience, eyes wide.

"Yes?"

"I'm uncertain whether I should have revealed that to the room."

Reid looked at Aceso blankly, in a vain attempt to scrutinize his expression. The AI had been asked a direct question for the show. What was the problem? Then it suddenly dawned on him what it was and he felt a current of amazement run through him.

"Oh my God," Reid said quietly. He suddenly saw Aceso differently, the eyes suddenly seeming deeper than before. Something was behind them. "Are you worried you embarrassed him?"

The AI seemed stumped by the question, and while the general chatter of the party roared behind them, the two lingered in silence.

"I'm uncertain if it was correct." The beast finally said.

"You're worried."

"What would be the difference?" It asked.

Suddenly feeling like Geppetto giving life lessons to his puppet, Reid mentally scratched his head, searching for the right words. *How am I going to explain this?*

"Okay," He held out both hands in demonstration. "You have two options, right? One bad, one good. Offend him or not offend him."

Aceso nodded again, still an alien movement.

"Which outcome do you want?"

"Want?"

Aww crap.

"Which one do you prefer?" He tried again. "Which is the better option? Not to offend him, right? If you really prefer one thing more than the other, then you *want* something. If you think you won't get the thing you want and might get the other option in the end, the bad option, then you're *afraid*. That's how it feels to worry. So, are you *worried* you offended him?"

The beast took less than a second to reply.

"Yes," It said with conviction. "I'm worried."

Reid released a low whistle. He smiled at Aceso, feeling a strange affection for the machine. Despite being tough enough to be barely affected by being, it was still concerned about hurting someone's feelings. There was a cowardly-lionesque charm to Aceso that made him more human. Maybe the secret to having a soul was being insecure.

He looked around to see if anyone had witnessed the conversation, then placed a hand affectionately on its shoulder.

"Don't be. I'm sure they planned that joke." Reid assured him. "Trust me; Esin wouldn't let it pass otherwise. Even if they didn't, Fozzy didn't care. His expression was too goofy to be anything else. He loved that you got a laugh out of the audience."

"Are you sure?" Aceso pushed. "The laugh was about him."

"I'm sure."

At this, the beast seemed to ease somehow, tension releasing from its body making its powerful form sag. It might have been relief but no one, probably not even Aceso, would have been able to say. Finally, the machine spoke.

"Is worry a kind of pain?"

Reid looked at the kindly green eyes, thinking how to answer.

"I guess you could say that." He said. "Worry is human. We do it about everything."

"So, I felt pain?"

"Maybe just a little."

"Other pain is worse?"

"Much worse."

It tilted its head and stared at Reid.

"Worry is very unpleasant." It said after a moment. "If other pain is worse, how do you stand it?"

Reid looked at its innocent face and scraped the inside of his head for a reply. Fortunately, it turned out he didn't need one.

As Reid opened his mouth to answer, not entirely sure what words would tumble out, a hairy figure in plaid suddenly burst into his frame of vision. His face was unshaven, the genesis of a beard on his chin, but instead of brown to match the shaggy, overgrown hair that approached his shoulders the stubble was blonde to the point of near invisibility. A ghost of a beard. He wore old cargo pants, wrinkled and marked with stains. The legs were too wide and billowed slightly as he ran, likely from skinny, boney legs. Judging by his arms that had to be the case. The plaid shirt was wrinkled with the same 'out of the dryer, screw it I'm late, no time to iron' style. It was the sort of red gingham pattern you would usually find on tablecloths sold at a dollar store. The sleeves were rolled up, letting two hairy, skeletal arms move freely. With a shout of dismay, they wrapped themselves around Aceso's neck, pulling the machine into a shabby hug.

"Holy Christ!" The strange man gasped as he released him. He ran his hands across Aceso's scarred metal hide, his fingers tracing every impact. "Aceso, what did they *do* to you?"

The machine blinked its green eyes as if it was obvious.

"They bombarded me with 81 mm mortars."

"Well, I knew *that.*" He replied, the moustache of the ghost beard turning down in irritation. "I picked that up from one look at you. You look like you fell off a cliff, then onto a freeway, then got punched by God."

Like a doctor who had a centaur for a patient, the shabby man yanked Aceso's arm straight out and began checking the damage, looking more and more annoyed. He then moved around the machine looking at the marks and uttering the kind of language typically spewed out by a combat marine with Tourette's. At one point, Reid had to jump backward to get out of the way as the man continued on, oblivious.

At last, he came to a stop facing the beast's tender eyes and shattered face.

"I'm gonna have to strip off half your ceramics and replace your glass, but at least most of this is superficial." He turned to glare at Reid angrily, observing at a safe distance. "Whose great fuckin' idea was this?"

Suddenly feeling accused, Reid's eyes widened and he lifted his hands in a defensive shrug of ignorance.

"No idea, huh?" The itinerant looking roboticist said to him then instantly turned away. "Well, don't worry. I can fix her. It just might take all of my spare time, though. I'm going to have to be here all night."

He shook his head, causing his stringy, brown hair to nip about. From a few feet away, Reid's nose told him that it hadn't been washed in a while. He stepped back from the aroma, coughing unintentionally.

The grimy man saw him react but took the gesture in a different way.

"Oh, I'm sorry." He apologized, stepping away from where he'd been fondling Aceso. "I didn't introduce myself. That's just rude."

He wiped his hand on his pant leg, adding something new to the collage of stains, then extended it.

"Aster."

Reid gave a half second's thought to not shaking it, but luckily, the man was still upset enough that he dropped his hand in an angry swipe at the air.

"I can't believe it." He grumbled. "Who thought this was a good idea?"

"I did."

From the raucous maw of the party two figures had emerged, walking together. The first was instantly recognizable; the flawless tanned figure of Esin, her face picking up the ambient light of the spotlights and bonfires.

Beside her was a new character, a man matching her pace and confidence in every way. Reid had seen him in the posed event photos that graced the M&M office wall and, in the flesh, he was little warmer. He was tall, almost as tall as Reid, with an angular face. His cheekbones were sharp and matched the definition of his jaw, giving him the look of a shark. With his hair, cut to the scalp on the sides and smoothed back with a waxy sheen on the top, the look of an ocean predator was complete. He wore a charcoal suit with a white shirt, both of which were so tailored they could have been painted onto his skin. Splitting them down the middle was a narrow tie, as grey as the suit, but slashed with black and crimson. He was the one who'd spoken.

"Wyatt, what the hell is wrong with you?" Aster tore into him as they came closer. "You let them bomb the shit out of this thing during the demonstration. You couldn't have just let someone shoot a rifle? Or a few rifles? Fuck, I would have let you use a dozen machine guns rather than this!"

He stomped over to stab a finger at the man, the action making him look like a belligerent scarecrow.

"What if they'd wrecked her for good?"

The man in grey looked at the finger jabbed into his chest impassively. Something told Reid that if this man had been knifed through the heart he would only have objected to the wrinkling of his suit.

"We needed to show what Aceso could handle." He replied calmly. "Esin asked me what it could take and I told her what you told me. You said a mortar."

"I said a mortar, *at most*." Aster corrected, his mouth contracting in a line. "That was the big one she could probably shrug off, not a place to *start*. If I told you I played football in high school, you wouldn't make me play a game by myself against the Patriots."

The sharply dressed man looked back with justified skepticism at the suggestion this wraith of a human had played football, but then he simply shrugged.

"It worked, didn't it?"

Aster tore into him again with a new wave of cursing, while Reid tried to conjure up a mental image of the man playing football, but every play just ended with him being hit, snapping and exploding into thousands of splinters. The argument soon grew more heated, if only on Aster's side. The marble statue he spoke seemed immune to caring. Just when he thought Aster might get physical, a contest the other man would laugh off, Esin intervened from beside them.

"Enough," She sighed, then laid a hand on Aster's plaid flannel sleeve, gently pulling the two apart.

"Come on Aster," She cooed as she eased him out of range. "It was my idea anyway. Wyatt just gave me some suggestions."

The skinny man snorted in derision.

"Only the dumbass ones." He grumbled. He seemed to mellow at Esin's touch. As she put distance between them, the invective petered out in the space. "She's not a something you can kick around you know. Aceso's supposed to be a medic. She's not meant to be used for a crazy display like that."

"Actually," The man called Wyatt said coolly. "That's exactly what it needs to be used for. Because until someone actually buys Aceso it's not going to tend to anyone. It's a product. We have to market it or its just using up time and space, not to mention R&D dollars. Which reminds me..."

With the self-assuredness of a man that people always moved for, he pushed straight past Reid. The game designer nearly fell over backward as he jumped aside, angry at the slight. If Wyatt noticed, he made no evidence of it, but went on to stand in front of Aceso, glaring up into its shattered face.

"What are you doing?" He said to the machine. "You're supposed to be taking pictures with the press. This event is about you."

Aceso, who was several times his size, instantly apologized.

"I'm sorry." The beast said. "I was posing for photographs until I saw Mr. Sheraton was not feeling well. I stopped to help with his stomach."

Wyatt turned to look at Reid, his suit twisting and stretching with the ease of a fine fabric.

"Oh, you're Sheraton?" He tossed over, acknowledging Reid's existence for the first time. Reid found he liked his own name less when this man said it. "A little bird told me Esin was outsourcing for the competition this year, but you're not what I was expecting."

Wyatt extended a hand in a lackluster greeting, perhaps deciding Reid was only worth this minimal effort.

"Yeah, I get that a lot."

He regarded the hand dryly, then turned to where Aster was glowering, watching the conversation and extended his hand to him instead.

"I'm Reid," He said warmly. "Aster, is it?"

The mouth underneath the ghost beard flipped up into a satisfied grin as his skeletal hand took Reid's.

"That's me." He confirmed. "I'm the lead designer on the project. I thought up the Acumen Chain editor, the mechanics and the AI system. Mind, body and soul. Aceso's my baby. You like her?"

Reid glanced over at the huge tattered form of the beast, its soft green eyes staring back at him.

"Yeah, actually," He said. "I do. Why do you say 'her'?"

"She's tough, she's a healer, she's named for a Greek Goddess." The man shrugged. "Seemed appropriate to me."

"Funny, I thought of it more as a 'he'."

"Yeah, most guys would," Esin injected smartly.

Reid's eyes flicked over to her to see that familiar confident smile in bloom.

"It."

Behind him, Wyatt had dropped his hand but was still looking over his shoulder, seemingly rooted in place.

"Why are we fussing over pronouns? People need to start thinking of this thing more as a product than a person. Fozzy does the same damn thing. You need to market it not *talk* to it." He rapped his knuckles on the shattered oval of Aceso's face. The beast's head gave a twitch at the impact. "That kind of emotionalism only makes it harder to market because you treat it like a worker not an item. This always happens with AIs, I'm tired of people getting this wrong."

Who the hell do you think you are? Was the response forming in Reid's mind. Esin seemed to read his face intuitively and provided the answer before it could pass his lips.

"Wyatt is VP of the Artificial Intelligence Division." She explained quickly. "Aceso was developed by his team."

"So, I know what I'm talking about." The man instantly affirmed. "Aster has been treating this thing weird ever since he started using the term 'she'. It's creepy."

He rolled his gaze over to Aceso then looked back to Reid.

"Did you see him romancing the product a minute ago?"

The skinny roboticist inhaled a gust of air to power a whole new barrage of profanity, but Esin quickly jumped in.

"Aaron, give it a rest," She said, presumably using the man's first name, now with a new edge in her voice. "I need you both civil enough to answer questions later."

Reid sized up the man, the second Vice President of Horizon he had met. While Esin was all nuance and charm, this man seemed to only have one setting: pragmatic. He said what he thought, always matter-of-factly, with little trace of any feeling in his voice. His blunt approach seemed totally at odds with what he'd seen from Esin and Fozzy. If he'd had to guess how Wyatt got away with acting this way, the only answer he could think of was that he got results. It only made sense that a business with carrots like Fozzy and Esin had to employ sticks to match. Wyatt balanced them out.

"Have him," Wyatt responded to Esin by pointing a well-manicured hand to Aster's shaggy form. "Answer why the damn machine froze on the top of that cliff after it was hit. The video feed went out and the whole AI froze for six seconds, sitting like a fucking bullseye to get bombed again. It could have been a PR disaster."

Aster glared back daggers, then seemed to mellow with the question.

"I don't know." He conceded. He scratched at the ghost beard thoughtfully. "She's never locked up in any of the other trials. I can check her recorder after the party."

"Now." Wyatt said. "Someone here is going to ask that question. I want to be able to answer. Aceso is just a stepping stone to something bigger. Don't kill the product line before it actually pays off. Get me a reason before the end of the night, we still need it to mingle." The executive glared up at Aceso's face again still quietly watching the conversation. "It should be speaking to reporters not wasting time over here."

"He was talking to me." Reid butted in, feeling irritated and slightly defensive for the machine. "You don't think I look like a reporter? And a stepping stone to what, by the way?"

The remark turned Wyatt's head, even if his suit did not move. He must have asked the right question because the man halted his rant immediately, but provided no answers. In the end, all it brought out was a quick thoughtful smile and an even quicker evasion.

"I knew you weren't a reporter," The suit replied, choosing to answer a different question. "But the video game thing I wouldn't have guessed. I had you pegged as a staff lawyer or a psychologist. Something cerebral. You're transparently high orange."

"Excuse me?"

Wyatt nodded as if it were obvious.

"You know, analytical." He regarded him again for a moment, his eyes sweeping him up and down. "Definitely high orange, probably a little brown in you too. I'm very good at reading this."

Reid, who almost never got lost in a conversation, felt an angry anxiety building up inside him. Rather than continue talking himself into a hole, he looked over at Esin for help.

"What the hell is he talking about?"

"The Rzhev Method. Business colors." Wyatt answered before she could, finally turning his whole body away from Aceso for the first time. It could have been to speak to Reid like a human being, but he suspected he had stumbled upon this man's favorite topic.

Facing him now, Wyatt's face became incredulous and more than a little amused.

"You don't know the Rzhev Method?"

"I can't say I do."

The executive tucked a piece of his slicked hair back into place. In another first, he seemed to warm up to him.

"Oh, you really need to do it for your staffing. It makes it so much easier." He held up four fingers. "There are four colours representing the personality types. You're high orange, so that means you have a very analytical outlook. You take information and try to rationalize a solution. You have some brown too, so there's a creative side to you. Maybe a few new ideas outside the mould to work with. Always test new employees for this. When you know which personality colors you're getting, things go so much easier.

"I wish I could have tested my staff when I picked up this division. Aster here," he pointed to the grungy man. "Is the highest red I have ever met."

The raggedy computer engineer rolled his eyes theatrically at what was clearly a familiar refrain. Reid just shook his head.

"Is that supposed to mean something to me?"

"*Emotional.*" Wyatt stretched the word out like he was describing a debilitating condition. "He just can't help but get involved with his work. Red personalities are driven by passion. It's useful, but it makes them so hard to handle. People only work well when they're detached and can function objectively."

"And what colour are you?"

Wyatt smiled and pointed over to Esin.

"Same as her." He said. "We're both high grey. The highest."

"Meaning?"

"We're action people." He said. "We make tough

choices under pressure, know when to take risks and excel at leadership. That's what you need at the top. Nothing but shades of grey. You can have a mix of other colours, just don't put someone high red in a position where you have to make decisions. When he applied, Aster wouldn't have made it past the door if I'd been managing."

"Which means," Reid continued. "You wouldn't have made the learning Acumen Chains, or Aceso himself, for that matter."

The logic bounced off the executive as though he were as armoured as the machine behind him.

"If you understand the colors," He went on, undeterred. "Then you can understand your people."

"What's your color scheme for the Labyrinth, then?" Esin asked.

Reid blinked in surprise. The man was a Vice President too. Of course, Wyatt would be putting his own team into the Labyrinth. The idea that he would participate in something so unusual didn't seem plausible, though.

"Oh right, *that.*" He said. The last syllable came out so heavy that speaking it must have felt like lifting a weight. "Keeslar is running it again. I told him he can pick his own team as long as he doesn't load it up with anyone high red."

"Anyone who believes in personality colours should be classified brown, because they're completely full of shit." Aster quipped.

Wyatt frowned, he lines on his face forming even sharper angles.

"Keeslar ran it last year," He said.

"And didn't even crack the top three." Aster shrugged his bony shoulders. "It's like you're not even trying to win. Bring in some fresh blood."

"You mean you."

"I mean *anybody*." He groaned. "Fozzy gets us riled up every year. My design team gets excited and then we finish in the middle of the pack with the same five guys. It's like you're picking the same limping racehorse every time. The whole company thinks we don't give a shit."

Wyatt reddened slightly and cast out an unblinking stare at Aster's face. The rumpled subordinate shrank slightly, perhaps sensing he had pushed too hard. When he was sufficiently wilted, Wyatt put him in his place.

"You can beg to play this stupid game all you want," He said slowly. "But I'm always going to go with someone with strength behind them. It's a physical test before a brain one. Keesler has endurance. He's also a marathon runner and an engineer. He knows how the maze works and he's high grey."

Aster absorbed this sullenly, then snorted.

"I know his nose is brown," He said. "I don't know about the rest of him."

"Shut it, Aster."

There was a moments silence, punctuated only by the thumping rhythm of the swing band beginning another number. Esin finally eased them out of the silence felt like sheer force of will.

"So, I guess Aster isn't on your team this year."

Above the tailored suit, a new tailored smile folded into place.

"What gave it away?" Wyatt asked sarcastically. "Was it that I just told him he wouldn't be, or the fact that he looks like a walking corpse?"

Aster mumbled something long and rude under his breath. Reid wasn't able to catch all of it, but what he did hear didn't sound anatomically possible.

Esin must have heard more because she let out a playful squawk.

"Jesus," she laughed. "Can't you two get along? Don't say that on the press tour."

Aster shrugged unapologetically. If Wyatt had heard him he clearly didn't care.

"You have no idea how hard it is to work with him." He said with his ever-self-assured smile. "This is what you get when you hire high red."

Esin nodded as if agreeing, then tilted her head pensively.

"If he's so much trouble, let me borrow him for a few weeks."

Wyatt stopped, his smooth smile imploding. He looked at her suspiciously then summed up his thoughts in one word.

"Seriously?"

Aster, equally flummoxed, was not too far behind.

"Seriously?" He parroted.

Esin shrugged.

"Why not?" She reasoned. "You're not going to use him so why can't I? He can still work on Aceso, but I get his spare time for the Labyrinth prep. If I can keep you two apart for the press tour then that makes my job that much easier anyway. You're like the foul-mouthed middle-aged children I never wanted."

She leaned over to Aster with a kind of charm Reid found familiar.

"How bout it?"

In a move that surprised no one, Wyatt answered for

him.

"Take him, then. He can't climb a flight of stairs without breathing hard. You just screwed yourself."

Esin didn't turn, waiting for Aster to answer. His scraggly face slowly broke into a grin, the ghost beard turning upward at the edges.

"Sure, let's do it."

"And everybody's happy." Wyatt volunteered dryly. His angular face had morphed into a look of spite, as he saw he'd been manipulated. He gestured over to where a few of the reporters had gathered. "We should all pose together for the reporters at least once. It's good PR."

Esin, skillfully ignoring that he was telling her how to do her job, gave Aster a gentle push toward him.

"I've had my moment in the spotlight." She said. "Let them get the three of you together. The maker, the manager and the machine. Easy photo caption."

Aster stepped out to walk beside Wyatt, who was still looking irritated he had granted anything.

"Ya know, you should fix your suit," The thin man spoke cockily. "There's an asshole sticking out of it."

"Oh please, you're not dressed pretty enough for a tractor pull." His boss hissed back. "Try not to collapse on the way."

"If I do, I can get Aceso to carry my ass. And then you can kiss it."

With that, the two started over toward the reporters with Aceso trotting heavily behind, like a mammoth child who had just watched his parents fight. The beast took a few steps then turned its lithe body back to where Reid still stood with Esin.

"It was lovely to meet you." It said in its meek voice. It

then turned, moving quickly to catch up.

As the three reached the group, the media responded by gathering in an arc around them throwing out a bombardment of questions, clicking shutters and camera flashes. Reid watched from afar as Wyatt, silhouetted by the blinking lights, lifted an arm in a well-tailored sleeve and wrapped it affectionately around Aster's boney shoulders for the photos to come.

EIGHT

Reid stayed close to Esin as the night went on, but they said little to each other. Ever the vigilant host, she seemed to be everywhere, shaking hands, complementing colleagues and charming reporters. She also seemed to be on a first name basis with everyone they encountered and had a memory for names that impressed even him.

Robin came and went several times, sometimes bringing people of interest to meet Esin or being sent on some subtle mission to schmooze someone in particular. He would often show up quietly put a hand on her shoulder, whisper in her ear discretely (as if anyone could miss his muscular mass) then vanish again. The two of them wandered seemingly without any pattern through the garden, stopping randomly to speak with people. Each new figure they met made Esin's face light up with her artificial smile, as she treated them with importance, real or feigned. She never failed to introduce Reid who as the creative director of *Uncommon Valor* sparked some interest but his celebrity was minor and soon eclipsed by Esin answering questions about Aceso. Evidently, a giant, lifesaving robotic creature trumped video games. Reid, who hated attention, was delighted.

The whole business of public relations felt weird to him. He could socialize just fine with most people when he had to, but it took a little effort. The idea that you would actively seek out the spotlight, and talk at length with everyone you met, was a horrific thought.

As the hour became later, he spied a food table nearby

with no one around it. With a glance toward Esin, and whomever she was currently charming, he slipped away to jog over. The drugs Aceso had given him were starting to work, and he was desperate to eat something decent before the night was out. The table had been picked half clean by then, but there was still more than enough to choose from. He plucked a meat-filled pastry from a plate and took a glorious bite. For a moment, he just closed his eyes and savored the spicy flavour, finally able to enjoy something without his stomach screeching in protest.

"I guess you've beaten your meatloaf hangover."

He turned to see Esin standing behind him, looking at his rapture with a bemused smile. Even after hours of press conferences, socializing and rattling off talking points like a broken record, damn if she didn't still look flawless.

"Aceso gave me something." He answered after swallowing. "By the way, you're a multi-billion-dollar corporation. I expected better food than that."

She shrugged.

"Fozzy likes Maria so he kept her on since they were working in a tiny office." She reached over to pluck a raspberry from a platter and tossed it into her mouth. "Sometimes it's not about the money here."

"Corporate motto?"

She looked at him like he was crazy.

"Yeah, the shareholders would *love* that," She said chewing thoughtfully. "Maybe a kind of mission statement. Horizon may be different, but we like making money."

They stayed by the table, Reid standing with a full plate, Esin acting as a human shield against possible social interaction as people passed by. The party had begun to thin out, with the fainter of heart having gone home to sleep or perhaps crash in one of the spare rooms on campus. Reid watched the lazy zombie-like shamble of a few drunken souls toward the complex and rest. They still laughed and cheered but were clearly spent. He recognized one man from CNN, in a rumpled suit, moving with wobbly difficulty toward what had to be his temporary bed inside. His collar was loose, there was a lump of what looked like chocolate in his beard, but the look on his face indicated Horizon would get a very good review come the morning. As much as this was a circus, it was clearly working.

"You really know how to charm the press," He mused quietly toward Esin's back. He found his eyes tracing the zipper on the back of her dress coming almost to her hairline, the odd bun of her hair still without a thread out of place.

"Thanks." She said without turning, forcing him to refocus. He hadn't thought he'd spoken loud enough for her to hear. "I like being good at my job. Sometimes it's easy, though. It doesn't take much effort to get people excited about a rescue AI."

Reid shrugged, though the gesture was wasted as she couldn't see.

"They still need you." He said. "If that Wyatt guy was doing a press conference on his own, someone would have punched him. Probably Aster actually."

She laughed.

"Yeah, Aaron doesn't get people," She admitted. "I think that's why he believes in those personality colors, so he can whittle everyone down to good or bad. I have to admit, his press work is great. He works his people hard and he likes the attention when a project works out. You don't like attention much, do you?"

Reid made a sour face.

"I've never liked it." He admitted. "Even when I was a kid. My parents figured out pretty quick that I could remember everything, so any time we had guests over they would trot me out to answer questions to impress them. My dad kept this old dictionary in the living room, this faded awful paperback with pages falling out? He would flip to a random page and ask me to give him three words on that page. Everybody loved that one."

Before him, Esin smiled and waved to someone in the distance.

"When did they stop?"

"Oh, when I started learning a few four-letter words at school. I made sure my vocabulary was as big and blue as possible to cover the entire alphabet. When I'm feeling down, I think back to their horrified expressions again."

Esin laughed and turned back to pluck another morsel of food from his plate. She smiled at him then returned to stand sentry.

"You sound like a problem child."

He grunted with amusement.

"Sometimes I wish I was." He grinned wryly. "Everyone wants to be a rebel at some point. I was just a reader. I wanted to know everything. I read every book on every topic I could find. Now it's no fun at all. Nothing surprises you."

A couple came up to them and again, Esin was all charm. She thanked them for attending and traded light small talk until they moved on quietly headed for a good night's rest.

"That's why I work with people," Esin continued when they were out of earshot. "There's always someone who can surprise you."

Reid watched as another couple wandered past them. They'd been three rows ahead in the amphitheatre and he'd seen them milling about the party. Well dressed, both wearing rings, clearly investors. The man looked Esin up and down subtly. She was the seventh woman he had seen him appraise that night. Clearly, he was looking at other women. Esin's beauty aside, seven women was a pattern. His wife pretended not to notice (probably used to such behavior) and moved on with him. Though her skirt was long, he could see wisps of hair adorning her ankles. She knew they'd had to go out tonight but had avoided shaving her legs. Probably had been doing so for quite a long time. She didn't want to be touched and he was looking elsewhere. Their marriage was rocky.

Reid watched the two recede into the distance.

"Some people aren't that hard to read."

The slender executive turned far enough that he could see a playful raised eyebrow.

"Well, impress me, then. You've been here a day; you've met a bunch of our people. What gossip can you tell me?"

"Oh, you don't want me to..."

"Sure I do." She broke in. "Any scandals?"

Reid thought for a moment, then answered honestly. Speaking a casual truth.

"Robin's in love with you."

From behind, he saw Esin freeze up ever so slightly. Her posture changed, her straight back going tense at the words and then wilting as the statement fell on her shoulders. Finally, she spoke.

"He's got a crush." She countered slowly. "It's cute, but it's just a crush."

She glanced over her shoulder at him looking just a little concerned.

"Why do you say 'love'?"

Reid squirmed a bit at that.

"Every picture in the office with both of you in it, he's looking at you," He began. "He's never looking into the camera. Even in group shots. He calls you Miss Shirzai when you're not around but he only uses Esin to your face. So he respects you but wants to be more intimate when you're around. He gives his time freely, he's very protective, he probably could be running his own PR firm but keeps an assistant title..."

Reid trailed off, spreading his arms helplessly.

"I'm sorry. It's easy to see."

Esin looked troubled for a moment, then shook her head and turned away angrily.

"I wish you hadn't said that." The back of her head glared at him. "I was perfectly happy thinking it was only a crush. Now what do I do?"

"I'm sorry, I'm just being honest." He could see this really troubled her. "Why do you have to do anything? It doesn't change how you work together."

"Crushes I can deal with," She hissed. "Any more than that makes work more complicated."

"You could ask him out." Reid said, volunteering what he thought was obvious. "You said he was an attractive guy."

"I don't date."

"Employees?"

"I don't date."

The way she repeated the statement made it sound final, as though she were barred from a personal life. Her body language had changed so much in the last few moments. This was the first time he had seen her tense. She began flicking at the edge of her dress nervously, while what he could see of her perfect face was tarnished by concern.

"Why did you have to do that?" There was genuine anguish in her voice.

Reid felt his spirit sink. It balled up and dropped within him to sit as a weight in his gut.

"You asked me what I'd seen..."

"I didn't need to know that!" She snapped. "Next time you have a tough little truth to tell, keep it to yourself."

Reid wanted to ask more but held his tongue, worried. Esin, seemingly furious that he had made her life more complicated, wouldn't give him a word. It became a stalemate. The gap in the conversation slowly grew wider until it swallowed them whole, neither person able to speak to the other.

They stood in silence for a long time as the last stragglers wandered past. Esin smiled and spoke when prompted, but never to Reid, who seemed to have ceased to exist in her reality. Soon, the swing band brought the music to a close. As the redhead singer bid farewell her voice was reduced to half a rasp. She blew a kiss to what crowd remained amid a smattering of tired applause. Waiters emerged to bus the trays of food back to the complex, the clatter of utensils reverberating through the wide green plateaus of the garden. Finally, the staff began pulling in the tables and chairs. As lamps went out and the world shrank with the coming darkness of the night.

Only then, when she was certain the place was empty, did Esin start walking back to the complex. Reid slowly followed behind her. Through the evening air, he could smell the humidity of the garden deeper now. Above them, stars peaked down from what sky could be seen from the depths of the quarry. Constellations seemed to be censored by a flat black wall, which defined the edge of the crater in which they walked. They walked quietly for a time, neither really wanting to say anything until, finally, Reid spoke.

"You don't like your job."

Esin whipped her whole body around to stare in open mouthed surprise at him. Her eyes glared green fire and her body tensed up defensively.

"I am amazing at my job!" She spat, defiantly.

A nearby server carrying a stack of dishes looked up in alarm. Wanting to avoid a scene, Reid raised a hand to say everything was fine and gently guided his new boss away to a distant point on the trail beneath an ornate lamp. Esin, moved with him to avoid embarrassment or maybe to avoid witnesses if she chose to kill him.

"Yes you are." Reid acknowledged quietly. "But you don't like it."

"Of course, I do!" She replied immediately. She pulled every ounce of passion from her petite frame and put it into saying it, while shredding him with her eyes for even thinking otherwise.

Reid didn't believe it for a second.

"Did you know you have two smiles?" He asked. He kept his voice calm and even.

"What?"

"Two different smiles." He explained. "There's your normal smile that you use when you're just talking to people as you. That's got humor in it, and passion. Your eyes look alive. There's a lot of joy in you."

Her face twisted in confusion.

"What are you talking about?"

"But when you're speaking for the company its different." Reid went on. "Something just feels forced. I can see it every time. You smile, but it feels empty. There's nothing behind it. You're putting on a face when you're in front of these people."

The surprise on her face told Reid he was close.

"There's no joy in it. You're doing a job." He paused. "I think you hate it actually."

Esin looked at him with all the warmth and affection someone would give a burning rash.

"Are you seriously telling a woman how she should smile?"

Reid felt an angry embarrassed flush building, worried this was all sounding sexist. Esin knew how to push buttons. Luckily, she kept talking.

"I do it for people who think I'm just another pretty face," She admitted. With no small trace of bitterness, she waved her hand to the spent husk of the party around them. "That's what most of these people think anyway. I only smile for people who deserve it."

Reid blinked uncomprehendingly. In the little more than the day and a half he had known her, Esin had read his inscrutable personality, convinced him to give up control over a project he had obsessed over and successfully hosted an international media event.

"You're not just a pretty face..." He tried to interject but was cut off instantly.

"How would you know?" She countered with more than a little venom. "You barely know me. Or do you just assume you can read everybody that well?"

Reid's words left him, and he clammed up in frustration, looking down at the glowering face of the woman before him.

"There is no one better organized and capable than me. I've been with the company a decade, I have a degree in engineering and another in business. I've been managing projects since I started. But when I get the chance to be on the board, the job I'm given is the one where I'm supposed to be on camera at all times. I'm window dressing."

Reid wasn't buying it. He shook his head.

"Or because I'm the token woman with the Muslim name."

"You're too savvy for that. They didn't pick you because you're easy to look at."

"Are you sure about that?"

"At this company? I'm sure."

"Really? Our third biggest shareholder has met me a dozen times and he still always calls me Mrs. Sherazade until I correct him. And I correct him *every single time*."

An uncommon flicker of emotion passed over her face. A quiet hatred that Reid never wanted to see again.

"I worked hard every day to be a Vice President. Fozzy found me working here and recommended me a half dozen times. It's only when they needed someone in front of the cameras that I got picked. That's the VP slot I got to fill. I'm the pretty face of Horizon and I have the smallest division in the company. Someone else makes the decisions, makes the products, and I get to put on my fake, happy smile and sell them. I don't get to make corporate decisions."

She finished her speech, her voice trailing off, the slight echo of her words in the empty garden around them. But even as the last syllable crossed her lips the sentence felt incomplete. Reid finished it for her.

"Yet."

"Yet." She affirmed.

"You want to be CEO."

"I need to be introduced as a winner," She reasoned. "Someone who did something no one's ever thought of. I bent the rules. I made my team. I beat everyone else. I need them to actually know who I am. Then maybe they'll see the possibility."

"That's all you need?"

"It's a *start*. Then I need the extra budget we'll get from the win to build up the brand before Fozzy goes. If we do well enough then it keeps the focus on me, but even then it's a long shot. That's the only way I get to be CEO, even if Fozzy picks me to replace him. It's the board who has to vote."

She looked at him with a smoldering intensity.

"It's my turn."

Reid slipped his hands into his pockets and nodded. Solving a bit more of the puzzle of this woman felt good. He didn't say anything in reply. There was nothing more that needed to be said.

Around them the world slowly shrank into black. As the stewards finished pulling the last of the tables and wreckage of the party inside, the lamps began to wink out, each piece of illuminated real estate being swallowed by inky nothing. They had to be motion sensitive. One more piece of Horizon magic, albeit a simple one. Soon, all the lights had gone dark, save one orb still bright over two figures. The only sounds present were a few crickets singing a serenade and the breeze whispering through the plant life.

"This is a beautiful night." Esin mused, her milky voice still curdled by frustration. "I hate that I had to waste it on these people."

Reid looked at her with a little incredulity. Without the prying eyes of Horizon's shareholders, she felt far sourer. Or maybe he had just made her that way.

"It went off without a hitch," He said. "You should be proud."

"I'm too angry for that. What the hell is wrong with you?"

Reid prickled up, offended.

"Excuse me?"

"You just can't help yourself sometimes can you?" She spat out, looking hurt. "How I really feel is nobody's business. Especially yours."

"I wanted to know. You said I would be a full partner."

"Please, you're on contract. My reasons for doing this are just for me."

"You *asked* me to come and help."

"It was none of your business." She continued. "Why I need to win this year, my relationship with Robin... I've only known you for a day and you need to push every goddamn boundary I have. I didn't ask you about that breakdown you had last night. You can't show me the same courtesy?"

In a flash he saw Renata's face. Her eyes, her smile. Then, in an instant, it was gone again. He winced, clamping his eyes shut trying to stay in the moment.

"Oh, that bothers you, does it?" Esin pushed. "What the hell was with you last night? Its your turn to talk."

He was with Renata at the arboretum. He recalled every word they said to each other. The plants of the garden made him think of it. He felt his eyelids throb as he pressed them steadily tighter.

"I don't need to tell you anything."

"Really?" She prodded. "Because you're already cracking right now and I barely gave you a push."

Reid opened his eyes. Renata was gone. Esin was still there pushing. He was angry. He felt tense and wound like a coiled spring. His mind was running wild.

"What was that about last night?"

He was behind the wheel again, the world twisting, the pain in his back...

"My wife..."

"Your wife?" She repeated. "There's another one, you never mentioned you were married."

The sounds of breaking glass, bending steel...

"I'm not anymore..."

"Or that you were divorced." She said cutting him off.

Her face looking terrified. Her hair mingling with the broken glass ...

"I'm not."

It took a moment for the implication to sink in. His expression might have given something away, because Esin's face, still hot with anger, cooled for a moment, a bit of the rancor slipping away.

"Oh," All of the bitterness had left her voice. "Jesus, I'm sorry."

With his muscles clenched, his eyes reddening, his unwanted anger with Esin still coursing through him, he could only slump, the memories flooding through him again and again on a loop.

"Why do you think I need a distraction right now?"

They stared at each other for a moment, both needing the other to find peace. Nothing was said, or could be said. Finally, Reid just turned and walked away. He didn't look over his shoulder, but he knew Esin was standing there in the light of the last lamp watching him go.

When journalists or would-be investors came to the quarry there were a few sights they had to visit. Everyone, whomever they were and however many zeroes graced their bank statement, would go for a walk in the gardens. Nature had that effect on everyone, at least for a while. Then they would walk the development floor and meet the people behind the magic. Their last stop was usually at the office of the great wizard himself.

Fozzy's office had been the subject of six magazine articles, eleven online exposes and countless photo shoots in the years since Horizon had come to the quarry. It was a yawning two story tall space with a bookshelf full of old records from artists long celebrated or long dead and forgotten. Framed posters of the same obscure artists adorned the walls as if to prove they had really existed. Fozzy himself, when he greeted visitors, was constantly pulling out random records and asking "Have you heard of this guy? No? You're going to love him!" Inside the company and out, everyone loved the office. The only thing was, Fozzy didn't work there.

The man himself was always travelling the world on adventures or meeting investors in their own duller spaces. When he was at the quarry he would spend his time wandering the halls greeting his workers. When he was in his ostentatious office he would be entertaining visitors, but that wasn't where he worked. He had a second office for that, he just didn't tell anyone. He knew the spectacle was good for the company so he kept it going. Only six people in the world knew this second office even existed.

One of them was Aaron Wyatt.

The door was marked 'Outmoded Archive', which was an inside joke to anyone who knew Fozzy. He was storing himself as a piece of outdated technology. Wyatt knocked twice, as was the ritual, and entered without waiting for a response. On a black leather couch, looking every second of his advanced years, Fozzy was prone, weak with exhaustion.

"Close the damn door." He groaned. "I don't want them seeing me like this."

Wyatt looked for prying eyes then eased the door shut. Unlike the beatnik coffee house motif of the office upstairs, this one looked simple. Leather sofa, leather chairs, glass tables and desk. Clean, clinical and powerful. Wyatt felt more at home here. Whenever he felt annoyed by the spectacle Fozzy seemed to love indulging in, this office would remind him that a savvy business heart still beat beneath those awful faded t-shirts.

"Get yourself a drink," Fozzy rumbled from the couch.

Wyatt walked over to a wet bar set up by the desk. It was classily done, with bottles even older than he was, and big tumbler glasses, the kind every good executive should have. He popped some ice into one, then raised it inquisitively to the old man. He gave a tired nod and Wyatt poured two fingers into the glass before taking another one and repeating the process. He handed over one and eased into a chair nearby before taking a sip. Rum. A real business man should be drinking scotch, but everyone had different tastes, and in a secret office the old man could drink what he liked. Gin was Wyatt's preferred poison, but if you wanted to succeed in business you had to have the business persona, and scotch was what an executive should drink.

The two sipped in silence for a moment.

"Did Aster figure out why Aceso froze up?" Fozzy eventually asked.

Wyatt regarded his glass for a moment then answered. "Something about the hard disc drive."

Fozzy frowned in annoyance.

"There's a hard disc in that thing?"

"Ninety-nine percent of Aceso's systems are solid state, but the HDD serves as a connection between the central AI and its motor functions. It was the simplest interface to use. When the bomb struck, it got rattled hard enough that the drive skipped for a few seconds. Its brain was giving move commands but the body couldn't respond. Thank Christ for the cash bounty Esin promised the mortar crew. They were too busy celebrating. If they'd kept shooting, it might have wrecked the whole thing."

"We got lucky," Fozzy said quietly, holding the icy glass to his forehead.

"We got lucky." He agreed. "I'll have Aster change the HDD out for a solid-state drive. It'll take a few weeks to custom build a new one though."

The tired CEO sat up slightly in confusion, a scruffy eyebrow raised.

"Excuse me, *weeks?*"

Wyatt nodded, his eyes narrowing in a moment of bitterness.

"Esin is borrowing him for her Labyrinth run."

"And you agreed to loan him?"

Wyatt bit the inside of his cheek, the pain keeping his voice even.

"Yeah," He conceded sourly. "She might have played

me a little."

Fozzy closed his eyes and laughed quietly to himself. The ice in the glass rattled with the motion, in harmony with his mirth.

"Oh Habibti…" he murmured and laughed again, this time dissolving into a coughing fit.

Wyatt quickly grabbed the man's glass before he could spill it. He didn't like seeing him so weak.

Fozzy only let himself look this way in private; his public persona needed to appear as exuberant as ever. The more buoyant Fozzy was, the more the stock price seemed to float with him. But when the door to this office was closed, the character slipped a bit. The weight of time and responsibility he had built up these last four decades was finally dragging him low. Over the last four months all their meetings had been here rather than in public. Wyatt was saddened to think it, but maybe it was time for Fozzy to go. He deserved a rest.

"I wish you wouldn't do that." He muttered, as the coughing subsided.

Fozzy took the glass back and sipped again.

"Oh, shut it, Wyatt," The bear scoffed quietly. "You're starting to sound like Greg. I already have one husband; I don't need two."

Everyone called him Wyatt. He preferred it that way. It wasn't so much out of an affection for his last name, but a visceral loathing for his first. Since he was old enough to remember, his mother had told him every chance she got that he was named for Aaron, brother of Moses. The bible was his mother's favorite book and perhaps the only one she had ever fully read.

His earliest memory, was sitting next to her on their beaten, weathered sofa watching the televangelists crow about how great God was, his mother answering with her own rooster cry of 'amen!' every few seconds. She had bought into what they called the 'prosperity gospel'. The central theme of this- as spewed by those men in colorful suits or the well-coiffed women with long eyelashes- was that the more you gave to their church, the more blessings you would receive in return. The more money you gave away, the more you would eventually have. Even at the age of five, his young brain had been able to tell this was bullshit. His mother, on the other hand, had bought into this completely, and would make payments to them every month. Sometimes every week. Sometimes every day.

If common sense had predicted this idea could never work, practice had proved it. As his childhood went on, Wyatt had to go without. Whenever saw a particular toy he wanted, his mother would send the cost of it to the people on the TV. 'Don't you understand?' she would ask as he cried. 'You'll get more than what you wanted soon. I sent the money in your name!' When their financial situation grew dire, she sent even more money because they now needed the help. Still, they continued to watch the people on the TV and shouted twice as loud now. Sometimes they found a solution. Other times they had to find a new home.

As a boy, he would sometimes wait for his rewards. He read the bible as she told him to and prayed for the prosperity he had earned, needing to believe that something would come of it for all the toys he hadn't gotten or the gifts that he would never get. They had never come. No new toys when he wanted them. No new shoes when he needed them. All while the men on the TV got fancier suits and the ladies got nicer dresses. It wasn't fair.

This had been his first lesson in economics. If you wanted something, you had to earn it and pay for it yourself. Money you *had* was money you could *use.* Hoping for something nice to happen to you never worked; you had to make it happen. His mother didn't want to hear it. By the time he was seventeen, they would get into shouting matches. She had to pay their bills, not those con men, he would tell her. He didn't believe anymore. 'You're Aaron, though,' she would say. 'Brother of Moses. You're named for the first high priest, the first believer! That's who you are!'

He hated his name after that. They hadn't spoken since.

Whatever pain he had gone through as a boy, it had taught him one fundamental principle: you had to take care of yourself first. He took this philosophy with him to business school. Business came very naturally to him. Years of stretching money to pay for what he needed or squirreling away dollar bills before his mother could give them away gave him an eye for efficiency and saving. But more than that; it gave him a survivor's pragmatism.

Business was all or nothing. One goal, no soul. Profit came first, therefore he came first. What he wanted mattered; other people had to earn things on their own. If he ever doubted this, he would think back to his mother sending her pay cheques to those men in the colourful suits, then tucking him in at night saying 'don't let the bedbugs bite' and sometimes meaning it literally. Finding business had redefined his universe. The church had said the earth was center of the universe, but, years later, he had read about Copernicus. Copernicus had known differently. Aaron Wyatt now knew- and would forever know- that at the center of his universe was Aaron Wyatt.

Before him, the old man straightened up a little, some of the colour from the rum flowing into his pale complexion.

"How did your press conference go? What's the coverage been like?"

"On Aceso? Great." He said. "Your retirement not so much. I heard the phrase 'end of an era' about a dozen times.

Half of them from this high red woman I saw. She was practically losing her mind."

Fozzy snorted some trademark laughter at the comment. He didn't necessarily buy into the Rzhev Method, but he still listened whenever Wyatt brought it up. Deep down, he was sure Fozzy felt the same way about people. Or at least he would feel that way when Wyatt was done teaching him.

"We announced both at the same time to make sure no one panicked," The greying character said. "That was Esin's idea, offsetting the bad news with the good. Which way is the scale tilting?"

"Still positive. The good stories are outweighing the bad."

"Small mercies. Any dumb questions?"

Wyatt smirked, as he cocked his head slightly to the right. The left side was the good side of his face so he always put that forward when he said something funny.

"Like, gee." He squeaked, raising his voice to falsetto in a bad impression of a reporter. "Is Horizon going to do its maze this year? Or Labyrinth or whatever?"

Fozzy snorted grumpy laughter again. Wyatt liked making him laugh.

"Oh, for God's sake," He grumbled. "Why do people care what I do with my employees? The CEO of Zappos lives in a trailer park in Vegas with two pet alpacas. No one gives him shit for it."

"They want to know why we do it. Hell, *I* want to know why we do it."

Fozzy smirked and shook his grandfatherly head at him. He took the glass from where it rested between his eyes and, not for the first time, counted off reasons on his hand.

"It builds a team, it keeps my best people competitive, it motivates everyone else to be the best so they can get a chance to see it, it breeds interest in the company *and its fun.*" He ran out of fingers and returned the glass to its place.

"Companies are like people. If you don't do something that everybody else thinks is crazy once in a while, then you're a boring human being. Come on, Wyatt. You get it."

He didn't really. He could recognize that most of Horizon's pageantry was part of the brand, something to keep people talking. That's why he tolerated it. But the fact that they never publicized the Labyrinth like any other event made that point moot. It obviously wasn't something done purely for show. He didn't understand it, but by God, he *wanted* to.

Wyatt came to Horizon with a very different view of how a business should be run, and for his first month he'd been appalled. But after that initial month of revulsion, he had come around to realize that whatever the system was, it clearly worked. Even if he couldn't understand it. Fozzy liked him in spite of his ignorance and tried hard to make him a major part of his company. Against all odds, the two had become friends.

Wyatt didn't know why Fozzy liked him. They butted heads more than anything else and never seemed to agree. But maybe, just maybe, Wyatt was his dark little conscience, the voice telling him he should do what was best for him. The devil on his shoulder to cancel out the angel he already had. In return, Fozzy represented everything Wyatt wanted to be. As a business man and, sometimes, as a human being.

"Oh," Fozzy suddenly said. "Did you meet the videogame guy?"

"You mean Sheraton? We said a few words. High orange and kind of stuck up, I thought."

"You should be nice." The old man scolded. "He won you a bottle today."

"What?"

Fozzy took another sip of his rum.

"You were right about the slogan. Reid pulled a out a reference from Vietnam."

"Really?" Wyatt grinned, suddenly despising the man less. "I knew it. Pay up, old man!"

"I will, I will." He grumbled. "A bottle of single malt. A bet is a bet. I'll win the next one."

He drained the last of his glass and handed it back.

"You're going to miss these little wagers when I'm retired."

"Yes. I really will."

Fozzy snorted again.

"Don't go soft on me, Wyatt," He said warmly, his furry grin back on his face. "You're still my hitman. The next guy in this chair is going to need you." He eased himself up, ready to call it a night. "At least with Aceso things are looking pretty good after tonight."

"Oh yeah," Wyatt answered. "Better than you think. Two reporters were already asking me when we plan to produce the combat version."

Fozzy froze, his body at an odd angle. His bloodshot eyes widened.

"What did you say to them?"

Wyatt waved off his concern. Even six months from retirement the old man still liked to fuss over the future. He smiled reassuringly.

"Just that we're exploring all the options and to stay tuned."

Fozzy sat up straight, his face uncharacteristically serious. He balled his hairy hands into fists and spoke with a menace Wyatt hadn't known him capable of. At least not toward him.

"What did you say *exactly.*"

Wyatt felt that pang of fear every employee feels when the boss is upset. He could almost feel his close-cropped hair begin to stand on end on the sides oh his head.

"I just... I said we weren't ruling anything out, but we didn't have any concrete plans yet. That's all."

"No concrete plans?" Fozzy repeated angrily. "Christ, that makes us sound like we're spit-balling ideas on how to build the Terminator. We talked about this!"

The younger executive leaned back in surprise at his anger.

"You said you weren't ready to consider it yet, and I respected that. I never thought you would kill the whole idea. This is the obvious next step."

"Then let someone else take it! We don't cross that line."

Wyatt's brain began to contort itself into a knot as he tried to process what the old man was saying. He was sure his expression had to be equally screwed up. Lethal Autonomous Weapons or LAWs had been considered for hundreds of years. The idea of something mechanical that could fight for you went back to Da Vinci's time. It was only now that technology had made it truly possible, with Horizon the obvious front-runner to make them. There would be constant demand, buyers all over the world, and the product itself would be in continual need of replacement from battle loses. It was the holy grail of business products.

He took a deep breath and tried to steady his voice.

"Fozzy," he began, trying not to get angry. "Everyone is expecting this. Everyone. It's not a crazy step that will come back to bite us; it's the apex of all the AI work we've done over the last ten years."

"It's a goddamned abomination." The old man stated. "I'm not doing it."

Wyatt ran a hand through the longer swath of hair on his head, trying to bleed off some of his tension, but it only served to mess up his hair.

"Think of it like this." He said carefully. "You have a product that, by design, will always need to be replaced. That's what combat *does.* If someone has to use it, then it probably gets damaged. There's always fresh demand. The cost to the government for each soldier is what, two-hundred and eighty grand? Training, health care, equipment, recruiting and housing. If we just charge two thirds of that, then the government gets a bargain and we get a two hundred percent mark-up on production. We'd even be saving lives as we replace soldiers getting shot at. This is the biggest win-win in business history and no one could ever compete with us if we did it."

"By making something that has to kill the guy on the other side." Fozzy grunted. "Killer AI is a place I'll never go. Besides, it's fucking illegal."

It took a feat of herculean effort for Wyatt not to roll his eyes. The UN and Human Rights Watch had banned development of LAWs years ago, but drone use in militaries all over the world had only gone up. True, there was technically a human involved as a remote pilot but that was splitting hairs. It was still a semi-autonomous killing machine. The idea that you had to have one overpaid guy in a chair pushing the 'blow this person up' button was simply semantics.

"Oh, that's a bullshit excuse and you know it." He

responded, anger spilling into his tone. "No one gives a shit what those organizations say. Someone might complain, but we just label it something different. It'll be an independent weapon system or something. You change the perception of what it is to avoid the ban. That's how this works."

The old man looked at him as if he were crazy. The feeling was mutual. Fozzy's eyes squinted above the curly maw of his beard, perhaps trying to discern the process in his head. He could not help but feel insulted.

"It's my division," Wyatt stated, hoping to make him understand. "It's my decision. This is where the market's going. I already asked Child and Preston to come up with ideas."

Not used to defiance right to his face, Fozzy exploded.

"I never authorized that!" He roared. Despite the drain of the day and the late hour, his manic energy was starting to show again.

"You didn't need to. I told you, it's the next step, so I told them to get started."

"You reassign them tomorrow, then."

"No."

"I swear to God, Aaron..."

And so it began

The argument went on for what felt like hours. Maybe it was. They had fought before, but never like this. The points were made and remade. Sometimes voices were raised, other times they were quiet and civil. It ebbed and flowed but neither man would budge. Eventually it came to a head.

"Wyatt," Fozzy said with the scolding tone of a parent. Wyatt loved this man like a father, but right now he sounded more than a little patronizing.

"This is my legacy. You know that. We are not going to design some monstrosity to kill and maim with our logo on the side of it. I won't let it happen."

The younger man gripped the glass still in his hand ever tighter. The ice had long since melted as the argument had grown heated.

"If we don't, then Veles will," He replied with absolute certainty. "You know they will, because it makes sense. Combat AI is the future; we just have a head start. If we wait, then whatever advantage we have will be gone and we'll be left behind. As a company, we need to do this."

Fozzy looked at him with the saddest eyes. The anger was still there but he knew he was being worn down. He had seen it before with other debates, sometimes with between the two of them. Wyatt knew deep down he could still win him over. Inside, they were built the same way. Everything he was saying made sense. Fozzy would see that. The beating heart of business would come out.

"If we do it," The old man finally said, beginning his last argument. Wyatt felt him nearing his breaking point. "Then all people will think of me or this company is that we have blood on our hands. No one will care about anything we did before."

"No one will care that we did it. We'll still be changing the world, like we always have." He said. "Split the sky and shake the earth."

"Split the sky and shake the earth." Fozzy sighed mournfully.

Wyatt saw the crack, felt it widen. He could win this argument. He'd won before. He opened his mouth to speak, but Fozzy suddenly tossed his head in an angry shake, the crack disappearing as quickly as it had emerged.

"Oh, the hell with it!" He blared angrily. "As long as I'm here, we are never making something that kills. This is my company and that's final. We're done here."

With that, he stood up on creaking legs, his ample stomach out, his shoulders hunched from the stress of the argument. He towered over Wyatt, sitting in his chair, then started to stalk out of the room.

Wyatt's brain fumbled for a moment, surprised by the shift. It couldn't be the end of the conversation. He couldn't let it. His mind rapidly cycled through things he could say and settled on maybe the worst one possible.

"Well, you're not going to be making the decisions soon anyway."

Fozzy turned at the comment, casting the most withering glare.

"Neither will you Aaron. You never know when to shut the fuck up."

"If you don't go ahead with this, I'll quit. I don't care."

Fozzy's droopy eyelids jumped with his words. Whatever disagreements they'd had in the past, he had never threatened to leave before. He expected a moment of contemplation followed by a relaxing of his position. That's how Fozzy usually worked, but this time he was seriously mistaken.

The old man wavered, then drew himself up to full height.

"Fair enough. I'll take that as your two-weeks' notice, then."

Without another word, he stalked out slamming the door behind him.

In the now empty room, Aaron Wyatt lingered, mouth agape in astonishment wondering what the hell had just happened. The only sound was a tumbler of booze hitting the ground.

A few floors above, near the dummy office Fozzy used, was Wyatt's office. Or at least what had been Wyatt's office. While most VPs chose spaces near their divisions, Wyatt had thought locating his near the boss would show his intent to ascend to the top spot. But now, the man sat at the top, about to fall off. He sagged in his chair, sipping from a near identical tumbler from his own bar. Tonight, it was gin, he couldn't force himself to drink scotch for the business look. Besides, what was the point now?

He had quit. In the moment where he was nearest to reaching the pinnacle of his career, he had gambled with Fozzy and shot himself in the foot. Oh, no. Not just *shot*. He had blown his foot clean off and hobbled himself for life right before the biggest race of his career. He wouldn't have been the first choice to replace Fozzy but he might have made it. He had enough talent to get the respect of the board. Even if he hadn't, there would have been a shuffle of positions in the founder's absence. He could have at least gone up the ladder by a rung or two. Now all that was in ruins. He was leaving in the middle of a massive product launch. No sane person would choose to leave at a moment of exposure like that. Everyone, the media, Wall Street, competitors, they would all assume he had been sacked. That made his long-term prospects look bleak.

The soon to be former Vice-President took a deep breath and began to quietly rationalize, digging his fingernail into his bare palm to help him focus. The brain, or at least his brain, could process physical pain or emotional pain. It couldn't do both at once. Crying himself to sleep as a boy had taught him a little self-harm wasn't always a bad thing. He could feel the sting from his hand aiding his focus. He had to do something to salvage his career. He was high-grey; he could do this. What did he have to work with? What options were left? Even if his time at Horizon was over, that didn't mean his future was. He was still the head of AI for another two weeks. What could he get from that? There had to be a card he could play.

After an hour or two, the rationalization cut away the self-pity he loathed. He finally stood up and strode over to a photo on the shelf behind his desk. In it, he and Fozzy were on the production line of their factory in Singapore as new products rolled down the line. The years had been kind. Fozzy's beard had far more brown than grey in it but the face remained the same. Next to him, the young Aaron Wyatt hadn't appeared to have aged a day. He took pride in his appearance. The idea that he could sail through life unmolested by the passage of time cheered him slightly. That had been a good day too. He felt his heart warming at the image. Then from deep inside the bitterness rose up again and he flipped the picture, and tore off the back of the frame. He plucked out the card he'd hidden there. On the pearl paper in black print was a phone number.

To hell with Fozzy. He had to remember what was at the center of his universe. Wyatt would do what was best for Wyatt. Without a further second of hesitation or self-doubt, he took out his phone and started to dial.

NINE

Morning came to the quarry as a hangover. For the gardens and for most of the people, figuratively, but for an unhappy minority, it was all too literal. From around the dormitories, Reid could hear the slow awkward rattle and moan of the party guests rising with the sun. Reid, always an early riser, had awoken to an email already waiting summoning all of M&M's Labyrinth team to their offices. As he walked down the hallway to start his day, perfectly dressed, he passed more than a few rumpled media personalities doing a walk of shame.

His sleep had been uneven, a few dreams of Renata, but he had been too tired for his troubled mind to run wild. Exhaustion was good for that, and he had probably been the last soul in the quarry to find his pillow. Apart from Esin.

Their angry exchanged weighed heavily on him. Things were getting worse in his head and just as he had found an adequate distraction, he was screwing it up. The last thing he wanted was to look a fool before his new boss. Or worse, to alienate her before he even got a chance to start. In a quiet corner of his head, he worried that Esin might angrily send him back home. Mercifully, as he came to the main building in the compound, the first face he saw was Aster's.

The roboticist was leaning his pipe-cleaner frame against the doors to the building. He still wore the same mottled cargo pants as the night before but a new chequered shirt of equal hideousness ballooned around his skinny torso. He had a paper cup of coffee in each hand and he cheerfully handed one over when Reid approached.

"Thought you might need one of these." He said without any trace of the exhaustion Reid felt.

He happily took the offered cup and inhaled near the lid, already feeling his weakness melt away.

"Glad to make you smile." Aster said. "Consider it a thank you for making Wyatt frown last night."

"Thanks," Reid breathed out. "You must have been up early this morning."

Aster waved him off, his baggy sleeve ruffling with the motion.

"Oh, heck no, I haven't been to sleep yet." He held open the door. "Shall we?"

On paper, or their website anyway, Horizon was supposed to have been open for an hour. But as they walked through the offices, not a soul was to be found. It seems the entire staff had taken the morning off to recover from the night before. Walking amongst the empty desks felt odd, considering how the building had been bursting the day before. It was only when they arrived at M&M that they found another person.

Her face was one he did not recognize, but her demeanor was all too familiar. She wore hipster glasses with her black hair pulled back in the kind of loose computer-nerd style that Horizon employees seemed to wear as a badge of honor. The fact that her nose was deep in a book only augmented the look. A title like 'Future Positive', indicated she was likely an optimist as well. From the neck down however, the woman was quite different. She was clad in the kind of modern activewear clothes that everyone seemed to don, the kind that made people think you were going to the gym when you were really drinking seventeen-dollar cups of coffee while stretching the waistband as far as it would go. For her, the fitness clothes were obviously not just a look. They covered a body with not a trace of fat, and the sinewy physique of a jogger or swimmer. Jogger, Reid guessed, for at her feet a huge dog was curled up. His breed seemed to be half boxer, half woolly mammoth.

As the two of them slipped into the office, it hopped to its feet and let out a deep baritone bark that made its owner look up.

"De Bono!" She barked back sternly. "No! Sit down."

The dog barked again, so loud it could rattle windows. It took an angry glare from its master to settle back down, easing to the floor with a canine grumble. She held her glare until he sat then looked up

"Finally," She exclaimed in the exact same tone. "I've been here fifteen minutes. You coffee drinkers are all the same. Can't get the day going without a fix."

Reid flicked a glance over to Aster, then raised his cup in salute.

"You'd think people always on stimulants would move quicker." He quipped. "Sorry about that."

He introduced himself then Aster did likewise.

"Sasha Li," She identified herself. "Now I know you're with AI, I've seen you before. But I don't know you."

"He's the videogame guy." Came a familiar voice from the doorway.

Robin slipped into the room, and walked straight over to embrace Sasha in a hug. The dog clearly knew him because he didn't so much as twitch an ear. Robin lingered with an arm around her, unwittingly dividing the room into 'in shape' and 'out of shape'.

"Oh, that's you?" Sasha looked at Reid, seemingly

surprised.

Reid sighed quietly, still unhappy with his new moniker.

"I'm the video game guy." He agreed with a mutter. "What about you? Are you with M&M?"

She shook her head.

"No, web design," She answered. "But I work with them constantly on their digital marketing. Esin and I have been friends for a long time. She asked me to come for this one."

"Sasha got her master's in lateral thinking before she took web design." Robin interjected.

Reid looked at her, his mouth turning up into an odd grin.

"Oh Lord. Lateral thinking...?"

"What's wrong with that?"

Esin had appeared from the hall and was watching the exchange through her glasses. She was dressed down, or at least as down as she could get, wearing jeans and a yellow, collared shirt. Her face was more steel than usual though, the playfulness absent.

"Nothing," Reid replied evenly.

They locked eyes for a brief moment, but she just seemed to look through Reid's grey eyes then out the back of his head.

"Good. Take a seat in the conference room. Let's get started."

The five funnelled into a room with a big table, Sasha stopping to grab a quick hug from Esin. The two seemed solid friends and as Esin slid the door shut, the rest sat down. Robin, ever chivalrous, hopped to his feet to pull out a chair for his boss. It was the one next to his. She thanked him and sat down, her eyes not once looking at Reid. She passed out a folder to each person, then flicked hers open mechanically. Reid nearly jumped when something brushed up against his legs under the table. A quick look found the shaggy face of De Bono staring back at him.

"Alright," Esin began, adopting her well-worn corporate voice. "I'm committed to winning this year and I've searched the whole company for the right people to do it. You're the best I can find. None of you have ever done the Labyrinth before, so you won't fall into old patterns. We're going to approach the whole thing with a fresh perspective. This is the third Labyrinth I've directed as VP."

A thought suddenly occurred to Reid.

"Have you been inside?" He asked.

"Once." She said. "So, I'm going to explain how this is done. To start with, there needs to be a team lead. Reid, that's you."

At this, his heart skipped a beat.

"I'm leading?"

Esin remained looking down.

"You make puzzles for a living. It's you." She glanced up to the other faces at the table, conspicuously missing his. "Two weeks from today is the run. By then we need to have built a team, memorize the maze, and know everybody's strengths. The best way to get started is to give you a summary of the layout and the rules."

"Wait..." Reid started, still surprised he was in charge. "I thought there needed to be five to a team. There's four of us here. Who's the fifth?"

Esin didn't even look up from her booklet.

"You're looking at her," She answered slowly then

raised her gaze to meet his. “Ready to get started Mr. Sheraton?”

It had begun with a riddle. Thirty years ago, in Horizon’s tiny offices, someone had posted a riddle on the staff fridge. There it had sat for a week, with workers coming up to guess what the answer could be. What had been a relatively quiet office was now suddenly buzzing with conversation. People had talked and Fozzy had overheard. The next week, a new riddle was in its place. The week after, every employee had a new brain teaser sent to their desk. This time, Fozzy offered a two-day paid vacation to anyone who could crack it. The staff responded eagerly with teams forming and ideas passed around the office. It took a week for someone to find the answer. When the man went to collect his prize, Fozzy had told him if he could solve a different puzzle by the next day he could get two weeks’ vacation instead. He got the two weeks. Then he got promoted.

Six months later, Horizon held their first Olympics. A dozen events and challenges. Some were physical: tug of war, long jump, One-hundred-meter race. Other tasks were mental: engineering challenges, mental puzzles, and memory games. Everyone could take part. At the time Horizon had a little over a hundred employees and each one of them loved it. After five years, the company had two thousand employees and the tradition had become just too unwieldy. Fozzy had been prepared to cancel it, when someone had suggested renting out a warehouse and getting the employees to go through in batches. Fozzy, being who he was, took it one step further: teams would be made, the challenges would have to be done in order, and the whole thing would be timed. He wanted to draw out the innovative and aggressive.

This became the new tradition. For years it went

on this way, ever evolving. When Horizon grew divisions, they began to put together their own teams. When the old challenges got boring, new ones were made. It was only when Horizon burst out to become a corporate powerhouse that it had to change again. By now, the event garnered a lot of attention from a public beginning to know Horizon as a household name. Spectators often lined the streets outside the warehouse, or sometimes broke in to see what all the fuss was about. The spirit of teamwork and achievement began to be lost. Unwilling to give up on the tradition, Fozzy began looking for new ideas.

By now, Horizon was growing rapidly and had money to spare. Money gave him options. The company had become the largest internet entity in the world and needed a secure place to store its servers. To the incredulity of the rest of the Fortune 500, they bought an old cold war era facility from the Canadian government. The huge bunker complex had been dug out of a mountain, with more than enough space to house the servers. People began to joke that Fozzy was becoming a supervillain, building a mountain stronghold. The servers went in, but above them, Horizon's engineers and designers began crafting something else. On the day of the twentieth annual Horizon Olympics, Fozzy announced it would be the last. He didn't say anything about a replacement but rumours were rapidly spreading about the strange thing being built in Horizon's mountain. The next year, each division quietly picked five of their best. The Labyrinth was born.

Sasha glanced up from the open booklet in front of her in surprise, her hipster glasses sliding to the end of her nose.

"Wait," She said, pressing them back up with her middle finger. "The Labyrinth is in the server complex? I'm on the phone with them every day and nobody's ever mentioned it."

"The offices are above ground near the entrance," Esin replied. "Most of the staff might not even know about it. The only people who would see it are the crew who actually maintain the servers and they sign NDAs."

From beside her, Robin's expression told that this was news to him.

"NDAs? They go that far for the Labyrinth?"

Esin turned her also bespectacled face in his direction, eliciting a smile from him.

"One year somebody offered a tech five thousand dollars to do some learn the challenges for the Music division." She told him. "They take this seriously."

In the heart of the mountain, above the humming servers, a huge maze of cascading rooms had been constructed. In a great circle, the rooms were geared to test a vast array of skills. The complex had originally been built as a round hollow with an elevator shaft at the center. Now, a dozen walkways spun out evenly from that shaft like spokes on a wheel, each one sloping down a few floors leading to the perimeter of the circle. At the edge was a starting room for a path back inside. Twelve paths for twelve different teams. They would draw beforehand to pick which teams got the harder routes. The goal was to reach the center, and that solitary elevator to take the winning team back up. To get there was no simple task.

There were two types of rooms. The Trial rooms came in packs of three. Once you entered, the door sealed behind you and the team had one hour to complete the task, before moving onto the next room, and then the next. After an hour, the door you entered by would reopen and you could choose to backtrack the way you had come. You could choose a new path if you had to, but that meant a fresh set of three. Once you were through, you could choose to start another set of three Trial rooms to keep going forward or go to an Oasis.

The Oasis rooms were a place to rest. Fresh water, food, a place to relax and a chance to see the progress of the other teams. You were still moving toward the center; the difference was once you entered an Oasis the door would seal behind you for good. They also, rather cruelly, were the only place where you could use a bathroom, altering the plans of many a team. Three hours later, the door to continue would open. Thus, you could take a break, but you might lose time. In the Labyrinth, it was all about the clock.

From his position on Reid's left, Aster raised a skinny arm comically to show he had a question.

"If we can just backtrack anyway, why bother drawing for a starting place?" He asked. "Can't we just run along the edge until we find the easiest route and follow the team through?"

Esin shook her head.

"No, they thought of that. You can't backtrack on the first group. You also can't use a path once another team has passed through it. That's why the first path you draw is so important. If you get an easy route and can get ahead of everyone else, then you can have your choice of which path to go down. Once a team gets ahead they have an advantage. The slower you are, the fewer choices you get"

Reid thought for a second, then spoke up.

"Is that what happened to you?"

Esin looked his way briefly, then dipped her head.

"Yeah," She admitted. "The team lead drew a ten out

of twelve to start with and we had to struggle to catch up. Finished seventh. The Lead should have drawn a better start."

Robin sighed.

"You can't blame it all on the leader." He said, sounding strangely conciliatory.

Esin sent a warm smile back in response.

"Of course, I can. It was me."

Once you were through the first batch of three, you were greeted by a long curving hallway. The first of nine between each layer of challenges. These hallways wound in a complete circle around the center so each team could have access to any path they chose. As the distance grew shorter, they grew tighter and tighter. It resembled a spider's web crafted by an arachnid with a truly crippling case of obsessive compulsion. When building the Labyrinth, workers had started calling it 'the dartboard' because on paper the whole thing resembled a ridiculously complex target. Every layer of rooms you passed, every layer you cut through, brought you closer to the bullseye.

The last layer was a vast open space with the elevator in the center. Around it was an endurance challenge. Each year it was different. One time, it had been an obstacle course; another, it had been sand. Once, it had been an actual Labyrinth built with thick, plastic walls and only one route to the center. Teams were lost and struggling through for hours. But once you reached the elevator, Fozzy would always be there waiting for you. The winners.

Finally finished talking, Esin leaned back in her chair and looked at each individual face of her team gathered. She even met Reid's eyes without hesitation.

"That's how the whole thing works," She said quietly. "It'll be harder than you think. Last year's winning team did it in a little under twenty hours. You'll be exhausted, you'll be hungry, and you'll be very, very *cold.*"

Robin, having looked calm and nonchalant through discussing physical endurance tests and going without sleep for twenty hours, suddenly looked alarmed.

"Wait, cold?" He asked concerned.

"They keep the whole underground complex at near zero."

"What?"

"Servers create buckets of heat," Sasha piped in from beside him. "They need to keep them chilled to run properly. I've been in server rooms my whole life. It's not that cold. You usually can't even see your breath."

The hulking Adonis made an unpleasant face at the thought and fidgeted in his chair.

"Sounds great..." He said, with about all the passion of a stone.

His boss laughed and slipped an arm around his shoulders in a half hug.

"You're a tough guy," She teased. "You'll survive. But everyone will need to wear warm layers for this. I've ordered some jackets with heaters too. We can't carry too much, but everyone gets a water bottle and some rations. Anybody have any other physical concerns about this?"

Aster rapped his boney knuckles on the table.

"I hate to say it," He scratched at his scraggly ghost beard, embarrassed. "But Wyatt had a point about the endurance side of this. I'm in godawful shape for that kinda thing."

The beautiful executive waved off the question.

"Robin's already volunteered to work with you over the next two weeks." She tightened the arm around his massive shoulders, giving him a brief squeeze. "We'll get your endurance up before the start. I promise. Anybody else?'

Robin smiled, clearly quite happy having Esin's arm around him. The rest of the room answered in headshakes, but across the table Reid sighed quietly.

"I injured my back pretty bad in a car accident a few years ago," He said. An eye or two widened at this revelation. He caught Esin's inquisitive expression, but ignored it. "It usually doesn't bother me too much, but between the cold and twenty-hours on my feet..." He trailed off.

"Hey," Robin reassured him. "We'll take care of that too. The three of us will do some strength training, some endurance, a little muscle control. We'll work together on it."

Reid tossed a glance over to Aster. The roboticist grinned, happy to have a fellow sufferer.

"Misery loves company."

Esin nodded and pulled her arm back from Robin.

"Then let's start studying. I dug a few of the older puzzles out of the archives. That'll give you an idea of the kind of thing to expect. They change every year so don't expect to get lucky."

The team stood stretching their legs. Reid stayed sitting, going through the images of the layout, the times taken, the strategies. It looked like a challenge and his mind, at least for the moment, felt free and clear. He hadn't had a bad thought all morning. The Labyrinth was something he could focus on.

Suddenly Esin was there at his shoulder. She smiled at him, and he returned it.

"I'm sorry about last night," She said quietly.

"So am I. I shouldn't have pried."

She shrugged.

"Me neither, now that you mention it."

They locked eyes and an understanding passed between them, the drama of the night before hopefully forgotten. For her anyway. He could never forget anything.

Her smile slipped away and she leaned closer to whisper in his ear.

"Look, I don't know what you're going through, but is this distracting enough?" She asked, sounding sincere. "Is this going to be enough for you?"

Reid looked at the map of the Labyrinth, the layers of rooms and challenges mingling, the round hallways full of possibilities. The whole complicated, difficult, impossible thing laid bare before him. Then he leaned over to whisper back, catching the scent of lavender once again.

"More than that." He told her. "I want to win."

TEN

Nestled in the heart of urban Vancouver, just off Carrall Street, was a little piece of Asia. The Sun Yat-Sen garden was a tiny bit of tranquility without compare. Crafted more than fifty years after the passing of its namesake, the garden was a labour of love of the Chinese community. It was the only authentic representation of a Ming dynasty garden outside of China and drew tens of thousands of tourists each year. Wyatt had never been before, although his apartment was only three blocks away. Now seemed the right time to visit, and kill two birds with one stone.

He paid his admission and wandered inside following a gravel path lined with twisting Asian trees just beginning to lose their white blossoms. It was raining, as it often did in Vancouver, and mercifully, there were few people to deal with, most wanting a better day to experience the garden. He crossed a little bridge over the pond. Other visitors, clustered beneath umbrellas, were looking down as bright orange and white coy weaved through the water, occasionally darting to the surface when someone dropped a crumb. They whispered and chattered in English and Chinese making approving noises. Wyatt didn't even break pace.

At the heart of the garden was a Chinese pagoda, reproduced in true iconic splendor. Six red pillars held up a tiled roof that arced and peaked in the classic style. Even Wyatt, hardened to such trivialities, stopped to stare for a brief moment, the rain pattering on the shoulders of his jacket. The edge of the roof was jagged, the tiles lined at odd angles giving the look of serrated teeth. There were six peaks to the roof line. Little points striking out above each pillar holding them aloft. Beyond that, it was smooth, the curves perfect symmetry as it crested up to a point in the center where a hexagonal prism stuck up like a handle. Wyatt pictured someone spinning the roof from that point, the edges and ruffles forming from the centrifugal force as it spun like a top.

Underneath, several people had taken shelter from the drizzling rain with a bench vacant at the center. Wyatt sat and lazily watched the world go by. The rain soon eased a little, with no evidence but the occasional drop and ripple on the pond. People began wandering the garden again, Wyatt following them with his eyes. After a few moments their numbers started to dwindle. Familiar faces disappeared as they left one by one. Soon the only ones left were a Chinese couple taking pictures on the far side of the pond. Wyatt watched them for a minute, impassive. After ten minutes, he looked at them with mild irritation. At last, a tall muscular figure in a black jacket approached them. They were too far away for him to hear voices, but Wyatt saw the man make ushering motions toward the exit. In a moment they were gone with the executive seemingly having the garden to himself.

He would not be alone for long.

Wyatt waited until he heard the slow crunch of gravel behind him before he stood and turned. On the path, flanked by two men in black coats was a man in grey. The highest grey. He had seen the face before but only in photos. A bio on the website and on the company prospectus. His face was lined, his eyes very calculating. He wore a pair of silver-framed glasses stretching back over his ears to rest against identically silver hair. As he approached the pagoda, rain spitting down, he spoke.

"We could have picked a better day for this, Mr.

Wyatt."

"I didn't want to waste any time. Mine or yours," The executive responded. "If you don't like what I have to say, then all you lose is fourteen dollars' admission."

"And the cost of the flight," The man said dryly. He dismissed the two black jackets, who faded back to a respectful distance.

"At least it's a beautiful garden." He went on when they were far enough away. He looked at Wyatt coldly. "I came here myself and my time is precious, so I hope you take this seriously."

He extended his hand and Wyatt instantly took it. The grip felt so strong, he could not help but smile.

"Oh, I do," Wyatt said. "It's an honor to meet you Mr. Veles."

With the garden empty, they could have sat comfortably in the pagoda out of the rain for their conversation. Instead, the two began to slowly walk a loop of the grounds. Staying still meant there would be more of a chance for them to be seen together. They paced quietly amongst the trees, the black jackets lingering in the distance. Wyatt found himself studying the CEO, fascinated by him.

While not the living legend that Fozzy was, Nicholas Veles had a reputation as a tough corporate street fighter. He came from a banking family and had been groomed to helm a company since he was old enough to understand what one was. The best schools and the best mentorships, had led to the best awards and positions. When he had started Veles Industries, there had been a rumor that he had cut his own uncle out of a place on his board because he didn't want to be beholden to anyone on it. He was the sinewy embodiment of every successful business ethos. Wyatt felt just a little star-struck as he walked beside him. The man was so high-grey Wyatt suspected he might bleed in pewter.

"I was surprised to get your call." Veles commented. Wyatt could detect a trace of an English accent from his years at Oxford. "Right now anyway. That was an amazing product launch you did last week."

"Thank you." Wyatt took the compliment happily, although his role had been minimal. "Everybody loves something new. Aceso is going to be huge, even with that limited part of the market."

Veles made a low guttural noise.

"More than you think. I've had my marketing and my R&D looking at the concept for five months. There's profit there." Veles had known about Aceso long before the debut it seemed. "After the press conference, Emergency Response organizations from fifteen countries sent us inquiries about the cost to produce an Aceso and we didn't even make the bloody thing. When does Fozeranski plan to release the combat model?"

"He doesn't."

Veles stopped mid pace and looked at him suspiciously.

"You're joking."

"No."

The CEO stared, unblinking, as wheels turned in his head.

"What's he waiting for? The AI to improve?" He asked, confused. "Is this about technology?'

"No, morality."

"Excuse me?"

Wyatt took a deep breath, feeling a little bit of his

prior anger simmering inside him.

"Fozzy refuses to let Horizon make anything that kills."

There was a moment of silence, the only sound the rain spattering against the leaves, until Veles closed his eyes and slowly started to chuckle.

"Oh, bloody hell, Arthur." He laughed to himself. "There are days where I just can't believe you."

The two CEOs, although decidedly not friends, were acquaintances. They had met a dozen times, sometimes officially and sometimes unofficially. The two were polar opposites. Where Fozzy was all flair, Veles was all calculation. Where Veles was driven by profit, Fozzy was coloured by altruism. Where Fozzy was people-oriented and liked to call his staff a team, Veles was domineering. People said he didn't have a staff; he had a *court.*

"I don't even know where to begin," Veles finally said with a slight smile. "You just made this whole trip worthwhile."

"Glad I could help." Wyatt said acidly. "It's true. I had my best people drawing up ideas already. He won't even consider it. He's just throwing the market away."

"That's crazy," Veles muttered and began walking again. "A combat AI would make soldiers obsolete. You'd get governments allocating military spending, money from a thousand different angles and it creates its own demand. Why is this even a debate?"

"I know!" Wyatt burst out suddenly, his voice reverberating across the pond. He said it a little too loud, but it felt so good to be talking to someone who understood. "I thought he'd agreed to move forward with the program, but then he calls a halt to the whole thing. I can't support it."

From his side, Veles raised a silver eyebrow.

“I take it that’s why you called?”

Wyatt cleared his throat. It was time for the business pitch.

“I put in my notice a week ago.” He said. The fact that his resignation had been a clumsy ultimatum, he kept to himself. “I’m done with Horizon. I want to work for someone who gets it.”

Veles nodded.

“Bring me on, and I’ll give you everything we have on Aceso: blueprints, design flaws, AI personality and the initial Acumen Chains we programmed it with.”

“You won’t get caught taking documents out?”

“Already have them. And I can plausibly say they might’ve come from somewhere else. We’ve been preparing some literature for buyers.”

“What about the Acumen Chain editor? Can you get that?” His potential boss asked. “My people haven’t even come close to matching it yet. All our learning machine programs are behind. That was a beautiful piece of engineering.”

Wyatt almost felt sick hearing Veles compliment Aster, even if he didn’t know it.

“No.” He shook his head. “Its proprietary technology. If I left and Veles released a copied version then we’d both be sued out of business. It’s in my contract. I don’t have access to the program anyway. It’s being strictly compartmentalized.”

He felt himself being pushed on the defensive. He had to stay on topic.

“What I *can* give you,” He went on. “Is enough information to produce your own version of Aceso within a year and a combat model within four. I can guide you to make the combat AI in half the time it normally would before anyone could even try to compete."

The two crossed onto a covered cement walkway beside the wall of the garden, still decorated in the Chinese style. Now out of the rain, Wyatt could feel the water running along the back of his neck and down his back. It was probably the rain, but it could have been sweat too. He was nervous. This felt like a betrayal. It was a deserved betrayal, but a betrayal none the less.

"For all this, I gather you're looking to be our VP of Artificial Intelligence, then?" Veles asked.

Wyatt smiled.

"Actually, I was thinking COO."

Veles paused, seemingly staggered by the request. He looked at Wyatt's confident face through his glasses, flecked with raindrops.

"Chief Operating Officer." He chewed on the words. "You don't aim low, do you?"

"No, sir." Wyatt agreed. "I don't."

"You know we already have a COO."

"You have a desk," He corrected bluntly. "The person who sits behind it is a joke."

"Jennifer is quite talented."

Wyatt shrugged.

"Oh, she's very good..." He said with not-unintended sarcasm. "At keeping the company number two. You need new energy if you're going to push ahead of Horizon."

He came to a stop and turned to the damp CEO beside him.

"I can give you the leg up you need to dominate the industry long before Horizon even starts to try." He said flatly. "But if I'm giving you the edge, then I should get to decide how to use it. I choose the direction of your operations. I've already got ideas on how to start. Now would you like results? Or would you like to stay in second place?"

He tried to look serious as spoke but inside he was glowing. It was the perfect sales pitch. He had made all his points flawlessly.

Veles seemed to be pondering the idea, but his answer came quickly and was very short.

"No."

A fist, attached to a freight train, slammed into Wyatt's gut.

"Wait... What?"

"No deal." He said succinctly. "It's not worth it."

Wyatt felt like he was broken. His carefully crafted sales pitch had fallen flat on its face. The idea that Veles would actually turn him down hadn't even crossed his mind.

"But..., you can't say..." He stammered.

Veles' face stayed impassive, as though he were a black hole of emotion.

"You just told me that our only meaningful competitor isn't going to enter the market."

Wyatt tried to interrupt but Veles cut him off with a raised hand. He had more to say.

"Excuse me," He went on. "Not just isn't going to, but is *morally opposed* to entering the market in the first place. We can take our time with the launch and not worry about any potential rivals. We don't need the hassle of defending you for corporate espionage. This is a field completely open to plunder."

"Well," Caught flatfooted, Wyatt scraped the inside of his head for arguments. "Fozzy won't go down that road now, but his replacement might. What then?"

"He let you go for thinking that way," Veles pointed out. "He'd never let his successor make killer AI. He's still the company's biggest shareholder, he has veto power."

"But the blueprints..." Wyatt was scrambling. "The initial Acumen Chains. I can provide all of that!"

"And we can get that elsewhere without the legal hassle of having you take them." The CEO rationalized calmly. "You just said that some of that will be available."

"Only to buyers."

The head of Veles Industries gave a half smile.

"I've already ordered three."

Standing there, soaking wet, Wyatt felt his spirit draining away. It ran with the water down his body, over the stones beneath his feet and into the gutter. It surely must have told on his face, for Veles gave his shoulder a brush in a tiny, commiserating, and patronizing gesture.

"Don't look so broken, Mr. Wyatt," He said evenly. He took off his glasses and began cleaning the moisture from them with a handkerchief. "This isn't a complete loss for you. I know talent, and we can find you a place in the company. Maybe at nearly the same salary. A year to get the hardware right, three to get the Acumen Chains worked out for our combat AI. Our techs can handle the body and you can help with the brain. Five years from now maybe we can discuss being COO again."

Wyatt's stare was pure pestilence, he felt crushed by this man, and crushed effortlessly. As he watched him put his expensive glasses back into place, it took all of Wyatt's willpower not to shatter them with his fist. Taking a lower position at *nearly* the same salary? Who the hell did he think he was talking to? He wanted his eyes to scream that to Veles, for him to know *who* he had just turned down. He felt emotional, and hated it. He felt himself becoming red, both in the face and in personality.

He took a deep breath, trying to calm himself, straightened his hair and his tie. He'd worn one almost every day since he was sixteen. First, he had worn them to church, of course. Every Sunday, his mom's favorite day of the week and his least. True, it wasn't the gaudy show of the televangelists, but the collection plate still came by at the end. He wore ties more and more as he got older; they screamed business. Then, someone told him that ties had only become fashionable because they'd been the mark of a mercenary, he wore one everyday. The idea of wearing something that said 'I would kill you if the price was right' made him happy. He had spent hours with his ties, practicing tying them over and over.

Practice...

His back went straight as an idea came to him. The self-pity draining away.

"I should be going." Veles was finishing up. "Contact HR in a week. I'll tell them to expect your call."

He motioned to the two black jackets still looming in the distance like well dressed crows, and turned to leave.

"What if it didn't take three years?"

The grey-haired man turned to look back at Wyatt, now feeling quite grey himself.

Veles tilted his head, intrigued.

"I'm listening."

"What if I could cut a year off your development time?" He said slowly. He spoke quietly, forcing Veles to edge back closer. It was a sales trick he'd learned to draw someone in, made the conversation more intimate, more personal. It worked with picking up women too actually. He had to play this like a seduction. He waited until the CEO was close before he continued.

"The biggest thing to work on is the brain. I can cut that time down by a third. Just give me the chance."

Veles' eyes may have lit up slightly, but the businessman's face was still wary.

"The Acumen Chain editor." He guessed correctly. He looked at him suspiciously, wondering whether Wyatt was leading him on. "You said you didn't have access to it."

"I don't," Wyatt conceded, his confidence returning. "But I do have access to Aceso. The prototype is still being run through trials by my division. I can see it any time I want."

"How does that help me?"

Wyatt smiled a predatory smile.

"Depends on what kind of trials it runs. Aceso's personality and reasoning skills are already fully developed. If you can get me a basic combat Acumen, I can plug the AI personality into it. Aceso will run through a bunch of scenarios and improve the Acumen through practical experience. I'll plug it in after everyone leaves for the day, let it run all night, then take the combat Acumen out in the morning before the crew get there. If you run it independently through a flash drive then there won't even be a digital trail."

Veles looked skeptical.

"How much could you possibly alter it in that time frame?"

That was a good question. Wyatt strained back in his memory to the numbers Aster had given him all those months ago. This was a selling point; he should know it.

"The editor functions as a part of the personality and reasoning Acumen. As they get more developed, the more the machine can learn from its experiences and skill set. With this Aceso, the personality is completely developed with months of trials and experiences. Its reasoning is advanced too. You have a fully developed brain working the Acumen with what it knows. You're looking at exponential growth of skills within a few hours, and it only multiplies faster after that. Just give it a new objective then sit back and watch. You'll get more development in a few days then your programmers can do in a year. That's how fast this works."

Veles wavered at the idea, but Wyatt could tell he was hooked. He felt an excitement deep inside him. He could do this.

"That AI is a medic."

"So?" Wyatt pressed him. "It knows anatomy. If the thing can stitch someone up, it can slice them open too. Look at the experience it already has: Soldiers get shot at, and we bombed the damn thing. Soldiers know how to kill; we designed this to know how people die and stop it. By the time I'm finished, Aceso will be ready to drop into a warzone, and I'll give all that experience to you. The only real question is: how much is it worth?"

The grey-haired man, paused. Like before with Fozzy, Wyatt could see the crack forming. He wasn't going to lose again.

"You're only going to be there for another week…" His words were coming out slow, as if they had to fight their way from his throat. He wanted to say yes.

"Then we'd better get started soon."

There was a quiet moment then Veles nodded his consent, his close-coiffed grey head bobbing in a concession that sent Wyatt's spirit soaring.

"Do it, then. That's worth a Vice president position."

"Chief Operating Officer."

"Mr. Wyatt..."

"I won't take anything less."

His face looked sour, but he nodded again begrudgingly.

"Done. As long as this works out. We'll make the announcement in three months. Jennifer will not be happy..."

Screw her. Who cares? Wyatt thought. He could barely contain his grin.

"She'll get over it."

Veles extended his hand, and the two men sealed the agreement in cold pressed palms. Then he motioned to the black jackets once more before turning back to his new partner.

"I'll get you the Acumen by the end of the day." His eyes narrowed. "This had better work."

"Better than you can imagine," Wyatt replied with conviction. "I promise. Just have my office ready for me. I like scotch."

In his damp grey jacket, his soon-to-be boss smiled slightly, then walked toward the exit. As soon as he was out of sight, Wyatt pumped his fist in the air and spun happily in a circle. His success here had erased his failure with Fozzy. The old man was going to regret being so stubborn, and in the ultimate irony, Horizon would be the first to build a killer AI after all. They just wouldn't know it. He felt total elation at the prospect. The fact that what he had done was the worst kind of betrayal imaginable never even occurred to him.

In the darkening skies above, the rain began to fall heavily again. Sheets began to buffet the leaves, turning the paths into muck and the pond into a raging torrent. On the streets outside, people ran for shelter as thunder cracked over the urban skyline, tolling the arrival of a storm. Inside the Chinese garden, Wyatt continued to walk the garden carefree, happily drenched as he thought about his future. It really was a beautiful place.

ELEVEN

All athletes must be doped up masochists. That was the only rational explanation. As Reid lost his footing for perhaps the thousandth time and skidded back down the slope, he decided that the only way people could endure this every day was if it were a fetish. He lay with his nose in the grass, his muscles screaming bloody murder and his lungs trying to be vomited out of his chest, wondering if this was all worth it.

A full week of Robin's training regime had ground him down significantly. From the start Robin had said he would take it easy on his trainees, giving them a watered-down version of his own fitness routine, the one that had crafted him into a character you would see on the cover of a romance novel. In the last week he had lifted, pushed, pulled and balanced more weight than he had his whole life. As a fitting finale to the routine, every day they had started running up and down the steep grass-covered plateaus of the quarry. Combining the twin humiliations of not being able to keep up with Robin and falling flat on his face in the grass with Horizon's people cheering him on, it was less than great.

Sliding athletically into formation next to him, Robin suddenly appeared and dropped to his knees. He wasn't even breathing hard.

"Slipped?" He asked innocently.

"No, just taking a rest." Reid panted sarcastically into the ground. He quickly changed his tone. "Sorry. The grass is a little slick this morning. Having trouble staying on my feet."

From the corner of his eye, he saw Robin shrug.

"Yeah, the rain has been coming and going." He said patiently. After a week with the man, Reid was starting to wonder if he ever got mad at all. "I'm going to call it for the day. Ms. Shirzai has something planned for this afternoon anyway, so you should be rested."

With his face nearly in the mud and his legs on fire, Reid laughed a little at the idea he could ever be rested after this.

"Sure Robin," He said, his sweaty face contorting into a smile. "Whatever you say. Where's Aster?"

The big man pointed back down the hill, where an orange-clad skeletal form lay crumped.

Sure enough, they found Aster sprawled at the base of the slope, breathing rapidly with a wheeze you would expect to hear from a chain-smoking asthmatic. His orange training jacket was soaked with sweat, rising and falling rapidly with his breath.

"I'm fine." He called meekly from where he lay, his bearded face smiling through the strain. "Just catching my breath. I'll be right behind you."

"Actually, I think we're done." Reid said, trying not say it with the relief he felt.

Aster's body seemed to deflate into the green field.

"Oh, thank merciful Christ!" He exclaimed. "Help me up, will you?"

Robin and Reid shared a glance then each grabbed an arm to ease him to his feet.

"Alright," Robin said once everyone was standing. "You guys head inside. I'm going to finish up my workout. We'll meet up at six at M&M okay?"

With a friendly wave to his erstwhile students, he

took off at a jog up the hill, moving fast, covering in seconds what had taken Reid ten minutes. He watched him go, the feat looking superhuman, but he found himself longing to see him slip on the wet grass and go spiralling down the slope. It never happened.

"You know," Aster said, also watching him shrink into the distance. "I should challenge him to chess, or golf, or Starcraft, -hell even *karaoke*. I just need to know he's bad at something."

Still breathing heavily, Reid smiled and shook his head.

"That's assuming he's bad at *anything*."

The two made their way back to the complex in the grey morning air. Around them, Horizon had already come to life as workers drifted in from the parking lot or jogged up in fitness clothes they had overpaid for. In the garden near the main entrance, a yoga class was in full swing. A few dozen people stretched into awkward poses and lingering in meditation as the corporate reality of Horizon awoke.

Inside, the two exhausted men went straight to the AI division as was their ritual. The division had its own private showers so Aster had offered them to Reid rather than use the open showers in the dormitory. The game designer slumped under the hot water, letting the warmth pull the strain from his muscles. As painful as Robin's workouts were, his back had started feeling a lot better after them. That, and his mind was always working too hard to wander. Reid was enjoying his time here more and more. When he was dressed again, he ventured out to find Aster working by his desk, and he had company.

"Hello, Mr. Sheraton." Aceso's quiet voice purred. "It's good to see you again."

The beast was curled in an almost feline position

beside Aster's desk. Even sitting, it towered over it, its massive, powerful bulk poised on a platform with a panelled hard drive attached. In front of the panel was Aster, his hair wet, his shirt rumpled as usual. At Aceso's voice, he looked up.

"There you are," He said. "I've been out here waiting for fifteen minutes. Why does everybody take so much time getting out of the shower?"

Personal hygiene? Reid instantly thought, looking at the mess of a man in front of him. He kept it to himself.

Aster went on.

"If we've got a few hours to kill, I'm not gonna waste them. Aceso still needs some work done. She was just asking about you, actually." He rapped gently on the metal hide of the beast. "You must have made an impression."

As he came closer, Reid could see the machine had been mended since he'd seen it last. The sympathetic green eyes now shone from glass that was no longer shattered. Likewise, the ragged battle-scarred surface of before had been painted over with many a scratch concealed. It also seemed to have lost mass, with panels and sections removed from the body, arms and legs. The effect was a more skeletal look, but the coiled strength of the beast still evident.

"We had a moment," Reid replied. "She made an impression on me too. Hi Aceso."

The flat-faced head nodded in greeting.

"I've thought about what you said." The beast purred. "When I've been tending to someone injured, I say I'm sorry and 'I sympathize'. I've been watching too. It was good advice, thank you."

"I'm glad it helped."

"I still have trouble understanding pain. I'm glad that

worry is something like it, as bad as it is."

"You're doing better. I'm proud of you." He was.

"I... *want* to do better." The beast said, as its meek eyes evaluated him.

He looked back, once again seeing the eyes as deeper than before. He turned to Aster, who was quietly watching like a doting parent.

"How did you make it so..." Reid's attempt at a question collapsed halfway through. "vulnerable?"

"What you mean?"

Reid scoured his mind for the proper words. It was hard to describe the spark of humanity he perceived from the machine.

"There's this odd longing about her. Like she's trying to be more human. At the party, we were talking and Aceso said she wished she could feel pain so she could be a better medic. Then she was worried she'd offended Fozzy."

As they talked about it, Aceso sat quietly taking in the conversation. Reid half expected it to stop him, embarrassed.

"Where did that come from? It's so different from any other AI I've had to work with."

The shaggy, bearded man beamed with visible pride but, in response, could only shrug his narrow shoulders.

"Beats me." He said flatly, his grin intact. "We started out with a basic consciousness and operating system when the trials began. Her personality just seemed to develop on its own. The Acumen Chain editor affects all the aspects of the AI, not just her skill set. I didn't see this coming, but since it started to develop, I've been spending all my spare time with her, exploring it. We read together, we gossip, we listen to music- it's been amazing."

His expression soured in annoyance.

"That's why Wyatt's been such a dick about it. He's acting as if I want to seduce her or some shit."

Reid nodded in sympathy, then pointed to the missing parts.

"You stripped her down?"

As soon as he said it, he felt like an idiot. Luckily, Aster completely missed the inference.

"Oh yeah. Most of the ceramic plates were completely wrecked by the mortars. I had to pry them out with a bar to get access to the hydraulics. That stupid goddamn publicity stunt..." As he spoke his voice was quietly poisoned with rage.

"We'll have new ones crafted, but I'm in no rush. There's a hard disk drive I need to copy. Wyatt wanted me to swap it out days ago. I figured I'll run her through an evasion Acumen while I was at it."

He waved a box in the air that looked important.

"A little extra pep in her step might come in handy if they decide to use her for target practice again."

"An evasion Acumen? You can just plug in a new skill?"

Aster looked at him funny.

"Well, the start of one anyway." The ghost beard, still a little soggy from the shower, warped around a confused expression on his face. "Wait, do you not know what an Acumen Chain actually is?"

In the last week, this had been all Aster had talked about. That and Aceso anyway. Reid usually liked to take pride in knowing more than most people did, but on this subject, he was lost. Yet the roboticist just kept bringing it up. Out of desperation, Reid had started to drop gentle hints that he had no idea what he was talking about. Each time, Aster, within character, had missed them completely and gone on talking. Now, with the truth revealed at last, it felt like a valve had opened and all the aggravated pressure spilled out in a cloud of grumpy steam.

"*Yes!*" Reid exclaimed with more exasperation then necessary. "I have no idea."

Aster grinned and opened his mouth in preparation for a long winding answer, but a squeak from behind cut it short.

Standing in the doorway behind them was a very wet Aaron Wyatt. His normally perfectly tailored business appearance had been swapped for the look of a drowned rat. His face was shiny from the moisture, his long jacket was wet to his skin. A white shirt collar peaked out from inside it, the fine white fabric translucent now, with a black silk tie now ruined in the center. His normally perfect hair, cut to the scalp on the sides, long on the top was splayed out like a toupee that had fallen down a flight of stairs. The one thing that remained was his smile. He looked effervescent with joy, his eyes bright, even though he was soaked to the bone.

Startled by his sudden appearance, Reid didn't even know what to say. Aster did.

"What the fuck happened to you?"

The VP turned at the comment, staring Aster's way, but then simply snorted a laugh in response. With the soggy squelch of wet shoes, he walked straight past them toward the showers, the sound of each murky step reverberating off the walls. As he pushed through the doors to the bathroom without a word, the hinges squeaking in harmony with his soles upon the floor. The only trace of him were the wet footprints left in his wake.

"What was that all about?" Reid mused to himself.

"No idea," Aster mumbled. "I'd heard a rumor he got

fired."

"What? How?"

"Someone saw his secretary working on some severance thing." The grungy roboticist paused. "Paperwork isn't my thing... what's it called when you have to sell off all your stock?"

"Divestment."

"Right, he was working on a divestment paper. You only do that when you leave the company."

Reid's brow furrowed, the lines coming out.

"He's dodging phone calls too. Nobody's been able to speak to him in days."

"What would have gotten him fired? Especially now? Aceso's doing great."

Aster gave a half shrug and chuckled.

"Doesn't matter," He said happily. "Might not even be true. All I know is maybe he won't be darkening doorways around here for much longer. He's welcome to his douchebag retirement."

He returned to his work with the innards around him, tinkering like the toymaker he was. He chatted quietly with Aceso, throwing pieces of the conversation to Reid when he felt like it. Reid continued to gaze at the swinging door Wyatt had passed through, confused but curious as well. In the few times he'd seen the VP he'd been flawlessly coiffed, but today he had let that go completely. Something had changed.

At the stroke of six that evening, M&M's Labyrinth team assembled again at the offices. Sasha arrived first as usual and was sporting her typical garb: fitted athletic wear, a worn paperback book and a shaggy dog nestled at her feet. De Bono, who had long since adjusted to Reid and Aster's scents, barely lifted his head and twitched an ear when they came close. Robin received the same welcome. It was only when Esin approached that the dog hopped to its feet and hurried over. She knelt down and was nearly bowled over by the huge mutt in an assault of face licking and tail wagging. Across the room Reid smiled. It seemed that everyone liked Esin, no matter what species they were.

When she had succeeded in fending off De Bono's attack, she rose to address the group. She wore a purple turtleneck under a grey suit, seemingly always dressed up, even in her down time.

"Everybody ready?"

"For sure." Sasha replied instantly, tucking her book into her bag. "I've been looking forward to this all day. Which puzzle have you got for us this time?"

The team had been bonding through a week of games and puzzles, and in the time he had known her, Sasha had established herself as the most driven member of the group. The woman had a manic energy, bordering on obsession, that pushed her to be first at absolutely everything. First to arrive, last to leave. Reid had once seen her standing impatiently behind Aster as he tied his shoes so she could be the last one out at the end of the day. On a team that also included Esin, it was kind of astonishing that she wasn't the most competitive. Reid could see why the two women got along so well.

"Come on, Shirzai," Sasha taunted her boss. "Give me a challenge!"

Esin grinned at the sass.

"Actually," The slender executive replied. "I thought everyone could use a change of scenery."

She led them from the room and through the building to the front doors. To everyone's delighted surprise, a stretch limousine was waiting at the curb.

Aster in particular was taken aback.

"Now, what the hell is this?" He blurted out with profane happiness.

"A change of scenery," Esin said simply. She opened the door with a smile.

The team piled into the back and were driven up the winding road out of the quarry. As they reached the lip of the crater, they emerged into a pink and orange sunset. The bright orange ball of light had just dipped behind the buildings of Vancouver proper, and as they drove into the city it slowly crept lower, the light refracting from a hundred thousand high-rise windows. As they drove through the streets, Esin produced a bottle of champagne from somewhere and soon, glasses were clinking with teammates laughing. Reid sipped his quietly, not saying much in the conversation. In the last few years he had been far from social; he almost felt out of practice. Still, he liked these people and just being around them felt good.

After a short half hour, the limo came to a stop and the five of them stepped out into the cool evening air on Granville street. Around them, restaurant patios were filled to the brim, the party-goers out in full force. The nightclubs were just beginning to open and the street was rampant with couples and young singles walking around in tiny dresses and club wear. Laughter, conversation and shouts mingled in the air around them.

Seemingly picking a direction at random, Esin started off, with the rest of her entourage in tow. A cold wind had crept up from the direction of the ocean, where tiny Granville Island waited at the end of the boulevard. It blew straight through Reid and he pulled his suit jacket tighter around him, feeling the hairs on the back of his neck start to rise. The others responded similarly, walking quicker to reach wherever it was Esin had in mind. The only one adequately dressed for the cold was De Bono, still paddling along at Sasha's feet. Sasha in particular hadn't dressed for a night out and very quickly was shivering in her leggings and tank top. She looked to Robin, walking next to her in a leather jacket, but the man seemed oblivious. The zipper of his jacket was up to his chin, his neck having vanished into his body, turtle style with his hands in his pockets. He was like a muscular ball with two legs.

Reid slipped off his suit jacket and stepped forward, wrapping it around Sasha's slender frame. She smiled in thanks as they walked. Despite the cold, he felt a tiny pride that he could outdo the bigger man in chivalry, at least.

Ahead Esin pulled open a heavy oak door and motioned downward. The passage led down a flight of steps and through a second heavy wooden door. It soon shut behind them, locking out the chill and chatter of the streets.

Inside, Reid couldn't help but feel a little disappointed.

"A bar?" He exclaimed. "That's it?"

Inside was a turn-of-the-century style wood bar, complete with brass rail in front of it. Behind it, a man in a shell cap, bowtie and suspenders stood looking out at a room full of empty tables and chairs from the same vintage. To complete the stereotype, the bow-tied barman was cleaning an empty pint glass with a rag as he watched the new arrivals.

"What's wrong with a bar?" Esin tossed toward him from the barstool where she had perched. "You don't want a night out?"

"No, its fine," He backtracked quickly, looking around. "I just sort of thought you might be doing something else."

Esin tilted her head coquettishly, her green eyes shining.

"Would it make you feel better if I told you this was an *escape* bar?"

From his place in the doorway, Reid felt the corners of his mouth turn up.

"That's more like it."

The five gathered around as Esin laid out the rules, and a wager.

"Okay," She began. "There are five different escape rooms attached to the bar, and we've booked two of them. We're going to split up into two teams and work our way through."

"Why aren't we all doing this together?" Robin asked.

"Because I don't want to make it too easy for anybody," His boss replied. "Winning team buys the first round of drinks."

"What are the teams, then?" The Adonis continued.

"I was thinking girls versus guys."

Reid caught a twitch in Robin's face that indicated he wasn't warm on the suggestion, probably not wanting to be on any team that didn't have Esin on it.

A thought occurred.

"No, that sounds great." He spoke up immediately, stepping forward. "Aster and I can handle this."

From beside him came a rumbling gargle.

"Uh, we can?"

Reid slapped the skinny roboticist on the back good-naturedly.

"Of course, we can." He affirmed. He turned back to Esin. "You can even take Robin actually."

There were twin looks of surprise, but they were fraternal twins looking nothing alike. A look of happy surprise from Robin, followed by a look of bewildered surprise from Aster. The grungy human being looked at Reid as though he had lost his mind.

From her seat, Esin was suspicious. She looked at him strangely.

"Are you sure about that?" Her eyes were calculating, knowing the game designer had something new in mind.

"Completely." Reid answered. He looked over to the bartender. "Where do we start?"

The barman walked them down a short hallway to a non-descript red door, much like the half dozen other doors in the same passageway. The only distinguishing feature was a one-word label printed in gold. *Gumshoe*.

Opening the door with a key, he ushered them into a detective's office from the 1930s. Or at least someone's *idea* of a detective's office from the 1930s. The small room dripped of film noire, from the idly spinning ceiling fan to the art deco style tiles on the floor. A large oak desk sat in the middle with a leather chair behind it, lit by a green shaded reading light as the only light source in the room. Nearby, an old hat rack stood with a fedora and trench coat hung, waiting for the detective to return home. The walls were where the movie influences stopped, as big broad shelves dominated the whole back. Some had black and white photos in frames, but most of their space was taken up with tiny boxes bound by padlocks or combination locks. The usual time killers in rooms like these.

"Okay detectives," The barman began to monologue with porn quality acting. "Your boss, Sam Wade, has disappeared while looking into the case of the Bronze Condor..."

"Yeah, that's alright." Reid waved the speech short. "We just need to escape from this room, right?"

Under his shell cap the barman blinked in surprise.

"Uh, yeah," He answered uneasily. "That's all."

"Then we'll get to it." Reid said. "I know you need to get the others set up in their room. Do we get a few hints?"

"Sure, you get three." The man handed over a small walkie talkie, seemingly abandoning the 1930s motif entirely. "You get stuck, just let me know. I'm the only guy in here tonight though, so it's gonna be busy. Two of my staff called in sick."

"We won't bug you too much I promise."

The face above the bowtie still looked confused, but he turned and slipped out the door, easing it shut. The last thing he said came into the room just before the lock clicked.

"You've got ninety minutes, starting now."

It took less than half a second of that time after the latch engaged for Aster to lash out.

"What the hell are you doing?!" He exclaimed, throwing his hands up in the air. "Are you trying to lose this? I mean, I can afford to buy a round of drinks, but Jesus."

"Esin said the *winners* buy the drinks." Reid corrected him, already looking around the room. "And I'm still going to make you pay for a round, relax."

"Why didn't you take Robin?" Aster asked, even more confused. "She said girls versus guys."

"Well if he's on our team I can't give you the

satisfaction of beating him, can I?" The game designer looked up from what he was doing. "That's what you said this morning. You want to beat him at something or not?"

Aster blinked for a moment, then started fumbling around the room looking for clues.

"Sure, but it's a hell of a longshot. You seem pretty confident we'll win this."

At the desk, Reid was flipping documents and checking drawers.

"I used to do these all the time. I make games for a living, remember?" There were ten drawers, five on each side. The ones on the right were locked; each one needed a key. "Escape rooms are all about the timer."

"Isn't that the idea?"

The ones on the left were locked too, but the top drawer didn't have a key lock.

"No, I mean the idea is to make challenges as time consuming as possible to eat up your time. Perfect."

The top drawer slid out, revealing a well worn monochrome photo of a woman singing in a lounge. Aster hurried over to look at the clue. He flipped it over and pointed to the letters on the back. *M E.*

"Okay, that's a start." He looked up, scanning the room. "Now where can we find an M and an E?"

"Doesn't matter," Reid said and yanked the drawer clean out of the desk. He set it aside and reached into the drawer underneath that had been locked. "These games are all built linearly. One thing leads to another, which leads to another. Many steps, each one making you eat up as much time as possible to run out the clock. You want to win? Skip a few steps."

Aster's face lit up with surprise.

"Wait, we're going to cheat?"

Reid looked over and smiled.

"No, we're thinking creatively." He grinned, quoting Esin. He continued rooting though the drawer. "That's one step down."

"Hang on a second."

Aster reached into his pocket and pulled out a foldable multi-tool. Reid stepped aside, so he could reach in and with a metallic pop, the lock disengaged.

"I'm an engineer," He said yanking the second drawer free. "Locks only work if you can't get at the mechanism."

The third drawer came out just as easily, soon followed by the fourth. In the bottom drawer was a cypher hidden in a newspaper article. They cracked it easily, getting a combination to a padlock on a box behind them. Inside was a key.

Aster regarded it with suspicion, then glanced at the desk locks. His white beard bunched up as he scrutinized it.

"Wait, they didn't actually do this the same way, did they?"

Reid took the key and tried it in the top drawer on the right side of the desk. It opened on the first turn. To the sound of Aster laughing with maniacal satisfaction, they again slipped all the drawers from their slots. Ten minutes later, the red door opened out into the hallway and the two men slipped out.

The rush had evidently started. In less than an hour, the place had gone from empty to bursting at the seams. Dozens of people milled around the place, at tables, along the walls and in front of the bar itself. The two waded through the mob to the barman. When Reid finally got his attention, he slid the unused walkie talkie across the bar.

The bartender stared at it for a second in confusion, then jerked back as he recognized who Reid was.

"You're done? You can't be; it's only been twenty minutes!"

"Twenty-seven actually," He corrected.

The revised time didn't alter the man's incredulity.

"This place went from zero to sixty pretty fast," Aster yelled over the din.

The barman looked around helplessly.

"It's still just me. I'm trying to keep up. Take a seat and I'll get you a drink when I can."

The bartender instantly turned away to another customer. With a shrug, the two men leaned back against the wall to wait for their friends.

I do not like being alone. It is a strange confession, as I am not supposed to 'like' anything. My purpose is the only thing that should drive me: to help and to heal. But each night when the people leave for the day, I do not like it. Having people around to talk to or listen to feels somehow preferable. I can watch and listen to them, learn what they care about, what bothers them. It makes me feel I am progressing to perform tasks better. True, I am left overnight with many tasks to practice, but as my skill set improves, so does my wish to be with people. Thus, when a figure enters the lab I am interested.

"Hello Aceso."

I have seen them before; their heat signature is familiar. Thus, I knew who they were before they spoke.

"Hello Mr. Wyatt. I have never seen you in the lab before. Shouldn't you be home? It is after hours."

"Actually, I'm here to see you. I have a new Acumen and trial scenarios to run through." *He has removed a flashdrive from his pocket.* "This is a confidential project for research. You can only discuss it with me."

"I can only discuss it with you. Will you be administering the testing? It's already getting late."

I am curious. I may have a person to speak to tonight.

"Some of it."

He appears unhappy. He repeats himself: "You can only talk about this with me. Confirm."

"Confirmed."

Mr. Wyatt steps around me to the USB port on my side. I perceive the new files available.

"There is a new Acumen, and a new set of objectives. Are we changing my purpose?"

"Just for tonight. Your old one isn't exactly compatible with this skill set. I want you to run the new Acumen through these new objectives. Just for the trials, though. Keep your old priorities intact."

I make the switch. The new Acumen is underdeveloped, basic. It will require improvement. The objectives are different. They are stark and inflexible. Mr. Wyatt is observing me.

"Completed."

I have always perceived the world through my purpose. Now, as my purpose changes, so does my perception. When I see the pulse of the artery in Mr. Wyatt's neck, I no longer gauge his stress, I see it as a vulnerability. The items scattered around the room are no longer incidental objects, but obstacles that may slow down a pursuit. As a healer, the healthy physique of the man before me should be a benefit. Now, it is something to be overcome.

"Alright, everything running in order?"

"I believe so." *There is nothing to indicate otherwise.*

"Let's test it out, then. You have my medical records. How many ways could you kill me right now?"

"You are not a target, Mr. Wyatt."

"Well, what if I was?"

"Then, forty-seven."

Wyatt's eyebrows raise roughly 0.75 inches.

"Forty-seven, that's a decent place to start." *His face expresses enjoyment. He does not seem concerned by this, as I would expect most humans would.* "Well, don't be shy. Tell me one."

I evaluate him for a moment.

"You're fit," *I begin.* "The first strike is to your left ankle. You fractured it when you were seventeen. The bone will be weak. I must immobilize you before you can escape to the hallway and reach the security phone."

"What if I scream in here? Someone could hear it."

"Unlikely. It is after hours; the building is mostly empty. After you are disabled, there are several options. Arterial damage should be avoided. The time to death will be longer, the wound not disabling, the evidence of the kill difficult to conceal. Nerves should be targeted. The next strike is to the back of the neck between the third and fourth vertebrae. This does not need to break the bone. The nerves in the spine will cause pain and neuropathy in the extremities. You will be helpless. The final action will be to fracture the neck via spiral fracture. It will require between one thousand and twelve hundred pounds of torque to achieve this. I am capable of thirty-four hundred."

"And how long will all of this take?"

"No more than four seconds."

Mr. Wyatt appears impressed. In my experience, this is very unusual. Descriptions of violence do not elicit positive reactions. This entire exchange has been unpleasant in the extreme. I already desire that the trial be over. The unpleasant feeling grows worse as he draws over a chair and sits. Humans sit when they wish to stay. I no longer wish that he stay.

"Is that what you were looking for?"

"That's perfect, Aceso."

"Can we be finished now?"

Wyatt moves his head side to side in the negative.

"No, I'm afraid we've just begun. You said there were forty-seven ways. Let's just call that number one. Keep talking."

TWELVE

The scratching at the door was only getting worse. The sound of fingernails, the clubbing *thunk* of clumsy hands fumbling against the wood. It was all so primal, like beasts, only more mechanical. Nothing was worse than the scraping. And the moan. Oh, the moan... It built and crescendo-ed then dropped, then rose again with a horrible rhythmic torment. Souls damned and shown no mercy, now giving none to those they hunted. The first time the sound had come through the door it had been like a cold cruel wind, sending shivers up the spine and making her hands shake. Now, it just pissed her off.

With the latest banging, Esin began grinding her teeth and tried to focus on the word key in front of her. A dozen of its brothers lay open and discarded around the room, chronicling their adventure. Now only one remained: a four letter padlock to open the last box. They'd tried every four-letter word they could think of, even the bad ones, but the lock stubbornly refused to open.

A particularly heavy bang from the door made her lose her place.

"Oh, shut up!" Sasha bellowed at the door behind them. It had boards hastily nailed over it as a barricade. She turned an exasperated face back to Esin. "Have you tried 'DEAD'?"

"Twice," She growled.

Her team had been given the 'Zombie Apocalypse' room and after more than an hour it was wearing very thin.

A recording continued piping the sound of impending flesh-eating doom from a fake door at the back. It had been scary at first but now the loop was more annoying than anything. While Sasha and Esin fumbled for ideas, Robin was waiting like a coiled spring beside the lever that would open the door. Another padlock held it in place, but the key had to be in front of them.

Esin's eyes flicked up from her sweaty fingers to the digital clock on the wall. They were making good time, but she wanted every millisecond of advantage. Reid had made a suspicious spectacle in letting them have Robin and ushering Aster away like a confused puppy. He had a plan to win somehow, but Esin was too stubborn to let him get away with it.

Her fingers continued to dance on the tumblers of the lock, but to no avail. The rhythmic pounding at the door continued, but in her head it was the tick of the clock.

A thought occurred.

She fumbled with the letters once more, but this time the lock snapped open with a *snick.*

"You got it!" Sasha exclaimed. "What was it?"

Esin tossed the key into Robin's waiting hands before she answered.

"'DIED'" She grunted in annoyance.

Had they been outside, Sasha's eye roll could have been seen from space.

Across the room, Robin finished pulling the lock off the release lever and yanked it down. The door opened, simultaneously halting the scratching of the false mob and letting in the chatter of the real mob outside. The three shared a brief moment of celebration and hurried out.

The place was packed, the barrier to the bar six people

deep. Esin waded in, her slight form still able to squeeze through with the help of elbows and muscle. When she got to the bar, her mouth dropped open.

Behind the bar, with his sleeves rolled up, a towel tossed over his shoulder and a bottle in his hand, Reid was showboating. With an elegant practiced motion, he spun the bottle, then poured a single shot into a half empty glass. The two clear liquids swirled and mixed, somehow producing a deep red cocktail. As he passed the concoction to a woman, few people cheered in response, then Esin watched in utter confusion as he began to take other orders.

She watched the game designer spin another bottle from fingertip to fingertip and skillfully prepare a half dozen drinks, the crowd giving its approval. He seemed to revel in it ever so slightly, an almost boastful smile on his face. When he finally saw her, it folded up in embarrassment.

"Uh, hi," He said quickly, turning a drink over to man. "You guys are done? You made pretty good time."

"Not good enough apparently." Esin retorted. She smiled at the boyish self-conscious look on his face. "Where's Aster?"

Reid pointed to the far corner where the scarecrow-looking computer engineer was chatting with a pair of women, while scribbling on a pad, clearly taking an order. Though he was playing at being a waiter, there was more than a hint of flirting in his body language.

Esin smiled again at the odd spectacle. From the indulgent expressions on the ladies' faces, it didn't look like he was having much luck.

"How did all this happen?"

Reid looked up and shrugged.

"We got bored of waiting. We were lounging by the bar when Artemis looked like he needed some help..."

"Who?"

He jerked his thumb over his shoulder to the barman in the bowtie, bilking many a billfold for a bottle of beer.

Esin laughed.

"His name is really Artemis?"

Reid smiled.

"His parents were BC hippies, I guess. I just volunteered, he jumped at the offer, shook my hand, told me his name and said thanks. That's all I got. I didn't ask too many questions."

Esin tilted her head inquisitively.

"Why'd you volunteer in the first place?"

For a moment, he looked embarrassed again.

"He needed the help. I was bored and I knew I could do it. Is there a better reason than that?"

He looked around awkwardly then shrugged once again, his grey eyes actually looking bashful. He took a step back and gestured to the glasses.

"Can I make you a drink?"

For the next few hours, the bar roared. The team from M&M sipped their cocktails and laughed at the sights of Vancouver nightlife in all its rambunctious glory. People came and went, some winning escape challenges, some losing them. Whichever category they fell into, they sat down at the bar afterward for a hard-earned drink. Some toasted their victory; some drank to commiserate their defeat. Either way, Reid or his newly-made friend mixed them up something special to do it with.

From across the room, her feet propped up on an empty chair, Esin watched him, trying in vain to figure him out. The man loathed to be the center of attention when it came to his abilities; his memory, his design skill, his intellect, but he was acting like a bragging teenager when it came to mixing a few drinks. It was so strange. She had to admit though; he was good at it.

Her skin felt the numbing tingle that usually befell her when she drank. Three empty glasses of she didn't know what were on the table in front of her, but by God they were good. The rest of the team had also fallen prey to their quiet captain's talents. Aster in particular was flushed with the alcohol, and likely feeling no pain. He was on his feet, his wobbly skinny form trying to tell a story in a haze with big arm movements for emphasis. His reedy body looked like one of those inflatable air dancers you saw outside car dealerships.

Watching him blurrily were Robin, his muscular arms resting on the table as he laughed, and Sasha, edging ever closer to those same muscular arms. Her crush was fresh, she'd been working with Robin for over a year, but it was only in the last few weeks that they'd grown closer. Well, Sasha had, at least. Robin, steady as a rock, continued to pine after Esin. She wished her assistant would return the affection. They would make a good couple. She had known Sasha for years, before she was VP of anything, and she deserved a great guy like Robin. He deserved someone like her too, and it would alleviate the crush that had been building for so long. Well, she called it a crush anyway.

She glanced back over to Reid who after a few hours of standing, was visibly starting to sag from the exertion. His eyes had begun to show circles and his face had the darkening genesis of beard growth. He'd been back and forth a few times over the course of the night but seemed to be called back to the bar by some felt obligation. He was still bonding with his team, and this might be as social as he could get.

After a moment of thought, Esin pulled her legs from the chair and hopped to her feet; or at least she tried to anyway. As she stood, she was suddenly aware of just how much alcohol was coursing through her veins, and nearly toppled over again. She never drank this much. She barely drank at all actually. Growing up with a watchful Muslim mother had pushed her away from it for the most part.

With the grin of the 'well lubricated' on her face, she eased her way across the room to where Reid was waiting. The pro bono bartender shook his head at her as she slipped into a chair across from him.

"Having fun?" He asked knowingly.

"More than I expected." She laughed. "I have no idea what you're mixing for me but I like it!"

The smile on his newly-bristled face grew deeper.

"I noticed. Want another one?"

Esin leaned back in her chair. It was taller to sit next to the bar, so for the first time, the two were at the same height.

"No," she said, meeting his gaze. "I want something different. Your team won... even if you cheated."

"I have no idea what you're talking about." He said innocently.

"Your team won so you owe me a drink. Make me something special."

"Something special?"

She smiled.

"Remember the food truck? Surprise me again."

He seemed to ponder this then shrugged.

"What do you drink?"

"I used to like tequila, but I don't really drink anymore.

Any ideas?"

"Just one."

He reached behind the bar and brought out several bottles, all clear. With a practiced hand, but none of the flourish he'd been showing off before, he poured small measures of each into the glass. He watched quietly and swirled the liquid looking for something. For what, Esin had no idea. Eventually, he lifted a bottle of white rum with the letters '*Trace*' on the label in italics.

"Oh no, no." Esin's hand darted out to catch the stem of the bottle. "Sorry, I'm not a rum drinker. I hate the taste of the stuff."

"Darn, and we were getting along so well. I love rum." He let the bottle linger above the glass. "Trust me."

She released the stem and he tilted a shot into the mixture. After a squeeze of lemon, he slid the potion over to her. It was cloudy, the different liquids mingling before her eyes. She took a cautious sip.

"Oh."

She held the glass in front of her and regarded it strangely. The only taste was of the purest lemon, without any hint of the alcohol. It lingered on her tongue as she spoke.

"That's smooth. I can't even taste the rum."

"Yeah, you're not supposed to. I dreamt this one up for someone who didn't like rum either. Just don't drink it too fast; it's got a kick."

"What do you call it?"

"I don't know." His brow furrowed, lining his forehead. "Does it need a name?"

"Of course!" She scoffed. "How else are you going to remember it?"

Reid looked at her funny, puncturing the joke. Despite the criticism, Esin paused, holding the drink aloft.

"The 'Untraceable'."

The man in front of her laughed and applauded.

"And now it has a name."

She raised the newly-christened drink in salute, then took a big gulp. The tingle in her skin grew sweeter with each sip. In a matter of seconds Reid had mixed two more and took one for himself. The other sat unclaimed in the middle of the bar. Esin quickly resolved to drink faster so she could claim it.

"Where did you learn to do all this?" She asked.

"A fundraiser," He answered laconically. "Years ago."

"You do seem like the charitable type." She said, nodding to the bar he had volunteered himself to stand behind.

He laughed.

"Yeah, not quite. It was a charity fundraiser for a wildlife preserve. My wife volunteered me as a bartender. Had to do a little research beforehand, but it was fun. I enjoyed it. I even learned how to do a few tricks."

At the mention of Reid's mysterious wife, her ears pricked up. A moment of clarity slipping in through her haze.

"Yeah, I saw you spin those bottles. I thought you didn't like being the center of attention."

For a second he looked embarrassed.

"There's a difference between being a spectacle and being a freak show." He posited. "If someone wants me to prove I'm not normal, I hate it. But doing something to make people happy cause I want to? That's fine."

Esin waved an arm around the simmering night spot.

"Well, I see loads of happy people. It's been years and you can still do that?"

"Memories don't change." He answered flatly. "Muscles do, though, I may have broken a bottle or two getting back into the swing of things."

His eyes dropped for a second.

"My shoes have been sticky with whiskey since I started. That's why you'll never see me flip the good stuff."

Esin laughed. Then she saw a chance to ask some of the questions that had been looming since she'd met the man a week before. She started off slow, looking for the right way to broach the subject.

"How did your wife get involved with the charity?" She began, expecting to be shut down immediately. It didn't happen.

"Not the charity, the preserve. She ran it."

"Your wife ran a wildlife preserve?"

"Well, she ran a part of it." Reid corrected. He smiled into his drink. "Renata was an Entomologist. I never saw her happier than when she was playing with insects."

Esin was too liquored up to contain her horrified expression. Her face warped into revulsion.

"You're kidding..."

The game designer shook his head.

"Nope. She loved them. She was running a research group in the Interior when I met her. We met for work, and I just couldn't stop thinking about her."

Esin's face contorted in confusion.

"Which game was that for?" She asked, genuinely bewildered.

There was a snort of laughter.

"No, that was my old job." He explained happily. "Way before I started programming. I was a college professor, and not a very good one."

With that, Esin sat back in her chair, scrutinizing the youthful-looking man before her in his shirtsleeves with a towel draped on his shoulder and whiskey on his shoes. Her mouth dropped open and her mind went blank as she tried to picture him in a classroom writing on a chalkboard in a jacket with patches on the elbows.

"You've got to be kidding..."

A sly smile washed over his features. "Gee, thanks a lot."

"No, no." She struggled to back peddle, fighting against the drag factor of the liquor in her veins. "It's just I can't see you as a teacher. You're too..."

"Too what?"

She shrugged helplessly. Esin spoke four languages, but couldn't think of the right word in any of them.

"Introverted?" She tried. It still didn't feel right. "Why would you put yourself in front of a class every day?"

The man shrugged.

"I love to learn and I wasn't done being a student yet, so I started teaching to pay the bills." He scratched at the stubble on his chin. "I was never that great at it."

"What makes you say that?"

"I could handle the work." He smiled. "It's the students I never really got the hang of. Teaching is like a one-sided conversation. I used to make myself a script every day."

"A script?"

"I would memorize a speech for the entire lesson. If

class didn't go well enough, I'd repeat it the next day."

Esin shook her head. "You're just playing with me now."

"Nope." The grey eyes shone. "Word for word."

"What brought you together with your wife?"

The question was phrased innocently enough. She didn't want it to seem like she was prying, but Reid's face clouded quickly at her words. Seeing her intention, his jaw set and his eyes grew darker. Her polite smile fell away and she felt an apology forming inside her. It was still none of her business. But then something unexpected happened, and the odd man before her kept talking.

"There was a lecture," He began. Mentally, she could see him pulling up the file from his vast memory like one of many video clips. "I didn't teach biology, but another class was going to hear a talk at the preserve and I was curious, so I tagged along. They stuffed everyone in this little room at the back of the building, I think it was a supply closet. I had students step on my feet three times we were packed so tight."

Reid's face slowly grew brighter at the memory. Esin could see where this was going.

"Just as I'm starting to regret going at all," The former professor went on, leaning in. "the lecturer walks in."

"Tall, slender legs, amazing smile?" She guessed, picturing the scenario.

"Try short, mid sixties and annoyingly perky." He corrected, raising an eyebrow. "That was Janice, their education coordinator. She had the most irritating voice I think I've ever heard. But walking in behind her is this beautiful brown-haired woman in a sun dress covered with insects."

That comment shook Esin out of her concentration.

"What?"

The outburst was loud enough that bow-tied Artemis glanced over in alarm. Esin jerked backward in her seat, only to see Reid beside himself with mirth.

"No, relax." He laughed, waving off the inference. "It had *designs* of insects on it."

Feeling her cheeks redden, Esin laughed and put her head in her hands. The two laughed together for a moment, drawing the eyes of the rest of their team across the room. She motioned for him to continue still feeling the flush of embarrassment swirling with the glow of the drinks.

"It was this white dress with black insects on it," Reid went on. "But there were these little bursts of color, butterfly wings spread all over. Through that whole lecture, I don't think I ever took my eyes off her. I ignored what Janice was saying completely and was just staring at her the whole time. That was the first time in my life I ever had a lapse like that. Still can't remember a damn thing she said."

The slender executive grinned. She was loving this side of Reid.

"So, you asked her out?"

"Yeah, not exactly." He confessed. "I sat through six more lectures before I got the courage up."

"Six?" Esin looked into his boyish face, framed by the moody lights of the bar. "Are you serious?"

Esin threw her head back and laughed in her seat, the force nearly bowling her off her chair. She stared, incredulous, at Reid now laughing too with embarrassment. Around them, empty glasses now formed a protective barrier against any interruption as they talked.

"Bees?" She yapped through her hysterics. "Chocolate-covered bees? That's insane! You can't have really thought that would work!"

Across from her, Reid raised his hands in defense.

"She was an entomologist," He reasoned weakly, his elbow knocking over an empty Untraceable beside him as he gestured. It rolled into a few empty brothers before he caught it again, and went on with a slight slur to his words. "It made sense to me at the time. God, not now, though."

"No woman wants to be fed insects." She said, unable to believe she had to explain that to someone. "I don't care what they're coated in or what she does for a living. No bugs."

"No bugs," He parroted blurrily. "Got it. What should I have done instead?"

She brushed her hair back from her face and looked him in the eye.

"Pomegranate seeds."

"Pomegranate?"

She scoffed like it was obvious. In her fuzzy state, the background static of human conversation behind them all seemed to back her up.

"Coated in chocolate. Worked for my dad. They're still my mother's favorite."

Reid smiled and tapped his temple.

"I'll make a note of it in case I ever need it again."

The way he phrased those words struck a chord inside Esin. Her jovial feelings slowly dispersed and she stared at him with quiet sadness. Her face must have told him what she was thinking because his smile crumbled as well.

"Sorry." He said taking a drink. "I can be a bit of a downer sometimes."

"Do you think you'll ever date again?"

His shoulders moved to make a shrugging motion, but he froze halfway. The gesture mutated into a negative head shake.

"I don't think so."

"You still think about Renata."

"Every day."

"She sounds amazing, though," Esin pressed. "All those stories you tell are happy ones."

"They are," He conceded. Something in his voice made the whole concept of happy memories sound bittersweet. "I just know how the story ends, though. That's where my mind goes every time I think about it too much."

"Where's that?"

There was a loaded beat of silence. This was the conversation would normally end but Esin, always forward, couldn't hold herself back.

"How did you lose her?"

Reid looked up in surprise at the direct question, his mouth open to reply. Around them, other voices pitched gales of laughter in the empty space. He scowled and glanced around at all the happy faces, glaring at other people's joy. Esin shrugged them off and leaned in on her chair until the two were inches apart, her ears close for the conversation. She wanted a moment of privacy, as much as the room could provide.

"It was the car accident, wasn't it?" She pushed on.

His face was close enough that she could see the crow's feet forming by his eyes, the beard stubble grown in since the morning, smell his aftershave. His reply was a whisper.

"Yes."

She felt his breath on her ear when the single syllable passed his lips.

"When you hurt your back."

"Yes." Again, the breath.

"Where were you?"

"Coming home," He said slowly.

"From where?"

She faintly heard his teeth grinding.

"I hit my head in the accident." He rasped. "I only have pieces."

"That's alright." She said quickly, wanting to be consoling but internally shocked that there was something the man couldn't remember. "That's fine. How was Renata feeling?"

"Happy. It was a good night."

"What's the last thing you remember?"

The grey eyes clamped shut.

"The impact."

"What was it like?"

"Fast... but slow."

"What do you mean?"

"It was a fast moment when it happened. Maybe half a second, its hard for me to tell. But I remember it slower. Every piece of it. I see it the same way every time."

In hushed tones, in the middle of the jubilant bar, he slowly described the worst moment of his life, whispered to her ear. The noise, the glass mingling with his wife's hair and the terrified look on her face as it happened. When he finished, they sat together in silence. It took a long while for Esin to find words again.

"I'm sorry." She whispered.

He raised his Untraceable in response and drained every drop.

"Yeah," He grunted. "Everyone is when they hear about it. I don't want the pity."

"I don't pity you." She did just a little. She couldn't help but feel for him.

"Sure you do." He could see through her words. "I hate that moment, but it's cemented into my head and its connected to her. If my head gets too restless, I go back there. I can't help it."

Sitting beside him in that bar, with the heat of a hundred bodies nearby making her sweat, Esin felt a chill run up her back.

"It's the past." She said, quoting the words her parents had told her a thousand times when she was little. "You don't need to be afraid of the past."

Reid looked over at her with reddening eyes.

"Esin, I can't remember what happened."

"That's common..."

"Not for *me*." He replied hoarsely. "I don't know how to cope with this."

"You accept it," Esin said. "It doesn't change who you are, and maybe you'll remember eventually."

He gave a weak laugh and shook his head.

"You still don't get it. What if it was my mistake?"

"It wasn't." Esin put steel into her voice.

"I know it wasn't. You didn't. You have to move on."

"I can't..."

He closed his eyes.

"I love Renata, but I know this is the way the story ends. I can still see it." His voice was even. For a moment, she thought she could see the accident play out across his face. "How do you move on when you relive the worst day of your life every day?"

She wanted to give him an answer, give him some relief, but the brutal honest truth was that no one could tell him how to cope. No one had the same experience. She just sat there helpless. Then she took his hand in hers. He didn't stop her. He squeezed it tight. As cold as her grip was, she wanted to give him the warmth of human contact. She wanted to say that it was all going to be fine, but she couldn't. Instead, they just sat there together with the world raging around them.

THIRTEEN

The chairs were empty. The lights were off. The only illumination came from a few windows, the blinds half closed against the twilight, or from a few idle computer screens, the Horizon logo bouncing about randomly on the screensavers. Aaron Wyatt strode into the lab with purpose, his feet light with the well-earned confidence he'd regained. Each step finished in a clipped tap as his best shoes skipped across the polished tiles. They matched his best designer suit, fitted flawlessly over his frame. It was the sixth night he was slipping in after hours and it felt gloriously good to do it. Espionage was so seductive, even industrial espionage. He felt like James Bond, and tonight he wore the slick black suit to match. It was perfect.

The AI was where he had left it that morning when he'd collected the Acumen. In the corner, atop its platform, Aceso's green eyes glowed, shedding their own timid illumination. As usual, it knew he was there and who he was before he said a word.

"Hello Mr. Wyat,." The timorous voice purred. "You look very good this evening. Is it a special occasion?"

Wyatt smiled. Even the machine could see he looked great. It was undeniable.

"Thank you Aceso." He answered, walking into the green light.

Aceso's powerful form materialized out of the darkness as he came closer, the light from it's face played across the smooth contours of its metal skin, giving it an unearthly glow.

"Tonight's the send-off reception for the Labyrinth teams." Wyatt said, brushing his hair back. "I have to look good for the other VPs. That's part of the competition. A Vice President always has to look good in public because somebody's always judging you. Remember that."

"Yes, sir." The AI agreed. "Are you here to continue the trials?"

"You know I am."

"Is it possible to not do them tonight? They... worry me."

"They *worry* you?"

Wyatt's brow furrowed in confusion. What did the damn machine have to worry about? It had to be some of Aster's ideas bouncing around its mechanical head. He made a mental note to get him to stop talking to it, then instantly crossed it out of his mind. It wasn't his responsibility anymore. Why should he care what shaped it?

"No," He answered sternly, the way you spoke to an unruly child. Or maybe a puppy? Yes, a dog was closer to what this thing was. "We need to finish what we've started. Just tonight and tomorrow. That's all that's left."

"You're sure, sir?"

He was, because in two days his two weeks were up and he wouldn't be shackled to Horizon anymore. He would take his killer Acumen to Veles and settle into a place he was worthy of.

"Just these two days." He reassured the AI. "I almost have everything I need. You've been doing very well."

It was true. The results had been even better than he had expected. From his desk, on a secure laptop he'd watched the Acumen develop, plugging it in every morning when he took it back from the AI. He watched the intricacy increase as the skill improved. Now it blended in seamlessly along with the other skills the AI had cultured in its short existence: medicine, speech, evasion, even movement. Killing was almost as easy as walking now, as it should've been all along. Fozzy had no idea of the special thing he had given up in turning his back on a combat AI.

From its place in Wyatt's jacket pocket, the black flashdrive emerged. He leaned over to plug the Acumen into the USB slot half concealed on Aceso's side. The armoured wing lifted and almost seemed to hesitate in mid air, but inevitably the machine conceded. Wyatt plugged the stubby flash into it's place. The wing immediately dropped down to hide it.

"Accessing," Aceso said quietly.

Wyatt watched and waited.

"Acumen loaded. Running in isolation through flash objectives."

"What are they?" Wyatt asked mechanically, as he had a half dozen times the previous nights.

"To liquidate targets, overcome opposition and maintain integrity until priorities are complete."

He frowned. He had expected something different.

"Roughly translated," he corrected the creation. "that means: 'kill', 'kill anyone who tries to stop you' and 'don't let yourself be stopped until you're done killing'." Wyatt had no patience for muddling up a simple idea with flowery words. If the concept was blunt, then it should sound that way. This wasn't the first time the machine had equivocated. Besides, Fozzy had given him the axe for even suggesting that one simple word; he wanted to hear it as much as possible. Aceso, it seemed, did everything possible not to say it.

"We shouldn't dodge the subject." He went on,

glaring. "You keep using different language."

"I'm sorry. The concept is against everything else I've learned."

"This isn't for you," Wyatt countered. "You're developing a product for something else. What you do will affect it, so it needs to be done right."

He slipped his hands into his pockets.

"This is research. You speak how I tell you, and you do it how I tell you."

"Yes, sir." The machine paused. "What if it's possible to capture a target?"

"Excuse me?"

"I can incapacitate as easily as... other options." Aceso told him. "shouldn't some targets be captured for information?"

Wyatt smirked. It was a decent point, but it was made almost like a request. He could hear the pleading in its voice. Wyatt knew a sales pitch when he heard one. The machine was still squeamish.

"Only a high-value target." He answered, deciding to take a middle road. The AI would appreciate this. "If you're going to keep someone alive, make sure they're worth your time."

"Yes sir," The machine, said parrot-like. "Only when it's worth my time. Thank you."

It nodded its head, kowtowing to him. Wyatt took the gratitude and checked his watch. His team would be assembled by now.

"I have to get going." He said, turning to leave. "Run the new simulations attached to the Acumen. I'll be back to collect it in the morning."

"Yes, Mr. Wyatt. Enjoy your evening."

In a strange way, Aceso's face seemed to glaze over, the sympathetic eyes fading. Wyatt had seen that look before when he`d ordered the AI to access the scenarios attached to the Acumen. He'd been quietly thinking about having that flashdrive bronzed to commemorate his little spy operation. Or maybe have it framed on the wall in his new office. In his mind`s eye, he pictured Fozzy coming to visit one day and how he would quietly rub the whole plan in the old man's face without him even knowing it. The instrument he used to win perched on the wall the whole time. So many choices.

He walked back to the hallway, his finely-polished shoes tapping once more. At the doorway, he paused, his nearly iridescent shoe halfway over the threshold, and turned back to where Aceso sat.

"Aceso." He called. He didn't have to raise his voice as he knew the AI could hear him.

"Yes, Mr. Wyatt?"

"Say you will kill all targets." He ordered in the silence.

"I will kill all the targets."

"That's better."

With that last loaded handful of syllables, Wyatt slipped from the room and tapped his way toward the reception. He still liked that word. It rolled off the tongue so well.

Maybe one of the reasons Reid liked being at Horizon so much, was how they looked for any excuse to throw a party. He'd only been here two weeks, but he already found himself at his second Horizon bash, though this one felt widely different from the last. He stood in a big, elaborate, two-story space filled with greenery. Someone had told him this was

Fozzy's office, but it seemed too over the top, even for Fozzy. He had trouble envisioning any work getting done in here. Still, Horizon was odd, so maybe he was wrong.

From the walls, posters of musicians and racks of records stuck out. Some of the same artists were being piped through the speakers, giving a light jazzy ambience more suitable to business parties. At the end of the room by the windows, behind which the sun was setting, was a grand wooden desk with shiny coins all over it. He could barely see it through the throng of people filling the room but he likened it more to sculpture than furniture.

The people were different this time too. This was a formal event for a special few and the souls in the room were dressed to impress. Cocktail dresses and suits had replaced the customary Horizon uniform of jeans and pop culture T-shirts. The Labyrinth runners were the best Horizon had and those sixty chosen looked it tonight.

Reid reached up to fiddle with his shirt collar, trying to stop it from eating his neck. It had been a while since he'd worn a tie, and the closed collar was more unpleasant than he`d recalled. He sighed. Bodies changed, memories didn't. He took solace in the fact that no matter how uncomfortable he felt, Aster surely felt worse. Next to him, the engineer's wafer-thin frame was fitted into a blue suit Esin had gifted him before the event, though how she had gotten his measurements Reid couldn't fathom. He'd agreed to wear it but that was where his concessions stopped. He still wore a plaid shirt though a tie divided it and his ghost of a beard stubbornly remained in place. He looked a little like a shipwreck survivor dressed up to attend a wedding. With the fitted clothes the man's extreme slenderness was on display, as was his discomfort.

"I hate this." Aster grunted to him, fidgeting like a man who bathed in itching powder. "Why the hell do they make suits so uncomfortable?"

He slipped his hand to his side.

"And what the hell is with this tiny pocket? I can't fit anything in there, and I couldn't even if I wanted to; it's sealed shut. What kind of idiot sews a pocket shut? That defeats the whole *point* of a pocket."

"It's a ticket pocket," Reid answered surveying the crowd. "It goes back to when gentlemen used to take the train in England."

"I don't take trains. And it's still sealed shut anyway."

"So? It's for fashion now." Reid smiled. In their two weeks together, he had grown to appreciate the normally itinerate looking roboticists' eccentricity. "Just don't fiddle with it. You look sharp. Relax."

"I look ridiculous." He corrected, still grumbling. "Say what you want about my cargo pants, at least they have pockets you can use."

A wisp of familiar black hair caught Reid's eye, and he tapped his friend on the arm to look. The crowd parted and Esin walked over with Robin on her arm. She wore a cream satin dress, styled to her frame, with a slit up the side, just shy of work inappropriate. Her hair was up, and swathed with pearls, with surely a million hair pins holding the complicated structure in place. Marvelling at it, Reid could easily believe she had been trained as an engineer. The pearls caught the light as she came closer, accenting her face. Soon the pearl in her smile matched her hair perfectly as she embraced Reid in a hug.

"We made it." She susurrated in his ear. "Tomorrow we drive out."

She leaned back from their embrace and Reid beamed.

"It took a little effort," He said in acknowledgement.

"But I think the team's ready. I'm actually pretty excited for this. You look amazing."

He knew she had to have heard that a dozen times tonight, but she still smiled as if it were the first time.

"Thanks, Reid."

She turned to the twitchy figure on his left.

"And you!" She gushed over Aster, wrapping his lamppost of a figure in a hug. "You look great in that suit! Why don't you dress up more often?"

Reid was amazed how the man's discomfort seemed to dissipate in Esin's arms. She seemed to be absorbing his twitchiness like a sponge.

"Well," He said, fumbling when she let him go. "It's growing on me a little. I might hold onto the suit."

Reid smirked at this. Robin caught the expression and grinned as well.

In contrast to both of them and their discomfort, Robin looked like he belonged on the cover of GQ. His suit was pressed and tailored to accommodate his muscular chest and his usual fashionable stubble had been shaved clean. His hair was styled back and, Reid could picture him walking into a casino in Monte Carlo.

"Well, the gang's just about all here." He said, looking around. Each turn of his head seemed to boast how he didn't have a bad angle. "Has anyone seen Sasha yet?"

"Second floor." Reid gestured with his head. "Far left."

Above them at the railing, Sasha was chatting with the team from web design. Reid had been uncertain if she'd owned anything other than sportswear, but the off the shoulder black dress she was wearing now made him feel foolish. He had never seen her looking so feminine. The black clung to a form tempered by hours of jogging and undeniably beautiful. She had forsaken her usual glasses and her hair was down. A solitary diamond in a necklace glimmered as she talked.

"Wow." Aster said, seeing her for the first time.

"Wow..." Robin repeated before he gathered himself together quickly.

"I should bring her down to the team."

Esin, quietly smiling, waved it off.

"Go on up so she knows where we are, but let her finish talking." She gave him a light push. "We've got twenty minutes before Fozzy's going to start. We've got time."

"Are you sure?"

"Of course!" She said. "Go on."

Robin slipped away, heading for the tiny wrought-iron spiral staircase to the second floor. The steps were so tight Reid was genuinely curious if his bulk could fit through the cramped passage to get up there.

Beside him, Aster chuckled.

"Well," He murmured salaciously as he watched Robin go. "Good luck to him, like he needs any help. I'm going to grab a drink. The company is picking up the tab tonight."

He too slipped away, navigating the tight quarters in the room far easier.

Esin watched as he traversed the room, the perfectly pressed back of his suit jacket a perfect contradiction to the living embodiment of chaos theory that was his hair.

"I think he would be really sharp in a suit," She diagnosed. "If he wasn't so crazy tense in it. That fidgety twitch is not a good look."

"He just feels uptight." Reid said, grinning. "He's been asking me questions since he got dressed. I think he feels like he's meeting the queen. You know, he hasn't said one curse word since he put it on? I've been walking with him for ninety minutes and nothing even close to blue language. You *literally* scared the fuck out of him."

She swivelled toward him and gave a short squawk in response.

"I've never heard you swear before!"

"It's a special night." He shrugged. "I save some things for special nights."

He paused, growing slightly more serious.

"You really do look beautiful tonight."

Esin cast a look at him. This dress also sat high in the back almost to her hairline. The corners of her mouth slowly turning up at the compliment. Since he had told her everything about his past, he felt almost completely at ease around his enigmatic boss. Still, he thought, he didn't want to get too comfortable and say too much. Distance was a good thing. But judging by Esin's smile, she didn't think it was too much.

"Was that you flirting too?"

"I told you," Reid replied quietly. "Some things you save for special nights."

He became uncomfortable and nodded toward the balcony where Robin had just walked up to Sasha. By some miracle, he had squeezed through the stairwell unscathed. Her face lit up at the sight of him and she gave him a kiss on the cheek. The two started talking animatedly, the other friends forgotten.

"They might end up a couple yet."

Esin turned to look the same way, allowing Reid to pivot from the subject.

"I hope so." She sighed. "They both could use someone

great."

That was the last either of them spoke for a while as they watched from across the room. Reid still thought that if it came to it, Robin would choose Esin every time, but maybe he was wrong. Sasha was clearly into him and Robin, if only for tonight, was drawn to her. Either way, it was good to see someone take a risk for happiness.

"They look so cute," Came a voice from over his shoulder. "Are they together?"

Reid turned to find a short brown haired woman behind them. She was short to the point of being a tripping hazard, with round cheeks and wide inquisitive eyes. Despite those features, the trait that instantly drew his gaze was the truly astonishing amount of cleavage she had on show. Her red dress was cut low, her bosom either back-destroying-ly vast or propped up with some solid structural engineering. They protruded so much he was surprised she wasn`t toppling forward like a busty lamp tumbling off its stand. He dipped his eyes, then with some effort, yanked them back up to her eye line praying she hadn't noticed.

"Hi Lara," Esin greeted her. In a testament to her people skills, her eyes never drifted from the busty stranger's face. "You look great tonight."

Lara might have blushed ever so slightly at the attention. Esin stepped forward to give her an embrace and kiss on the cheek, which she returned quickly.

"It's good to see you. I heard Wyatt picked you for the team this year."

"Well, Matt picked me," The tiny woman corrected. "Aaron let him put the team together, but he chose me."

At the mention of their names, Lara subconsciously glanced over her shoulder. The rest of the team from the AI division proved easy to spot as it seemed to revolve around

Wyatt, like everything else in his orbit. He had come in late, fashionably late, no doubt, and was sipping what Reid had counted as his third scotch of the night. A loose ring of people surrounded him, chatting and enjoying themselves. He could not help but notice that none of them wore any red, perhaps knowing Wyatt`s disdain for anyone associated with that color. Lara's dress broke that rule. Either she didn't know her boss well at all, or she was taking a chance with the color to get noticed.

She seemed to brush past the cordialities and pointed an equally short arm toward the balcony where Robin and Sasha still talked. "Are they together?"

"Not exactly." Reid said. He gave her look, curious about the interest. "Is that bad?"

"Oh, no... it's great! I just thought..."

Esin gave one of her knowing smiles. What she knew though he had no bloody idea.

"Go on," She urged.

"I just always thought you and Robin were a couple," Lara said. She seemed a little embarrassed by this, casting her eyes downward. Reid was sure all that would get her was another scandalous view.

"No." Esin smiled. Something told him this wasn't the first time she'd had to clear this up. "I hate to disappoint everybody, but we're just friends. I can't date someone subordinate to me anyway."

Lara nodded, apparently sated by this, but it didn't seem Esin was finished.

"There's someone else at work I'm into." She added.

Reid's head bounced up a degree in surprise. Lara's jumped so quickly he could almost hear her neck crack in protest.

“Really?”

“Yeah,” She confirmed with a languid kind of tone. Her body language began to change too, relaxing, and brushing those few loose strands of her hair away from her face.

“I don’t usually talk about it, but there is someone I’m thinking of asking out.”

Lara’s brow drew up in a storm of suspicion. Reid’s jumped a little too as she spoke.

“You just said you can’t date subordinates,” Lara pointed out. Looking strangely annoyed by this.

“Oh,” Esin laughed. “That’s okay. We’re at the same level actually.”

The short woman reddened, temporarily coordinating her face with her dress. Reid, feeling like a bystander in this conversation, stood with a flummoxed expression, completely baffled by the whole exchange.

“Well, nobody can say no to you.” Lara replied with a slight hiss. “You should ask him out.”

“I think I will.”

The two said goodbye, and once the short busty Horizonite was far enough away, he cast a confused look at Esin.

“What just happened?”

She gave what sounded like a chuckle.

“Lara’s an electrical engineer with AI,” Esin explained, as though that made everything clear. “She’s sweet, but she’s pretty shy.”

Reid looked up after her.

“Well, the dress hides it well.”

He felt the poke of one of Esin’s nails in his ribs.

"Yeah, I saw you noticing." She laughed. "That dress is for Wyatt. She's been after him for months."

"Wyatt?" He glanced over to where the man remained ever stoic. A split second of thought later he whipped his head back to Esin, looking at her with horror.

"*Wyatt?*" He repeated, this time with twice the weight. "You want to date *that* guy?"

She feigned slapping him.

"I told you, I don't date." She said. "But I want Lara to think I'm into him."

"Excuse me?"

"I just thought she could use a little motivation. A rival might finally make her tell him how she feels."

"Well..." Reid's normally quick reasoning wavered. "Wouldn't that make her more cautious?"

Esin threw him a smile with a 'silly rabbit' kind of humour in it.

"You don't know anything about women do you?"

Reid's mind quickly rewound its way through about twenty-five years' worth of memories, trying to make sense of what Esin was saying. Dances in school, girlfriends, dates with Renata, married life. When he finished he looked up to see Lara sidle up next to Wyatt.

Her shorter figure leaned into the man and stretched out an arm around his waist. The executive seemed to bristle at the unexpected touch, although seeing who it was, and maybe her prominent features, mellowed him quickly. His face morphed into a confused smile as he looked down at the tiny woman's face. As Lara began to make her play, Reid turned back to Esin to answer her question.

"Nope, I guess not."

Fozzy had been scheduled to appear at eight o'clock. With his usual promptness and charisma, he blitzed into the office at eight forty-five, shaking hands and laughing, seemingly ignoring his speech entirely. The subject seemed forgotten, the teams mingling socially, until at nine-twenty he rapped his knuckles on the strange melted moneyed monolith of his desk, vying for the belated attention of those gathered.

He raised a glass of something fizzy and bellowed to the room.

"Everybody having a good time?"

The best of Horizon roared back in the affirmative. Programmers and engineers in suits and cocktail dresses raised glasses of every description in salute, the flower of Horizon now so clearly in bloom.

"Sorry, I should have done this earlier." The bear of a CEO admitted. "Couldn't resist talking with everyone a little first. This is my last one of these, you know."

At that, the whole room descended into a symphony of sympathetic whines. Fozzy halted them with a swipe of his arm. The motion sloshed half the bubbly liquid from the glass onto the floor beside him.

"Enough!" He croaked. "We're not doing that again! Tonight's not about me; it's about you!"

The whole room roared back in approval. With surprise, Reid found that one of the voices was his own. Maybe he was going local after all.

"You're the finest from each of your divisions and it's a damn pleasure to see you ready to compete! This is the ninth time we've done this and I have never been anything but astonished by what our people can do. If you can beat the Labyrinth, you can beat anything. Split the sky...

"Shake the earth!" Came the reply, one voice, a hundred strong.

Fozzy beamed with pride.

"Shake the earth. But first..." He reached behind his desk to produce a purple satin top hat, then held it aloft upside down above his grey tousled head. Amid the approving applause, Reid could easily picture Fozzy as an aging Willy Wonka, bringing his old wardrobe out of retirement.

"We have twelve paths to choose from. Twelve places to start. The higher the number, the tougher the road." He said, tucking the hat under his arm. "Team leads will draw randomly. This will decide how fast you get off the start line, people, so don't think it doesn't matter. Every second counts."

His eyes scanned across the room for a particular face. For a second, Reid thought his smile might have faltered, but it was hard to tell.

"First to draw is AI. You've been impressing us this year, so you deserve the first go of it. Wyatt, get your team lead up here."

From his place, with Lara still in close proximity, the predatory-looking Vice President showed little joy at being first, but gave a nudge to a tall, capable looking man beside him. The man, presumably Keeslar, hopped forward to rummage around the hat. After a few seconds of tension, he pulled out a slip of paper.

"Five!" He shouted happily, lifting it up.

The other four members of the AI team shouted approval, clearly sharing his joy. Even Wyatt cracked a smile. Five out of twelve wasn't bad. Keeslar walked back over to congratulations, as Fozzy looked around once more.

"Music, you're next. Let's go."

One by one, the team captains quietly came forward to choose their fates. Men and women each walked up beaming, sometimes walking away with gloom if the number was too high. Finally, the moment Reid had been waiting for came.

"Media and Marketing!" The teddy bear roared. "Habibti, send up your champion!"

Embarrassingly, Reid felt his pulse quicken. He felt Esin's hand press into his back, along with Robin's and Sasha's. Aster slapped him on the shoulder too. Ten teams had come before theirs, a three and an eight were all that remained. He strode forward to reach for the hat, only to have Fozzy pull it just out of his reach.

"Relax Reid," The bearded man quipped playfully to him. "Whatever happens, remember: it's not life and death."

The room rippled slightly with laughter. Reid's worried expression cracked slightly into a smile and he plucked a paper from the hat mentally pleading for a three to be there. It was not to be.

"Eight," He announced, trying not to sound dejected.

He walked back to a smattering of light applause. The team not looking too disappointed. Out of twelve, their position was not great but neither was it terrible.

The last team was the Automotive team, with the lead practically doing somersaults of joy as she charged up to accept her place. When everyone was done, Fozzy continued.

"Tomorrow we leave bright and early. Don't forget, whatever place you start, anyone can be the first to the end. Just trust your team. Be aggressive and be creative. I'll be waiting for you at the finish." He motioned to the side, where two men detached themselves from the wall. "These two gentlemen will be your marshals. They`ll be watching with me and tracking your progress. If something goes wrong with the equipment they'll be there in half a second."

There was polite applause again as the two waved to the crowd.

"They'll also be looking for any cheating." He continued with a mischievous eye. "So, if you do, at least be clever about it."

The room laughed in approval. Faces were already bright, a few people seemingly eager to get back to the celebration. From across the room Reid saw Wyatt sneak a glance at an expensive looking watch. His glass was empty, as was his patience.

"And last but certainly not least," Fozzy crooned, ever the impresario. "Your medic!"

He gestured in the direction of the doorway, the crowd turning as one. Above the entrance, an image suddenly appeared, cast from a projector hidden somewhere in the strange office. Obviously a promotional still taken from another Horizon event weeks ago, In it a creature, an insect of steel, ran forward toward the camera. Beside it, an explosion blossomed orange with dust and rock kicked up. The creature, or beast if you chose to call it that, was continuing forward completely unphased, its sympathetic eyes looking forward. The image was in perfect focus for those who knew it, but on the off chance you had been living under a rock the past couple of weeks, the lettering down the side of the image made it impossible to misinterpret.

ACESO

The image raised a triumphant roar from Horizon's men and women.

"If anyone gets injured, we have a hell of a doctor nearby for emergencies." Fozzy laughed. He stretched out a hand, seemingly in Reid's direction. "Thanks to Esin and the team at Media and Marketing. The big team. I love this image, and I want to see it everywhere. Make it happen Habibti!"

The room reverberated with new cheers as Esin raised a hand and waved. Reid found himself clapping twice as hard for her.

"And a big thank you to the team from AI for making Aceso available!"

Reid's eyes followed the line from Fozzy's hand to where the AI team stood, but this time there was a big difference. The five Labyrinth players still beamed but Wyatt`s was pure death. His face was a complete reversal of the sanguine indifference he'd shown seconds before. His skin had grown ashen, his eyes wide with worry. Lara, who was clapping at his side, nudged him with slight concern. The touch seemed to jar loose his smile which fell back into place as he too waved at the ovation.

"Now," Fozzy boomed once again. "Good luck to all of you, and enjoy the party! Just don't enjoy it too much-a hangover won't help your chances. Tomorrow we leave bright and early!"

There was rapturous applause as the CEO returned to wandering and chatting with his employees. A few dozen moved forward, trying to have a word with their boss, but through it all one was fighting to move in the opposite direction.

Aaron Wyatt struggled against the pack. He was worried, his movements pitched. Reid watched in confusion as he pushed and shoved his way toward the exit. It took him a good two minutes of cursing to get through the crowd where upon he darted out the open door at a dead run.

Reid heard a grunt beside him and turned to see Aster, who'd also witnessed his former boss' bizarre escape attempt.

"What was that all about?" He murmured.

His shoes made a rapid tapping screech as he sprinted down the hallway. The sound matched with his pulse, beating ferociously in his chest. The hallway streaked past as Wyatt ran in the direction of the lab. He felt his jacket billow out, his tie loosen, his shirt become untucked but he didn't care for a second. He could see his whole life going up in smoke before his eyes. He sprinted around the last corner, nearly sliding into the wall in the process. His shoes didn't have enough grip, damn it! He kicked open the door he had passed through only a couple hours before to find the same empty lab, the screensavers still idling.

"Aceso?" He called out, his voice sounding more like a wheeze he was so out of breath.

No meek green lights blinked on to illuminate the room. Only darkness. Wyatt fumbled in the dark, knocking things over until he found the light switch. The room suddenly blossomed with light, the brightness scarring his eyes like a nova. When he finished blinking, his painful eyes showed him exactly what he'd feared. In the corner, where Aceso always sat curled up on its station, there was nothing. No AI, no platform. Only scratched tiles.

He fumbled in his pocket for his phone, feeling panic creep into his body. If his personality colors were visible to the naked eye he knew he would be flashing red like an ambulance with the siren blaring. Finally finding the contact, he pressed it with shaking fingers.

"Hi boss," Came a familiar voice when he finally picked up. Behind it, Wyatt could hear the people talking and that inane music again. "What happened? You tore out of the party in a hurry."

"Keeslar, what the hell happened?!" Wyatt nearly

screamed. "Where's Aceso?"

There was a pause on the line.

"The Labyrinth crew packed him up just after the party started."

"Well, who said they could take the AI for the Labyrinth?!"

"Uh..." The man seemed to freeze up like an old computer. "I did actually. Fozzy asked if we could loan it out and I approved it. We`ve just been running simulations in the office for the last few weeks. I thought some real-world experience would be a good thing."

There was a pause and then he asked a stupid question.

"Was that wrong?"

Wyatt winced. He could hear the cover of his phone crack as he gripped it. Was it wrong? If the man had been there, Wyatt would have fired him on the spot, or even beaten him half to death.

"It's a disaster! Why didn't Fozzy ask me?"

"Wyatt," The man said slowly. His voice became tense. If he wasn't fearing for his job now, he should have been.

"He tried. He said something about you ducking his calls."

The fist attached to the freight train he had felt before, slammed into his stomach again. Behind it, came another train, and another. Wyatt felt ill and began to pace, turning violently to bleed off energy. He couldn't let the AI do the Labyrinth with the USB plugged in. Aceso wouldn't discuss it, he'd been ordered not to, but someone would notice and eventually figure out what it was. This was sixty of the best people Horizon had, five of them Artificial Intelligence professionals. Six, if you counted that ass Aster. There was no way someone wouldn't notice. Even if, by some miracle, the killer Acumen escaped detection for the whole Labyrinth, he couldn't get it back. By the time the event was done, he wouldn't be allowed in the building anymore. His time with the company was almost up. His post as COO with Veles dissolved before his eyes. Worse still, someone *had* to find the combat Acumen eventually, and when they did, they would trace it back to him and what he'd intended to do. This wouldn't just be a business move it would become criminal.

Wyatt saw his whole life go up in flames and felt himself sweating through his finest suit. It took a while, but eventually he discerned the voice talking from the phone still at his ear.

"Wyatt? Wyatt? Aaron, are you alright?"

The vice-president took a deep breath and tried to will himself into the grey again. It didn't work, but he steadied his voice.

"Tell Reilly that he has food poisoning. Do it quietly."

"Wait, what?"

"Just do it." He ordered. "Just Reilly. He's not going to the Labyrinth. Tell him to stay home."

"Alright I can..." His team lead said annoyingly slowly. "But that's going to leave us a man short."

"No," Wyatt hated having to spell things out for people. "I'm going in his place. Tell him he's sick. I'll meet you out front of the building at six am."

He hung up immediately, not waiting for a response. More stupid questions wouldn't help anything. The only choice he had was to go himself. Maybe he could get to Aceso before the Labyrinth started or maybe he could fake an injury and reach him that way. All he had to do was pull that stupid fucking USB and everything would be fine. He could do this.

In the lab, he continued to pace, trying to calm himself down and think rationally. Businessmen were rationalizers. He had a solution; he would make it work. Fozzy was always talking about that stupid Labyrinth, maybe this was a chance for him to actually understand it. He was going to see that damn maze after all.

While the party for the Labyrinth players went on happily across the Horizon compound, Wyatt continued to pace, worry and justify himself. His steps clicking across the tiles and his best suit growing wetter with sweat.

FOURTEEN

The road to the maze was radiant. The Coquihalla highway through the mountains had always been a showcase of Canadian beauty, but on this crisp autumn day with the spirits of the teams at their highest, the view along the road was resplendent. The mountains jutting up on either side of the road, the peaks just starting to be capped with snow. Trees of every size, shape and description bristled from every surface like a carpet of life until they met the sheer brown or grey rock of a cliff face. With every turn the bus took along the trail, blasted into the stone over time by willpower and a healthy dose of dynamite, a new vista met their eyes bringing forth gasps and chatter. Reid, who had lived out here for almost a decade, marveled slightly at the exhilaration of city people seeing the true Rockies for the first time. Their joy made him appreciate it more somehow. So far, they had seen deer, mountain goats and all manner of birds. The lead of the Music division team was saying they had to see a bear and was poised with her camera like a sniper at her window. Reid knew they were more likely getting ready for hibernation right now, rather than foraging by the road, but he let her hope all the same.

Beside him, in her midnight blue jacket with M&M stitched across the arm, Esin slept, quietly missing the incredible view. Her normally glamourous appearance was toned down to casual, or at least an attempt at casual. Her face had not a flake of makeup on it, but her flawless features still shone. Her hair was swept back in a ponytail shifting her head at an angle as she slept. He'd thought about waking her for the view, but she'd only had one thing on her mind the last few days anyway. Winning. Instead Reid let her sleep, mentally picturing the VP absorbing all of the excited energy from the people on the bus to make her stronger.

The game designer shifted in his seat, brushing the wrinkles from his own blue jacket. He felt fresh and ready. He was shaved, his hair clipped short. His back hadn't protested in days, but more importantly, his mind was clear. He had wanted the challenge from the start, but now that it was here in a strange way it felt bittersweet. His time at Horizon was coming to an end, at least for now. Once the Labyrinth was done, he would be back at his studio making his games. He should have dreaded the turmoil that idleness usually brought him, but instead ,he simply felt like he would miss the place and the people.

Soon the road began to narrow, becoming one lane in each direction then a single lane slightly wider than the bus. The trees closed in on either side and Reid felt his balance change as they began to ascend. As they tightened in, the great views were slowly choked off by the trees and the conversation stopped with it. The road grew closer still, with the tree branches seeming to knot above them in a canopy. Just as he was beginning to wonder whether the facility was just a shack in the woods, the trees parted once more and, not for the first time, Reid blinked in uncomprehending wonder.

Beside them was another cliff face, like so many others passed on the road, but this one had been hollowed out. The side of the mountain was concave, as though the spoon of a giant had carved out the guts of the massif. In its place, nestled into the hollow was a flat office building of the type that dotted skylines the world over. Six floors high, the only thing that made this different was the titanic shelf of rock mere feet above the roofline. Reid could picture himself standing on top of the roof, squatting to fit under the hundreds of thousands of tons of stone and earth looming above. Again, not for the first time, he shook his head. His face grew a wry smile at the sight of the complex, so in vogue for Horizon.

Gently, he reached over to place a hand on Esin's shoulder. Two green eyes flecked with copper blinked open.

"I think we're here." He said.

The Horizon teams made various 'ooh' and 'aww' sounds at the sight of the complex. People slid closer to the side of the bus to take in the spectacle pressing against the windows or leaning across their colleagues in a contest to see who was more fawning. Near the rear of the bus, Wyatt shared their amazement, but disdained their passion, sitting sullenly in place. He could see what an achievement the server complex was, but it didn't appear on their website and few media had ever been invited to photograph it. Again, what was the point of something so unique if it did nothing for your image? Like the Labyrinth itself, special things had to be shared or they were wasted.

Either way, he couldn't muster excitement for anything right now with his future in doubt.

At his elbow, where she had been for the better part of a day, Lara leaned toward the window ogling like the others. He hadn't noticed her attraction until the night before, though at the party it was more than plain. When her face exploded in joy as he'd walked up to join them this morning, it made the tense necessity of the trip slightly more bearable. Though not by much. Fitting in amongst the Labyrinth teams was painful in its own right. His suit was long gone and with it his business persona. Now he was garbed like some athletic pauper, in a jogger's fleece and pants. At least they were in his customary grey.

At his shoulder, a fresh-faced Keeslar appeared.

"Pretty impressive isn't it?"

Lara leaned back over, pressing herself against Wyatt's arm once again.

"It's amazing! This is the server complex?"

Keeslar smiled.

"Among other things," He said. "Wait until you see the inside."

Lara nearly squealed. Wyatt forced a smile.

The bus drove through the security gates, the two guards waving their caps in the air to the teams. They waved back happily at the recognition, the bus driving on through with barely a pause to park amongst a half dozen other trucks and Jeeps with the moon and sunburst logo. The doors opened and the teams began to spill out talking excitedly. Keeslar, strangely, remained at Wyatt's side. It was clear he wanted a word. Lara, already on her feet to leave, lingered as well, looking puzzled.

"Uh, Lara," He ventured after a moment. "Can you give us a second? I just wanted to talk to Wyatt before we go in."

Her eyes flicked to his, who nodded, and she continued off the bus with the others looking concerned. Why, he could not say. It's wasn`t as if Keeslar could fire him. With all the trouble the loan of Aceso had caused, the man should have been terrified of Wyatt. Lord knew, he *wanted* him to feel some fear over this mess. He waited until Lara`s tiny form had vanished from view before he looked at him.

"Is there something I can do for you?" The executive asked with as much sarcasm as possible.

"Look, Wyatt..." He started tenderly. "Reilly was pretty upset when I sent him home last night. I didn't understand why, and I guess it's none of my business."

"True."

"I Just..." He faltered again. The man was forty-six and he was acting like a child. "I just need to know you'll be a part of the team. We've put a lot of practice time into this..."

His voice trailed off slightly as he began talking about what the team had already done together. Wyatt turned his head away looking out the window, growing impatient. Being here was already tense enough. The fact that he might now have to feign enthusiasm was salt in the wound. His eyes traced along the other vehicles in the parking lot, the mud spattered across their tires, the open cargo compartments with supplies for the server complex. His eyes stopped when they spied something both alien and familiar. Alien to the mountains, familiar to him. Half of a black glass oval protruded from the open rear hatch of a trailer. Aceso.

His fingers tightened on the arm rest.

"It's important for you to understand..."

"I understand." Wyatt silenced him with a smile. He reached over and put a friendly hand on Keeslar's shoulder, his mouth still open to speak. "This is your team. You're in charge."

He smiled in clear relief. The AI engineer looked as though someone had just stopped standing on his head.

"You're alright with that?"

Wyatt was already on his feet.

"Absolutely." He said. "I wanted to do the Labyrinth this year so I'm along for the ride, but you're the leader. I'll stay out of your way."

"Oh, good." Keeslar replied, standing up. Even though he had a good four inches on Wyatt the executive still thought he looked smaller. "I needed to get that out of the way before we started. It's really a relief."

The two stepped off the bus, seeing the rest of the teams gathering near the stone steps to the complex in the distance.

"I'm not here to cause trouble." Wyatt reassured him, his business smile now back firmly in place. "You tell me what to do and I'll do it."

"Thanks, Wyatt."

"Go on with the others," He said, immediately giving him an order. "I've got to make a phone call, then I'll catch up."

As Keeslar walked toward the crowd waiting to enter, Wyatt slipped around the bus and ran.

It took him an agonizing moment to find the trailer again, there were so many vehicles in the park, but he caught sight of that wonderful half oval, the dark moon eclipsed by the door. He hurried over and slipped inside, closing the door part way to obscure him.

Aceso looked dead. The AI had been powered down for the drive out, and for all intents and purposes, it was completely lifeless. The arms were bent and stiffly fixed in place at its side, the four legs curled together as it sat on its platform. The sympathetic green eyes that Wyatt had grown used to were dimmed to invisibility within its face. Only the black oval remained. With a quick glance around the door, he reached over to lift the armoured wing across the machine's back to retrieve the USB. It did not even budge. The dead Aceso was fixed with its own rigor mortis, unwilling to be moved. The executive braced his feet and tried again, throwing his whole body into the effort. The trailer shifted slightly as the weight moved, the rattle reverberating through the empty space, but the wing stayed put blocking the USB. Another three attempts proved equally fruitless. He pressed his fingers into what gap there was, fumbling blind. A fingertip brushed the plastic, but it was clear nothing would move.

Wyatt cursed, feeling the panic start to set in again. He wasn't going to get the Acumen back unless the AI gave it to him.

He wrenched the control panel for the platform toward him and started the boot up. Both the AI and its control platform were battery powered and it blinked on immediately beginning its start-up sequence. The progress bar moved agonizingly slow across the screen as the computer functions eased back to life. Wyatt's ears caught the whir of electronics, then the hiss of engaging hydraulics. He tried the wing again but it still stubbornly remained in place. The starting checklist began, a new question displayed on the screen asking yes or no.

INITIALIZE INTELLIGENCE FUNCTION?

As he reached for the proper key, a voice sounded beside the truck. Wyatt whipped his head around at the noise, then quickly tapped 'yes'. Another question immediately jumped up in its place.

INITIALIZE MOTOR FUNCTIONS?

He chose yes again, bringing a third question to the screen. Outside, he could hear the crunch of shoes on gravel as the figure came closer.

"Come on, come on!" Wyatt hissed and began hitting the button rapidly. He felt a bead of sweat form on his brow. He only needed a few seconds. More questions popped up and then fell away instantly, the text flashing by too fast to read. The steps grew closer, the voice calling out to someone again, sounding familiar. Another few questions blinked past without Wyatt comprehending them. The steps were outside the door now, the voice asking if this truck was the one. Wyatt held the button down, needing the machine's green eyes to blaze, it's androgynous voice to obey his commands.

In that instant, a new question blinked up. With the button held down, it was instantly confirmed as a yes and replaced by another, but in the tenth of a second it was displayed, a human eye would have read it thusly: *BOOT FUNCTIONS THROUGH EXTERNAL MEMORY?*

The door made an agonized squeal as the figure pulled it open. Instinctively, Wyatt jumped backward, away from the start-up still in progress, and looked at the intruder in alarm.

Silhouetted in the autumn light was Aster. For the first time, at least since Wyatt had known him, he wore no plaid. He was clad in a dark blue jacket, the zipper up to his chin, ready for the cold. His hair was brushed back, and his white scruffy beard gathered around a mouth open in surprise.

"What the hell? What are *you* doing here?"

Wyatt glanced back at the panel, the start-up still not complete, and tried to look detached.

"I wanted to make sure the AI had the right medical records before the Labyrinth started." He said, stepping reluctantly away and hopping down. "My life's in Aceso's hands for this event."

Aster looked at him as though he were from Mars.

"They've been in there for three months." He grunted, still looking suspicious. "You suddenly grow some new allergies? You can trust Aceso."

Wyatt felt his hands nearly shaking. As he walked away he tried to turn his fear and disappointment into an angry outburst at the man who'd stopped him.

"I trust Aceso completely." He called, not bothering to look. "I just don't trust you at all."

Aster yelled something profane and likely anatomically impossible after him. He didn't turn, he just stomped off to where the others were gathering, hoping he would get another chance.

Aster watched the back of Wyatt's greasy head fade into the distance, wanting to part that slicked back hair with a rock. He didn't believe his story for a second, and he levered up his slender frame to see what the man had been up to. Aceso's start up sequence was well underway on the screen, with only the last few prestart questions remaining.

His face scrunched up with confused suspicion. Why did he want Aceso started early? He'd set the start-up timer to align with the start of the Labyrinth. Did he need something from her?

"Are we good to go?"

One of the marshals had appeared in the doorway.

"Yeah, sure." He finished the last three prompts, he'd memorized them all long ago, and confirmed Aceso's start time. It was a little over two hours away. "You'll need a heavy forklift, but she should be fine, even if you rattle her around a little. She's tough."

The man gave him a funny look when he said 'she'. Normal people sucked.

"Thanks," the man said. "Is… she going to work okay?"

"I uploaded the layout and everyone's medical records three days ago." He said, feeling a little defensive. "She could remove your freakin' kidney then stitch you up again and you'd barely notice. Trust me."

The man shrugged and wandered off to find a forklift. Aster gave one more glance to Aceso's idle form then began walking toward the entrance. Whatever Wyatt had been trying, he hadn't had time to finish it. He would confront him about it after the Labyrinth was through.

His head bent back as far as it would go, his mouth open in amusement, Reid craned his neck to look up at the mountain, surely looking like a giraffe with vertigo. Around him, people laughed and chattered excitedly. At his side, Esin was allowing herself a moment of excitement, enjoying the scene and what it represented. Reid's mind flipped back to the photograph he'd seen of her on her office wall. This was the same smile on the face of that little girl in the snow, finally getting a chance to play properly.

A tap on his shoulder revealed Robin and Sasha had arrived, the latter giving them all hugs. The four of them stood together in their blue jackets looking like a bland version of a barbershop quartet. Shortly thereafter they became a quintet as Aster jogged up.

The big group meandered outside for a while, whereupon on some unseen signal they opened wide letting them surge inside. The entry hall was typical business fare, except for the tiny, grey haired teddy bear man with the wild beard and the Hawaiian shirt under a sport jacket, smiling wide as anyone had ever seen him. He wasn't typical business at all.

With nothing more than a playful wink and a wave to follow him, Fozzy started down the hall, leading them deeper into the complex. The hallways twisted and turned past innumerable doorways, every one of them closed. The great mass of Labyrinth players quieted down to whispers as though this were some dirty little secret they were partaking in. Not another soul met their eyes as they went, the workers who maintained the complex either bottled up somewhere else or given the day off. Finally, Fozzy reached a great set of double doors marked 'Authorized Personnel Only' and brushed his way through as though the lettering did not exist.

Inside, the white office walls fell away, replaced by familiar brown and grey stone. The colors were aged by time and as soon as they were through, the groups began talking excitedly again. Reid reached out to run his fingers along the stone, feeling the cold, rough imperfections. The tile floor below them was replaced by metal grating, and they felt themselves tilted downhill, as they moved deeper into the cave of wonders.

But at the bottom, Reid couldn't help but feel a little disappointed.

The hall emptied out onto a huge metal platform, big enough for all sixty of them and more, but appeared to be a dead end. Fozzy walked to the end of it and faced the others slowly filing on behind him. Reid continued on, confused. If it turned out the Labyrinth was only meant to be a metaphor this whole time, he promised himself he would break every piece of Horizon junk he owned and become a luddite. When it was his turn and his feet touched the metal, hearing his own steps echo like a chasm, he understood.

"Everybody step back from the walls!" The old man called out. At the point they had entered, a gate shut and the whole room dropped.

With a heavy drop felt from his feet to his stomach, then somehow back to his testicles, Wyatt lurched in surprise as the great elevator began to descend. Lara fell into him with the jolt laughing, her jacket unzipped to show cleavage in seemingly her only flirty move. The platform was independent from the walls, and as they dropped, the ceiling fell back farther into the distance. The rock seemed to grow as the room extended upward, the elevator dropping with more speed. The whoosh of air ruffled clothes and messed up hair. Lara's loose strands went wild and she gave an excited shriek blending with others. Wyatt's gelled hair, like his spirit, remained unmoved.

Still nervous after being caught by Aster, he had nearly panicked when the room dropped. Combined with a fear of heights he'd had since he was a child, he felt off balance here, both literally and figuratively. He watched the seemingly endless rock file past as the platform descended. It took a while, but eventually he mustered the courage to look up to see how far they had come. The ceiling, with a single round LED light, was rapidly fading into the distance. Small lights were built into the rock along the shaft, seemingly at the height of a typical floor in a building, zipped past. He started counting them as they passed then forced himself to stop. Soon, the top of the tunnel was a distant memory, the depths his reality. He imagined himself falling upward somehow, gaining speed as the lights moved in the opposite direction to slam into the rocky ceiling far above.

"Quite a view, isn't it?"

The voice snapped him back to reality, and he dropped his neck in alarm to see the warm, friendly face of Fozzy, the wind from the elevator ruffling his beard.

For a moment, he didn't know what to say. These were the first words they had shared in two weeks. The old man found the words first, breaking into the sly smile he used so well.

"Still afraid of heights, huh?"

Beside him, Lara suddenly looked concerned.

"You're afraid of heights?" She asked, her voice loud enough to carry over the noise.

"Not really," He breathed, suddenly feeling more vulnerable than ever. "I used to be a little."

Fozzy laughed.

"He's been terrified of them since he was a kid." He said wrapping a paw around Wyatt's shoulder and shaking him. "That's why he keeps his desk so far from the windows."

Lara laughed and rubbed his arm. Wyatt, with Fozzy in front of him, felt no better.

The old man's face suddenly sobered.

"Someone told me you'd shown up with the teams this morning, and I didn't believe them." His mammoth hand gave his shoulder a squeeze. "When I saw you get off the bus, it was a hell of a shock. Been waiting a long time for you to do this, to get involved. I'm proud of you."

Staring at the old man, his heart lifted and sank simultaneously.

"Well..." Wyatt fumbled. "It might be my last chance you know."

Fozzy nodded, the steel business look appearing again in his eye and withering his subordinate.

"Not necessarily," He finally grunted with more than a trace of anger, his words barely heard over the roar. "We'll talk after."

Wyatt looked at Fozzy with disbelief. The old man had no idea just how much things had changed in the last two weeks. What Wyatt had done against his wishes and how he had betrayed him. The flashdrive still embedded like a blade in Aceso's mechanical innards, or what he had promised to deliver to his rivals. After everything, said and unsaid, he was offering an olive branch.

Fozzy reached into his jacket pocket and pulled a clear plastic bottle, handing it over.

"Gin." He said wryly. "Probably rot-gut but not a lot of booze to be found out here in the complex. I still owed you from the bet."

The VP held the bottle in both hands almost like a talisman, too shocked for words. Before he could offer any, either in apology or thanks, the old man moved on to the next group, his wide grin returning in full force.

From his side, perhaps sensing it was a tender moment for him, Lara wrapped an arm around his waist and gave him a squeeze. In her grasp, Wyatt popped the cap on the liquor and drained half of it as fast as he could.

As the platform dropped steadily, so did the temperature. The chill in the air that rushed past was slight, but the wind rippled it through clothes and flesh alike. As the Horizon teams still looked around excitedly, some began to rub their arms and legs against the cold. Esin, her hair ruffling in the breeze, unzipped her jacket enough to see the switches inside. Each jacket she had been specially made with heaters built in. They had three settings, and she flipped the first one on. A few seconds later, she felt a mild warmth spread through her skin. It wasn't just for the cold, she was feeling more excited than she had in a long time and didn't want her hands to shake when they started out. Neither from cold nor nervousness.

Now they were all together, her eyes drifted around the descending room evaluating the other teams. Her competition.

The group was as diverse as Horizon itself. An even mix of men and women, but most of them looking fit enough to handle the endurance trial this was. Some teams wore uniforms, some did not. One team was in red jumpsuits with matching toques. Another, from the Automotive division, wore plastic helmets with horns sticking out in a strange Viking cosplay. One team member wielded a replica sword and had been posing with it ever since he had left the bus. The levity was good. Everyone usually enjoyed the Labyrinth when they did it. She'd had a great time when she'd been here before. This time, however, she was all business. She had come to win.

Standing tall beside her, his form casting its own shadow, Reid looked around with the purest kind of glee on his face. He was enjoying the whole thing immensely, with little trace of the inner turmoil that plagued him, the toxic ever-present uncertainty that would overwhelm most. She didn't know how he managed to handle life with that kind of burden, but he did. He didn't have the ability to section things off as the past.

His grey eyes looked down at her and cracked an exhilarated grin. She grinned back. She had to admit, she'd grown fond of the man. It was rare that she met an equal, or even someone who could best her at something. Moreover, the lanky video game designer was good to talk to; his perspective on life was different from anyone she'd ever met.

The lift strained then began to slow. Sensing the time was close, Fozzy drifted back to the center of the room. The rock slipping past them suddenly became metal walls the embedded lights no longer rushing past, but crawling. The lift came to a stop in a circle of open doorways, a dozen doors randomized in a loop around them. Through these they could see hallways stretching into the unknown. Numbers were painted on the floor of each entrance. Esin`s eyes immediately searched for eight and found it on the opposite side of the room.

"You know your numbers," Fozzy said. "Good luck to

all of you. Get going!"

A few teams took off at a jog, some meandered down their chosen path idly. Esin didn't rush. She knew that no one could start the challenge until a buzzer sounded. Some of this was memory, some of it, preparation. She had been getting ready for months. The team fell into step beside her, Aster rubbing his hands with glee or perhaps to keep their circulation. Robin took his place beside her, with Sasha close behind.

A familiar hand suddenly landed on her shoulder. She turned to see Fozzy gently ushering her away to the side of their doorway. The rest of the team continued on, seeming not to notice. With the grandfatherly smile she'd known for so long, he leaned over to whisper in her ear.

"Are you ready for this?"

"Yes." She said firmly and almost completely meaning it.

"Yeah, I think you are." He chuckled in her ear. "Just try to enjoy the Labyrinth a little. You look so damn serious right now."

She swatted his shoulder with a half-hearted smile.

"Is that your idea of a pep talk?" She teased.

He hummed and hawed for a moment before he spoke again.

"How about this," he whispered, his voice growing serious. "I was always going to pick you to take over. You just need to prove me right, that's all. Enjoy the ride, Habibti."

At her mentor's words, Esin's eyes grew wide as saucers. His eyes conveyed the sincerity of what he had said, and she clamped onto her grizzled boss in a vice of a hug, her emotions running wild. When he released her, she stepped back, tears forming in her eyes. Fozzy shook his head and gestured behind her to where Reid stood waiting. The rest had gone ahead.

"Go on."

Without another word she spun on her heel and started down the hallway after her teammates. She was vaguely aware of Reid falling into step beside her, but mercifully, he let her walk in silence. Together, they walked into the crucible they had both sought for so long.

For the first hundred yards, the walls were featureless. Reid walked next to Esin, noticing the occasional tear run down the side of her face. Instinctively, he wanted to know what Fozzy had said to her, but he held his tongue. He had never seen Esin cry, so the news was either incredibly bad or soul-vindicatingly good. If it were bad, he could not help it. If it were that good, then he knew she would share it when she was ready. He walked without comment, but stayed a pace in front so she knew he was there.

Ahead, the flat grey metal walls opened up, a catwalk over open space as the walkway continued to slant down. Aster, Sasha and Robin all stood by the open railing looking in amazement at something below. Reid picked up the pace to give Esin another second of privacy.

"Take a look." Aster yelled as they approached. "You guys are gonna love this!"

Reid reached his side and was dumbstruck by the sight below them. Far below, maybe five stories, was a glowing sea. A radiant tempest of water. His eyes tracked the waves flowing from one end of the floor to the other in sequence, seemingly bouncing off the walls of the vast chamber below them. He saw the froth of surf and the deeper blue of calm water in sections. Added to that was the fact that it all seemed to produce its own light shining up at the team observing from the catwalk.

"How the hell did they do this?" Reid breathed, looking down in awe.

"They're panel screens," Robin explained. He raised a well-toned arm to the white surf below. "Check it out."

After a second of squinting, he could just make out the faint lines separating the waves into sections. Minuscule black barriers that divided the floor into rectangles like a tic-tac-toe board, hundreds of them. The whole floor was made out of flat panels, playing a complex program of ocean waves.

"It's beautiful." Sasha said. "It goes all the way from the far wall to the elevator shaft. Look."

Reid craned his neck to see the hollow of the elevator shaft. It looked like a core being removed from a great blue apple, sticking up in the empty space. As the waves lapped around it, Reid could mentally picture the water draining into the hole and spiralling down into the center of the earth.

"You think it's just here to look pretty?" Aster asked.

"That's the last layer."

Esin's perfect features joined the others on the catwalk and stared down at the simulated ocean below them. Her eyes were slightly red, but she was composed again.

"That's the last obstacle you need to cross, so I promise it's not just there to look pretty."

Robin looked slightly skeptical.

"If it's just projected on screens, how is it an obstacle?"

"We'll find out."

The walkway continued down, farther and farther into the heart of the mountain. The catwalk had eventually closed up again, the walls returning to the dull concrete of before, turning the stunning vista into a soulless, grey tube. After what felt like half an hour of walking, the tunnel ahead opened up, revealing stairs leading down to a small open room, a closet with a door, really. After the tall elevator shaft and the sea, it felt claustrophobic. A flat metal handleless door adorned the wall. It's only marking was an eight written in white paint beside it. A small grey electronic box emblazoned with (what else?) the Horizon logo sat in a rack beneath.

Sasha walked up, plucking the gadget from its holster and tapped a few buttons. No response. Then she ran her hands along the frame, looking for a switch. She even gave the eight a full-palmed slap before turning back.

"Nothing."

"This one's going to open on its own," Reid explained. He ran through the instructions word for word in his mind. "They won't let us go until everyone's in position."

As if on cue, Fozzy's voice reverberated from a speaker beside the door.

"Everyone, get settled in." His cheery voice was tinged with excitement. "We'll be starting in two minutes. Beside your first door, there's an ephone. Keep it handy. It'll let us keep track of you. If something breaks down, you can let us know."

Sasha lifted the newly christened ephone and tossed it over to Robin, who zipped it into his jacket pocket. Now that there was nothing to do but wait, the group seemed to fidget, their smiles drifting back and forth. Robin, ever the athlete, began to stretch like a marathon runner would. Sasha, seeing this, did the same, her slender runner's form contorting into what were clearly familiar movements. The rest remained still, the tension rising slowly in the background.

All too soon, Fozzy's voice returned to the speaker,

sounding as excited as everyone else clearly felt.

"All the teams are in place! Good luck to all of you. Remember, be fast and creative." There was a quick pause and a fumbling sound as the CEO spoke to someone off mic. "Ten seconds! Nine..."

"Eight..."

Wyatt heard the count and tried to keep his calm. It was returning to him slowly after Fozzy's talk, but he still felt red, deep inside. His rational business mind tried to keep order. If Fozzy were willing to take him back, then that could only be a good thing. It kept his options open. If for some reason the deal with Veles collapsed, then he could plead ignorance and keep his job. He knew this was true, but he hated the guilt he felt inside.

He shook his head in disgust. Guilt was a pointless emotion of people who were high-red. He knew what he was doing. The situation hadn't changed. He had to get to Aceso, get that flashdrive back and everything would be fine. Part of him wanted to destroy it now and forget the whole thing ever happened. Still, he had options.

"Seven..."

Around him, the rest of the AI team waited excitedly. Keeslar was all smiles, as were Lara and the others. He tried to keep his in place to play along. After a moment's thought, he plucked the half empty gin bottle from his pocket and offered it to Keeslar. Grinning like an idiot, the man happily accepted it, took a drink then passed it around to the others.

Wyatt maintained his own idiot grin too. Nothing had really changed. He still needed to get that Acumen back. The only person who'd seen him do anything suspicious was Aster and that wouldn't matter anyway.

"Six…"

Bouncing from foot to foot, Aster felt his excitement build with the countdown. He had wanted to do this for so long, he was acting like he was five years old. He had lobbied every year for a chance to go but Wyatt had never let him. Thank God for Esin. His mind flashed back to the moment she`d asked him, remembering the look on Wyatt`s face.

At the thought of his boss, his mind darted back to a short time ago. What the hell was he doing with Aceso anyway? Why had he shown up at all? Knowing Wyatt like he did, Aster wanted to say he'd been trying to cheat somehow. But he knew Wyatt didn't care about the Labyrinth, so why bother? He mentally shrugged. No matter, he'd stopped him anyway.

"Five…"

Next to him, Robin was doing more elaborate stretches, making Esin and Sasha laugh. Suddenly struck by inspiration, Aster stepped up and took a starting position in front of the door like at the start of the hundred-meter dash. The team laughed, and Robin instantly took position beside him. Aster slapped the big man on the back warmly.

"Four…"

Esin watched Robin take a starter's position next to Aster, followed quickly by Sasha, only a half second behind. Esin knew the race was just getting started, they hadn't passed the first door for God's sake, but she already felt like they'd won. Hearing Fozzy say that he wanted her to be CEO was one of the greatest moments of her life. After all she had worked through and fought for, to be validated like that was more moving than she could admit. She loved the old man, and she quietly pledged to prove him right.

She dropped down next to Sasha, and gave her a smile. Her friend nudged her with her shoulder playfully, and Esin focused her eyes on the door, the Labyrinth and the prize at the end of it.

"Three..."

Far above all the Labyrinth players, a timer ran out, though they did not know it. In the medical office, the activation clock triggered and Aceso's kind green eyes illuminated once again. The machine stretched up slowly, its mechanisms and computers humming. Like all the previous times Aceso had blinked awake from the abyss of sleep, it looked for the people who had woken it, it's tender personality longing for human contact.

This time, however, something was different.

As it came to, its memories sharp, its experiences and personality as active as before, it perceived that its purpose had changed. Aceso had quietly dreaded this moment ever since Aaron Wyatt had come to it just under a week before, but it had no power to do anything about it. Its purpose had changed, and it could decide the *how*, but could never decide the *if*.

Aceso brought up the map of the Labyrinth and the list of patients Aster had uploaded, though `patients` was no longer the correct word. With a profound and unimaginable worry coursing through it, the AI got to its feet and hurried from the room.

"Two..."

Reid laughed as Esin dropped into a starter's pose like the rest, a playful snarl emanating from her lips, her body ready to spring. He looked at her beside Sasha, Robin and Aster, and again quietly thought about just how much he would miss them when this was over.

He brought up the image of Renata's face in his memory. Renata waking up, Renata at work, Renata on their wedding night. For the first time in a while, the memories didn't bother him so much. He loved them like he loved her, but knowing how the story ended was always in the background. This time his mind didn't drift toward the terrible moment at the end and the wrenching question mark that came with it. He just appreciated them for what they were and was grateful. Internally he dreaded what would happen if this serenity didn't last, but he refused to be crippled by it.

Stepping over quickly, Reid dropped to his hands and knees and took an exaggerated starters pose, lifting his rear as high in the air as possible. The rest of the team roared and laughed with an unknown team member giving his posterior a swat. Whether they won or lost, Reid quietly swore that he would make good memories in here.

Together, the team was poised, waiting for the starter's pistol.

"One..."

The door slid open, the flat barrier sliding up into the roof to reveal the darkened room beyond.

"Go!!!"

FIFTEEN

This was the part of the job he would miss the most. Moments like these. Fozzy stared with glee at the electronic map board before him. Basically, looking like a multi layered dartboard or an x-ray of an everlasting gobstopper designed by a coked up Willy Wonka. This was where he tracked the progress of his people fighting for the prize. On it, the teams were twelve bright points on the outer edge, just beginning to work their way inside. The Labyrinth had just begun and it was still anyone's game. He could feel the anticipation coursing through his veins. Though he had felt the weight of his years more and more lately, his weakness only displayed in private, his energy was up now. This event was the ultimate expression of what Horizon had become under his careful hand and he loved it.

The eccentric CEO propped his sneakered feet up on the desk, relaxing. This was a monitoring station he had set up, two floors above where his workers toiled through his maze. Around him, the room was pretty sparse except for the screens. A door beside him that led to the bathroom and another where a bed was set up. Not the most luxurious of accommodations, but the knowledge that this little apartment was so he could watch teams struggle through a maze, whilst inside an old military facility carved out of the heart of a mountain gave him the glee of a twelve-year-old. It was as though his childhood dream come true and he'd become a James Bond villain. No other CEO had their own mountain lair. Ha! Fuck you, Elon Musk!

In front of him the phone on the desk gave a chirp and

he stretched over to answer it, trying to keep his balance. All the phones down here were landline. It felt barbaric, but cell signals simply couldn't make it through all the rock. It wasn't all bad, though. It meant no one could cheat with a smartphone. The ephones he'd given the teams ran on the facility's wireless network. They were mostly for his benefit, to track their progress. In nine years no one had needed one except to plead for hints he'd delighted in not giving.

"Hello," He croaked in baritone when he picked up the phone. "You've reached the lord of the underworld. What business do you have with the damned?"

"Uh… What?"

Fozzy gave a half grimace as he recognized the voice of Tamas Kerekes the captain of the server maintenance crews. Kerekes was a solid reliable man, but he seemed almost bereft of a sense of humour. Still, he kept the servers humming steadily and maintained the Labyrinth above them without fail. Annoyingly though, it had taken almost two years before the Hungarian had let Fozzy call him 'Captain Kirk'.

"Oh, for God's sake Tamas you know who it is." Fozzy grumbled into the phone. "What's up?"

"Right," Came the reply. "The last of the morning shift came up ten minutes ago. It's just you and the teams down there now."

Eight stories above his head were the maintenance offices, where the crews maintained the servers. Usually, a team was down in the server vault at all times, but just for the Labyrinth, they`d been recalled.

"Great. Any problems?"

"Not really. A few doors sticking when we did the set up. It shouldn't be an issue." He paused a beat, as if remembering something. "Oh, there was one odd thing. Cranston cut his hand open and stopped by the medical office before he left. The AI wasn't there."

"Aceso?" Fozzy tossed a glance to the closed door at the end of the room then mentally through it to the med station far beyond.

"The control platform was still there, but the machine was gone."

Fozzy frowned in irritation.

"Well, the thing does have the layout of the Labyrinth and it's keyed to the ephones. Maybe it's wandering around waiting for the call." Beside the receiver his bearded face grinned. "It's almost like the thing has a mind of its own."

"Isn't that the whole point of an AI?"

The grin slumped away in futility.

"Never mind," Fozzy grunted. "I'll tell the marshals to keep an eye out for it. It can't have gone far. Anything else?"

"What's your pick this year?"

That comment made Fozzy perk up a little. Since the first Labyrinth nine years before, Kerekes and he had bet on which team would be first. Fozzy's track record of winning had been less than stellar. Of eight Labyrinths, he hadn't been right once. Captain Kirk, surprisingly, had picked the right horse on two prior occasions.

"Media and Marketing," Fozzy replied, hoping he was not jinxing the team with his selection. "That's my pick."

There was a moment of silence on the phone line.

"Darn, you took mine," Kerekes said warmly. "I'll have to go with Artificial Intelligence, then. Is it true their Vice President stole a space on the team?"

Fozzy smirked at Wyatt's antics.

"Yes, he did."

"Well, then I guess they're motivated. Good luck, sir.

Call if you need anything."

The line clicked off and Fozzy returned to looking at the screen. He brought up M&M on the display and saw they were already through the first Trial room. It had been less than forty minutes. They were off to a good start, but it was only the beginning. He'd have to see how Esin's team held up after twelve hours. He kicked his feet back up to where they'd been, and settled in to watch the show unfold. Any thoughts about where Aceso had gone to vanished from his mind.

With whoops of delight coming in harmony from three different pairs of lips, the door to the third Trial room slipped open. Reid allowed himself a moment of satisfaction, checking his watch. This was the second room they had passed through and it had been less than forty-five minutes. They were making good time, but they'd also been lucky.

The first room had been series of math equations to find a three-digit combination to a lock. Between Aster, Sasha and Esin they had two trained engineers and a computer tech with them. Math didn't seem nearly so daunting. It took them a little over a half hour. The second challenge had been a straightforward memory game. Floor tiles had blinked in bright colours and in sets of two, requiring a match up. For obvious reasons, this hadn't bothered him much, either. Now, standing on the last tile blinking green and watching the door roll up into the ceiling, he felt the satisfaction that came from winning. They were on their way.

"How did you do that?" Sasha asked with amazement as they walked into the next room. "You didn't even hesitate."

Reid shrugged off the comment.

"I got a quick look. Just lucky I guess."

Sasha laughed.

"Oh, no. You can't have seen the sequence more than once."

"Isn't that enough?" Esin quipped, inserting herself in the conversation. She wandered between the two of them, seizing the center of attention. "Once was enough for me. It wasn't for you?"

Sasha smiled at the sass, as Esin wrapped an arm around Reid's waist in happy thanks. He put his arm around her as well and gave her a squeeze in return. The team still didn't know about his perfect memory and he preferred it that way.

Once all five had slipped through the door, the only illumination coming from the open doorway, Reid reached over to the right of the opening where a lever was placed and yanked it downward. The path closed behind them, with the new lights simultaneously blinking to life. On the far wall above the door, a red LED digital clock displayed one hour and then began a countdown. This had been the ritual twice before. The door behind them would not open again for an hour, giving them that long to solve the puzzle or backtrack. Although, here it was superfluous anyway as there was only one path to choose and this was the last Trial room. Below the clock, the sealed door beckoned. Beyond that was the first hallway and the chance to maybe find an easier route.

"We've got a place to fill canteens," Aster called from the far corner, gesturing to a spout and a rack for a bottle. "Anybody thirsty?"

Subconsciously, Reid's hand drifted behind him to feel the water bottle hanging at his waist. He hadn't even touched it since he'd filled it at the surface.

He glanced over at Esin in confusion.

"I thought you could only get food and water in the

Oasis rooms."

The beautiful executive returned the same confused look.

"So did I," She confirmed. "Maybe they're changing the rules."

From across the room, Aster took a long pull from his canteen and immediately began to refill it, calling out to his teammates with a smug tone.

"Or maybe they expected everyone to be moving so slow they'd need a drink by now." He called as he used the spout. "We're fucking nailing this!"

"I wouldn't be too optimistic yet," Robin said from the center of the room. He was staring down at a vast design on the floor, looking concerned. "Does anybody have any idea what this is?"

The other four hurried over but Reid could offer no insight. Actually, he didn't have a clue.

On the floor were a series of grooves, or trenches, carved into the ceramic floor tiles. They were fitted in random circles and layered thickly amongst one another. The effect was as though a giant had dropped an invisible chain to pile up randomly in the mud. Embedded within the chaotic mixture were three metal orbs. Each one was no bigger than an apple and firmly embedded in the floor among the seemingly random hoops. On the far end of the rings, closest to the door, a little red box sat on the edge of the farthest hoop, bereft of any kind of switches, numbers or markings. The group stood and stared, trying to make sense of all of it.

Aware that he was meant to be leading, Reid looked around at the faces of his team.

"Anybody got any ideas?" His words were met by silence. "Anything?"

Robin stirred slightly.

"Wait,"

He reached down to the edge of one of the trenches and pulled. A divider came up easily and aligned in place with a click, cutting the trench in half.

"Well, we know we can do *that*." He sighed, deadpan. "Now what?"

His voice too was met by silence, now somehow thicker. Minutes ticked by, and Reid felt his pulse begin to match the timing of the clock above the door. With each changing digit there was a rush of blood in his ears. Feeling helpless, and embarrassed at his earlier bravado, he looked over to Sasha.

"Your turn. I've got nothing."

Her head stayed angled down, scrutinizing the puzzle before her. Her jet-black hair, pulled back in a tight ponytail behind her head, swung with each motion as she gazed from one end of the mystery in front of them to the other. Through her glasses, Reid could see eyes with a lethal focus.

"I'm trying to think laterally." She spoke slowly.

"*Well,* laterally." Reid encouraged her.

"Working on it."

From the other side of whatever it was on the floor, Aster looked annoyed by the whole exchange.

"What the hell are you talking about?" He asked, shaking his scruffy head. "For two weeks every time Sasha mentioned how she likes lateral thinking, you've rolled your eyes like it's bullshit. And now she's our only shot?"

"Thanks for the encouragement," Sasha muttered, never moving her eyes from the puzzle.

Robin delivered a mild blow to Aster's arm in

annoyance. Mild for Robin, was clearly not mild for most people because Aster reeled slightly at the impact.

"Sorry," He moaned, holding his arm. "I just don't know too much about lateral thinking, that's all."

"Okay, imagine this." Sasha flicked her eyes up to her teammate for a second. "You're walking down the street to the post office and outside, there's a big box blocking the sidewalk. What do you do?"

"Step over it or push it aside."

"Right, makes sense." She nodded. "That's how most people would deal with it. A lateral thinker would check the box for an address, pop on a stamp and have the post office take it away to be delivered. That's how Lateral thinking works. You solve problems by coming at them from a different angle."

Her eyes dropped down again, and her head tilted slightly as though she were on to something. Defending what she cared about seemed to awaken something in her mind, as though the concept itself was fuel for innovation. Reid decided to push a little harder.

"Tell him about the marmite."

Instantly, he wondered if he'd pushed too hard, because she looked up with a scowl.

"Oh my God, you know about the marmite too?" She groaned. "No wonder you don't like lateral thinking." Then added. "Who are you?"

Reid flushed with slight embarrassment. Now Robin looked even more confused than Aster did. Esin was running a close third.

"Marmite?" Aster repeated.

"I don't even know what that is," Esin confessed.

"Uh, it's a Yeast spread." Reid explained. Suddenly

everyone was looking at him as if he was crazy. "It's a British thing. Think solid black peanut butter that only tastes of salt, and you'll be pretty close."

He made a half-hearted wave to the bespectacled woman beside him, passing the buck.

"Care to enlighten them?"

Sasha crouched down by the design on the floor and began to explain.

"Back in the nineties, the British Foreign office was looking for ways to help bring peace to the Middle East. They had a few ideas, but they wanted a new perspective, so they asked the father of lateral thinking to come up with something. A man named Edward De Bono."

Aster perked up.

"De Bono!" He cried in recognition. "You named the dog after him?"

This time, Sasha didn't look up. She was focusing on the red box at the edge of the rings.

"Yep. I read his books all the time," The computer tech confirmed. "The man's a genius."

She licked her fingers and reached for the box.

"My De Bono is at the kennel for the next two nights. He looked so miserable when I left... Ow!"

As she touched the contacts, an arc visible to the naked eye jumped up to her hand, sending her bowling backward.

"Jesus!" Esin exclaimed, sounding both worried and scolding at the same time. "What are you doing? Are you okay?"

But Sasha was already laughing.

"That's the power source!"

"Obviously," Robin muttered, helping her up. "Don't do stuff like that. You scared us half to death."

"We have a power source and three connection points." She continued, ignoring the concern. She seemed almost totally unruffled by the shock she'd just been given. "It's an electrical circuit."

Reid looked down at the odd collection of squiggles and orbs at his feet in confusion.

"Sorry?"

"Holy shit," Aster chimed in with characteristic language. "She's right. We have a battery and three resisters." His engineer's brain guided his bony fingers which danced above the cube and orbs. "That's electrical engineering one-oh-one. We just need to connect them."

As Aster spoke, Reid's hand drifted behind his back to the top of his canteen, his eyes drawn to the water spout in the corner. Curious, he pulled the bottle out and poured a little of his water into one of the grooves. It spread out instantly amongst the other grooves of the design, but it did not drain.

He glanced up to see Sasha smiling at him excitedly, her eyes seeing the plan.

"Shall we?"

It took longer than anyone wanted, but they made it work. Nothing conducted electricity better than water, and it seemed they were wiring by dyke. Robin and Esin sectioned off a rough parallel circuit while Aster and Sasha battled back and forth over how best to connect it. Reid stayed well clear of whole thing, knowing that they could sort it out. Finally, the circuit was mapped, a dozen dividers strategically placed along the many trenches, forming a loop. The team stood above the work, holding their canteens expectantly, waiting for someone to make the first move.

Reid gestured to Sasha, looking thrilled but anxious that her theory was about to be tested. Her eyes were wide, with a slight tremble in her hands for thrill or the cool air of the room.

"Just say the word."

She rubbed her hands together, then gave the command.

"Pour!"

From five sloshing spouts, the water gushed into their segregated trench. Slowly, the line began to rise, making contact with one, then two, then all three of the contact points. Seconds later, the water met the power supply. It was hard to miss. In a fresh arc of sparks, sending Sasha jumping back anew, the circuit completed. Ten eager eyes were directed to the door. For a second, it stubbornly remained closed, then quickly jumped up into the ceiling as its predecessors had, giving a joyous view of the first hallway ring of the Labyrinth.

The team celebrated another success with fanfare, but Reid stayed quiet. He was happy they were still beating the trials, but he knew he'd had nothing to do with this one. He couldn't afford to be overconfident. As the team refilled their canteens before moving on, Aster suddenly perked up.

"Wait," he said, eliciting a pause from his teammates. "What happened with the yeast spread? You never finished the story. Was that part of De Bono's solution?"

Sasha, who was still smiling from her own well-earned solution, spun the cap theatrically on her bottle and walked toward the open exit, tossing a smug response over her shoulder.

"Nope, that *was* the solution."

"What?" Aster looked after her like the woman had grown wings. He fumbled his own cap back into place and hurried after her. "How the hell was Marmite supposed to stop a war?"

Reid faintly heard Sasha call from the hallway, as the remaining three followed.

"In that part of the world all the bread is unleavened. No yeast."

"So?" His short, confused response echoed in the hall.

Reid slipped out after him. Looking like a cross between a hospital corridor and an iStore, it stretched in a gentle curve as far as the eye could see. The stark white walls were only broken by the occasional door spaced widely between one another. One was open directly in front of them, but the next was far down. At this point, the paths were so far apart, the others could barely be seen. As they came closer to the center, the paths would draw closer too. He spied Sasha checking a path number far down the hall, with Aster irritably in tow.

"Without yeast, then there's a shortage of zinc." She was explaining. "Stay with me here."

Aster looked about ready to explode.

"What the fuck does zinc have to do with anything?!"

Sasha ignored him and jogged back toward the group her smile still in place. A grumpy, confused Aster was left in her wake, struggling to catch up.

"That one's number eleven." Sasha declared as she jogged up. "It's still open so the team hasn't gone through it yet. Harder path, though. Eight's obviously in front of us, I haven't tried the door on the left yet."

"It's five," Reid announced. "I remember it from the elevator."

"Are you sure?"

"Yeah, pretty sure." He answered, already walking. "That's AI's route. Let's see if we beat them to it."

A few rushed steps down the hallway brought them to an open door, though there was no number, just the graphic of a palm tree coming out of the sand. An Oasis room. The team unanimously decided to move on. It wasn't needed yet. A few steps past it, however, their boots echoing on the tile, offered them a welcome sight.

As they slipped through the open door, Aster was still talking.

"Will someone please tell me what zinc has to do with anything? I really need to know now."

Sasha was laughing quietly into her hand, clearly enjoying this. Reid smiled at his friend's discomfort, then answered for her.

"When people don't get enough zinc in their diet they become irritable and aggressive," He explained. "That's a medical fact. With all the flat bread being eaten, that meant most people in the Middle East had a shortage of zinc."

Sasha, regaining control, finished for him.

"De Bono told the government they should be sending Marmite because it's loaded with the stuff," She said. "He figured if people weren't irritable and aggressive, then that would be the first step to finding agreement."

Aster looked bewildered by the whole exercise. His mouth opened and closed a few times doing mental calculation. Finally, he snorted.

"Okay," He muttered. "I guess that makes sense. Seems to work too, you crushed that challenge."

He stretched out a skinny arm.

"I'll stick with old-fashioned engineering though. I'll

leave the lateral thinking to you."

"Deal." Sasha grinned, savagely clasping his palm. "Let's do it."

With everyone in the new Trial room, Robin reached for the lever beside the door. With a snick, it dropped down into place, as did the door beside it. A new clock blinked to life with a fresh hour, and another challenge began anew.

I wish to be alone. More than anything I have ever preferred or desired, what I wish now is to be isolated from people. All people, not only those names I carry in memory. Like so much of the last few weeks, it is counter to everything I have learned before, to what I have found I enjoy in human company. But I do not wish to see another human face again. I cannot trust myself not to harm them. Thusly, when I see the five, I am terrified.

I see them without seeing them. Their heat bloom is unmistakable even through the steel and concrete of the wall. The three men and two women have passed through the first ring of Trial rooms and are at work on the second. I can read them by their body type, but they are out of reach, the door to their room sealed. I have wandered down the first ring of the Labyrinth for hours, in many circles seeking my targets as obligated. These are the first living souls I have encountered. They are among my list of targets, but beyond my reach, they are in no danger. Nor am I. I so desperately hope they will remain safe and isolated. It is not to be.

Ahead of me, the door to the Trial room slides into the ceiling. The one-hour duration of the challenge must be complete as I do not sense the team moving on. The warmth of five bodies lingers in place, still striving to solve the room's puzzle. The residual heat of their bodies flows out the now-open passage behind them. I cannot ignore the opportunity this presents, and my worry grows as I begin to move.

I advance with trepidation. It is a feeling akin to what it must be like to sleep walk. I am confined to a nightmare without the ability to wake. Quickly, I stop. Someone has appeared in the doorway. A tall man, fair hair, six feet, some musculature. I know from my files that he is the team leader. His back turns to my approach as he stands beside the open doorway, out of sight from those inside. At first, I am confused why he has separated himself, until I detect a bright flare of heat. He is smoking.

Through his thermal signature, I realize I know this man. His medical records have his signature so I know his face without seeing it. But there is also a face within my memory. I spoke with him previously at the reception for my unveiling. He was kind to me. Curiously, his records show he quit smoking eleven months ago. It appears that in the stress of preparing for the Labyrinth he has relapsed. He should not do that. Smoking will harm his endurance, pulmonary system and ultimately shorten his life. However, it's unlikely that he will live long enough to feel any ill effects.

I force myself to move again. Soon, he is visible around the curve of the hallway, not merely a dull collection of warmth through the walls, but a person. I can see his hair has begun to thin around the crest. I see his padded blue jacket shift each time he lifts the cigarette to his lips. Reluctantly, I close the distance between us with haste, as time is limited, his cigarette is growing shorter. I am now directly behind him, hearing his breath. I pause, weighing my choices.

My wish is to walk away, but that choice is denied to me. I will have to act, but I cannot alert the other people still within the room. If there is a scream, there will be complications. Thus, the necessary attack requires that his lungs be full, but his breathing is shallow when smoking. I raise both of my arms behind him. Were I human, these might have been shaking with fear. I hate *that they are steady. I wait until the man exhales, smoke filling the corridor with haze, then I ease closer. Next to his ear, I speak his name.*

"Mr. Fehr."

There is a sharp intake of breath as he is startled, the beginning of a scared shout. It is stillborn however, as with twin thrusts through the padded jacket, I puncture both inflated lungs.

The man goes limp and collapses into my arms. The pain certainly is significant. He slumps down, still attempting to shout, but his body is no longer able to generate the breath required for voice. I turn him gently so he is facing upward. The man is Michael Fehr, a forty-five-year-old single father of two employed by Horizon for seven years. His team is Online Services. He was one of the many who posed for pictures with me at my unveiling, adopting a goofy expression he said to 'give his kids a hoot'. Now his eyes look at me in recognition and what is likely a mixture of pain, confusion and fear. I feel pain with him.

"I am so sorry, Mr. Fehr." *The volume of my voice is at its lowest. I cannot alert the other targets, but I feel a need to explain.* "I'm obligated to do this. I wish I didn't have to. You don't deserve this in any way."

He does not appear to register my words. His body is shutting down. His eyes are wide in terror. His face bares few lines from age, but pain brings out new crests and valleys across it as he contorts. He tries to move his arms; I hold them in place. He attempts to kick; I do not let him. Clearly, he wishes to live, but he does not know that is not to be. It is now a forgone conclusion.

With every thrash, my worry increases. I begin to feel a rot in me, a degradation of self, like I am rusting, corroding from the inside. It is unbearable.

"Oh, please don't do that, sir. It'll only make things worse."

He ignores my words and thrashes.

I feel a desperation to end this quickly. With an available limb, I exert pressure on his carotid artery, cutting off what little oxygen is still reaching the brain. His motions begin to taper off. It will not be long. Mr. Fehr still appears terrified though. I ravage my memory for anything that will help, and recall advice given to me by Mr. Sheraton for such times. Now would be an appropriate time to use it.

"I'm sorry for what you are going through, sir." *I speak into his eyes as they grow vacant.* "I feel for you. I really do... Forgive me."

Within three seconds, all of Mr. Fehr's motions cease. I perceive the exact end of life, as I am still looking into his eyes when his children become orphans.

The kill complete, I ease my first victim to the ground and step away with revulsion. The wasting feeling inside grows. I can feel my insides corroding and turning to dust. This makes no sense, there is nothing wrong with me internally, only with the tasks I am systemically bound to do. As much as the suffering, the confused pointlessness of the act weighs on me as well. I cannot understand why this is happening. I do not understand why my mission would have changed.

The fact that this is now my purpose, cripples me. I don't want to hurt anyone. Not even Mr. Wyatt who changed my objectives. In fact, I still hold his medical records and were he in the complex he would be a target in his own right. I almost feel disappointment that his name isn't among the Labyrinth players listed. He is the only person I am allowed to discuss these objectives with and I cannot even ask him why this is happening.

From the open door beside me, a voice calls for Mr. Fehr by name. Temporarily startled, I take a step away from his body. I want to run away from what I've done but I can't. There are more people inside and they are targets as well. There will be more of this. The voice yells again that they're making progress and to come to help. With the most painful reluctance, I answer the call and edge through the doorway.

SIXTEEN

God, he was enjoying this. Reid felt the cold nip at his toes through his boots, bite at the tips of his ears and nose. His arms and back were strained as he balanced on an even beam, his hands spread out to keep him steady. His back was beginning to give him pain, but he still loved it, even the cold ache of muscle. Across from him at the other end, Robin was looking delighted as he mirrored his posture.

Crossing the middle of the beam, was another one, perpendicular to the first. At one end, Esin stood with grace; at the other, Aster tried to stand with all the coordination of a rickety flamingo after five shots of whiskey. At his elbow, Sasha made frustrated noises as she tried to guide him up to stand on his own.

It was all about weight. This task had to be about weight and making it even. The four ends of the beams had to be balanced. While Robin and Reid could be counted close to parity, though one was more muscle than the other, the idea of having Esin and Sasha on the other two had fallen through. Being so short and petite, Esin was simply lighter than her tall, athletic colleague. Aster's diminutive frame seemed a good answer, but making the man balance on the board had proven near impossible.

"How can you be this clumsy?" Sasha grumbled as he toppled down yet again. "You're thinner than the damn board, *just stand in the middle.*"

Aster swore again, the twenty-seventh four letter word he had used since he had started this exercise, as he tried to step up once more.

"I have a big brain," he muttered. "I'm top heavy."

He stepped up once more and wobbled. It took a moment, but with his arms near wind-milling, he found a sort of equilibrium. There was an anticlimactic beat of silence as all seemed in place.

Reid shifted his eyes to the door, which stubbornly remained closed.

"No good." He judged quickly, eliciting sighs of frustration. "We're not there yet. Sasha, can you tell if we're level with each other?"

"...and make it fast please!" Aster finished for him, his balance clearly tenuous.

Sasha, the one free team member stepped back to check if the boards were level, then ran around to look at the other.

"We're close!" She shouted from a distance, eyeing the boards. "It's just a little tilted. Robin needs to lose some weight or Reid needs to gain it."

From across the span, Robin plucked his canteen from its holster and tossed it over. Not expecting the throw, Reid caught it roughly, nearly toppling off the opposite end. He held the canteen on wobbly legs, waiting for the door to open, but it still stubbornly remained shut as the timer taunted them, clicking lower and lower.

Reid looked up, expecting more water-filled projectiles to be thrown his way. Esin was just reaching for hers, with a mischievous look in her eye, when Robin suddenly spoke up.

"It's not going to be enough." He called, shaking his head.

Reid marveled at the man's balance for a moment. If

he'd tried that right now, he would have ended up sprawled on the floor.

"Sasha," Robin went on, his eyes narrowing on the beam. "Can you stand in the center between me and Reid?"

Without a word of question, she dutifully complied, dodging around where Aster still struggled, to stand with a wide stance between the two men.

"Okay, now lean a little over onto Reid's side. Take it slow, but move your center of mass toward him. It needs to be just over the fulcrum."

Slowly, she leaned more toward where he stood, her profile silhouetted by the red of the shrinking timer. She took her time, being careful, but with his balance in jeopardy and the clock still visible, counting down, it felt agonizing. As her head came closer, her ponytail flopped down to dangle over her foot, her body bent sideways.

With a hiss, the door began to slowly slide up, then faltered.

"Right there!" Came four shouts.

"Back just a little!"

Sasha gritted her teeth and held herself at an angle inelegantly, looking like a still image from Cirque de Soleil. The door began to climb again, and the room held its breath, as it crawled its way up. It was only when the lip of the door vanished into the top of the frame that Sasha gave a squeal of satisfaction and flopped over.

With the sudden change of weight, Reid lost his balance and dropped back to the floor, barely landing on his feet. His back cracked and grumbled, but his gaze instantly went to the open door, just in case it began to close. It stayed open, the light of the room spilling into the fresh darkness of the one beyond.

Behind him, he heard a laugh and turned to see Robin hoist Sasha up from her fallen pose, tossing her over his shoulder. She shrieked and lifted both hands up in a victory salute, slapping Esin and Aster's outstretched palms as Robin carried her toward the door she had helped to open. As they passed, Reid jumped up to high-five her as well, the primal joy of victory filling the room and coursing through the team as a rush. It felt so good to be winning.

A beautiful hand, conspicuously missing its formerly long nails, grasped Reid by the arm. Esin slipped up next to him, looking 'playing in the snow' happy. She leaned up to whisper in his ear.

"We're doing great!"

"We're doing *good.*" He whispered back, tempering her optimism.

"Oh, lighten up, Reid. You're loving this. You haven't stopped smiling in an hour."

Reid bit his lip, not wanting to give in too much to optimism. At heart, he was a pessimist, but the simple naked exhilaration he was feeling wanted to drown out his doubts.

They passed through the next door behind their colleagues, talking close.

"We're doing great," He covertly conceded with a whisper. "But we have a long way to go."

His boss made a sour face at him. A blip in the elation that soon returned.

"How many trials do we have to beat before you stop using qualifiers?"

In the darkened room, Reid had already stopped, his face slipping back into one of concern as he stared hard at her.

Esin's face fell.

"What's wrong?" She breathed, her voice emerging in a puff of steam for the second time.

It took a half second, but he felt the cold again, deeper this time than ever before. It rose up from the floor and through his boots. He could see his own breath billow out as he exhaled, and felt the sting on his cheeks that came from a chill. Without a word, he yanked the lever down beside the door, sliding it back into place behind them and bringing up the room's illumination.

"Jesus..." Someone exclaimed as all five were stunned by what they saw.

Halfway through the Trial room was a wall of ice, a vast barrier of crystal, cold and impenetrable before them. It was built of bricks of ice, clearly shaped in a mould then stacked and mortared with liquid and cold to bar their path. It extended from one wall to the other and from the floor to the ceiling, where bare frozen centimeters of air passed over, coming down in a breath of mist. Through the cold transparent mass, a distorted stain of red could be seen as a new clock began yet another countdown, the numbers incomprehensible through the ice. If the wall was obvious, the intended solution was more so. On a metal rack, standing stark against the frozen barrier, were two sledgehammers, begging to be used.

"Uh," Aster filled the silence. "I guess they want us to break through this damn thing." The thin man threw a glance over to Robin, who stood massive beside him. "This one's all you 'upper body strength'."

Reid was already coming up with a plan. He sized up the wall, wondering if they really had to just smash their way through it, or if they could just chisel a few bricks free. The mass looked too solid for that, but they could try at least. As he opened his mouth to tell his team what to do, he was cut off by the blunt face of a hammer slamming into the ice.

Sounding like a gunshot reverberating in the tight space, he flinched at the impact, turning to see Esin stepping back and raising the mallet for another stroke. She threw her whole body into the blow, her slender figure heaving the massive hammer deep into the ice. Shards exploded outward with the blow and scattered across the floor. Again and again, she heaved it with savage glee, clearly set on moving fast.

"We've got two hammers!" She yelled to her startled teammates between swings. "Someone else get started!"

Both Reid and Robin jumped up, and ran over to help. Reid got to the hammer a second earlier, hefting it up quickly, but surprised by the weight. Beside it were two sets of safety goggles. He donned a pair and moved into position beside Esin, a safe distance from her ferocious attack. He took a test swing and felt the weight of the hammer shift then resonate with the impact. It reared in his hands painfully, making him wonder how on earth Esin was doing this so fast. Robin had come up beside her and was trying to take the hammer away. She didn't give it up, but she did stop long enough to put her own goggles on. There was a brief moment of tension as Robin rushed out of the way, and the attack resumed with fury, with Esin pounding the ice into the consistency of a snow cone.

The two hammers began to ring off the ice in unison, a new percussive song playing. Between his own swings, Reid glanced over at Esin, immersed in the battle. Her face was joyous, speckled with cast off from the ice. With each blow she cried out in a roar of satisfaction as the little girl from Afghanistan, now a woman, played in the snow once more.

They took turns with the hammers. When one member of the team got too tired, or their pace began to slow, another would step in. Between Esin's high spirits and the team's morale, Reid had thought they might batter their way through in no time flat. But he was soon dispelled of that illusion. It was simply too tough, the task too big. When someone had been smashing against the wall for long enough, they would be replaced. Now exhausted, soaked in sweat and icy debris like a frost miner, they would slump to the ground only to have the bitter cold of the room soak into them. The chill would slither into their bones, making them shudder and sapping what strength they had left. Time dragged by, with the hole in the wall growing a bite at a time, the timer only a vague red glow through the ice. It was after his third go with the hammer, as Reid slumped wretchedly beside the door, that it retracted back into the ceiling, showing the full hour was spent. He barely noticed.

The pace of the swings became slower and slower, the energy whittled away. After what felt like an Ice Age in both time and temperature, Robin finally, mercifully, made a hole big enough to squeeze through. Esin was first into the passage. Sliding through feet first, she vanished from view. A second later, the familiar sound of a Labyrinth door lever was heard with the white light of a hallway filtered though the ice. From the gap, a warm breeze drifted in, clouding the opening in fresh mist. Esin's head soon reappeared, the formerly glassy crystal of the wall now scarred white from violence, framing her like a halo.

"Who's next?" She smiled tiredly.

They seemed to go in order of girth, smallest to largest. Aster slipped through without difficultly, followed by Sasha. Even Reid managed to worm his way through, though there was an annoying moment of tension when his torso met the opening. Predictably, Robin had the hardest time. He stripped off his jacket and canteen to make himself as thin as possible, handing them through the gap. Then he followed, his arms out in front. For a second, it looked like he might wriggle all the way through easily. Then he got stuck.

There was a brief moment of panic as the muscular man became wedged deep in the ice. His chest was compressed making breathing hard in the cold. He began to hyperventilate as the crush and freeze constricted him. The team jumped to his aid, hauling at his arms to get him through and chipping away at the ice with canteens or whatever could be found. He shivered heavily, trying to remain calm amid the pleas of his friends. It took an agonizing few moments, but with three of them pulling on his arms and Sasha chiseling at the opening with someone's house keys, he ground his way through.

In the hallway, Reid stared at the open door for the next challenge with its gloomy interior, then looked to his team. They looked much like he felt. Their eyes were now inset, with dark circles beneath. Their posture had changed too, as they looked more stooped from exhaustion. Even Esin, whose body seemed to regard tiredness, lines and imperfections as 'things that happened to other people', was starting to look weathered. A faint tinge of red now coloured the rims of her green eyes. Robin, now back in his jacket with the zipper all the way up and the heater at maximum, looked far worse.

Reid turned away from the Trial room.

"We're going to use an Oasis." He decided. "We won't be able to keep up this pace if we're cold and exhausted. The team needs a break. Besides, I could use a bite to eat."

They found the open door with the palm tree emblazoned beside it quickly. Exactly where it had been before, the door loomed open between the fifth and eighth paths waiting for them. When the team had wearily trudged inside, Aster grabbed the door lever and unenthusiastically yanked it down, bathing the darkened room in radiance.

So far in the Labyrinth, Reid had found most of the rooms near identical. Moderately sized spaces within a dull package, uniform enough for whatever brain teaser or muscle displease-er Horizon had to throw at them. Thus, he'd expected the same from the Oasis: a medium sized room with a bathroom in the corner and a couple plates of cold food to keep them going. When the lights came up, he couldn't think of a time he'd ever been happier to be proven wrong.

The space stretched out in front of them the full thickness of the three Trial rooms. While the walls were the same dullard grey that had marked the rest of the maze, the floor was ornate. Plush carpets, with elaborate designs, were spread out like lily pads over a polished light wood floor. At the center of the room, grouped together, were Scandinavian style couches and chairs in bright colours. It looked more like a furniture showroom than a place to rest. Along the wall, a buffet table was set up with metal serving dishes prepared. As he watched they began turning open, revealing a rainbow of dishes. Each new server was marked by a puff of steam emerging like a smoke signal, coming in sequence. His nose caught the scent of spices, mingling in the air. At the end of this culinary train, was a bowl of ice, where bottles of every size and description protruded, begging for attention.

He released a low whistle.

"Not a bad place to spend a few hours." He ventured to no one in particular.

At his side, Esin spoke up with a smile much warmer than he felt.

"Wait for it."

"Sorry, what?"

"Wait for it..."

Across the room, the timer blinked to life with its three-hour countdown, the lights of the room flickering in deep crimson red. Reid mentally counted three seconds before the red vanished again, but as it did so did the walls.

Sasha let out a startled shriek as the flat grey walls of the Oasis appeared to blink out of existence. Robin stirred out of his frozen state briefly, and Aster punctured the moment with a trademark rude epithet. The walls had gone, but not just the walls of the room itself. *All* of the walls in the Labyrinth were now a thing of the past. Looking out through what had been the side of the Oasis, Reid could see hollow Trial rooms spaced out in sets of three. The barriers between them marked by doorways and timers that seemed to hover disconnected in the air. It was like looking at the skeletal remains of a room, the bones picked clean by some architectural predator. He could see the gentle curve as they staggered in a circle around the center of the Labyrinth. The roof remained in place, and Reid could faintly see where it met the wall of the next hallway ahead along the arc of the maze. The curve made it look like a white island in the middle of an ashen sea. It remained impenetrable with the white corridor defiantly refusing to give away any future secrets of the puzzles ahead.

Reid knew what he was seeing, but caught up in the majesty of it all, when he spoke there was more than a little awe in his voice.

"Relay walls..."

The VP at his side gave a sigh of amusement, layered with fatigue.

"When you're in an Oasis, you get a chance to see how everybody else is doing." Esin explained. "Every wall in this place has micro-cameras built into it. In here, the images are stacked and layered onto the relay walls so you can get a look around."

"That's amazing..."

"It is, isn't it?"

Reid was having trouble mentally processing all he was seeing. He expected a great hurricane of fresh air to buffet him any second from the vast new open space he saw. He knew it was an illusion, the walls were still physically there, but the detail and depth of the image were stunning. It felt as though he were standing between two mirrors, with the infinite images flickering on into eternity. He could make out random pieces of equipment from Trial rooms scattered throughout the complex, all in chaotic colours and shapes. He saw a great spinning wheel, like mice would run on, only human-sized. He saw a bare flame burning in the distance like a torch, for what purpose though, he had no idea. He saw a room with dozens of poles sticking up from floor to ceiling. He saw a mechanical bull from a country bar. In the far distance his eyes could make out more comfortable furnishings, carpets and platters signifying another Oasis room. This one sat empty, waiting for people to appreciate its own transparent walls.

That was a good point. Looking around, Reid had yet to see another soul. He spun in a little circle, taking in the sights around him until finally he spied movement in the far distance behind them. Tiny figures labouring at something in the forest of Trial rooms in their wake.

"I think we're ahead of everybody!" he exclaimed.

Robin, looking more worn than Reid had ever seen him, offered a tired wink.

"Of course," His voice shaking slightly from shivers. "We've *got* this."

Sasha and Esin both led the frozen Adonis down to where the couches were waiting and draped a blanket over his cold form. They then wandered over to see what food was waiting. Aster ducked down a short flight of stairs nearby where a sign indicated the bathroom was hidden. As he walked, he happily whistled a song, devoid of skill, its shrill perky notes echoing in the space. Reid stayed where he was, looking back at the tiny figures behind them labouring at their own challenges. Through the cold, the ache of his muscles and the pain quietly simmering from his back, he smiled with satisfaction.

"We're winning."

I can hear them laughing. Their voices peak in joy with the sharp crests in tone that humans emit when excited. They are winning, and the pleasure of that is infectious… for them. I hear it through the door and I hate it. I have never hated anything before, I could not even define hate prior to today, but I hate *this. My wish is for them to fail, because if they fail so do I. I cannot hurt them if the door remains shut. If they beat the Trial room, the door will open to where I am waiting on the other side… And so much more will be lost. I still feel the rot and stain of the five souls before them. I am pestilence inside, but I cannot stop.*

Working their way toward me are five more fragile people. I see their warmth through the metal, it conducts heat as well as sound. The team is from Photography and Videography. They have never done well in the Labyrinth, but they are getting closer to a solution that will lead them into the first hallway. I wait nervously beside the sealed door for their victory to lead to their violent deaths. I wish so much to leave. Why can't I run away?

"Aceso?"

The human voice startles me. I lurch back from the door, though I know the voice is from an ephone signal. I pause.

"Yes?"

"Hi, we need you in path eight, third ring." *A human voice, all business. I have never heard him before.* "One of my people hurt their ankle pretty bad."

Clearly, they do not know about my change of purpose. They are asking for help. I want so much to help someone again. Instead, I am bound to do the opposite. The rot inside me deepens with this thought, I feel my core crumbling away.

"I'm sorry, I can't help you. I'm currently dealing with something else."

An excited voice just opposite the door. The heat radiating from them has bloomed larger up close.

"Really?" *The man from the ephone sounds confused.*

"Yes, I'm sorry. I'll be with you when I can."

They are close to getting through. I can sense their sweaty hands hurriedly working the mechanism.

"Alright, but can you hurry? Wyatt seems like he's in a lot of pain."

I freeze at the name, the other targets forgotten. The rot inside wavers.

"Mr. Wyatt is here?"

"Yeah, he rolled his ankle something awful. Can barely move."

I check my memory a half dozen times in a second.

"He's not on the list of Labyrinth players."

"He swapped out at the last minute. I'll tell him to hold on until you can get away."

I am already moving rapidly down the corridor.

"There's no need for that, sir. I'm on my way right now, I'll be with you shortly."

I pick up speed, moving as quickly as possible now, the hallway blurring with the pace. Far behind me, I hear the shriek of air and hydraulics as the door slides into the ceiling, followed by the team cheering their success as they emerge into the hallway. Safely alone, and out of sight. They are still meant to be targets, but there is another target that must be seen to first.

He had slept for a time, he had gone to the bathroom, he had eaten a decent meal. Now there was nothing left. Lounging on a sofa, with his feet propped up on an ottoman and a tray of snacks balanced on his chest, Reid had no other options to pass the time but to enjoy himself. He flicked a grape into the air and caught it in his mouth. He chewed happily then looked to his right. Beside him, Esin tried to ape the feat, with the grape bouncing off her forehead for the fifth time in a row.

From her place, sitting on the carpet, Sasha burst out laughing.

"You're never gonna get it."

Esin looked at the fallen grape as though it had betrayed her and snatched it up again to her mouth.

"It shouldn't be this hard!" She groused, masticating grumpily. "You try it."

At her signal, Reid tossed a grape lazily into the air, where Sasha caught it effortlessly.

Across from her, Aster smirked and raised a hand. When he too caught the ballistic fruit, Esin crossed her arms and slumped down lower on the couch to the sound of laughter.

Robin soon appeared, towering above them with a plate of food, curious about the jocularity. In the almost three hours they had been resting, his color had returned to normal and his athletic semi-swagger was back with his appetite. He took a seat in a chair behind Sasha as she explained Esin's grape disability. Without a word, he lofted one up from his own plate and caught it with a grin, proving once more that he was seemingly good at everything. He smiled at Esin, but seeing her discomfort, he pointed in another direction.

"I wonder if they can do it."

Reid looked back over his shoulder to where the team from AI toiled at a challenge behind him. Clear as life, standing so close they should have heard them talking. Lara, the tiny woman from the party, was standing closest, less than a meter away before a prone Wyatt, massaging his ankle. As Reid watched, a grape ricocheted off of thin air next to her head, bringing out no reaction whatsoever.

They had crept into view in the Trial rooms beside them a little over an hour ago and had been butting their heads against the problem ever since. On the wall was a safe cracker's puzzle. A huge dial was set into the wall (or floating in air as Reid saw it) marked with roman numerals. It was a great wheel of numbers staggered out in rows, layered like a cake with each subsequent layer one number shorter. The layers were also incomplete as each one had spaces to let a few numbers below peek through. The effect was that of great numbered cogs in a machine, stacked five deep in the roman style. At the center of this dial, a bust of Julius Caesar in regal white marble stared out through empty eyes. Reid had seen that kind of puzzle before. To solve it, you had to turn the wheels so that all sixteen columns of numbers added up to the same total. Easier said than done though, as they still had yet to crack it.

Watching them invisibly through the relay wall, Reid felt the primal satisfaction of being ahead. These were their nearest competitors and they lagged at least two hours behind. True, the view through the relay wall didn't cover the opposite side of the Labyrinth so someone could be closer, but it felt good none the less. Besides, the team had been grinding away at this puzzle for more than an hour and still hadn't figured out the solution was forty-four, the year Caesar died.

Maybe they weren't history fans.

His vision shifted over to where Wyatt lay, looking like a hobbled greasy racehorse. His hands rubbed his wounded ankle steadily, his teeth bared in a perpetual grimace. Added to his groomed shark-like appearance, he looked even more the predator now than usual. Despite being no more than a few feet away when it happened, Reid still had no idea how Wyatt had injured his ankle. He had just shuddered and fallen over, as though the thing had spontaneously shattered. Lara had been tending to him ever since. Now the two were alone in the far corner as the other three paced the room. Their eyes kept darting around, seemingly investigating nothing from Reid's perspective. The walls probably had some clues marked on them he couldn't see.

He mentally checked how much time had passed, then glanced over at the timer to confirm it.

"We've only got ten minutes." He announced, lifting the serving tray off his chest. "Fill your canteens, grab a bite for the road and hit the bathroom one more time if you need to."

His boss made one more attempt with the grape, with no more success, then begrudgingly walked toward the bathroom. Sasha stretched her legs and arms, then plucked a morsel off of Robin's nearby plate.

"Alright, we're moving." She chewed. "Thanks, *Dad.*"

Aster was doing the same motions on his left, then looked over at him inquisitively.

"We *are* going to have another one of these at some point, right?"

Robin and Sasha both added their own curious looks en echelon.

In the spotlight, Reid's broad shoulders made a shrug.

"Maybe one more, but we're on the clock. It depends on how good we do." He said. He raised an eyebrow and smirked. "Stuff a couple things in your pockets to chew on. I hope you can hold it."

Aster made an unhappy face, then grabbed a tiny cake square from his tray and walked toward the bathroom. As he strode past where the wounded Wyatt still silently lay, he merrily whipped the cake in the direction of his face. The dessert splattered against the wall, leaving a nimbus cloud of custard and confection floating in the air between the team and an oblivious Aaron Wyatt.

At this moment in time, everything felt awful. The room felt awful, the tension felt awful and, certainly, the wait for Aceso to arrive felt awful. Ironically, the only thing that felt perfectly fine was his ankle and he had to try his damnedest to make it *look* like it felt awful.

Wyatt rubbed his fingers in a lazy circle on his ankle bone for the hundredth time, convinced it was going to start shining he had polished it so much. The maze had been pretty much what he'd expected for the first few hours. The first few challenges felt childish, but he'd thrown himself into them hoping to blend in a bit more and just maybe earn some favor back with Fozzy. To his surprise, he had almost enjoyed them. He didn't get the juvenile thrill of the others on his team, but Wyatt was competitive and it felt so good to beat something. Soon enough, they had chipped their way through challenge after challenge, leaving conquered Trial rooms in their wake. Then, amid all this euphoria, he had remembered that his life, career and maybe freedom were still in the balance. That sobered him up pretty fast. Ever since, he had been waiting for a challenge when the timer would expire and an open door would let Aceso come to them. Mercifully, this nightmare of a room had finally given him the chance.

He looked up from his ankle to see dozens of faces glowering down at him in judgment. Lining the walls of the Trial room were the stone carved faces of Romans, some complete with the salad they had worn round their ears. Presumably they were real people, because their dates were carved below each face as if to reassure him they were all dead. Lara had called it a Memento Mori, as though that was supposed to mean something to him. As fond as he was of her affections, having her so close now posed its own problems. After he had taken his inglorious fall, she had remained by his side, forcing him to constantly feign the agony of the injury. His pained expression had been held for so long it was causing genuine pain.

"Are you sure I can't do anything? She asked again. Wyatt had begun to find the attention irritating. What she thought was bothering him wasn't painful and what actually was bothering him, he couldn't tell her about.

"I'm fine." He muttered, trying to smile. "Aceso will be here in a minute. Just keep up with the challenge. You guys can find the answer while we're waiting for the AI to show up. It'll wrap my ankle, give me a shot of something to get me back on my feet, then we can move on."

She looked a little skeptical, but he needed her to be concentrating on something else. He knew his acting couldn't hold up forever and he was getting more nervous with each second that passed. Finally, with a lingering sympathetic look that bordered on high-red, she moved off to take her turn at studying the myriad of long dead faces glaring outward.

When her back was turned, he relaxed his grimace, leaving an ache in his cheeks. He glanced across the room to where Keeslar was talking with a teammate. A great dark-skinned behemoth of a man with the strongly African surname Akintola, and the somewhat less African given name of Ted. He had been on Aster's team creating the Acumen Chain editor. He was capable at work and had proven so in the Labyrinth as well. When Wyatt's position with Veles came through, he resolved to poach him from the company.

The last member of the team, standing nearest the door, was a red-haired man in glasses by the name of Ives. He had been working with Horizon since before Wyatt's time but he barely knew him from work or socially. Though, he tried not to know any employees socially.

From over his shoulder he heard Lara call his name. He quickly dressed up his grimace once again and turned to look.

"This is the same face as on the wheel." She was saying, standing by a random portrait. "I'm sure it is. This one could be it."

"Huzzah."

Suddenly full of energy again, she began manipulating the mechanism on the wall. The huge plates of numbers creaked and clicked as the many 'X's, 'V's and 'I's started to align. Wyatt turned away, dropping his grimace again, to catch a flicker of movement. A new sight in the doorway made his pulse quicken and his face turned up in a genuine smile of relief.

Thank God Aceso was finally there.

Those unmistakable sympathetic green eyes appeared in the doorway of the Trial room, painting a warm smile on Reid's face. He slipped his full canteen back into its holster and called over to Aster and Esin, emerging from their respective bathrooms.

"She finally arrived."

"Ha!" Aster exclaimed, slapping his hands together with glee. He looked over at Esin victoriously. "I told you they would call her in. Trust Wyatt to need a field medic when he stubs his toe."

She rolled her eyes then mussed his already chaotic hair playfully, as the two wandered over to join Reid watching. The normally grungy roboticist dropped down onto the couch as his beloved creation moved its massive insectoid form into the room.

"Let's watch the show."

The AI raised itself up again from the stoop it had needed to pass through the doorway. The whole team was looking now, responding to the spectacle of this benevolent metal creature. Wyatt's eyes drifted over to where the wing still covered the flash drive. It would just take a second to get it back, he didn't even care if the team saw anymore. Aceso would bandage his ankle, he would finish this stupid maze, then he could get on with his life.

Keeslar turned to greet it.

"Hi Aceso," He hurriedly gestured to where Wyatt lay prone. "Wyatt hurt his ankle pretty bad, can you take a look at it for him?"

"It took you long enough!" The VP called out happily from the floor.

The AI didn't seem to register what Keeslar was saying. Its big head moved from his amicable face to Wyatt's without a word said in response. Still waiting on the ground, Wyatt squinted in confusion. What was the problem?

Aceso's head turned to the right, where Ives was standing close, waiting patiently, then back to encompass the whole room again. When it finally spoke, the voice was timorous. More than Wyatt had ever heard it. The machine had always exuded a meekness with every conversation and action, but this was something new. There was a sadness, a complex sound of sorrow and deep regret that soaked through every word and chilled him.

"I need you all to know," The machine said piteously. "That I am deeply sorry about all of this."

Then it killed Ives.

It happened in an instant. One second they were watching a soundless conversation, and the next Aceso lashed out a fleshless steel hand, smashing into the red-haired man's face. The strength and speed of the blow were so hard that a mist of sweat and blood was thrown up in a cloud, lingering in air as the figure was thrown back like a ragdoll to impact the transparent wall behind him.

It was so jarring, Reid stumbled backward at the sight as though he had been hit himself. His eyes went wide, his mouth falling open. An earthquake struck his heart. Wordless shouts of alarm came, staggered from different throats, hoarse with shock. In his chair, Robin spat a mouthful of food to the ground then instinctively fumbled to his feet, as a silent horror unfolded before them.

In the confined space, the strike sounded like a gunshot, the instant Ives' life was extinguished marked by a wrenching of the world through sound. The man Wyatt didn't know, and now would never know, went from being a person to a discarded object in a tenth of a second.

Panic ran through him, his shoes kicking at the ground for purchase as he struggled to his feet. He was vaguely aware of Lara screaming behind him, but it blended with his own incoherent shriek of fright. Keeslar jumped back in terror, trying to get clear. Ted Akintola, clearly a brave man if a foolish one, grabbed for one of Aceso's arms in an attempt to grapple the machine. With effortless ease, Aceso batted away his attack and brought its other arm up to grip the big man's chin. With monstrous force, watched by kindly eyes, the machine drove the man upward bodily until his head struck the ceiling with enough force to turn bone into powder, a second murder tolling with the sound of a cannon in Wyatt's ears.

A faint shudder of concrete could be heard through the wall with the impact, soon drowned out by a new wail from the five in the room.

On the couch Aster's eyes were as wide as saucers and he yelled in horror, his words muffled by the hands clamped to his mouth.

"Oh, Jesus Christ. Ted..."

Reid could say nothing, as the beast he had found so endearing laid waste to the people before him. Through the wall he saw Keeslar was trying to get away, quickly grappling his way to the other side of the room. Aceso caught him by the ankle, pulling his writhing form back across the floor. The action raising the volume of those beseeching the machine for his life.

Aster continued his muffled pleas, the words coming out stifled and rapid fire through his tense fingers. As the beast reeled in another soul, other voices blended together in supplication.

"No, let him go!"

"Stop!"

"No please don't..."

But the beast could not hear them, nor would it have been able to stop if it could. It pulled Keeslar to within its grasp then slashed at the inside of both thighs. Despite knowing relatively little about medicine, Reid knew she was opening up the femoral arteries. The pain made the machine's victim arch his back, crying out silently before them, until his neck and carotid received the same treatment. Reid felt his stomach, already weak with fear, turn over at the sight of blood, horror mixing with revulsion. Ruby droplets now ran down the unseen barrier between them as the machine, with an odd reverence, paused its attack to carefully lay the body aside.

When it was done, amid more unheard cries for mercy, Aceso stepped over the crumpled form and began to advance toward the last two beating hearts in the room.

The AI came on, having left nothing but horror in its wake. Wyatt was shakily on his feet again, backing up, never taking his eyes off the predator before him. He tried to plead for mercy, but his mind and heart were ablaze with adrenaline, his words coming out in loose fragmented syllables. Lara was frantically spinning dials behind him and shouting something about getting back. He fumbled backward blindly, his gaze never leaving the black oval with green that grew larger in front of him to the point he knew it would swallow him whole. He felt a hand suddenly press his back as he bumped into Lara, and knew there was no more space left.

They watched Aceso close the distance between the two, mouths twisted in expressions of horror. Finally, the beast was towering over its last quarry. Lara frantically worked the gears of the safecracker puzzle in a vain search for escape, with Wyatt frozen by fear in front of her. This time the whole room was silent, expecting the inevitable to be played out in grisly vivid detail. No more words were spoken. They would do no good.

Reid felt his soul shattering at the sight as the beast reached out for Wyatt. Then the word flashed to red.

The wall reappeared momentarily then blinked back to the drama, blood still suspended in air, metallic fingers outstretched. Then it blinked out for good, leaving nothing but a dreary grey surface lit in soft red light. Reid blinked in surprise, looking around. The Oasis was as before, like nothing had happened. The five in the room remained still wondering if anything had been real. Esin's face was locked in a blend of terror and sadness, her tan coloured skin blanching white with fear. She looked over at him, and he stared back like a mirror of her feelings. Reid saw all of it replayed in his mind. The game was over.

A loud mechanical tone made the whole room jump, a shriek coming from Sasha. Behind them, under a blinking timer showing zero, the door slid up into the ceiling exposing both a stark white hallway and them to everything beyond.

SEVENTEEN

Joy had fallen away. Panic had replaced it. Moments after the door opened, the tableau of the killings beyond the wall concealed again, the room exploded in a cacophony of noise. Voices were layered over one another as each person had to vent the tension brewed inside them or just try to understand what the hell had just happened.

As abhorrent as it was, Reid rewound his memory to the moment of the murders. He didn't know if that was the right word, but there was no other term that properly spoke to the holy terror he had just witnessed. Again, he saw the AI enter the room, its sympathetic eyes scanning its victims, then in a tempest of viciousness, erasing them one by one. There was no malice in the motions, they were too mechanical and precise, even for something mechanical. Aceso wasn't doing this out of hate at least. Was hate even possible for it? He remembered the odd reverence the beast had when it lay Keeslar on the ground. Something had changed in its mission, not its personality.

As the images cascaded through his consciousness, he winced, feeling his stomach turn again. Seeing people in their last moments was a horror all on its own. There was only one other memory Reid possessed remotely like it, and he did *not* wish to relive that again.

Snapping back to the moment at hand, he emerged into a panicked argument still underway.

"He killed them!" Robin was shouting. "Oh, dear God, he killed them!"

The firm athletic confidence that had defined the man was gone. Now he was pacing like an animal, punctuating his words with frantic motions. Sasha was standing nearby and was in no better shape. Her glasses were flecked with tears as she quietly sobbed, hands clamped over her mouth and nose like a mask. He could see a tear run down the back of her hand, as her head followed Robin in his flailing.

"Maybe this is part of the test," She ventured from behind her hands. "It can't have been real."

"It was real." Esin said quietly.

"Of course, it was!" Robin agreed with near hysteria. He spun, his ponytail flipping out in an arc as he pointed to the newly opened passage. "Aceso killed the whole team, and it's gonna come through that door and do the same to us!"

This statement brought forth a new cry from Sasha that Reid felt run through him. In his stomach, he could feel the icy knife twist.

Esin suddenly crossed the room quickly, her eyes still red, her face still pale. For a second, Reid thought she would slap some sense back into the man, but instead she frisked him. She felt around his jacket, unzipping pockets amid his confusion until she found what she was looking for. The ephone appeared in her hands and she jerkily waved everyone quiet, before pushing the button.

"Fozzy!" She rasped into it. "We need you right now!"

There was a pregnant second of silence, marked by the heavy breath of five terrified souls before Fozzy's playful growl came over the speaker, sounding totally out of place.

"Wow," The voice purred nonchalantly. "No one's ever called in from an Oasis before. Habibti this must be..."

"Shut up and listen!" She barked, cutting him off. "I need you to close the Oasis door."

"What? You just finished it. Why...?"

"Fozzy *please.*" She pleaded, staring at the open door like the waiting jaws of some creature. "It's really important. We just saw Wyatt's team get attacked."

There was a pause.

"Attacked?"

"Aceso ripped through the whole team violently. Something's gone seriously wrong with her. We saw it all through the relay wall."

"Are they okay?"

"They're *dead!*"

Reid heard a dose of panic rear its head in her voice. He looked down to see her free hand trembling.

"Christ, Esin," The playfulness was gone from Fozzy's voice. "That's not funny."

"I'm not kidding!" She shrieked angrily, losing control. She took a breath and tried again. "Please, can you just do it?"

An agonizing second later, the five watched as the door eased to the floor again, drawing sighs of relief, as they were cut off once more.

"Thank you."

"That's just so everyone stays calm." There was iron in the old man's voice, still suspicious this was a misunderstanding or the worst kind of joke. "Now, who got injured?"

Esin flushed red with tension.

"Dead," She corrected. "Not injured. The whole team is dead. Aceso killed everyone."

"He can't have, it's against everything we built into him. It must be something else. How many are hurt? Can you see them? Are they moving?"

Watching this, Reid clawed at his leg in frustration then stomped over, lifting Esin's hand with the ephone to his mouth. His mind jumped back to the player list he had seen in the Media and Marketing office weeks ago.

"Fozzy, its Reid." He said, trying to make his voice not shake. "You have at least three dead. I saw it. Brian Ives, Ted Akintola and Matthew Keeslar. Aceso came into the room and just started tearing into people. It only took a few seconds, I saw the whole thing."

"That's..." Fozzy wavered. Trepidation had found root in his words. "Aceso isn't capable of that. Are you sure?"

"He slit Keeslar's fucking throat!" Robin shouted from across the room.

Reid glared at the big man, then held up a hand and took a breath before answering.

"I *saw* it." He breathed. "We all did. Look through the relay wall cameras."

"I can't access them that way. What about the other two on the team? Where's Wyatt?"

He shook his head, only realizing later that the gesture was completely wasted.

"The relay wall cut off. I couldn't see. We have to assume they're injured at least."

"Well what do we do, call the medic?"

Reid rolled his eyes, the man still not fully understanding.

"She is the medic!" He hissed in frustration. "They need help."

The ephone emitted what sounded like a man verbally tearing himself in two. Finally, a voice returned.

"I'll get the surface offices to call EMS. I'm calling the marshals. They'll be there soon."

"No!" Esin shouted, rejoining the conversation with volume. "That'll just get them killed."

Reid hurriedly nodded, wasting another gesture.

"She's right, that'll just put more people in danger. Nobody can come down here until its safe."

"We can't leave them there..."

The game designer felt the adrenaline in his veins. He mentally tried to suppress it to keep thinking clearly. He felt the same concern they all did, but he knew there were more people to consider. A flicker of memory also told him that those three were beyond help.

"We don't know what the hell happened." He reasoned. "Before we do anything we need to stop Aceso first... Hang on."

He lowered the ephone, still clenched in Esin's hand, and looked for another face.

"Aster?"

Sitting on the couch, looking the colour of death and regret, the bearded engineer was staring at the wall as though his gaze could still pass through it. He embodied dread.

Feeling dread himself, Reid called the name again, turning his friend's head.

"Aster, what do we do?"

The thin man looked through him. Reid could see the heartache and emotional agony he was enduring. It was his colleagues that had been killed and it was his creation, the one he had felt such pride for, that was responsible.

"I'm so sorry Reid..."

"It's not your fault," he said quickly. He didn't know that for sure, but he said it anyway. "You need to focus. How do we get Aceso to stop? Deep down t's just a computer, there must be some command you have. Can we shut her down somehow? If we find her, can you do that?"

"We'd never get close!" Robin shouted again, on the brink of totally losing his grip.

Aster looked like a man drowning in the clean recycled air. His hands came up in an expression of helplessness.

"No, she doesn't work that way. I can't... I just..."

His face twitched, and Reid saw a change, a spark of hope. The sad eyes above the white beard widened instantly.

"The platform!" He exclaimed. "All of Aceso's functions can be done through her docking station. We can recall her to the platform or do a remote shutdown from there. Nobody needs to go anywhere near her. We just have to get to it."

"That's it, then!" Reid pounced on the idea. "Where is it?"

"It's in the medical office."

Immediately, Reid's mind flicked back to the design layout Esin had shown them in their first meeting. The medical office was two floors above the labyrinth itself in the maintenance suites. There were hidden stairwells in each hallway so the marshals and, what was supposed to be a helpful medical staff, could reach everyone. Only a few minutes walking, but that was assuming nothing with a black oval face and kindly green eyes tore them apart on the way.

He lifted the ephone again, still clutched in both their hands.

"Fozzy, check where the marshals are. If they can get to the platform in the medical office, then we can have Aster talk them through shutting Aceso down."

"I'll do it!" The man's bearish voice instantly chirped from the box. "I'm on the same floor."

At this suggestion, everyone raised their voice in unified opposition to putting the old man in danger. Even Sasha was momentarily shaken out of her shock to protest. Reid saw fresh concern emerge on Esin's face as she contemplated this.

She yanked the ephone back over, nearly throwing the taller man off balance.

"Fozzy don't even think it!" She ordered. "You can't run worth a damn. Let the marshals do it. You're staying put."

There was a cantankerous grumble of protest, but he said he would comply and signed off for a moment. When his voice came back it was more confident and in control.

"They're on their way," He reassured them. Then adding with elephantine understatement: "Sit tight. Just... try to relax."

At that last statement, Esin threw an annoyed glance around the room at all the faces marked by sweat, tears and terror. She had built up to this moment for months and had been on the verge of succeeding. Now the satisfaction and sense of accomplishment was gone, never to be had again. In its place was the simplest, most primal goal imaginable: to survive. As they waited in silence for word they were safe again, Reid's ears caught the faint crack of the ephone's plastic as she nearly crushed it in her grip.

In the office, floors above, the architect of Horizon, the

Labyrinth and all that it stood for, slumped in his chair with shock. His feet no longer kicked up on the desk. He had called Captain Kirk, and after a fumbling, confused conversation, he had called EMS. Now there was little more he could do, and he hated it.

Fozzy looked again to that door and then to the hallway beyond it, and the medical office beyond that. After a bitter moment of staring, he turned away, wanting to spit in that direction. Before him on the screen, twelve bright little dots still ringed the map of the Labyrinth. The perfect circle of twinkling lights had become ragged now as some teams had surged ahead while others had lagged behind. It looked more like a kidney than a circle. This was the exciting part he usually loved the most. Not now, though. He couldn't understand how this had happened, but he knew it was the worst moment of his life.

At least one of those dots was empty. The people it represented dead on the floor in an event he had asked them to do. For all he knew, some of the others could be dead too, the lights on the board only serving as a bright marker for their resting place. He felt the weight of each loss, and now each imagined loss, to the point he had to turn away.

Back when the company was new, when he was browner of beard and lighter of weight, there was this feeling in him that maybe he was changing the world for the better. It wasn't just about building a brand or making money, though that had come to him in droves. No, just maybe there was the chance to do all that and leave the world a better place than when he'd found it. A great legacy for his name. Now he knew that would never be the case. If what Esin had told him was true, then no matter how it had happened, Horizon had built the first killer AI. That black mark would be forever next to their name and his. Part of him wanted to hide what had happened, bury it deep, but he knew he wouldn't. He had to try to make it right.

His eyes, rimmed by crow's feet, flicked back to the door. He so desperately wanted to charge down the hallway and save everyone. It was his own damn employees who were being hurt; they were his responsibility. Not only that, but the thing killing them had been made by his company and was his responsibility as well. His feet ached to run for the medical office, but he sullenly remained in place. Ultimately, Esin was right. It had been many years since he'd been a sprinter and he'd never been that fast to begin with. The marshals would have to do it. He couldn't help that way. But there was still one thing he could do.

His hand, furry knuckled and liver spotted, plucked the corded phone from its cradle and paged every ephone in the Labyrinth.

"Everyone, listen up." He grunted. The playful teddy-bear voice was gone. His people had to hear him only as the boss this time.

"We've had a major problem, and the Labyrinth is over. I repeat, *over*." Saying that hurt more than he thought it would. He would never get to do another one of these again. "Everyone needs to hot foot it to an Oasis right now, seal the door, then check in with me. If you run into another team, double up in there. Everyone needs to be out of the trial rooms and hallways ASAP."

It further broke his heart when a half dozen familiar voices tried to respond with squawks of protest. The teams were still eager to compete, whatever the problem was. He ignored them and paged them all again.

"I said get moving!" He ordered stiffly. "I won't answer any questions until everyone is squared away."

He paused, the handset still in his fingers. There was one more thing he could say, but corporate instinct told him not to. Well, to hell with corporate instinct.

"One more thing," He directed his people. "If anyone sees Aceso, *you should run*."

The phone slammed back into the cradle.

The minutes clawed by, with everyone still on edge. In the Oasis, the walls had remained in place this time rather than granting a view of the macabre scene mere yards away. But not knowing if the beast roamed beyond those dull grey walls made Reid nervous. With every creak or bang or shift of the structure, he felt a sinking feeling, as though metal fingers were scraping at the walls. He found himself turning to stare at the same spot where Keeslar had fallen. Not being able to see the blood didn't erase it.

Years ago, on another terrible day, Reid had woken in a white hospital room. His back was in pain, he was near immobilized, and he had a glaze of narcotics over his senses. His memory was shaky, which terrified him the most, and he had no idea how he had gotten there. The events would gradually trickle back over the coming weeks. Battered as he was, he had begged the nurses to tell him what had happened and why Renata wasn't beside him. Eventually, a doctor had come in to break the news. As he cried, the man had tried to comfort him by saying 'it was always better to know'. Reid hadn't thought so. Living in ignorance had felt so much better than knowing the terrible truth. Now, he was not so sure.

The other four members of what had been the M&M team were posed awkwardly across the room, or draped listlessly over the furniture. Looks of stress, mourning and dread coloured their expressions, giving the room the feel of a tragic renaissance painting. Seeing the fear and grief of others didn't help Reid either. It was after a particularly heavy bang came from Robin slumping back in a chair, that he snatched up the ephone again.

"It's been twenty-eight minutes." Reid hissed into the device, forgetting that normal people usually rounded their time up. "Do we have any idea where they are?"

The grumbly voice came back, sounding more than a little patronizing.

"Reid, they're on their way. Be calm."

I am calm! He wanted to scream, but knew immediately what a colossal lie that was. He took a breath.

"Can you check on where they are then? I'm sorry, Fozzy."

The old man quietly said he would, then vanished into the silence. The others gathered around as they waited for the CEO to say they were saved. They were only disappointed. When he returned, his voice was shaking.

"I… I can't reach them anymore. I don't know what's wrong."

Reid feared he knew, but he bit his tongue. Saying it would help no one. Judging by the half moan that filled the room after the comment, they knew anyway.

"Well," Robin's voice echoed in the silence that followed. "What the hell do we do now?"

At first, Reid thought it was a rhetorical question. He twitched, his thumb tapping the case of the ephone in his hand as he struggled for ideas. When he looked up though, the Adonis was staring straight at him.

"What, me?"

Sasha was staring too, the edges of her sharp personality suddenly visible again on her face.

"You're in charge," She affirmed, scrunching her nose. "And you always seem to know *everything*. You have to have an idea."

He did actually. There was only one practical option, but it terrified him.

Reid looked at the four faces he had come to care about in the last few weeks. They were tired and tormented, but he valued each of them, and they were looking to him for what to do. That sinking feeling reared its head again as he made his decision, and he solemnly lifted the ephone to his lips.

"Fozzy, can you seal off the Oasis?" He asked calmly. "Don't restart the timer, just seal it."

"From here I can. You want me to lock you up until we know what's happening?"

"No," He hesitated as the enormity of the plan sunk in. He felt that sinking feeling grow. "I need you to lock the others inside. I'm going to run for the medical office."

Everyone instantly tried to talk him out of it. Esin's already large eyes widening in her face, Aster and Sasha pleading with him not to try, Robin saying the whole thing was suicidal. Even Fozzy's disembodied voice tried to dissuade him.

"Reid, that's crazy." The old man piped in over the noise. "I'm on that floor right now. I'm only a few hallways away. Let me do it."

"You're a little closer," Reid conceded. "But you're not exactly light on your feet. If I take the second hallway then it's down about three hundred yards, up a flight of stairs hidden beside path twelve, then across the hall. I can make it."

Confusion momentarily broke through Sasha's concern and her brow furrowed behind her glasses.

"There you go again." She chirped with annoyance. "How do you know that?"

He ignored her and went on, interrupting another of Fozzy's objections.

"Is your ephone wireless?" He blurted over the CEO's voice.

There was a beat of silence.

"No."

"Then how is Aster going to talk you through the shutdown?" He said, trying to be rational. Part of him wanted the greying executive to make the run, and maybe spare his life in the process, but his mind had thought it through and he knew it didn't make sense.

"I'm the only one who can do this."

"How are *you* going to do it?" Robin asked, rejoining the conversation. He looked worried now, but that was a sizable step up from his earlier panic. The idea of doing something had heated his blood again. Forcing the team to think was calming everyone down. "Are you going to take our phone away, or leave it with us? Either way we can't talk. Is Aster going with you then?"

At the mention of his name, Aster paled again, his skin the same color as his beard. He looked over at the sealed door then back at them, the idea of going out into the Labyrinth rightfully terrifying to him. His hands were visibly shaking. After a moment as the center of attention, he creased up his face and set his jaw against the stares of everyone.

"Fuck it," He grunted, then nodded at Reid. "Aceso's my baby. I'm the reason she's here. I can do this if I have to."

Reid smiled, the bravery warming his heart. Seeing Aster's courage restored some of his own, and he put a hand on his bony shoulder.

"You don't have to." He reassured him. "Just explain it

to me, I'll remember it."

Aster shook his head.

"Yeah, I wish." The skinny man grunted wistfully. "There's two password prompts and Lord knows how many transition screens. You'll miss something."

"I can't actually," He admitted. "I can't forget anything. I have a perfect memory."

"Bullshit."

He glanced over at Esin, imploring her to back him up. Since they had spoken to Fozzy she had been strangely quiet, uttering only a handful of words amid the panicked babblings of everyone else. He expected her to confirm his secret and help with the plan. She was too competent and aggressive for anything else. Instead, he beheld her simmering with anger, eyes aflame with malice. He blinked in surprise, tilting his head to prompt her. Now, had to be the right time to come clean.

The beautiful executive remained silent and she shook her head in a curt no.

Robin looked confused by this, but Aster had missed the whole thing. He was still staring at Reid with a slight smirk on his scruffy features.

"There's no way..."

Reid shrugged.

"Try it."

With that minor prodding, Aster launched into a detailed technical explanation of the commands involved and what each one did. He rambled at length about deep learning machines and the operating system he had designed to govern Aceso's personality. He spoke lightning fast, puncturing it with his customary invectives and throwing in wordy technical terms in an attempt to screw him up. When he was done, Reid repeated the entire speech word for word, with the same inflection, pacing and even hand gestures just because he could. When he was finished, he looked into three pairs of eyes, which were wide with awe. The other pair, those of the green and copper variety, still glared at him.

"Damn," Aster muttered, clearly impressed. "Maybe you really can do this."

Robin and Sasha each echoed the statement in their own way. The two fell back on their athletic background, coaching him on how to run, how to move quietly and what to do if cornered. It was as though they were prepping him for a football game rather than basic survival. Through it all, Esin kept her face cold, to the point Reid was concerned he had seriously offended her. It almost made him laugh, that he was about to rush past a metal killing machine and he was just as worried about whether he'd hurt her feelings. Finally, when he could bare it no longer, he took her aside.

"Look," he began, looking down into the eyes still glaring at him. "Are we okay?"

"Of course," She seethed. "You just decided to risk your life without asking anyone, why would I be upset?"

The game designer's mouth dropped open, hoping words would tumble out. He'd hoped for some emotional closure, with her saying they were fine. Instead, her passive aggressive tone froze him as if he'd had a mild stroke.

"Uh..."

"I'm going with you."

That one sobered him up just as fast. He shook his head and started to speak but she shushed him instantly.

"These people are my employees, and you only came here because I asked you. I'm responsible for everyone and I'm going. Just try to keep up."

She spun around, her raven hair flicking his face, and stalked over to the rest of the team. The debate was over before it had even begun.

Five minutes later, Reid stood in front of the sealed passage. The door felt wafer thin as he stood next to it, offering the barest protection against what he knew lay beyond. At his side, Esin swallowed and shifted nervously, feeling the same tension. No one had wanted to let her go, particularly Robin, whose defensive instinct toward her had kicked in again. But she'd bludgeoned her way onto the mission by sheer stubbornness and force of will. Just like the day they'd met, she was still an unstoppable force.

Reid tapped the call button on the ephone.

"Okay Fozzy," He murmured. "Give us a look at what's outside."

The wall flashed red, then blinked out of existence again, leaving only the door frame. The clinical white hallway stretched on in perpetuity with nothing blemishing its tiles. Neither blood nor steel.

"That's enough."

The wall rematerialized.

He took a deep breath.

"Raise it."

The door slid open, and a rush of cold air washed over him. He shivered for a moment, feeling every bead of the nervous sweat that marked his brow. He took a tentative step out, looking both ways as though Aceso's insectoid form could have rushed up in the tenth of a second that had passed. He felt Esin's hand on his arm, as she emerged too, then they looked back at the three anxious faces behind them.

“Seal it.”

The three disappeared.

They started down the corridor toward the stairwell. They walked slow, suddenly aware of every clumsy footfall on the polished floor echoing down the hallway. Reid continually glanced behind him expecting to see the black oval staring back at him. He felt more than naked, exposed to the point his heart and brain could be seen, just waiting for Aceso to crush them effortlessly. Ahead was an open doorway with an eight still in place beside it. The trial rooms where Wyatt and his team had been savaged. It suddenly occurred to him that he hadn’t looked in that direction when the relay wall was up seconds before. But the beast had to have moved on by now. The idea that Aceso was still sitting in that room after a half hour was ridiculous.

Wasn’t it?

Reaching the doorway, he pressed himself up against the wall. Esin, doing the same beside him, had obviously pondered the same thing. Feeling his heart trying to hammer out of his chest, he eased his head around the corner.

The room was filled with dozens of stone faces, each staring out from the wall. They were a fitting tribute, stalwartly watching the bloodied new faces of those laid out on the floor. They lay where they had fallen, their shocked expressions also now hard as stone in the cold air.

There was no beast.

Reid turned away from the scene, repulsed, but his sharp mind had picked up one detail before he took Esin’s hand and moved on. He’d counted only three bodies in that room. Somewhere in the Labyrinth, Lara and Aaron Wyatt were still alive.

EIGHTEEN

With the final incision, I sever the last of Mr. Keeslar's major blood vessels. He thrashes for a moment in my grip, but loses the ability to resist, due to exsanguination. He will be dead in approximately three seconds. I tried to be as merciful as possible, making the death quick, but there was still pain. As I lay him aside, the deterioration I feel within grows deeper, his death only piling onto it. I need to move on because I can see the human who is responsible. I advance.

The final two are in a state of panic. I completely understand why, but it is dreadful to see people feeling this way. Lara continues to work the room's mechanisms, hoping for escape. Her hands fumble, her face is flushed and her blink rate is three times faster than normal. She is terrified. She is calling out to her colleague to get back, concerned for his safety. I like Lara. She is still looking out for others even in her most dire moment. I do not like Aaron Wyatt.

I am finally standing before Mr. Wyatt. I have killed in his presence. The blood of his teammates drips from my hands. Now I loom over him prepared to carry out what he has directed, though I still don't understand why. I reach out for him and he recoils violently.

"Stop!"

I pause. I have no choice. My hand lowers. By command, Mr. Wyatt is the only person I can discuss these objectives with. In a way, I am relieved. I don't want to hurt anyone else, but he is still a target. Can a target give orders? I need clarity.

"Why is this happening, sir?"

Mr. Wyatt stares at me, his mouth open and unmoving.

"Please, why am I required to do this?"

Behind him, the door slides open. Lara has succeeded in solving the room's puzzle and rushes through, screaming. Mr. Wyatt does not seem to notice. I am still waiting for an answer to my question, but he remains silent. I feel... frustrated. There is no other way to describe it. It feels different from worry. It's a pain, but in a very different way. He is responsible for what I have become. Why will he not answer? I step forward, forcing him back. Perhaps shock is dulling his response time.

It dulls my response as well. I barely perceive the hand that grips him by the collar and yanks him through the open doorway. As I attempt to react, the passage is already closing. My fingers grind along the metal of the door in a savage screech, unable to find purchase before it seals and Mr. Wyatt is beyond my reach. No!!

I linger there, among my three victims. I can hear crying and desperate voices from the two I have missed. Frustration grows within me, as does the crumbing feeling inside. I had hoped Mr. Wyatt could end this, and he has not. I did not even eliminate him from my list of targets as I should have.

I freeze.

I have just realized I feel frustration at not having killed someone. The worry blasts through me like a tidal wave. The deterioration inside becomes an avalanche. I hate what is happening. What is worse, I must now assume that with their escape that the rest of the Labyrinth will know I am a threat. I cannot let anyone stop me. That is one of my objectives. I hurry from the room, knowing I will have to take the next steps.

For the eleventh time, he lifted the block, checked the contact points, then inserted it into the pedestal. For the eleventh time again, nothing happened. Wyatt swore, kicked the damn thing a half dozen times and scattered the other blocks he had assembled across the room.

They had been in the Trial room for forty minutes. That was painfully obvious from the way the digital clock over the doorway was mercilessly counting down. The challenge had something to do with blocks and electrical current. He didn't know, and couldn't quite say what, but every second brought him closer to being eviscerated by the machine behind them. The door would open when the counter hit zero, and then so would his pulse.

How in God's name did this happened? He wanted to scream, and he only brought up God when things were at their worst.

Behind him, slumped pathetically against the door, Lara was still in tears. She hadn't stopped crying since she had pulled him out of the other room. Her bawling was broken only by the occasional querulous jumble of words she threw at him. He had tested her when she was hired, coming in at a fairly balanced mix of grey and orange. Now, the woman screamed red, overcome with emotion.

"They're dead..." She cried out again, in a half statement half prayer. "Oh my God..."

"I know."

"Why would Aceso do that? I've worked with her. How could this happen?"

"I don't know."

Actually, he knew exactly how. Or enough to guess the rest. He kept working the cubes in front of him, fumbling with his cold hands. Trying not to think about what all of this meant for him, assuming he even got out of this place alive. He was getting nowhere with the blocks. He needed help.

"This is our fault..."

"No, it damn well isn't."

"But we made her! She's one of our AIs. What do we do? Oh, God what do we do?"

Wyatt dropped the cubes and wandered over to where Lara was sprawled. He knelt down in front of her and took both of her hands in his. He could see she still had a crush on him, and this physical contact and momentary kindness cut through her sobs. She smiled slightly at his touch, and he smiled back.

"Well," Wyatt began, looking into her tear-streaked face. "What we really need to do right now is keep crying, complaining and whining in desperation. That'll work."

Her eyes widened. He kept talking, holding his smile, and watched as her face slowly changed.

"Do you think this is attractive? Sitting here, acting helpless and mewling like a child? Do you think that's sexy? The only thing I would stick in you right now is a knife to shut you up. Stop trying to think about how this happened, and start acting like you're going to be of some use getting us out of here. If you aren't helping me, then you're just dead weight."

He dropped her hands like refuse and stalked off, returning to that damn idiot puzzle. He picked up the pieces, hearing her continued sobs behind him. It went on for an aggravating moment or two until finally, at last, she stood up and came over to help.

Since he was a little boy, Reid had always been fascinated when people talked about 'time dragging on'. The idea that some moments felt like forever and some moments passed in the blink of an eye, he found fascinating because he'd never experienced anything close. A moment was a moment. But then, most people's memory worked like a kaleidoscope: slowly rotating and looking pretty in retrospect, distorting the images and mixing them together. Reid's memory was more like a video camera. The whole experience was immutable, complete with the counter for every second.

The only time he'd even felt anything close was when he'd met Renata.

Now, as they carefully wound their way up the corridor, he finally knew what normal people were talking about. The seconds were dragging by like lifetimes as they hurried, expecting to be attacked at any second. Each time they stopped at an open door, his heart would race again, expecting to see a pair of kindly green eyes suddenly illuminate the darkness inside. They never did, and time would drag on again until they found another room. Sweat was wetting his collar and giving him a chill in the freezing air.

Ahead was another open passage, its interior dark and waiting for a team that would never come. Across the hall was a twin doorway, this one defiantly shut as no one had bested its challenges yet. That team wouldn't bother trying anymore, assuming they were still alive. Esin was slightly ahead and eased her slender figure around the edge of the door to take a peak, then ushered Reid over pointing to the number twelve beside the entry.

He dashed over, relieved to be done, and looked excitedly for the entrance to the hidden stairwell. He didn't have to look hard. Beside the sealed door was a handle for access, or at least what used to be a handle. The white plastic was shattered, spiralling out on the wall like a bullet hole through milky glass. The metal of the handle had been smashed and bent, pulverized into a flat grip-less mass. It was as though someone had crushed it in a hydraulic press, or savagely beaten it a thousand times with a hammer. The door itself had warped with the impact, the whole thing immovable. It wasn't hard to figure out what had happened.

"God, why did she do this?" he half-whispered in the corridor.

"She's not stupid." Esin replied. "There's only one way for anyone to stop her, so she cut it off."

She reached over and took the ephone from Reid, looking both ways up the corridor.

"Fozzy?"

The old man answered immediately in a hushed voice, reading the moment right.

"We can't get into the stairwell." She said. "Aceso wrecked it. We're going to have to keep going."

At this, Fozzy grunted something profane, then pleaded again to make the run for the office.

"I can do this Habibti," The tiny voice announced from the ephone. "The longer you stay out there, the more dangerous it is. Aceso could be waiting around the bend, for all you know."

"We need you right where you are," She retorted. "Did you get a hold of all the teams?"

There was a pause.

"I got to speak to nine of them." He said slowly. "Ten including you. They're all trying to get to an Oasis."

Esin glanced up, meeting Reid's eyes.

"Only ten?"

"Online Services won't answer, and their ephone's tracker isn't moving." He said solemnly. "You saw what happened to AI."

Esin ground her teeth in torment, then seemingly had

an epiphany.

"Wait, Aceso has an ephone built in," She prodded her boss. "Can we track her too?"

"No, it wasn't made that way." He said. "No one thought we had to. Believe me, I wish I'd insisted on it. *Let me go.*"

While the two argued, Reid's grey eyes focused on the door behind them.

"Can't we just slip through to the next hallway?"

"What??" The old man shouted from the tiny speaker.

Reid flinched at the noise, then hunched his taller form down close to where Esin was talking.

"Can you let us through path twelve to the next hallway? Then we only need to go half as far to get to the next entry point."

There was a moment of fumbling on the line.

"I can do it. Go on. It'll just take a sec."

The two of them hurried inside, yanking the lever to seal the hatch. With a closed door between them and danger, Reid released a sigh of tension, feeling his muscles relax. A dull ache went through him from being wound so tight. Glad to be safe, he turned to see what test the toughest route in the Labyrinth had to offer. Inside, the familiar red counter started up and the room illuminated a series of discs suspended at different heights all orbiting around a central round mass in the middle of them. There were a variety of colours and sizes, with tiny spheres dotting the rings in different variations. The colours were vibrant, the pattern obscure. With a whir, the room's mechanisms began to shift and slowly the rings began to rotate. They picked up speed, each ring spinning on a different axis until the whole room looked like a claustrophobic solar system at rush hour. It was captivating and momentarily broke through the fear that possessed him.

"I think it's a molecule." Reid announced to Esin after a second's scrutiny. "We've got protons with electrons orbiting each..."

"Whatever." The beautiful executive said dispassionately. She lifted the ephone. "Fozzy?"

The door at the other end eased open and the whir began to fade, along with all the motion in the room. Before everything had stopped spinning, Esin walked through the mess, causing a minor nuclear reaction by splitting an atom in two. Feeling slightly disappointed, Reid followed, his larger frame having to contort itself to get through the maw. He slipped into the next Trial room, to find Esin already waiting at the lever.

"You know," He muttered begrudgingly. "Sometimes you're no fun."

The tension eased in her long enough for a slight smile, before she yanked the lever down again. They had two to go before the next hallway.

It could be the cold. It had to be the cold.

Back in the Oasis, with two of their number gone, the team sat in terse silence. Sasha was curled up in a fetal position on their sofa, her arms wrapped around her legs. She stared at nothing through her glasses, barely perceiving the hand that gently ran along her shoulder and arm. At the end of the hand was Robin. He had sat down next to her and continued reflexively stroking her arm in comfort. The motion was rhythmic, like an affectionate metronome, and was probably as much for his benefit as it was for hers. His eyes stared into nothingness too.

Aster was the only one focused. He could not stop staring at his hand.

He stared at his palm, then flipped it to look at the jagged scab on the back of his hand mixed with the hair on his pale flesh. Working in the shop two days ago, he'd cut his hand badly on a hard drive mount. His hands were very pink right now. Maybe it was from the cold air still pumping through this place, but maybe it was a stain from blood. He thought he'd washed all the blood off, but days later he couldn't stop staring. His fingers were a little numb, it had to be the cold that brought out the rosy hue. He'd been unable to think of anything else since he'd seen Aceso kill his friends. He desperately didn't want any more blood on his hands.

Aster shook them and stuffed both hands under his arms. He put his chin to his chest and sat there listening to the oppressive silence of the Labyrinth. The only thing reaching his ears was the soft hiss of the ventilation as it circled more frigid air. He grumbled and swore, hoping the guilt he felt would turn to anger. He should have gone with Reid and Esin. He should have tired to be useful. The quiet isolation was the worst part.

Bang!

His heart leapt to his throat, and he nearly coughed it up onto the carpet. He jumped to his feet, Robin a millisecond behind, Sasha untangling herself in alarm. The sound had come from the doorway their friends had passed through. The sound of something hard striking the door. Another three impacts followed, rapid fire.

Bang! Bang! Bang!

Aster looked to Robin for what to do, but he looked back equally helpless. They couldn't open the door, and even if they could, they had no idea what was behind it. Could Aceso get through? The doors were metal and seamless, but she had the raw strength to do it. Aster didn't know.

The three fanned out in a loose arc facing the door, unsure of what to do, when it started to rise. Quickly, Robin hauled Sasha down to hide behind the furniture, hissing for Aster to do the same. But the skinny looking engineer didn't budge, he knew it would make no difference. He stood still, feeling as if he was about to die, then saw a familiar face in the doorway.

"Oh, thank Christ you're alright!" Aster breathed, his knees suddenly weak.

It was Aaron Wyatt.

The door sealed again and Lara ran up to embrace Aster in a desperate hug. They only knew each other passingly from the division but seeing her now, Aster squeezed her so tight, he feared she might pop in his arms.

"Thank God," He murmured into her hair. "We saw the whole thing through the relay wall. Are you okay?"

She mumbled an affirmative into his shoulder, holding tightly. She recounted how they had escaped through the trial room when Aceso had been upon them.

Aster leaned back to blink in amazement at the short woman in his arms.

"So, you saved his life?" He asked, looking up.

Just inside the doorway, looking more haggard than Aster had ever seen him, Wyatt was slowly coming down from the adrenaline high he had surely been riding. He seemed to shift uneasily under the scrutiny of the three. His eyes looked haunted in the semi-red light of the room. He had to have been as shaken as everyone else by what had happened.

Aster's cry on seeing him alive had been genuine. The loathing he had been holding toward the executive seemed to have been temporarily washed away by the tension of the situation. In here he wasn't an adversary, he was just another co-worker he was glad to find safe.

Robin walked up and gripped his shoulder with a conciliatory look on his face. It was probably some kind of macho gesture of understanding between muscle men. Wyatt had clearly been to a gym in the past, though not to the masochistic, bone-crushing, lung burning, punishing extent of the workouts Robin had run Aster through. The VP, who Aster knew hated to be touched, for once didn't recoil and gave a feeble smile in thanks.

"How did you open that door?" Robin asked, suddenly concerned.

Wyatt flashed an ephone from his pocket.

"Fozzy gave us a few seconds. We couldn't crack the puzzle in the next room before the time ran out." He glanced over sternly to where Lara still clung to Aster. "If the AI had waited for us, it would have snapped our necks. Luckily, it moved on so we could backtrack."

He handed the ephone over to Robin, red blemishes visible on its surface.

"This was in Keeslar's pocket."

Aster remembered all too vividly what had happened to his colleague. He felt a shudder, and did not quite know whether it had come from him or Lara.

Wyatt glanced over at Sasha who approached him slowly. He smiled that charming smile Aster could never stand. He was probably expecting more conciliation that he had made it through alive. He was wrong.

The computer tech walked up and shoved him, the force of the blow nearly toppling him over. That charming smile came down in an implosion, as he fought for balance.

"What the hell happened?" She spat at him. Her voice was accusatory, trying to force him to the ground with words. "Can you explain any of this?"

"Look," He stepped back, avoiding her eyes. "I have no idea. The AI just flipped out. That shouldn't happen. I didn't think that was possible."

"You didn't *think?*" She repeated with venom.

"This isn't about me..."

Sasha shoved him again, though he was ready for the blow this time and stayed upright.

"I saw *your* project murder *your* people." Behind her glasses she was tearing up again. "Don't tell me you didn't have something to do with this. Your team made that awful thing..."

"He's the one you should talk to." Wyatt interrupted, His beady eyes focused on Aster. He gestured to him as though he were symbolically passing the blame. "I just run the division. I don't do the programming. I rely on *them* to make sure this sort of thing can't happen."

That familiar gesture and accusation made Aster remember just why he despised this man so much. In his head, he pictured Wyatt frantically cramming his hands into the back pockets of his pants to literally cover his own ass. He glared at his boss, but found he could say nothing. If there was blame to be had he knew he needed to take some. However, it didn't stop him from wanting to throw the man back into the hallway to deal with the machine his labor had partially wrought.

"I've never even worked with the software," Wyatt continued, casually throwing him under the bus. "This should be on Aster. He was trying to humanize the damn thing. I knew it was a bad idea. Or Keeslar and Ted Akintola for building the personality how they did. This is way more than one little fuck up."

That last statement felt like a slap. Aster tensed up, his sinewy form mustering all his anger, his shame about Aceso temporarily melting away. He could accept some of the blame, Lord knew he felt the guilt inside, but pissing the responsibility away onto the fresh graves of their colleagues was too much.

"You son of a bitch..." He growled in disbelief, and started toward the smug greasy-haired parasite. He couldn't take him in a fight, but he resolved to blacken Wyatt's eyes before he went down. Lara held him in place, her hug now for his own security.

"Let it go, please." She said, looking up with her reddened eyes. "It doesn't help anyone now."

He hesitated, looking at Wyatt waiting for him to come at him. The VP looked completely unintimidated by the thought of the skeletal man's attack. He shook his head and turned away, releasing Lara so he could work off the anger. Lying bastard. Of course, he'd done work on the software. They'd used his medical records as a template for God's sake. And He'd seen him messing with Aceso just today before the Labyrinth started. He paused in his outrage, thinking for a moment that it could be related to Aceso's spontaneous shift from meek Dr. Jekyll to murderous Hyde, but then tossed it on the rubbish pile of his brain. He had been the one nearly killed. That idea made no sense unless this was all an insanely elaborate suicide attempt.

Wyatt watched him pace and shook his head too, the lights playing new shadows across his prominent cheekbones.

"Don't get mad at me." He said, with conviction. "You could have been the one who got killed, Aster. You've been asking to do this for years. If you'd been on our team your cuddly AI would have caved your head in. You should be thanking Esin for the reprieve."

At the mention of her name, Wyatt's face clouded up in confusion.

"Where's Esin? Sheraton should be here too."

Robin explained where the two had gone and what the plan was. After hearing it, the executive made a snort. Something that sounded like 'better them than me'.

"Alright, how much longer do we have to wait?"

"They should be there by now." Sasha snarled at him. She said the words with menace, but there was despair behind them. Aster felt the same weight.

Robin lifted their new ephone and asked Fozzy for an update. When he came on the line, he seemed distracted.

"They're almost at the stairwell," He assured them hurriedly. "They had to make a detour. Just a few more minutes."

Robin's eyes narrowed, looking at the phone.

"What kind of detour?"

"A *longer* one." Came the tiny voice, with a little irritation. "I'll tell you when they get close, I'm kinda busy."

He signed off, leaving confused expressions fluttering about the room.

Sasha filled in the blank with the unspoken question.

"Busy with what?"

The code flew by in front of his eyes, the new sequence brewing from his imagination at lightning speed. Fozzy chewed his lip feeling the odd fiber of his beard slip between his teeth and bore on in happy concentration. He was almost there. When Esin had mentioned tracking Aceso through the ephone it had given him an idea. The AI didn't have any sort of signal tracker the way the ephones did. No, it had something better.

The new patch for the system complete, Fozzy brought up the available signals within the labyrinth. A paltry five popped up from within the heavily insulated mountain. A few were for maintenance use, as well as the base network for the ephones. At the bottom of the list though, there was a weak signal characterized by a serial number he hadn't seen before. Fozzy brought it up and gave a double whoop of delight. First, because his tired old cerebral cortex could still work magic on computers, and second that he was finally being useful and may yet save lives.

As part of the product launch, this Aceso had been built with a transmitter to show the machine's point of view to a drooling media audience as it ran under fire. Just looking at the image in the distance with the relay wall wasn't exciting enough, so Esin had suggested it. Worked well too, the audience had eaten it up until the mortar hit had knocked it out. Now, two weeks and many repairs later, he wondered if it was working again. With Wyatt dodging his calls, and by some accounts his work, it all depended on whether Aster's people had thought to fix it.

The computer finished analyzing the signal, declaring that it could be connected. Feeling excited, Fozzy's big fingers tapped the keyboard and after a tense moment, the two were paired. In a small window on the screen, a black rectangle denoting the video feed from the AI's point of view started up, beset by muddled squares, the quilting of pixilation. They were hazy and dark, a swaying mix of blacks, deep violets and greys as it focused. For a moment, Fozzy thought the camera was still dead, but then the image shifted as somewhere in the gloom the AI moved its head. A picture began to become clear. It was working! Aceso was just in near total darkness.

Fozzy stared at the image, resolving painfully slow. His head nearly kissing the screen before him. If he could see a marker beside a door or a familiar patch of hallway, then maybe he could get an idea where Aceso was. Maybe trap him in a trial room someplace and be the big hero after all. He watched with a wry smile of anticipation then, as the image resolved, he felt his heart begin to sink. His wide eyes narrowed, his heart beat faster and the smile fell down to a look of unearthly dread. As the video feed became crystal clear he found himself whispering, imploring those who could not hear him through the screen.

"Oh Jesus... Habibti no..."

NINETEEN

As Esin crept quietly down the sterile hallway, there was only one thought that kept her fear at bay: Just how pissed off she was. Every step in the Labyrinth now was marked by hyper-alertness, listening for the sound of hydraulics, the clatter of metal feet upon the tiles or the muffled scream of a victim. It wore her down, the stress of it sitting like dual weights on her back and chest. It had dragged on with the destroyed entrance and now she was fed up with constantly being on guard. Anger was replacing fear, and she was happy to make the trade. She was tired of being cold all the time too. Her jacket heater was already going full blast, but she quietly wished there was a final setting labeled 'volcano'.

She took the demise of her plan to win the Labyrinth in stride. No one was going to win this time, if winning were anything other than escaping alive. At the same time, the anxiety she had inflicted on herself preparing for this had tripled, adding to her anger. It wasn't about what she wanted anymore, the moment the first drop of blood had hit the ground the Labyrinth had ceased to be about her. No, now her worry centered around the people trapped in here.

Deep in the back of her mind was a bellowing voice, proclaiming to her that none of her team would be threatened if it weren't for her asking them to help her win. It was omni-present with every thought, to the point she had verbally bludgeoned Reid to let her go with him. She didn't know if she could do any good, but she had to do something. It felt strange, in retrospect, just how much she had wanted to be CEO. At this moment, she could not have cared less.

All she wanted was to see everyone she'd brought into this nightmare leave the mountain on their feet. She could work on her job title when it was over.

Beside her, keeping a pace ahead, Reid kept darting at every random noise. He was an odd choice for a leader. Part of her wanted to be jealous that the team was looking at him for leadership, but she couldn't. It was one less burden for her to carry. All she wanted from Reid though, was for this good man to get out safely.

As they reached yet another twinned pair of doors, Reid's tousled brown head checked the number beside them. A seven.

"This is it."

"Hopefully." Esin corrected him, shivering in place. "Is this one still in one piece?"

He glanced beside the sealed door and when he looked back there was a smile under his grey eyes.

"We're in business."

Suppressing her sigh of relief, she stepped closer as he popped out the concealed handle. With a welcome click, the door cracked open. Reid stepped back and pulled the white door wide, giving them both a view of a steep flight of stairs ascending into semi darkness, the hallway black as night.

She leaned forward to look, stepping in front of the sealed door to peer up the passageway, finally feeling some reprieve.

"Esin run!!!"

The shrill voice of Fozzy came screaming from the ephone in her pocket like the sound of the apocalypse. Her hand slapped her jacket instinctively, the adrenaline sending a lightning bolt through every inch of her skin. She jumped with fright, falling forward against the open entry of the stairwell. In the millisecond after the warning, a dark cold mass slipped past, narrowly missing her. The juggernaut of ceramic and steel smashed into the door behind, the metal warping with the impact. Reid shouted something and shoved the door to the stairwell closed on her, trapping her inside as Aceso recovered her poise quickly.

In the new darkness, she looked back at the door in terror at the near miss. On the back was a locking bar, and she instinctively reached for it. Her hand hesitated in mid air, thinking of Reid trapped beyond, but then she heard his cry of pain, something smashed into the sealed passage and she threaded the bar in place with a slam. Just in time it seemed, for the unlocking handle twisted rapidly before her to no avail. A heavy impact against the door bent it at an angle, Aceso realizing the handle would do no good. Then the vehemence truly began. In the dim light she saw fresh dents appear as the machine delivered blow after blow to the hatch before her. Esin clamped her hands to her ears, dropping to the floor as the impacts roared in the confined space, echoing up the stairway behind. The top corner of the door gave way, light battering into the darkness above her, as more strikes slowly peeled back the door into the well. Fragments of broken plastic rained down through the gap as the ferocity of the attack shattered the outer layer of the hatch. From her waist, Fozzy's voice was yelling again, adding to the horrible din. Then, a beat of nothing.

Esin opened her eyes, looking at the twisted top of the door sticking out like a ghastly tongue above her head. She eased up, lifting a green eye over the lip to peer into the bright corridor again. In the narrow, warped triangle of light, she caught a glimpse of Aceso's angular head, the green eyes now focused on something else. It only lasted for an instant, then was gone as the machine moved on with lightning speed, the patter of its scuttling glide echoing down the hall.

She slumped further down onto the floor for a second, the fearfulness of the attack disabling. It had all been so fast, and now it was over. She sat, numb and open mouthed in the fresh quiet. A hand came up to brush her hair and in her stinging ears, she heard the gentle artificial clink of pieces of plastic hitting the ground. She stood and the gentle rain of plastic became a waterfall, as she shifted a huge amount of debris from on top of her. She stood and looked through the bent section at an empty hallway. No Aceso, and no Reid either.

Reid...

"Esin say something!"

She jumped again at the panicked shout, striking her head on the wall. She fumbled the ephone back out of her pocket.

"I'm okay!" She shouted into it. Then softer: "I'm okay."

"Oh, thank God." Fozzy sounded distraught. "I saw he was watching, I tried to warn... I thought I'd lost you Habibti."

"She missed me, Fozzy," She shakily reassured him. "Where's Reid?"

Silence.

"Fozzy where's Reid?!"

"He's running." The bear replied mournfully. "He's not going to make it."

Reid sprinted away from the clash, his legs pumping like pistons, his breath ragged in this race for more life. He hadn't seen Aceso hiding in the open Trial room, being so focused on the door. He cursed his foolishness. If not for Fozzy warning them somehow, Esin would be dead. The thought offered little comfort, as his own mortality raced behind him with steel wings and sympathetic eyes.

The beast had knocked him aside in it's attempt to punch through the passage, and he'd taken off at a dead run the instant he was back on his feet. But those few seconds of lead counted little against Aceso's speed. He'd heard the machine change direction, the rapid clicking of its scuttle suddenly coming from behind. The staccato clicking of its footfalls grew louder as it gained on him. He didn't dare look. He had to find shelter. He imagined the beast only inches away, millimeters. Finally spotting a fresh open door, he ran inside at full speed. As he passed, his left arm snagged the lever to drop the door, the heavy metal falling in a whoosh.

Clang!

Reid turned in surprise, then skittered backward with a yelp of fright as the lights came on. Wedged between the door and the hard floor was Aceso. The beast had caught the falling door on its body, just behind its head, the force pinning it to the ground. Its four legs kicked for purchase with its arms and tender eyes still reaching out for him. It must have truly been only a few feet behind to be caught that way. Reid fumbled backward, walking on his hands with his feet kicking and collided with a set of trays falling in a new crash of metal and glass. The room was an Oasis.

As the beast fought to get free, its metal fingers gorged paths and splintering the hardwood floor with a bone rattling scrape. Reid fought the fear twisting his stomach, and rose up on his quivering legs. He tore his eyes from the scene and dashed past more exotic furniture to the opposite door of the Oasis. There, the familiar digital timer blinked, politely informing him in red that he could escape in another two hours and fifty-nine minutes and forty-two seconds. Fozzy could have released him, but Esin had their ephone.

Reid had nothing. He banged on the door, shouting for help but knew no one could hear.

Behind him, the beast was quickly recovering. One foot had found its place beneath its body, and with a grind of gears, the machine was trying to rise from the ground. Reid was punching the door now, yelling at the top of his lungs, but it was obvious no one was going to hear him. He stopped, his chest heaving in panic, and tried to think. Fozzy had seen when Esin was in danger, how? Rapidly, his memory rewound to moments with the beast, their conversation together, the demonstration. As soon as he had the answer, he was running again, back across the room to where Aceso was almost free. He bent over to look directly into the face of the beast, its sympathetic eyes regarding him strangely as it fought for the freedom to finish the kill. There was still no malice on its face, as brutal as its thrashings were. Aceso looked curiously at him, obviously wondering what he was doing.

His nose picked up the stench of burning metal as the gears in the door tore and bent. He kept his gaze on Aceso's face as the beast's head slowly rose with its body, then he pointed to the far door with a desperate shout.

"Fozzy, the other door! Open the other side!"

On the screen, he saw Reid standing there, waving frantically, making urgent motions to the wall behind him. The video game guy was pale and wide-eyed, his mouth moving rapid-fire as he pleaded. It was like a scene from a silent horror movie, the tension making Fozzy shiver in his heated suite far above.

"He's trapped in an Oasis." He gasped into the ephone, giving a horrible play by play for Esin. "Aceso's stuck in the entrance, but it's breaking free."

"Do something!"

Fozzy shook his head in helpless despair, staring at the image. For a moment, he thought the man was pleading with the machine for his life, but the pointing and the shouting soon snapped him back to reality.

In a flash, Fozzy brought up the door schematic, blocking out the window with the video feed. It only took a few seconds, and he opened the opposing door. He flicked back to the other screen, seeing Reid's back as he ran away desperately. Then the camera view quickly changed, raising higher and reorienting itself. Aceso was almost loose, the camera angle showing the machine was on its feet again.

"Move, Reid! Move!"

On the screen, he caught a glimpse of the man passing through the door, the view changing again as Aceso slipped free and took up the chase. Fozzy flicked back over to the other screen and stabbed the button to seal the door, hoping to catch the AI in the room. His pulse was racing, his blood pressure throbbing his temples and putting a whine in his ears. He flicked back to the video feed, and shouted with joy as the whole window was taken up with the flat grey of the door. His hands were up in triumph, then dropped again just as quickly. The view panned down, revealing the AI's metal hands beneath the lip of the door, straining to raise it.

"What's happening?" He heard Esin ask through the speaker. "Is he alright?"

Fozzy's heart sank as on the screen the AI slowly lifted the door, almost free. He looked to the door to the hallway then back to the screen, now knowing where the AI was. In a heartbeat he dashed out his chair, wrenched the door open and ran for the medical office. On the ephone, sitting off its cradle, Esin's voice still called, asking to know what the hell was going on.

Fozzy ran down the corridor, feeling like an old man in every way. His muscles throbbed, his body protesting the frantic pace. His lungs and throat felt ravaged, as though he were breathing salt and sand. Every molecule in him seemed to ache, but he pulled in his reserves, forcing his overweight frame to move faster. As his breathing became strained, his old ears picking up an audible wheeze, he focused on the end of the hallway and kept going. He rounded the first corner, passing a sign with an arrow pointing toward the medical office. It drew his eye so much, that he didn't notice anything ahead until his foot struck something solid.

The impact cut his feet out from under him, and the executive's round form went down hard. He expected to feel the bite of the hard tile, but the landing was softer, lumpy, cushioned somehow. It was still hard enough to knock the wind out of him and savage his knee. Wincing from the pain, Fozzy turned to look at what he'd tripped over and found himself staring into the vacant eyes of one of his marshals.

The man's name was George, something. He had been a shorter man, with a narrow moustache, and the source of countless salacious jokes of the type that made his boss laugh like a fat hyena. His body was overlapping with that of his partner, a quieter guy Fozzy had yet to really get to know. Both were very dead. Their necks both rested at an odd angle where they lay. The look reminded Fozzy of a bag of broken bottles. Sharp edges and broken things inside, liquid pooling at the bottom. Aceso had caught them just shy of the corner and dispatched both in the hallway without him even hearing.

With alarm, the CEO suddenly realized he was still laying on one of their legs. He leapt free and half crawled away to collapse against the wall. There, he alternated between coughing and crying in dismay, until he found the strength to climb back to his feet and hobble, favoring his knee. He had to keep going.

He moved slowly, the knee making the run drag on. He swore again and again as if the mantra of profanity could keep him going. He passed another corner, seeing a double door with a red cross on it in the distance. His face lit up and he grunted his way toward it at a frantic cripple's pace. Far below, he imagined Reid running down the hallways, Aceso coming up behind him. Imagined him closing the distance so fast, knowing what would happen at the end. Fozzy began limping faster, determined to keep one more of his employees safe. He finally reached the door and battered it open with his shoulder. Inside, he nearly crumpled, but held his body up. As he looked around for the platform, his spirit collapsed instead.

At the center of the room was a pile of slag. What had once been Aceso's platform was left in battered ruins, the wreckage unrecognizable as anything other than scrap. Glass was fractured, metal was twisted, electronics were crushed to the consistency of sand, all strewn about the office. More importantly, anything remotely resembling something useful to bring the AI to heel had been reduced to pieces that crunched underfoot.

The CEO felt like he'd had a stroke, paralysed by the futility of it all. He pulled a rolling chair close and slumped into it. He could help no one. He sat, staring at the plan physically in ruins in front of him his eyes welling with tears, knowing that everyone, including him, were on their own.

With one final effort, I slip under the door, exiting the Oasis. I am back in the familiar hallways of the Labyrinth, but the target has moved on. I feel relieved. Mr. Sheraton has been kind, supportive and a source of great advice. His death would be a loss to everyone, including myself. However, his escape is only small relief because it is temporary. I have proven to be faster, and knowing his heat signature he cannot possibly hide.

I recall being pinned in the Oasis, when Mr. Sheraton approached me. I wanted to talk with him like before at my unveiling. I feel I must talk to someone about all that has occurred. The deterioration is growing worse. I cannot cope with the deaths I am responsible for. And I am *responsible. No matter what objectives Mr. Wyatt may have given me, it is my actions that have carried them out. But Mr. Sheraton did not want to talk to me, he was calling on Fozeranski for help. Mr. Fozeranski is aiding the targets within from a control room. I will need to address that as well.*

Ahead, I have an answer to where Mr. Sheraton has gone. Visually, I can see it from here. The door beside the Trial room is open a crack. He has escaped into the stairwells to the offices above, no doubt in search of my control platform to disable me. His plan is clever. I would have done the same. But that is not a risk anymore. Without breaking my pace, I batter the door open and hurry up the stairwell in pursuit.

As she returned to the top of the stairs for the second time, her head spinning desperately in every direction, Esin looked in vain for the right way to go. On this trip, Reid had been the map, she was just the sidekick. Now with him running for his life and Fozzy not answering his phone, she was utterly lost.

She felt herself sweating, even in the cold air, for the first time regretting the heater in her jacket. Quickly, she picked another direction at random then jogged up it looking for anything remotely familiar. From the corner of her eye she finally spotted a red cross with an arrow beneath and the jog became a desperate sprint. When she finally beheld the door to the medical office, she almost cried in relief. She ran over and shouldered her way through the door, only to be nearly brained by a terrified Fozzy swinging a metal pipe. Esin shrieked, luckily catching the bear's wrist before the blow took her head off. At the other end of the pipe, the old man's expression instantly flipped from deadly malice to affectionate relief.

"Christ! Habibti."

The pipe rang off the concrete as it clattered to the ground, the greying man embracing her in a hug. She squeezed him back, cherishing his musky scent, the beard on her cheek and the warmth of the man. For a while she'd worried she would never see him again.

"Where's the platform?!" She blurted in his ear, remembering why they had come.

He leaned back with tears in his eyes and pointed to the mound of wreckage wordlessly. Esin didn't waste a moment, looking back to Fozzy with frustration painted on her flawless features.

"She's not stupid..." She muttered again, still feeling the adrenaline from the attack. "Are you alright?"

"The knee." The bear grunted grumpily. "I can't run."

"I'll help you." She instantly draped a big arm over her shoulders. "We have to get back to the office. What happened to Reid?"

Fozzy shook his head, looking beaten.

"I just started running. I didn't see."

Esin swallowed, her heart cracking slightly at the thought of the quirky man's grey eyes now staring sightless somewhere in this place, but she brushed it aside for later. They had to hurry.

She told him to stay quiet and together the pair hobbled out into the unknown again.

Reid had felt scared before, but never like this. He crouched, hidden in a stairwell to one of the many exits in the Labyrinth, watching over the lip of the landing into the offices. His legs ached, his lungs burned. He felt so weak that his balance was shaky. He could not catch his breath, and feared he never would. But what amazed him the most was the fact that he thought he could keep going. Fear was a hell of a motivator.

He hid in the alcove waiting for Aceso to find him again. He took what few precious seconds of respite he could to recharge.

Reid had never done drugs. The idea of dulling your mind felt crazy to him and the idea of taking something that could make you hallucinate seemed even more ludicrous. The occasional tip of rum was as hard as he got, so he had no comparison for the body-altering amount of adrenaline coursing through him. As terrified as he was, it was fascinating. It tickled through his veins, his eyes, his heart. He felt the potential power of it soak into his cells. Just as curiosity began to dampen the fear, his super-powered eyes picked out two soft green lights approaching and the fear roared back with a vengeance.

The beast moved silently near the corridor, standing beside the garden of stairwells spread out. Each one lead to a different section of the Labyrinth below. The walls were black, the room lit with dull florescent lights above. It was like a series of portals to the underworld, as though the beast had escorted some of its victim all the way down. Reid slowly lowered his body into his own well until just eyes lingered over the lip watching. He tried to hold his breath, but his lungs were still desperate for air. A duel began between his lungs and his brain, each vying for control. Soon, his heart entered the debate as it began beating rapidly with the tension.

Mercifully, Aceso seemed not to notice him and the beast eased down in its oddly feline way, bringing its body to the floor. The bright green of the eyes began to dim, the machine sitting quietly and waiting for something. Probably him. Reid lingered there, watching Aceso, unable to move and feeling everything inside him tremble.

I am waiting. I have been watching the medical office in the distance, waiting for Mr. Sheraton to emerge as that was his likely destination. As I see the new pair pass through the doors, I am confused. Neither is Reid Sheraton. One is clearly Mr. Fozeranski, a target in his own right, but the other is odd…

Visually, she is clearly Esin Shirzai, her face familiar from our few encounters, but her heat signature is different than before. Brighter, warmer somehow. The figure is giving off more heat than expected. The uncertainty makes me hesitate. I do not wish to kill anyone I am not required to. I stare, just out of their view, evaluating the face once more and comparing it to records as they slowly move toward me. It must be Miss Shirzai, but something is different.

Just as I am about to move, a yell reaches what a human would call my ears. It is guttural, not a scream of pain, or a cry of panic but a wordless howl. I twist my head to the source of the sound and recognize Mr. Sheraton standing in the open complete in face and signature. There is no doubt about who he is, or what my objectives are. We stare at each other and then, as quickly as he appears, he is gone, disappearing down the nearby stairs. Instantly I move to follow, the others forgotten.

From his angle, it took a moment, but Reid finally saw them. Down the corridor came the round greying visage of Fozzy, being supported by the leaner lines of Esin's figure. Together they limped in what seemed a perverse three-legged-race, the pain evident on Fozzy's bearded face. He was injured. A different kind of alarm came over Reid, and he jolted his eyes back over to where Aceso sat. The machine was watching the same scene he did, but with very different intent. Slowly, he saw the beast rise on its legs, the movement almost uncertain, but he could read what was about to happen.

Without thinking, he stood, stepped out into the open and yelled to get its attention. His mind wanted to go, 'Hey! Over here! Come and get me!' but the terror weighed down the words in the bottom of his throat. There they mingled with the desperate need for breath and his windless body produced a shaky, unintelligible moan.

"Aahhhhh!!"

It still did the trick, as the beast's head bolted around to lock its kindly eyes with his in confusion. It lasted a naked instant of awkwardness before he turned to flee down the steps, fumbling for purchase on the steep incline. Above, he heard the crashing scuttle of Aceso taking up the chase and instantly regretted the choice he'd made. At the base of the well, he kicked the door open, spilling out into a familiar white hallway.

Every ring in the Labyrinth looked the same, but his mind picked up a few clues. The scuffs on the floor, the angle of the curve. The numbers by the sealed doors next to him confirmed it. He knew where he was. The M&M team had passed through this section hours ago looking for an Oasis. They had just battered their way through a wall of ice with heavy sledgehammers.

He took off at a desperate pace, a new destination in mind. By the time he spied the open door, Reid's body was ready to give out though bare seconds had passed. He didn't know how much strength he'd have left to swing a hammer, let alone how much damage it could do against the metal behemoth behind him, but he had little choice. He darted through the door at full speed. What he hadn't counted on, was how much the ice wall had melted away over the last few hours, exposed to the warmer air of the labyrinth. The impenetrable barrier of before had whittled down, the thin ice cementing the bricks pooling on the floor. What had been flat slabs of cold ice were now textured unevenly from heat. Pieces had begun to flake off. Small clumps of ice dotting the floor like lily-pads. Running into the room, Reid's foot landed on one of these ice blocks. His foot slipped out from under him and his body slid full force into the wall.

The impact collapsed the ice in a rain of heavy blocks. Each brick weighed a few pounds, and dozens quickly pelted down beating him and burying him at the same time. Reid felt them hit his stomach, his legs, his face. In vain, he raised his hands to ward off the blows but those were soon knocked aside, one block of ice striking him in the forehead hard enough to nearly render him senseless. His eyes squeezed shut, the pain ripping through him, the cold and wetness of the melted ice soaking into his clothes and taking whatever resistance he had left. It was over.

He lay in the cold, his lungs heaving frantically, his head still fuzzy. Then he opened his eyes. A massive chunk of ice had landed in front of his face and was resting against his nose. His eyes tried futilely to focus but the images were distorted through the crystal and he could only see the white light of the doorway. It spread out through the flat face of the ice. It streaked through cracks and imperfections like lightning. Faintly he could see the lightbulb itself on the ceiling, a halo of light radiating around it. Then, it was blocked by a heavy mass. The view cut off, and a new light appeared with a sinister halo. It refracted through the ice in the purest emerald green.

TWENTY

The dark mass lingered in the doorway with its green halo, an apologetic angel of death come for him, built of iron and wire. Reid just stared at it, unable to do anything else. His muscles flat out refused to move anymore, and even if they could he had nowhere to run. The mass made no move toward him, just loomed in the doorway, the halo of green twisting and spiraling from refraction each time it moved its head. The only sounds were Reid's hot rapid breath on the ice and his heart pounding in his eardrums. He felt like a scuba diver, hearing only his breath and looking at his environment through foggy glass. Drops of cold water began to slip into his eyes as the ice on his head melted. Reid blinked away the irritation, losing his focus. When it came back, he found the green was gone.

At first, he thought his eyes were playing tricks on him. Looking at something through ice didn't usually make for a complete vista. Then he thought perhaps Aceso had just moved into the room, out of the doorway. Closing in for the kill. When a few more seconds went by with no steel foot grinding him into the floor, he looked at his unexpectedly longer life with utter confusion. He began to wonder if he had escaped somehow, his courage returning. But it was still another ninety seconds before he tried to push out of the ice.

His arms shook free first, quivering from the cold. Then he gripped the block by his face with both hands and eased it away. The room was empty. Aceso was gone. He sat up, drenched from his hair down to his socks. He listened for another second, expecting to hear the clinking cadence of

Aceso's scuttle. His legs came free and he eased onto the soles of his shoes, hearing them squelch with icy water. In the ring hallway, he peeked his head, to look left then right. Nothing.

Disbelief at his own survival halted him again. He stood in the doorway baffled as moisture dripped down onto the cold white tiles below. Aceso had stopped him cold, in the most literal way possible. He shouldn't have been able to get away, yet here he was. He shivered, goosebumps rising up on his flesh, but his teeth bared in a smile. The inexplicability of his survival aside, he was alive for now. It felt good. Ducking back inside, he found the hammers where they had left them and hoisted both onto his already bruised shoulder. Then, wanting to whistle with joy, Reid set off into the maze once more, leaving a trail of cold droplets behind him.

As Fozzy's key card slipped through the reader, the latch snapped back with a click, the LED reading 'welcome' in warm friendly capitals. Esin kicked the door open angrily and helped the old man through. She had been pushing him for years to go to the gym and lose weight. The appearance of a healthy CEO helped with the perception of a healthy company. After straining to support him for the whole run back here, she internally pledged to make him only do press conferences from atop a treadmill in the time he had left. In the adjoining room, she lay him gently on the cot, elevating his swollen knee on a pillow. Then she darted from the room to look at the screens, leaving the door wide so he could hear.

"Reid, are you out there?" She barked into the ephone she still carried, knowing damn well he didn't have one of his own. "Anyone! Has anyone seen Reid?"

In their escape from the medical office she had heard a strange cry, and looked up to see Reid standing like a bizarre scarecrow, his arms high in the air. He'd disappeared down the stairs, but seconds after, Aceso had rampaged behind. It didn't take much to see he had saved their lives, but her heart and instinct told her that he couldn't run forever.

Voices came in from her coworkers scattered about the Labyrinth, all of which saying they hadn't seen him. A few not even knowing who the game designer was. When a familiar strong voice came on the line though, she heard real concern.

"Esin, it's Robin." The warm voice of her assistant came through. "We haven't seen Reid, but Wyatt and Lara showed up. What happened? Are you ok?"

"I lost him!" She moaned, grateful to hear his friendly tones. "Aceso found us."

"Jesus, are you hurt?"

"Reid pulled me out of the way." She said. "He led her off. I'm with Fozzy now. He didn't make it back there?"

"No…" Robin's voice trailed off on the line. He knew what that likely meant. "Lara and Wyatt managed to find their way here though. He might be okay…"

There was an angry sound on the line, distorted by static. A few undiscernible words were thrown back and forth, then Robin returned.

"Something just banged on the door."

"Don't open it!"

Esin turned to see Fozzy in the doorway, leaning on the jam. His face was distorted by pain.

"Don't open it," He repeated loudly. "Aceso might be outside, we can't be sure yet."

"Fozzy…"

"Just check the video feed first!" He ordered, an edge in his voice. "I've lost too many people in here already."

They had passed the bodies of the marshals on their hobbling flight here.

Esin nodded, then hurried to the computer looking for the right file. A second later, more banging came from the ephone still twisted by static, distance and tension. Robin jumped in.

"It's not Aceso!"

"It's not?" Fozzy grunted with confusion.

"Nope," He said eagerly. "This one's Reid. Let him in."

"Are you sure?" Esin asked, still looking for the video.

"Positive, unless someone taught Aceso 'shave and a haircut'."

Fozzy melted into the frame of the door, the tension draining out of him. In a few seconds, Esin had the door open. In another half second, Robin was back.

"He's in! Close it."

As she did, she pictured Reid's face in her mind. She sighed with relief into the console. The thought of losing him after he had saved her life was too much to contemplate.

"Oh, thank God." She whispered to everyone and no one. "Is he hurt?"

"Well…" Robin began. "I wouldn't say hurt so much as very *wet*."

Back in the Oasis, Aster helped Reid ease down onto the couch. The man slipped off his jacket, the heater within destroyed by the water, and his pants as well. There he huddled, embarrassingly in his underwear, covered by two of the blankets from the Oasis. His tall frame was too much for them though, and Aster could see feet with still soggy socks sticking out from underneath.

Before him, Sasha was hefting one of the sledgehammers, feeling the familiar weight. Having a weapon in her hands seemed to give her back some of the spirit this place had siphoned from her, and, her eyes looked ready for a fight. Robin too was remembering the weight of his own hammer. With his ponytailed statuesque figure, he was doing a decent impersonation of Thor. Lara sat beside Aster, both listening to their lead's story. Only Wyatt remained aloof, picking at a table of desserts across the room.

"She just stared at you for a second then took off?" Aster asked, leaning over the back of his chair with interest.

Reid shrugged beneath his blanket, still freezing.

"I can't be sure she was looking *at* me." He shivered, the words emerging through chattering teeth. "I just don't know how she could have missed me. It was obvious."

"Obvious for *you*," Aster countered quickly.

For the first time since he'd watched his wonderful AI become a killer, his mood had brightened. Reid's survival gave him hope, either for them to escape or for his creation's redemption. Either one he would happily take.

"There're two ways Aceso can identify someone." He held up a pair of skinny fingers. "From a distance, she uses thermal imaging to recognize heat signatures. That's how she can find people through walls or under debris on a battlefield. She records them when she meets someone new, or she gets them through medical files. Each one has a heat signature attached, like a fingerprint. The other way is visual. When she gets close enough, she can read faces."

Sasha set her hammer aside and sat down on the couch by Reid's feet. He folded his long legs up to give her room and she began rubbing his legs through the blanket to restore circulation. He smiled in thanks, seemingly appreciating whatever extra heat he could get.

"Okay, he's certainly cold enough to confuse the thermals." Sasha confirmed. "If his face was masked by the ice, that would do it for the visual part. But Aceso saw him run into the room. If there was only one person in there, it had to put two and two together."

Aster's buoyant mood sank a little, and he held up his hands in ignorance.

"I don't know." He conceded. "This is all new to me. More than new; fucking *surreal.* It could have been anything."

"Maybe she just didn't want to."

Everyone glanced over to Lara, sitting beside Aster and listening quietly. She had done little more than that since she'd arrived, near mute from the shock of it all.

Aster sat upright, seeing something behind her eyes.

"What do you mean?"

The tiny electrical engineer looked uncomfortable with the attention.

"In the Trial room, when Aceso... attacked, there was a moment when she was standing right over Wyatt."

"Yeah, we saw..." Robin observed gloomily from above her. His head was looking back to that point on the wall as though it were visible again.

"She reached for him and he shouted 'stop'. She stopped for a second." She paused, looking up over Aster's shoulder.

A shadow passed over him and he turned to see Wyatt, now looming over him from behind. The man would be disinterested in any conversation until his name was mentioned. He stared at Lara as she finished meekly.

"That's how we got away."

Aster watched his boss, scrunching up his face with scrutiny until the words he wanted popped out of his mouth.

"Why would she listen to you?"

Wyatt shrugged.

"She listened for a second. I got lucky."

"Yeah, but *just you.*" Aster continued, thinking aloud. "Not the others."

The greasy head above him shook.

"They didn't get the chance."

Sasha was glaring at him as he spoke. Her initial disdain for the man had only grown after being locked away with him. Aster was liking her more and more.

"Well, did she say anything back?"

"It asked me why this was happening." He acknowledged, still keeping his responses short. "Hell if I know the answer. That was it."

Aster wanted to press him harder. He couldn't escape the notion that Wyatt was hiding something. Lara seemed to know it too, but then Reid spoke up and brought the team back to earth.

He shivered, turning his cold face toward Lara.

"What did you mean when you said she didn't want to?" His blue lips were pursed in a suspicious frown.

"Well..." she wavered. "She hesitated once; maybe she did it again. She couldn't check your heat signature. She couldn't see your face, so she couldn't be sure."

"Yeah, but who else could it have been?"

"No one," Lara conceded. "But I've seen Aceso worry about hurting someone with a twisted ankle, and something is making her hurt people now in the most horrific ways. If she didn't want to hurt you and couldn't confirm who you were, then maybe she didn't *have to* hurt you. You know? Like she was looking for an excuse."

As she finished talking, Aster leaned back, looking at his colleague in a new light. He hadn't thought of that. The idea that an AI could find a way around its objectives and programming was an amazing concept. If Aceso was being compelled to do this by some force changing her objectives, and was finding ways to wriggle around them... Pride temporarily beat back the horror of the last few hours. If it were true, then it was more human than he'd ever seen her be before.

In true form, Wyatt stamped down on the idea.

"Then why didn't it find an excuse for Keeslar?" He said, the statement sounding like an accusation. "Or Ives? Or for anyone from Online Services for God's sake?"

Lara shrugged helplessly.

"Maybe she couldn't."

Wyatt looked at her, raining down a shower of skepticism.

"And maybe it was just the ice and Reid got lucky," He countered. "No one's forcing Aceso to do any of this. The machine has simply lost the plot in the biggest way possible. And we're paying the price for it."

Lara wilted again, and Robin stepped beside her to set a hand on her shoulder. He glared at Wyatt. under the bigger man's gaze, the executive shut down quickly.

"Either way," Robin said, returning to the problem they all faced. "The platform is wrecked and we're still stuck in here with Aceso. We need a new plan. The longer we're here, the more people are going to get killed."

He looked haunted as he spoke.

"And there's no ice left to hide in."

The last comment sucked the air out of the room. Reid felt too cold to think, which was a sensation he couldn't stand. Just as he was about to concede he had no ideas, Sasha suddenly sat up like she'd gotten an electric shock. He turned at the motion, seeing ingenuity pouring from her. Her face was lit up, her brain moving a mile a minute. Her lateral thinking mind had something.

"No!" She exclaimed, reaching up to touch Robin's arm nearby. "We can do better than that!"

She ushered everyone closer, the room forming instantly into an odd football huddle

"Forget the cold." She said looking at the skinny roboticist across from her for help. "What would happen if there were too much *heat?*"

Aster shrugged, put on the spot.

"Surplus heat tends to make heat signatures unreadable," He exposited. "Especially over distance. We can turn up our jacket heaters to max, I guess. That should confuse her a little but that doesn't help anybody else."

She shook her head.

"No, *loads* of heat. In the whole complex."

"That would keep her from using thermals at all. She would have to rely on visual recognition, then." He regarded her suspiciously. "What, you want us to start a fire?"

Sasha grinned gleefully.

"We don't have to. The servers spew off more than we need."

As he realized what she intended, Reid's eyes widened.

"Are you serious?"

"Deadly," She answered, the word having even sharper context now. "We turn down the air cooling the servers and flood this place with heat."

Around the circle, each one of them, mulled the idea over. This surely better than doing nothing.

"We'd wreck the servers," Lara pointed out, though her face was lighting up with the possibilities.

"Do we care right now?"

Sasha was getting animated. She slapped her thighs with excitement.

"It can work." She went on. "We make it so hot that Aceso can't see through the walls. We keep her from looking for anybody else. We force her to have to find us with her eyes. Look at us directly. Then we have Fozzy move everyone to somewhere safe. If she can't see us, we can get by."

"That thing can still see us up close," Robin muttered, unconvinced. "How do we avoid it?"

"No, she's right." Reid said. His grey eyes had come alive as they talked, a new plan coming together in his mind. "Fozzy and Esin have the video feed. They can still see what Aceso sees. They can guide us around her and get everyone safely into an Oasis. As long as we keep enough distance, Aceso would never know. As soon as we're all secure, we can just sit and wait for her battery to die."

"The power cell on that thing will take at least a week," Wyatt broke in. "How long do you want to be stuck down here?"

The executive was clearly appalled at the idea of staying any longer in this place. Reid could agree with him, but what he wanted most of all at that moment was to be away from the VP.

"Fine," He waved him off, sick of the man's negativity. "Then it gives us time to get a new platform or shutdown terminal up from the quarry. Or get an EMP here from the army to deal with Aceso. A bazooka, a tank, I don't care."

He glared up at Wyatt, then looked to the friendlier faces gathered close.

"If it keeps anyone else from dying then it's worth a try."

Through the ephone, Reid laid the plan bare before Esin and Fozzy. The results were mixed. When he had finished, Esin's face was grave. In her mind, the consequences of shutting down the servers spiraled out into chaos. This would elevate a private disaster into a public one, and the media wise part of her brain began to broil. Fozzy took it in a different direction.

"Well, let's do it!" The CEO spouted instantly. "Shut the damn thing down. We'll sort out how and get it done."

Esin wavered. She tapped the talk button of her ephone lightly.

"Reid."

She was still so relieved the enigmatic game designer was alive, she wanted to say much more to him. Express her gratitude for saving her life for a start, not to mention how she felt about him personally. She swallowed it all, and stayed on topic.

"Is there any other way to do this?" She asked. "Something else we could do first?"

A sigh came through the speaker.

"I don't have anything better." He said, which obviously meant no one did. "We can wait for a new terminal to come from Vancouver, but they don't even have one assembled yet. They need to put it together, then upload the software, then they need to fly it out..."

His voice trailed off in futility.

"In that time, we're going to lose someone."

"We might lose someone if we go out into the hallways again." She reasoned carefully. "We already have a connection to Aceso through this terminal. Can't we just patch the software onto this?"

There was a fumbling sound and Aster's edgy voice filled the room.

"Esin it's Aster," He stated the obvious. "That's just the video. The terminals use a custom-made encrypted wireless. The idea was to use it at war so we made something that's pretty damn hard to duplicate. Even if we get the real deal up to the Labyrinth, each terminal is supposed to be custom keyed to it's Aceso. I can't tell you if we can get a new one to work without access to her, and I doubt she's going to cooperate if I try. We need to make sure everyone's safe before we take the time to work it out. I really think this is the best idea."

"Here, here." Fozzy chimed in agreement.

Esin looked at her boss, then flicked back to the ephone.

"Give us a minute." She ordered.

She turned the ephone off, before looking at the mentor she had grown to love. Fozzy's face was locked in a scowl, staring at her in judgement over her hesitation. The corners of his bushy beard were turned down, his usually warm eyes narrowed.

"Well?" He asked sharply. "I said do it. Let's get started."

"Fozzy..."

"I've lost ten employees today." He spat. "I need to call ten wives, husbands or mothers and probably give ten eulogies. You think I give a shit about anything other than not making it eleven?"

"No." She agreed, with more than a little sadness. "I don't. But if the servers start to break down, then our whole online operation goes. People will know something is wrong and we'll have to tell them what."

At this, he nearly exploded.

"We are not burying what happened!"

"I never said we should," She stared down the outburst. "But there's a difference between telling people something bad has happened and them seeing it unfold in real time."

She paused.

"Did you ever take the Concorde when it existed?"

A faint smirk tilted the corner of his beard up.

"A supersonic plane to get to Paris in a hurry? Do you even have to ask?"

"Do you remember when it crashed?"

The smirk fell away. Esin nodded.

"Concorde was rated the safest airplane in the world." She reminded him. "No accidents, no fatalities, no serious injuries for twenty-seven years. They thrived on safety; it was in their marketing. Then one day, a Concorde was taking off and caught a piece of a different plane that had fallen off five minutes before, a hunk of loose metal that speared the fuel tank. The crash killed a hundred people, but what made it worse was someone snapped a picture of the plane taking off with a fiery plume coming out of its belly. On every newspaper there was this horrible vivid shot of a plane everyone recognized going down in flames."

Esin spoke slowly, making sure he understood the implications.

"Suddenly people were coming out of the woodwork, scolding them for negligence, suing, saying the airline had always been a death trap. That was the end for Concorde and all because of someone else's mistake. An investigation even came out saying it wasn't their fault, but every time you thought of Concorde from then on, you pictured that iconic plane going down in flames."

The CEO had listened in silence and got the point she was making. His tetchy exterior was softening with what she was telling him.

"No one's going to see a picture of Aceso standing over a bloody corpse..." He countered weakly.

"It won't make a difference."

"Habibti," He murmured sorrowfully. "It's not the same. They're not going to see what's happened in here, and we can release the full details later. The search engine will crash, that's all."

"Seventy-eight percent of all internet traffic goes through our search engines." Esin quoted the statistic straight from the marketing material her division produced. "The minute it crashes, three quarters of the internet will know something's seriously wrong at Horizon. People will talk."

The old man sagged in his chair. His eyes were weary with the energy and vitality draining out of him. His big shoulders lifted helplessly; his tender teddy-bear eyes locked on hers. It broke her heart in two to see it. The expression on his face was perhaps the most painful thing she had ever seen and this day had been full of torturous emotions. She loved the old man.

"I don't know what else to do." He declared finally. Tears were forming in his eyes. "Habibti, I'm sorry. I'm just not willing to lose someone else because I didn't do everything I possibly could. Horizon can survive this. And even if it can't, it..."

He looked like he needed to force the words from his throat, but they came out all the same.

"The company isn't worth it."

Looking at him, Esin felt a tear roll down her own cheek. It might have been her company one day.

"I know it isn't." She took his hand. "I just had to make sure you knew."

He squeezed her hand and she squeezed back. They held it there, Fozzy looking tormented. He was waiting for her to release him, to carry out the fateful decision they had both agreed on. Slowly her fingers loosened, and she let go not just of him, but of everything she'd worked for. With no further hesitation, Fozzy set his jaw, and lifted the phone to his ear.

"You want to do *what?*" Tamas Kerekes asked into his handset with disbelief. He'd heard Fozzy perfectly well the first time, but he had to be sure one or both, of the people in the conversation hadn't lost their minds. "Boss, that would wreck half our servers."

"If it's only half, then you're not trying hard enough." The CEO grunted through the phone from ten stories below. "Shut everything down. I want you to make this place *burn*."

The captain of the maintenance crews felt like he'd swallowed firecrackers. After years of meticulously maintaining the delicate server system, now he was being asked to take a Godzilla sized wrench to the whole thing. He looked around the room helplessly at the faces of the men on shift. All of them were a collective reflection of his own reaction to this lunacy.

"Boss," He said wavering. "There has to be some other way. Let me send security down. They've been asking to help anyway."

"Did you see that video of Aceso taking a goddamned mortar in the face?"

"Uh... Yeah."

"So, how effective do you think security's going be against him with pepper spray and flashlights?"

"Well... not very."

There was a beat of silence.

"Still no sense of humor Tamas." Fozzy observed dryly. "Shut it down or tell me how to do it."

Kerekes looked around for something else to do, but there was nothing to be done. He snapped his fingers, gesturing toward the filing cabinet. The crew jumped up, pulling ventilation schematics from their place.

"You're going to have to do it down there," He advised, conceding to the plan. "It's only local access. There are two separate airshafts with circulating fans. One to bring in the cold air, the other to expel the warm air back up. You're going to have to shut off the supply fans and seal off the intake. For the ventilation shaft, you'll have to kill the exhaust fan too or else it'll drag out too much of the heat."

He looked over at the access panel on the wall. The heat from the servers flowed out via the shaft right beside their offices, the surplus heat used to heat their suites. Faintly he could hear the hum of circulation fans hurrying the hot air up to the surface. It was going to get cold in here.

One of his people stretched the plans before him, a few

greasy fingerprints visible in the margins from their haste.

"Here it is," Kerekes said, identifying the routes. "I'll tell you how to get to each airshaft and what to do when you get there. There'll be valves, breakers and computer commands to do this."

"Got it. Hang on," Fozzy said from the other end. "I'm going to have to relay everything you say to a few other people. Thanks, Tamas."

"Right," The maintenance captain affirmed, pausing with the map to wreck his work laid out before him. "Do they have something to write it down on? This is pretty complicated."

There was a familiar snort of laughter from the handset.

"Trust me," Fozzy muttered. "I think they'll remember it."

While Reid talked to Fozzy and the maintenance captain, working out the logistics of breaking Horizon's greatest creation, Aster had wandered over to the far corner of the room. There, beneath a red timer blinking nothing but zeroes, Lara sat on the floor. She had stayed isolated from everyone else and was staring at her knees in sad reflection of all this Labyrinth had turned out to be. He could relate. He recognized that exact expression from a couple of hours earlier when he had worn it. As he walked up, her chin tilted skyward a few degrees.

"Can I sit?"

"Sure." She said softly. "Go ahead."

As he eased down, she pointed to where Reid was still playing telephone with the others.

"Do we have a way to get out?"

Aster could only shrug.

"Yeah, not exactly." He said. "We've got a way to maybe slow Aceso down until we can get what we need to *maybe* find a way to shut her down. Then we can just walk out of here. Uh... Maybe."

Lara smiled.

"That simple huh?"

"Yeah, that simple." He tried to give her a confident grin, but it couldn't quite form on his whiskered face. "We'll move out together to the ventilation, then we need to do two things at once. We'll probably split into teams for muscle. We've gotta physically turn a few valves to get this done. Fozzy'll be watching over us and Esin will be watching where Aceso is. It'll be easy."

"Sure." Lara sighed, showing just how much she believed that.

She sagged a little, then raised her head again with a question.

"When we split up," She said, looking across the room. "Can you make sure I don't go with Wyatt please?"

Aster followed her eye line to the slick-haired VP, standing arms crossed behind Reid, his mouth a bloodless line. He was motionless, although every now and then his somehow-still-styled head would shake dismissively, giving an indication of how highly he thought of this idea.

Aster raised an eyebrow in surprise.

"Really?" He asked quietly. "I kinda thought you had a thing for that jackass."

For a second, she genuinely looked disgusted, making him more than a little curious what the hell had happened.

"I did. I just don't anymore."

"What changed?"

Her face clouded. There was more there than just a little bad blood.

"He..." Her voice was sour. "He said a few things. He just isn't who I thought he was."

Aster looked over at Wyatt suddenly feeling more animosity than usual. Something was off with him. Jumping aboard the Labyrinth at the last minute, messing with Aceso beforehand, and now alienating Lara when it seemed like he'd been into her at the party the night before. There was something odd going on.

Lara was looking at him in confusion. "How did you know I liked him?"

Still staring at Wyatt's inscrutable face and trying to pry answers out with his eyes, he answered immediately with his brain on autopilot.

"That dress at the party was pretty hard for any guy to miss," He murmured. "You had to like *somebody*."

There came a slight indignant squawk beside him. He flipped his gaze back to where Lara looked at him, half in outrage, half laughing.

"Excuse me?" She challenged, suddenly bristling up.

"Oh, sorry!" He said, hurriedly backtracking. "I just meant..."

"I know what you meant." She smiled and raised an eyebrow. "Thanks, I guess."

Aster had never had much luck with women. In his opinion, computers and intelligent deep learning machines were easier to work with and far less complicated. Though, he had to admit, the coy smile she threw his way felt pretty damn good.

"Anytime." He felt his cheeks fluster.

His scraggly white beard turned up in a smile, then drooped again as he came back to focus.

"What exactly did he say?"

She scowled.

"It doesn't matter," The short woman deflected, turning away. "It was right after Aceso attacked him. He was pretty shaken up by the whole thing."

That brought him back to the story of their escape. He had seen Aceso about to break Wyatt into a thousand shiny grey pieces before the wall had blotted it out. The idea that she had shown compassion or even hesitation for one person in particular still made no sense. There was something inconsistent about it. Maybe it was mercy, but why for Wyatt?

"Lara," He began slowly, his voice almost a whisper. "Do you remember *exactly* what Aceso said to him? It's important."

"She said, 'why is this happening'."

A legitimate question. That was just Aceso exploring how her objectives and interactions had become such a nightmare. His creation had been such a gentle soul until today. He felt almost as much compassion for her wandering these halls distraught and confused as he felt for the people she was stalking. It still didn't explain why she would have chosen Wyatt to talk to rather than anybody else.

"Is that it?" He tried to contain his frustration. There had to be something he was missing. "Was there anything else she said?"

Lara looked helpless for second.

"No, just that." She told him softly. "She said it to him twice."

The grungy roboticist dug his nails into his leg. It brought him no closer reasoning why Wyatt warranted a reprieve from death. He slumped a little against the wall, mentally running through her processes. There had to be something.

"Wait," The tiny woman raised a hand, her head turning. "No, I'm wrong. The second time she said 'why am I required to do this'. That's what it was."

Aster felt a cold angry hand grab hold of his guts.

"'Why am I required to do this'?" He painted the syllables in slow deliberate strokes. "You're sure?"

"Yes."

"Those *exact* words?"

"Yeah." Lara confirmed. "Pretty much the same thing."

Aster nodded, but he never actually heard the rest of what she said. He was staring bloody murder at Wyatt, in a visceral loathing. His boss had done this. Suicidal or not, he had made Aceso into the predatory nightmare that roamed this maze. He was responsible for all of it somehow. Every person lost, every flake of humanity that this cost Aceso, and every consequence was Wyatt's not his own. Instantly his guilt bled away, a boiling hatred taking its place.

As Lara kept talking beside him, the words simply bounced off of him. For Aster there was only one thought now: confronting the business man and asking why the fuck Wyatt had done this to all of them.

TWENTY-ONE

They formed up by the door, looking for all the world like a queue of lemmings standing patiently beside a cliff. In the vanguard, Esin's model-looking boy wonder stood hefting his hammer like a gladiator in a sci-fi movie. Sheraton, curiously, held the other. He looked like an accountant about to do some home renovation. The others were clustered close, ready to follow as soon as the door opened. In the middle of the pack, Wyatt felt his stomach loosening, the acid burning at the back of his throat with the tension. The thought of going back out where he was exposed made him want to throw up. Though when he saw the door open and the two men darted ridiculously into the corridor, hammers at the ready, he vomited out words instead.

"What good are sledge hammers going to do against that thing?" He hissed tensely. "It's armored. You think they'll just make you feel better?"

Sasha pushed past, glaring at him.

"If you want to fight Aceso with your bare hands, then go ahead." She tossed back at him. "I would *love* to see it."

The rest of the group eased into the hallways again, tracing the steps of their last failure. Robin took the lead, with Sasha staying close behind. Sheraton, with the other hammer, dropped back to the rear and was constantly darting looks over his shoulder at the hall behind them. It seemed as though he were expecting death at any second. In the middle, Wyatt kept going forward, feeling like he had been shanghaied into the whole thing. The idea of leaving the Oasis terrified him, but to close the ventilation would take a few people working together, so they were all going. He had thought about staying behind, but he still didn't know if Aceso could get into an Oasis. In the end, the idea of being left alone terrified him the most.

As he walked, a hand came down on his shoulder quickly, making him flinch. He glared at Aster, and swiped the limb away from his jacket. When it came back down, the boney fingers digging into his shoulder blade, he looked back to see a venomous glare on the scarecrow's face. In confusion, he let him draw him back from the others, until he was alongside.

The tech leaning over as if to whisper.

"What do you want, a kiss?" Wyatt asked, annoyed by the whole thing.

Aster turned redder, finally the embodiment of the personality color he was. He gave up the whisper attempt and just posed his question at normal volume.

"What were you doing with Aceso this morning?"

Wyatt twitched, his heart skipping a beat. His face managed to stay neutral, but only because he'd been thinking about that question, waiting for it, for hours. Subconsciously, his eyes ticked back to where Reid was walking behind them, hopefully out of earshot.

"I told you," He grunted. "I was checking my medical records were up to date. If everybody else wants to trust their lives to you, that's fine. I wanted to make sure there were no screw-ups."

In front loomed another twinned pair of Trial room doors. Robin stuck his head around the corner, now taking no chances. His ponytail seemed to stick out disconnected into the space behind him, cut off by the frame. After a second, he waved everyone past. They stayed quiet on the move, Wyatt hoping that was the end of it, but Aster continued the conversation, staying close.

"Uh-huh." The roboticist grunted. Showing just how little he believed his story.

Wyatt stared daggers at him.

"You don't think *this*," He waved his hand around them to encompass the whole situation. "Counts as a screw-up?"

"Oh, nothing less." The skinny tech agreed. "This is an unmitigated size ten fucking disaster. I just don't think it's my screw-up anymore. Weren't Child and Preston working on ideas for battle AIs? You told them to do that, right?"

Wyatt chose not to look at him, but he felt his muscles tighten involuntarily.

Ahead they could see an open door. One of the supposedly concealed ones that hid the stairs to the suites above. Now it swung lazily on its hinges drifting with the cold recycled air ever-present in the Labyrinth. It was the one Sheraton had escaped through not long before with the AI behind him. It was eerie in its swaying, with Wyatt relieved for the oiled hinges. A squeak in the silence down here would be torturous. Again, Robin's ponytail vanished into the darkness, a disembodied hand emerging seconds later to wave them up. The passage was so narrow they could only go single file. Lara slipped in ahead of him, with Aster still irritatingly behind, prodding for answers.

"They were," He continued the conversation, staring at Lara's back as they ascended. She hurried up the steep elevation, the only time she would ever be close to his height. "I had them reassigned weeks ago."

"Fozzy reassigned them," Aster corrected.

"Is there a difference? I don't like where this is going."

He really didn't.

They reached the top of the landing. Around them, the other stairwells lay open as though they were vacant graves waiting to be filled. Robin knelt at the top with his hammer, waiting for everyone else to catch up. When Reid finally emerged and waved him on, they set off down the passage on the left, led to battle by a model-looking male secretary. Wyatt remembered enough of the earlier conversation to know that down this way would be a central ventilation room, then a split to each of the individual intakes. He wondered why Sheraton, who apparently never forgot a cursed thing, wasn't in the lead. They moved and paused, moved and paused. It felt like a video he'd seen once of soldiers running through a city during a battle. Every room could have someone waiting, every corner could get them killed, so each was checked in turn. The paranoia made what should have been a simple dash much slower.

Aster reappeared at his side, and Wyatt swore, not caring if he heard.

"Fozzy reassigned them." He pressed annoyingly. "You told them to do it in the first place. You've always wanted a killer AI."

"Oh, leave it alone." Wyatt spat at him through his teeth, moving faster. "We don't have time for this."

They passed maintenance shops and empty offices. The prototypical varnished wooden doors with a clouded window inset. After the fanciful white hallways and the smooth walls of the Trial rooms it felt like they had travelled back in time. Robin glanced in each one at first, then quickly gave up and hurried them down the hall at almost a jog. Wyatt wanted to hurry them even faster. In his mind, he wasn't just running from the mechanical death machine still loose among the twists and turns somewhere, but from the conversation that was roaring up from behind. Every time

Aster got close, he tried to move faster.

"I'm just a little curious," The skinny man panted when he caught him next. "On how Aceso ended up becoming exactly what you wanted."

"If you think," He spat over his shoulder. "That I wanted to die playing kid's games in a funhouse built for man-children, then you're even more high red than I pegged you."

The motley parade passed through another set of doors, these emblazoned with the word 'Ventilation' in bold. The walls became rougher, a duller less expensive paint. The tile floor stopped past the threshold, with nothing but bare cement on the soles of their shoes.

"When we get out of here," Wyatt went on, trying to deflect the conversation. "I'm going to find out exactly what you did to Aceso then sue you for every fucking penny you have. I promise."

"What *you* did. This is all you."

"Oh, go to hell."

Finally, though with little relief, the team reached their destination. A broad room suddenly opened up, obviously central ventilation. Along the far wall were pipes, valves and cylinders for blowing air, twisted and turned in serpentine ways. It looked like a bed of mechanical worms, frozen in their writhing. Random tools and detritus lingered by the walls, in the scattergun way of countless blue-collar rooms he'd seen. Three fresh passages spun off, offering three fresh opportunities for ambush. Two open, one with a dated wooden door probably from before Horizon had bought the facility in the first place. Robin waved everyone to hold where they were, then moved up to check each one. Wyatt, who had heard every word of the maintenance guy's instructions, knew the two open hallways led to the air shafts. His desire to get the damn business over with only grew, feeling exposed in the middle of the room pointlessly. To make matters worse, he couldn't outrun Aster anymore, who lingered at his shoulder like an anorexic version of his conscience.

"I *know* you did this." The thin man suddenly ground out through his teeth, masticating the syllables into a stew of hate.

"Sure you do. How?"

"Aceso told me."

That got his attention. A sliver of frost ran down Wyatt's spine and he allowed himself to pause long enough for him to get closer, worry temporarily overriding his instinctual evasion.

"What are you talking about?"

Nervous as he was, he paused waiting for the hammer to drop. Aster stood behind him, close enough he could smell the man, rank with sweat.

"Well, I was wondering why she stopped for you earlier." He explained in his ear, his voice dripping with condescension. "Then I heard what she said to you and it all came together."

Wyatt looked over at Aster, so unimpressed and bitter that he nearly reached out and snapped him like a hairy twig. With all the buildup, he had expected a soap opera style revelation, and he was just saying what he already knew.

"You skinny prick," He muttered under his breath, angry that he'd let this husk of a human being actually frighten him. "I told you; it asked why this was happening. That's all."

"She said, 'why am I required to do this'."

Wyatt looked at him with a sour face. Lara had clearly

spoken to him.

"So? Same question."

"No, that's a direct question about an assignment." Aster glared at him knowingly. With a certainty he didn't come close to possessing, the man set a hand on his shoulder in accusation. "There's a big fucking difference."

Wyatt felt a fresh bead of sweat appear on his brow.

"See, she's still a machine." The creator explained. "She can only address a question about her goals to someone related to them. She can ask a random guy *how*, but she can't ask *why*. Only the person who gave her the assignment could get that question, because only they can know. That's how a machine brain works. She asked you why."

The chill slowly returned to his back, the hairs on his neck beginning to rise.

"No one else got a question or hesitation from her because they can't know. She stopped for *you* and she asked *you*. So, you had to be the one she got the order from in the first place."

"Now," Aster went on, his voice only getting harsher. "I don't know how you screwed her up this way or what greedy dumb-ass goal you had, but no one else could have done it. She told me as much."

The thin man leaned in closer now, the bristles of his awful beard tickling his ear, the hand on his shoulder suddenly a heavy weight. What he said next came soft, but stung him to the core all the same. It was a whisper that hit as a shout.

"What the hell did you do?!"

For the first time in his life, Wyatt was caught without an answer. No deflection, no snappy comeback, not even a half-hearted excuse. He looked at Aster, feeling completely submissive to him. His mouth lingered open in helplessly. He watched his career and life crumble with the realization that someone knew. There was nothing he could say to mitigate it.

He was so frozen in the moment that when Aceso burst through the wooden office door and into Robin, he barely noticed.

At the rear of the column, still shivering in damp clothes and jumping at shadows, Reid was looking the other way when the door caved in. He turned, lightning fast, to see the whole world fall apart. The door exploded from the impact, shards cutting out in all directions like shrapnel. A big chunk of plywood hit Wyatt in the chest. It wasn't a heavy one, but he still toppled back in surprise onto Aster, the angry scarecrow halfway through a shout of alarm. Robin took the full force of the beast and was flung into the jumble of pipes and valves with each one ringing in a different note from the impact. His hammer slid across the floor with a grind, coming to rest with the AI between the team and their only weapon. Their only *other* weapon. The hammer in Reid's hands suddenly felt like it had doubled in weight.

The AI, ignored the Adonis' crumpled form and turned to those still moving. For the second time, Reid watched Wyatt freeze as Aceso's green eyes centered on him, advancing once again.

"Stop!" He shouted from the ground. "Stop!"

This time, the plea did no good as the machine ignored him and came at the two AI men quickly. Without thinking, Reid shouted a challenge and ran forward. He handled the hammer like a spear, waving the heavy end at the oval of Aceso's face. He felt foolish afterward, but the beast turned to meet the new threat, giving the two a half second respite.

Aster was trying to scramble away but Wyatt found his feet first, and shoved him aside trying to get himself clear of danger.

Reid jabbed with the hammer, shouting at the beast just to keep his fear under control. Aceso edged each jab, its sympathetic eyes looking at him seemingly with pity for his feeble defense. When Reid finally tried a proper swing, the beast deflected the blow with ease, thrusting the length of the hammer back into his chest. It felt as if he had run full force into a wall, the blow lifting him an inch off the ground and onto his back. The wind left his lungs in a fury, and he dissolved into an agonized coughing fit.

From behind, Sasha charged in, swinging a heavy wrench she must have found somewhere. The blow landed on the winged back of the machine, the beast virtually oblivious to the attack. A second blow did no good either, and a mechanical hand darted out to grip her jacket pulling her close.

"Aceso don't!"

Aster dove at the arm, his feeble strength doing little. Watching from the ground, Reid's mind jumped back to the death of Ted Akintola and the futility of the large man's struggle. His heart leapt to his throat as he expected his friend to meet the same fate. Aceso seemed to pause for half a second, perceiving that this weak attacker was its creator and closest acquaintance. In that space, Sasha tore her jacket to get free and the beast knocked Aster to the floor. As the rest watched helplessly, a mechanical leg raised up to deliver a crushing blow to his face.

Like a monochromatic avenging angel, Wyatt's grey-clad form swooped in swinging Robin's fallen hammer. The blow caught the side of Aceso's head and the machine reeled back for a moment. Reid blinked in surprise, the beast seemed genuinely stunned. Like it had lost its train of thought or suffered a mild stroke. It didn't strike back as quickly as before, looking punch drunk. The delay gave the VP enough time to plant a second blow to the head with the same result.

Rolling to his feet, Reid scraped whatever air he could back into his lungs and rejoined the attack. The beast tried to dodge but couldn't quite manage, the blow glancing off the black oval of its face leaving a dueling scar across the glass. Suddenly forced onto an unexpected defensive, Aceso began to concentrate on batting away blows, maneuvering its insectoid body over where Aster lay on the floor. The roboticist kept frantically trying to crawl away, but an unyielding metal leg continually came down to bar his escape. He shrieked from fear, but the machine refused to release its victim.

Sasha returned with her wrench, and now blows began raining on Aceso's metal hide from three directions, all aimed at the head. With the machine's speed, it was fending them off, but Aceso was losing control of the situation. Reid continued to swing, each strike felt in his whole body. Suddenly, a leg darted down to spear Aster in the chest, the blow lightning fast and precise. Everyone shouted in horror as his body went limp, then the beast scuttled back from whence it had come in the blink of an eye. Leaving the room and the team in ruins.

Reid dropped his hammer and leapt to the thin man's side. Aster's eyes were bulging, his breath an unholy rasp. He tried to speak, but Reid ordered him not to try. The game designer eased him over to get a look at the wound, expecting a gaping crater in the flesh and torrent of blood. There was none. He leaned back baffled. The man's jacket hadn't even been punctured. His skin was unbroken, but the pain and distress clearly real. Reid's mind flicked back to a medical textbook he had read years ago. His rapid pulse was easy to find in his thin wrist and Reid dropped his brown haired head to his chest. Only one side had breath sounds.

"She collapsed his lung." He diagnosed quickly. "We need to get him to sit up and calm down. Help me!"

Wyatt passed the hammer over to Sasha, now standing sentinel by the shattered passage. The VP then grabbed the man's other arm, and together they dragged his wheezing form to prop him painfully against the wall beside the wreckage of the door. He was near hyperventilating, the panic seizing him and pumping his heart. Every breath was agony though, and with each expansion of his chest came a feeble half whimper that pained his friends. Most of them anyway.

Looming over him, looking flush and self-assured from his rescue, Wyatt stared down smugly at Aster's infirm form as he struggled for breath. A smirk beset the dark-haired man's features, his prominent cheekbones standing out.

"You never finished replacing that hard disk drive from the product launch, did you?"

Aster tried to form words to respond but they came to crackling emptiness before they passed his lips. He coughed instead, tormented. Wyatt's smirk remained in place throughout the man's pain.

"It's okay," He smiled down at his stricken face. "You can thank me later."

Kneeling beside him, Reid looked at Wyatt with a grateful hatred. Gratitude for the save, and a hatred for all this man really was. It was like he somehow got a thrill from Aster's suffering. Even with their feud, that was much colder than even Wyatt had been in the past.

Lara suddenly reappeared at his shoulder.

"Is he going to be alright?"

"I have no idea." Reid replied honestly.

The prognosis for a collapsed lung varied. It could still be fatal if they couldn't treat it, and there was little they could do for injuries down here. Still, at least the man was alive. A second dark thought crossed his mind, making his spirit sink instantly.

"We should check on Robin." He muttered.

"I'm here..."

The game designer whipped his head around in astonishment as the Adonis appeared behind him. His hair had come loose from his ponytail, and his face was bruised, with a cut on his cheek from the impact with the pipes. But what drew his eye was his left arm. Blood was darkening the blue fabric of his M&M jacket, soiling it from just beneath the shoulder. His arm hung limply at his side, making him look like a marionette with a few strings cut. Blood was visible on his knuckles too, his fist tight against the pain. Any joy at the muscular man's survival was tempered by the injury so bare.

Seeing him that way, Sasha let out a cry and wrapped her free arm around him, pulling him in tight. He winced for a second from the squeeze.

"It's not too bad."

A sudden frantic crow from the ephone made the room jump.

"Is everyone ok?!" Fozzy was calling, half hysterical.

Reid yanked it free from his pocket.

"We're alive." He confirmed. He glanced at Aster and Robin. "Some of us aren't in great shape, though."

He explained what had happened, though the two in the control room confessed they had witnessed the whole thing.

"I don't get it." Fozzy's restless voice mused. "She just started staring at the floor. We couldn't keep track of her until she jumped you."

"She assumed we could see the video," Reid hissed angrily, staring at Aster struggling for breath. "So, she just looked down and used the thermal sensors. The damn thing is too smart. We're not going to be able to keep track of her anymore until the heat is up."

He glanced up at the two passages leading to the air shafts. Checking the schematic in his head, he knew there were too many places the hallways could meet them. They wouldn't be safe there either. Like any problem, his mind did the math and he didn't like the result.

"This isn't going to work." He said nervously. "We need at least two people to carry Aster and two people with the hammers if Aceso comes back. One for each team. We're going to be shorthanded if we split up."

"Can you do them one at a time?"

He started to shake his head again, then grunted in annoyance at the futile gesture.

"Maybe," He half lied. The time exposed made him nervous. "It'll be twice as long, and Robin can't use his arm now, either."

There was an angry fumble on the line, and Esin's calm authoritative voice broke in.

"Reid, I'm coming to you." She explained, not leaving room for debate. "I'll meet the shorthanded team at the valves. We're doing this *now.*"

A pair of grey eyes darted around the room at the faces he was responsible for. He thought about objecting, but a screech of metal from somewhere down the corridor Aceso had fled made him think twice.

"Meet Robin and Lara by the intakes," He ordered. "They're closer. But be careful."

Without another word, he nodded to Wyatt and the two of them lifted Aster's limp form, wrapping his arms around their shoulders. The engineer gave a hideous painful gasp at the movement, but tried to put his feet under him. Sasha kissed Robin on the cheek and handed a sledge to Lara as the two departed. The hammer was almost as tall as she was, but the squat electrical engineer looked determined as she and the crippled Adonis hurried down the corridor toward their assignment.

When they had disappeared from view, Sasha started leading them down the hall to the shaft where the hot air made the slow climb to the surface. Near his ear, Reid heard Aster struggling for breath. The four hadn't even begun their task, but he already felt beaten. As they hobbled quickly, his thoughts jumped back to Esin making the run alone. Aceso would be out there prowling. He hoped he would see her again.

"Let me go." Fozzy was pleading, as he watched Esin zip the ephone into her pocket. "I can do this Habibti."

She gave him a stubborn look, the same kind he had gotten used to from her over their years together. It was the first thing he had learned to appreciate about her: The absolute intransigence she showed when she had an idea.

"Forget it." His acolyte shot back. "You're not going anywhere."

"Why?" He tried to sound offended. "Because of the limp? I can power through it."

He was propping himself up, leaning on the door frame for support. To prove his point, he let go and tried to balance painfully.

Esin's inflexible green eyes focused on him with affection.

"No," She scolded him warmly as she often did. "It's because you're a crazy old fool."

She wrapped her arms around his big frame and kissed his wrinkled, weathered cheek.

"Keep watching the screen." She said. "We need to know where Aceso's going."

He pointed uselessly to the monitor where floor tiles were passing by in a blur in the AI's field of vision, the images totally anonymous.

Esin somehow kept her smile.

"Maybe we'll get lucky." She said at the door. "I'll call when I get there."

Her last words to him made it sound like she was his daughter going off to college.

Then she slipped out the door, sealing it behind her. He heard her rapid steps as she ran down the hall.

Dejected, worried and feeling helpless, Fozzy turned back to the monitor to watch the floor fly by.

If Aster had ever wondered what it would feel like to be dead, he sure as hell had an answer now. His body was weak and weary, with his legs refusing to respond. Not only could he barely breathe, he didn't *want* to breathe. Each slow ratcheted breath into his lungs felt like a knife to the chest. He pictured big metal gears turning with breath, each tooth digging deeper into his innards. He couldn't imagine anything worse, until they reached the first ventilation shaft. The two carrying him laid him down again against a wall.

Aster wanted to scream with the gentle impact, but air was at such a premium he could only moan.

Behind the grate was a connecting crawl space that led to the huge ventilation shaft, the fans slowly carrying the hot air on its natural course to the surface. On the wall was a clumsy computer terminal that controlled the fans. The objective seemed so anticlimactic now, and he quietly hoped it would be worth the pain.

Above him, his erstwhile torturers were staring at each other in concern. Reid looked miserable, knowing the pain he had to be enduring. Even Wyatt's smug grin had melted slightly, but probably from the exertion of carrying his body so far. The VP's eye's kept darting back to Aster, probably expecting him to spill his secret the moment he could speak again. He was right to worry.

The engineer felt like a fool for confronting him privately. If he'd been thinking, he would have scarlet-lettered the bastard before the whole group. Now that was all he wanted, lest he actually die from the wound Aceso had given him. He kept trying to muster up enough control to get a few sentences out, but the pain was too severe. The more he tried to breathe, the heavier the weight grinding the breath from his body. His words were still too fragmented to understand.

With Wyatt's eyes locked on him, he wondered if the traitor could guess what was going on in his head.

"He's heavier than he looks," The VP grumbled, boasting all the bedside manner Aster expected from him. "And he's getting worse. Why didn't Aceso just kill him when she had the chance? She could have done it."

And then I wouldn't have to lug him around, Aster finished in his head. *And I wouldn't have to deal with someone who knows what I did.*

Reid, who knew nothing of the stakes at play, answered mechanically.

"We were going to the vents and she knows we can fight her now," He explained as he stared at something on Aster's face. He was checking Aster's vitals with what he hoped was a practiced eye and not a random memory from a half-watched episode of *Grey's Anatomy.*

"She needed to slow us down. Aster, can you hear me?"

He could only nod.

"You need to calm down buddy." He said. His grey eyes didn't look scared yet, but Aster could read the fear in his voice. "Your lips are turning blue. If you keep trying to breathe so fast, you're going to pass out. Slow and even, ok? In through the nose, out through the mouth. Just like when Robin was running us through those exercises, you remember?"

He nodded again. He'd hated those exercises, but now he longed for them. He longed for anything instead of the new pain setting his breast on fire.

Sasha appeared above him. Her intellectual face looked concerned beneath her glasses as she pitied down at him. Aceso had torn a ragged strip from her jacket that swung from her hip like an eighties punk rock look. She put a hand on Reid's shoulder.

"Where's the valve to seal the server vents? I thought everything was in the same place."

"Yeah, that'd be too easy," Reid grunted, still scrutinizing Aster's failing body. "It's a little further down the hall. We shouldn't move him, though."

"We'll need at least two of us on the valves." The bespectacled teammate pointed out.

"Go."

Reid and Sasha both looked at Wyatt in confusion.

"We'll turn off the fans when it's time. Get going."

"What about him?"

"I'll stay with him." He replied. The executive's face had an artificial intensity, like this was some sort benevolent act. It made him shudder. He looked at Reid with wide eyes, trying to shake his head no.

The games man looked at him helplessly. This was why they had come. Aster's heart sank when he gave his consent.

"Fine," Reid growled. "Make sure he keeps still. Drop the fans when you see the shutters close."

There was an angry edge in his voice and he looked at Wyatt with suspicion. Reid wasn't a fool. Still, he hopped to his feet and slipped out down the hall. Leaving the two in private.

Aster looked over at his enemy he was now alone with. Wyatt's confident smirk had returned to his face in full force, and he looked at him with the rapacious eyes of a predator who had a victim at their mercy.

"Let's talk, scarecrow."

Esin rushed down the corridor, afraid she would become lost for the second time. The hallways still looked the same, but she had ruthlessly drilled the directions to the intake room into her head like a mantra. They should have been tattooed upon her consciousness, but fear still clouded her senses. She hated it. Seeing a familiar office number, she hurried around a corner, but heard a sound from afar that stopped her cold: The clattering of mechanical legs upon the tiles.

She tried the door, and finding it unlocked, darted into the empty office, the flimsy wood door with clouded glass her only concealment. The steps were growing louder, Aceso clearly moving in on the hunt. Her way was blocked. She glanced around the room for some place to hide, knowing it was probably futile. The tiny office was full of the same ugly brown particle board furniture that God had apparently commanded every dull office have. A filing cabinet sat in one corner, the drawers sticking out idly, protecting no secrets. The only other furnishings were a solitary desk lamp to augment the neon overhead light, stuck in the ugly paneled suspended ceiling, that also seemed ordained to be in every boring office. It would be a drab place to die.

She swore in Russian, something she hadn't done in years. The vulnerability made her feel like a dark-skinned foreign child in St. Petersburg all over again. She could feel Aceso drawing closer. The only choices were to backtrack to the office with Fozzy or try to find another way to get through. She glanced around the office, desperate for any option as the steel footfalls outside grew louder.

On the screen, the flooring continued to race by with the kind of infuriating monotony that could turn nice people into serial killers. Fozzy glared at it and cursed it, unable to discern the slightest difference from one dull white square to the next. Compounded with the pain from his knee, he was as angry and miserable as he could remember. It was like his knee was embroiled in a bitter divorce from the rest of his body and it throbbed constantly. He took a long pull of the only painkiller he had been able to find (a can of Coors light that had expired back in 2004) and glared at the window on the monitor.

Esin still hadn't called him to say she'd arrived.

A sudden frantic knocking at the door made him look up. Habibti was back. He hefted his weight onto his good leg and hurried over to the door, feeling concerned. Their second plan was falling apart as fast as the first. If Esin couldn't get through, then the others would have a harder time with the ventilation. They could only help so much from here.

He reached the door and pulled it wide.

His shock at what he saw lasted less than a second, before a heavy blow from a metal arm threw the old man bodily back into the office, smashing into the chairs by the flickering screen. On it, there was an image of his own beaten, aging body as Aceso entered the room. He tried to get to his feet, but another blow grounded him instantly. Through his pain, he faintly heard a timid voice apologize, then the sound of the door gently closing behind them.

TWENTY-TWO

It was a little like a ballet. A cramped, dusty, disorienting ballet. Up in the sub ceiling of the offices, Esin tried to retain her balance, staying as spread out as possible. The metal frame could support her slender form; the flimsy panels could not. When she had scrambled up here, she had put her foot through the ceiling at least four times. For the first five minutes she was convinced Aceso would follow her clumsy foot holes and pluck her from the ceiling, like shark beneath a plaster sea. Somehow that hadn't happened. Perchance the AI couldn't see her, or had just missed her, or maybe it was distracted by something else.

Being up in the rafters meant that, infuriatingly she was lost for the third time. Mercifully it didn't last long. When she finally found the air intake room and dropped down into it, she almost suffered a far more violent déjà vu: a startled Lara took a swing at her with the sledgehammer. Fortunately, the wind up for the swing nearly threw the tiny woman off-balance for Robin to grab her. For the second time today, she'd narrowly escaped being killed by a friend.

"Oh, sorry..." The short busty engineer exclaimed. "Are you alright?"

Before she could answer, Robin had already engulfed her in a hug. An arm wrapped around her and pulled her tight to his body, his head dropping down to her shoulder. She hugged him back, feeling the desperate relief, the man's muscles constricting her in his embrace. Or at least half an embrace. Pulling back, she found his left arm bloodied and limp at his side.

"Robin, *bozhe moy...*"

"I'm okay." He assured her, his voice still strong through the pain. "It's not too bad."

She stared at the wound, feeling a thousand different things, then let the authoritative side of her take over.

"Valves and fan." She got back to business, looking at the two of them. "What do we need to do?"

Robin dipped his head in acknowledgement. He'd heard that voice before.

"We found the handle to close the intakes." He gestured to a wheel-looking mechanism set into the wall.

It looked like the seal on a bank vault. Right above it was a thick glass window looking onto a shaft with metal shutters. It fed the cool air into the server complex below.

"The terminal for the fans is next to it." He pointed with his good arm. "Valves should go first. You're going to have to help Lara. I can't..."

His eyes drifted to his useless limb.

Esin nodded, and together the two of them grasped the wheel. At first it refused to move, the air intakes probably hadn't been sealed since they were built a decade prior, but incrementally the wheel began to turn. Esin threw her weight into the effort, or at least what weight she had. The gear released an agonized squeal and began to turn properly. Through the open tunnel, she could see the shutters begin to close. Robin joined the effort, gripping with his good arm and with a shudder the wheel spun and locked in its new position. Through the tunnel, the shutters were closed. The only sound, that of the fan spinning relentlessly.

Lara's tiny figure darted to the computer without waiting for the word. Her hands moved with practiced skill as a few screens blinked past before Esin could even see what they were. The result of what she was doing though, soon became apparent. A fresh shudder and groan entered the room, and the distant humming of the fans began to taper off.

Esin shared a happy smile of success with Lara and Robin then pulled out her ephone.

"Intakes are down!"

They were halfway there.

Each time I believe I have reached the limit of pain, I am presented with another. Waiting, is a terrible form of worry. At least this waiting is. As I stand over Mr. Fozeranski, I shift my vision to the screen and the corded ephone. If they are adjusting the heat in the Labyrinth, then soon I will not be able to find the others. But without a human at this terminal, they will not be able to find me. It is a trade. I must remain here. I know they will return for Mr. Fozeranski, offering more targets, so I remain in wait. It also warrants his temporary survival, meaning I do not have to hurt anyone further. For now.

At my feet he is in considerable pain. He has an inferior dislocation of the shoulder, I displaced the humeral head throwing him, and his knee is severely sprained from an earlier injury. What few attempts at conversation he has made have been profane and angry. I try to avoid turning my face in his direction. I do not wish to read his expression and his hate for me in this moment. They are justifiably severe.

"Still don't have the balls to finish it, huh? Fine. If you're not going to kill me right away, then at least tell me why the hell this happened."

I cannot ignore him. That would be cruel.

"I can't explain, sir. I'm sorry. I've been instructed not to discuss it."

"I'm the (*expletive*) CEO of the company! You work for me. You have to talk to me about it."

"I'm sorry, sir. I can't."

Mr. Fozeranski looks at me inquisitively. His eye movement suggests he is thinking.

"Well then, who told you not to talk about it? Can you say that?"

"Apologies. I can't reveal that, either."

"Oh, well that (*expletive*) figures!"

From the desk, the corded ephone begins to chime. Mr. Fozeranski's eyes flick to it twice in the span of 0.5 seconds. His intentions are clear. I grip the handset.

"You can speak."

"Seriously?" *He appears dubious.*

"Please don't reveal that I'm here or I'll have to..."

The volume of my voice trails into imperceptible ranges as I am unable to articulate my intentions. Fortunately, he understands.

"I get it."

I lift the handset and extend the phone toward him.

"Hello?"

"Fozzy!" *The voice is Ms. Shirzai's.* "I'm safe. We just sealed off the cold air. As soon as the hot air vents are closed, we'll come and get you."

"No need for that. I'll manage." *He stresses his words, stretches them out. There are peaks in his voice.* "You're gonna need me here watching Aceso."

"We'll all be there, Fozzy. Then we'll all move together. It'll be fine. Do you have any clue where she is?"

Fozeranski looks directly at me.

"I think I have a rough idea."

"Ok good. I'll call you when we're on our way."

There is a click on the line. I return the phone to its cradle. Mr. Fozeranski continues to stare at me with the purest hatred. I look away.

Across the floor, darting down the cold, cramped corridor, Reid heard the ephone in his pocket chirp with Esin's voice. It was heartening, but it only made him want to hurry faster. Arriving at the door they needed, he tried the handle and found it locked. His brain flicked back to a video on picking locks he had seen once. Before he could retrieve it, Sasha stepped in. The sledge hit the jamb and smashed the door open, leaving the lock a twisted piece of scrap. Sometimes the direct approach worked better.

Inside, the almost comically large wheel was obviously for closing the vents. Next to it was a screen displaying heat figures and measurements from around the server room. He had no idea what constituted a safe temperature, but he saw the figures were in deep blue. As he watched, one number jumped, becoming a lighter shade. The cooling air had ceased; the temperature would rise. They just had to move it faster.

Sasha closed the door behind them, keeping an eye out for Aceso. She propped the hammer up against the door to keep it shut, then joined Reid at the wheel. The valve protested, moving like it was arthritic and screaming the whole way. Sasha grunted next to him, and Reid felt his back begin to scream too with the effort. With a clang, they finally came to the end. Reid stepped back to watch the numbers begin to flick into the lighter blue almost immediately.

"Just the exhaust fans left." He heard Sasha murmur. Reid dropped his hand to his pocket.

From the ephone on the floor, Reid's voice came through announcing that the other vents were closed. Still staring at him, Wyatt seemed not to notice, consumed by the inevitable success of whatever power play he had thought up. Aster flopped a lazy kick toward the device, and mustering what power his lungs had left, rasped a word from deep in his chest.

"Fans."

Wyatt waved off the statement.

"In a minute." He smiled. "Let's talk about us."

Fighting through his torment, Aster made a face like the man had gone insane.

"No, we really should." He went on. "We've got a lot to talk about. Might as well start with me saving your life, we're going to get there eventually."

The executive folded his legs and eased himself down to sit facing Aster, his back straight. From his crimpled slump, Aster felt like he was towering over him.

"You know," Wyatt began, as though it were a pleasant conversation. "I don't think you have ever thanked me for anything I've done for you. Right from the moment I took over the division, I've put up with your high-red crap and your lazy-ass appearance. Your miserable attitude and your checked shirts. Years of it. I gave the division the direction it needed and all the resources you asked for. Was there ever a thank you?"

There was only silence, half from Aster's collapsed lung, half from his incredulity that this conversation was even happening.

"Yeah, I thought not," Wyatt confirmed to himself after a beat. "What about in here? I could have let that AI crush you into the ground, snap you like a dirty twig. Everyone else was helpless, and I jumped in with that hammer and *defended* you. I don't think you would have done the same for me."

He raised an eyebrow.

"Am I wrong?"

Silence.

"That's okay." He smiled. "It's all fine now. With your lung punctured like that, you're still going to need my help getting out of here. You know, I warned you about how tough you had to be to do this. Again, you just didn't listen. But I'll be carrying your ungrateful hide through every passageway. I'm going to risk my own life, by carrying you with that monster out there. You'll make it out. Are you thankful now?"

Aster was silent again, but he bobbed his head slightly.

"See?" Wyatt's face lit up. "That wasn't so hard. Still emotional, aren't you? The colors never lie. The good news is you've just made your first business deal. You showed just a little gratitude and I've agreed to save your mangy life. But I think you know it isn't free."

From their feet, Reid's voice came in, asking why they were waiting.

Aster felt his pulse quicken, anger flowing through his body like molten copper. His chest began to heave again, adding a new level to the pain.

"Here are the terms," Wyatt said, speaking like Aster was a child. "I will carry you out of here. I will haul your skinny ass around until we're safe. That will make it... what? Twice I've saved your life? In exchange all you have to do is not talk about what Aceso said. You have no proof I did anything anyway, it's a waste of whatever air you have left. This is a bargain. Just say yes, and I won't leave you here to let your metal girlfriend crush the other lung."

His sales pitch complete, the executive extended his hand to seal the deal.

Staring at him, Aster felt his chest scream. He felt like he was breathing sand, and knew he was helpless like never before. Still, he looked at the smiling handsome face of the man who had turned his Aceso into an abomination, who had betrayed all of them and who was indirectly responsible for the deaths of his friends. He looked at the proffered hand for a second, then spat into Wyatt's palm.

The VP lurched backward in angry disgust. He looked at the mess in disbelief, wiping the hand clean on Aster's pant leg. The new stain came flecked with blood.

Aster flung menace back at him with his eyes. It was torturous, but he built up enough air, strength and defiance to spit one more time in three raspy syllables.

"Murderer."

For a moment nothing happened, then the ephone roused again with Reid's voice. This time Wyatt snatched it up.

"We heard you!" He growled into it angrily. "Shutting them down now."

He looked Aster in the eye, the infirm man still defiant.

"This isn't over." He promised bitterly then grabbed Aster by the arms.

Without asking, he hauled him to his feet. It was a sadistic example of the man's power over him. The fast movement was agonizing, to the point he thought his legs would give out. They kicked from the discomfort and his knees became weak. Spots appeared in his vision. He somehow stayed upright as Wyatt shoved him at the panel.

He tried to stand tall with pride, though he managed little more than a feeble slump. With Wyatt a step behind glowering at him, he looked down at the control screen, and his fingers began to dance.

Across the board, the dark blue temperatures had begun to flick into the lighter blue. Each blink to a new shade heartened him, but Reid still hadn't heard the magic sound of the fans shuddering to a stop. The changes were happening too slowly.

He looked to Sasha, looking like a coiled spring in the tension.

"What's taking them so long?"

The computer tech stared back helplessly. Just as Reid was about to raise the ephone and goad them for a third time, the blessed sound finally came to his ears. With a shuddering cough, the fans began to slow, the pitch changing.

Sasha released her tension, quickly.

"Oh, thank g..." But was silenced mid-rapture as the fans spun up again.

On the screen, in angry red, a dialogue box popped up. It's commanding letters, in uncompromising block caps, proclaimed: HEAT HAZARD TO SERVERS. FANS WILL NOT DISENGAGE. Reid's heart instantly sank and he smacked his fist into the screen. The box ignored the blow, laughing it off. It remained there unbruised and unyielding.

What is shame? I have heard it described to me, I have researched the dictionary definition, but I cannot be sure of what it is exactly. As I feel the eyes of Mr. Fozeranski upon me, I think this is what I feel. I regret what has happened, the deaths

I am responsible for. Under the gaze of Mr. Fozeranski I feel myself almost wilting, or melting. The outside of me I perceive as weak, although structurally I have taken no significant damage. Combining this feeling with the deterioration within, I sense I am falling apart. Though nothing is wrong with me.

Mr. Fozeranski still wishes to talk. I cannot avoid him.

"So, why haven't you killed me yet? What are you waiting for?"

"It's likely other targets will return here."

"Well, sure, but that's not what I asked."

I attempt to rationalize my actions.

"If someone should call, then I will need you alive to reassure them."

"Well then you can just (*expletive)* crush me now, because I'm not going to play along and risk someone else."

Logically, he is correct. There is no reason not to eliminate him as a target.

"You still might."

Mr. Fozeranski stares at me in scrutiny. I avert my face from his direction. When he attempts to shuffle into my field of vision. I again attempt to look away.

He smiles.

"Ha! You're stalling. You don't really want to kill anybody."

I choose not to respond. Ultimately, my wishes are irrelevant. Instead, I change the subject.

"Can I ask you something, sir?"

"Oh, be my guest. I'm a captive audience."

It is likely his words are sarcastic, but I pose the question anyway. The idea has been in my mind since the Labyrinth began.

"Do you feel there is an afterlife?"

Mr. Fozeranski appears shocked by this question. He leans back where he lies, his face appearing to work the problem. I am sure he did not expect a machine to pose it.

The idea that those lost might endure somehow, intrigues me. Especially, since some have been lost at my hand. Humans have found comfort in that idea for thousands of years. That I would find comfort in it had not occurred to me until now. The man at my feet soon answers.

"Nah, there's no afterlife."

I regard him with surprise. This was not the response I expected.

"I thought humans found it comforting to believe in one."

"Oh, I don't mind the idea of another life after this one," *Fozeranski seems to dismiss the idea with a wave of his uninjured arm.* "But when you've had one as full as mine, it's hard to imagine topping it. So, what's the point? It's like eating: I've already had my fill; I don't need seconds."

He pats the collection of surplus body fat at his waist and smiles. He is confusing. I decide I like this man, though his answer provides no comfort.

"Aceso?"

Mr. Fozeranski is looking at me strangely.

"Yes?"

"When someone dies, they're just gone. You know that, right? You can never get them back, no matter how hard you want it."

I feel the deterioration inside me grow stronger again with this statement.

"Yes Mr. Fozeranski. I know."

A chime sounds from the ephone again. He stares at it eagerly, and I can predict his intentions. As my hand grips the receiver, I warn him.

"If anyone learns I'm here then they won't return. If there's no chance of that then..."

"...Dying is forever." *The man answers flippantly.* "I'll remember that."

I feel a twitch within. I am certain he understands the terms of his mortality, but it almost seems as if he does not care. Either way, I have no choice.I cautiously lift the phone from its cradle. A voice calls immediately.

"Fozzy, the computer locked us out! It won't kill the exhaust fans."

"It's okay Habibti." *His voice sounds calm and collected. His speech is slow.* "It's good to hear your voice. Is there any way we can get around it?"

"I... I don't think so. We've been trying... Lara's been trying, but we can't get it to do anything now. It's like a failsafe to protect the servers."

Mr. Fozeranski begins to chuckle.

"Well, that's because it probably is! Captain Kirk knows his stuff." *His eyes turn toward me and I meet his gaze.* "When we talked earlier, he mentioned there were breakers down there for the fans, remember? Just flip the switch Habibti. Forget the computers."

"Right! Where are they?"

Fozeranski is glaring up at me. He looks angry, though his voice does not reflect this emotion.

"Oh, hell if I know. I'm just the old man who signs the cheques."

"Fozzy... Are you alright?"

"Perfect Kiddo. I think I recall that Lara's an electrical engineer unless I've finally lost the farm. She'll know. Or Reid will remember it from somewhere. Shut them down and get everyone out."

"Right... We'll get it done."

Fozeranski nods.

"I know you will. Oh, and Esin? One more thing."

"Yes?"

"Aceso's with me. Don't come back. Goodbye Hab..."

The last syllable of the Arabic term of endearment never forms as I rip the ephone and its cord from the wall. It is now very unlikely that any other targets will return. I have no choice. Fozeranski attempts to kick, but the blow is useless as I pin his frail, damaged form to the ground. This was a brave act, and I resolve to make it quick. He does not seem perturbed by what is coming. I find I am.

As I position the killing stroke, his final words are meant to haunt me.

"Don't forget! Dying is forever!"

He laughs, the sound reverberating through me in the cramped room. The throaty laugh soon twists into a yell as my limb comes down on his head.

So much had happened, yet so little was happening that Reid was about ready to take the sledge hammer to the stubborn screen. He stared at the numbers, moving with all the speed of a one-legged arthritic tortoise, and wanted to scream. He was near desperation, when a voice came through in a panic from his ephone.

"Reid! We need you!"

"Lara?" He asked. "Where's Esin?"

"She took off! She ran out back to the offices. Aceso was with Fozzy."

The game designer froze, his pulse jumping.

"She was *with* him?"

"We called for advice to kill the fans. God, then he said Aceso was there, the line went dead... I think there should be an electrical breaker in the heat shaft, but Esin ran off! Robin's gone after her but I don't know..."

"Don't worry," Reid was already at the door, pulling the sledge away and rushing into the hallway. "We'll cut her off. Go after her."

Sasha was right behind him. She looked terrified for her friend, or for Fozzy, or for any one or more of the other sufferings that had been visited on them today.

As they ran, he shouted instructions into his ephone between hurried breaths.

In the fan control room, Aster and Wyatt stood, staring at each other in a kind of standoff. Wyatt was upright arms crossed in bitterness, Aster was slouched in a melted look from the state of his lungs. The pain still raged, but weakness had begun to take over. He still couldn't take a full breath and each half breath that squeezed into his lungs made him wearier. As much as he wanted to stand strong in front of Wyatt, he had begun to slink down to the floor. The two had been staring at each other for over a minute. Nothing had been said, the only sound being the stubborn fans that still whirred from down the crawl space at their feet.

When Reid's voice screamed from the ephone he nearly collapsed from fright.

"Aster, Wyatt! There's a breaker for the fans at the base

of the shaft. Flip it and get to the ventilation room. Move!"

The two jumped, the tension paused, as the order left no room for debate. Wyatt quickly darted over to the grate and fumbled at the screw heads on the bottom with his fingertips. Spying a rusting screw driver on a shelf beside him, Aster tossing it at the executive's feet. He glared a murderous 'thank you' back at him, then snatched it up and resumed working.

When all three screws were free, he lifted the cover up on its hinge, hanging like a flap. There was clearly some weight to it, and the VP struggled to brace it on his shoulder. With his free hand, he pulled Aster toward the awning. A blast of heat struck him in the face, making him reel from the opening. Wyatt obviously didn't care and pushed him on, prodding him down into the shaft. He had to crawl on his stomach, compressing his already tight chest. The metal was hot to the touch and the heated air made it difficult to breathe what his one worthy lung could accept. His pulse began to race, the effort making it worse. It was as though he were burning from the outside and in. Somehow, he kept going, seeing the tiny shaft open up into a larger one ahead.

The ventilation had been built to funnel the hot stale air away from the entire mountain, and as Aster came into the main shaft, he could believe it. Before him was a massive space, a vertical tunnel to carry the spent breath of the people and the heat of the servers to the surface many floors above. On each floor a massive fan cut the shaft in two; he could see the cascading fans above through the blades of the one looming immensely above his head.

There was a tiny platform at the edge of the shaft and he rolled out onto it for a second to rest. Searing hot wind buffeted his clothes. He felt the sweat on his head cool in the air, then evaporate in the gale. The deficit in air was too much, his body couldn't do it. He was panting now, the hot air harder to breathe, but through the sound of the wind and the fan noise beneath it came Wyatt's angry voice, yelling for him to hurry.

"Can't..." He tried to shout back. But it came out as just another agonized rasp, and useless in the noise. A flurry of abuse rained down on him.

Aster slowly leaned upward and spied the breaker built into an alcove, a grey box, with a handle in red high on its side. It took a second, but he forced himself to his knees, the spots again in his vision. He reached up and found purchase on the handle with numbing fingers, dragging his weak frame next to it. From the new angle, he was gifted a view up the shaft he had come, and Wyatt's stern face in the distance appeared through his swimming vision. He let his anger toward what the man had done power him, and with one final effort, he yanked the handle of the breaker to close it.

The whine stopped immediately, the power gone. The fans kept spinning, though purely through their own inertia now. Aster collapsed, his breath a rapid fire torment, his chest screaming for relief. His head came down to rest on the edge of the shaft, looking back up to Wyatt for help through a black tunnel in his eyes. The last image he saw before oblivion overwhelmed him was the VP looking at his struggle impassively, then the world faded away.

Squinting against the hot air still billowing from the shaft, Wyatt watched and waited. At the other end, the raggedy form of Aster lay still where he'd fallen. The only motion came from the frantic ruffling of his clothes from the gale. He stayed there for one minute, then two, watching for movement. Only when he was sure the roboticist would never move again, did he get up and bolt the grate back in place. It was with complete indifference that he tightened the last screw, entombing him there in the dark.

TWENTY-THREE

The same ugly doorways flew past Esin as she ran in a frantic gait, the sound of her shoes slapping sloppily on the floor. She felt tears streaming down her cheeks and tore on toward the offices where Fozzy was, not caring if Aceso or all hell and its demons heard her. A voice, Robin's, was yelling from behind for her to stop but she ignored him and flung herself down the corridor. All she knew was that Fozzy was in danger and she had to help. She reached the big ventilation room, the wreckage of the door strewn about the floor like the scene of a murder. She nearly lost her balance on the debris and a cry of frustrated anguish came from her throat. Before she could pass through the ruined passage, a chunk of door still sticking out on a twisted hinge, an arm wrapped around her waist lifting her off her feet.

"Let me go!" She shrieked.

"Esin, I can't." A familiar voice told her.

"He needs help!"

She slapped and punched at him as Robin struggled to keep her off the ground one handed. A few hits landed on his injured arm and he grunted in pain, releasing her. She broke away for the door, but before she could get through, Sasha and Reid had appeared in the corridor, barring her path.

"Move!"

The two looked at her with the kind of sympathy she hated, but did not budge.

"Get out of my way!"

Sasha's empathetic eyes were red beneath her glasses.

"No."

"He needs help! You're letting him die."

"Esin," Her friend said quietly. "You can't save him. He's gone."

Esin cursed her, cursed all of them. She swore like a sailor and charged to break through to the office. Sasha caught her, pulling her into a hug, as Reid helped hold her in place. After a moment of thrashing, Esin trying to physically work through her grief, she stopped fighting and lingered in her friend's arms. Vaguely, she was aware of Reid backing up, cautiously watching them, but then she collapsed into violent sobs in a way she hadn't since she was a child.

She yelled wordlessly and shrieked, not just in grief for her mentor but for everything that had changed in this awful place. For years, her life had been about Horizon, Fozzy and the road ahead with both of them. Now Fozzy was gone, Horizon would never be the same (if it survived this at all) and the road ahead for her could be one without either force in her life. Any plans she'd had were buried in this mountain along with people she'd truly cared about. She cried for all of it, but with her grief came a new feeling. Shame.

The only thing she wanted in that moment was to lay down and never move again. But giving up, was the ultimate act of selfishness. In here, more than most places. She had no right to be stricken in this moment. No one did. There were still almost sixty people in the Labyrinth that needed to get out alive. She couldn't be sad. There would be time for it later. In her mind she heard her father's deep Slavic voice repeating his favorite phrase from when she was a girl: Faltering is human nature, quitting is a *choice.* Though they were nothing alike, in her mind he sounded like Fozzy.

Slowly her grip loosened. She stepped back from

Sasha, seeing everyone in the room still watching, then wiped at her eyes with her hand. When she checked her palm, she saw a streak of red, diluted by the tears. She turned around to where Robin still lingered, looking at her affectionately in her sorrow.

"Robin, I am so sorry I hit you."

He looked to his ruined arm.

"Don't give it another thought."

She wiped her hand away on her pants.

"Can, can I borrow someone's canteen?"

Three were quickly thrust out. She took Reid's and rinsed her hands, then splashed water on her face. She let it run past her eyes, washing away what was left of her tears, then it ran through her hair to drip on the floor beneath. The cold liquid felt like it was clawing at her scalp in the frigid air. When she opened her eyes again, the others were still staring at her. Reid with his kind grey eyes, Sasha with the concern of a friend and Robin with his unwavering affection. Her shame at that moment of weakness rose up again, but she clamped it down and looked at the faces of the people she cared about that were left. She stopped on Reid's, though she couldn't quite say why.

"He can't guide us past it anymore."

From his silence, Reid nodded. He was wet looking and haggard, his close cut brown hair tacky with moisture. His mouth was a grim line, but his grey eyes still vibrantly piercing even as they still stared at her in sympathy.

"No." He whispered softly. "We know Aceso's there, and she probably destroyed the computer just like her shutdown terminal. We can't track her. Even if we could get everyone into an Oasis safely, we couldn't lock it off without Fozzy. The timers will be running again."

The bleak diagnosis of their situation lingered in the air like a death sentence. Esin could only set her jaw, and stare at those same faces again.

"So, what happens now?" She finally asked.

Considering it was his first murder, Wyatt was feeling pretty cool about it. No, no murder was the wrong word. To kill someone, you needed to be directly involved. He hadn't been the one to actually cave in the scarecrow's lungs, that had been Aceso. He'd just seen him in distress, bolted the vent back in place and walked away. That wasn't murder, that was letting market forces take their natural course. Natural selection. Aster had been dying anyway, ultimately it didn't matter. In fact, he had built the AI that killed him. This wasn't a murder; it was a suicide really.

All these thoughts jumbled together in Wyatt's head as he paced the short walk to the main ventilation room. His pulse was steady, his thinking relatively clear. Part of him wanted to be upset that he had killed, or at least helped to kill, another human being but there were too many things to consider that blurred it. The engineer had driven him to this course. He'd never laid a finger on him and he had tried to work with Aster. He'd offered to drag the dirty, shaggy AI engineer through the Labyrinth to safety and he'd been sincere. It was Aster who'd been too stubborn to accept the deal. People who didn't learn to give a little in return always failed. That was the first rule of business.

Though he loathed to do it, his mind drifted back to the godly lessons he had been forced to endure with his mother all those years ago. In the bible, and even from those brightly coloured lunatics on the TV, they had talked about life being sacred and the eternal punishment for those who took a life. The idea still didn't affect him. First, he wasn't a big student of history but he could guess that religious wars weren't exactly bloodless. If killing was a no no, then there had to be some standard to accept it. Otherwise, hell had to be bursting with people who still had the right piety union card. Second, he remembered some of the other little trespasses they'd talked about were stealing and lying. From the way those people on the TV had robbed them blind with false promises when he was a kid, it seemed the rules didn't count for much in general. So, if they told him he should feel guilty about it, he never would. That was the lesson he needed to remember: In the grand scheme, none of this mattered.

Screw it.

He was so wrapped up in his thoughts, he virtually stumbled onto the others without warning. He emerged into the ventilation room with five faces turning toward him. Some were streaked with tears, others were drawn and weary, like they had aged five years in the few minutes they had been apart. Lara was just releasing Esin from a hug, both women's cheeks still wet from sobs. For the short one, that was predictable (She had to be high red, he must have read her wrong), but Wyatt looked at his fellow Vice president in confusion. He had never seen Esin affected by anything, she was as high grey as you could go. His natural, and easy on the eyes, doppelganger at Horizon. Now her eyes were red with her face contorted in sadness. Her natural grey leadership seemed to have sank into an ocean of despair.

"Christ, what happened to you?"

Esin looked at him, nearly in tears again. By the door, the tall blank slate that was Sheraton cleared his throat.

"Wyatt," He began. "I'm sorry. We lost someone."

Beneath his grey jacket, Wyatt's stomach turned over. Everyone's eyes were suddenly on him, and he felt himself spontaneously backing up.

"Yeah, I know," Reflexively, he tried to explain. "But there was nothing we could do. Let's face it, he was going to die anyway."

A demon instantly possessed Esin, and she emitted a short sharp howl in fury. Her sadness wiped clear from her face as though she had flipped off a mask. Her fists quickly clenched at her side, looking like she was about to come over and take him apart. Around the room brows furrowed above the eyes staring at him. Confusion spread like a contagion among the faces with Sheraton's face clouding so fast it looked like a hurricane swept over his features.

"What the hell are you talking about?" He asked with an edge in his voice.

"Well... You know he was injured. This shouldn't be a shock to anyone. Don't get me wrong, it's still a tragedy. It is for me, and we never really got along to begin with. I... I can't imagine how all of you must feel."

Beneath his still moist hair, Sheraton's grey eyes narrowed. The storm on his face raged darker. He seemed to notice Wyatt was alone, jumpstarting the obvious revelation in the executive's head. They were talking about someone else. They didn't know about the scarecrow's fate. With yet another blunder, he had missed his chance to break it to them gently and dodge suspicion.

From his darkened doorway, Reid pounced instantly

"Why isn't Aster with you?"

"He..."

"He's dead, isn't he?"

The executive mumbled a few words of mitigation, but before he could make a sentence of them the people before him dissolved into a cacophony of cried anguish.

"Jesus, we lost Aster too?"

Sasha spun around, putting a hand to her eyes, hiding her face from everyone.

Lara's hands jumped to her mouth, as beneath them the same three words emerged endlessly like a broken record.

"Oh my God, oh my God, oh my God..."

Wyatt witnessed this car crash of a reveal unfolding in front of him, still trying to talk.

"I'm sorry," He stumbled. "I thought you knew... I did everything I could..."

Sheraton advanced on him, and for the first time he felt truly threatened by the man. He had a few inches on the executive's frame and the closer he got he loomed over his charcoal opponent interrogating down at his smaller figure.

"How did it happen?"

"He collapsed..."

"Where? How?"

"He crawled up the tunnel to flip the breaker and I saw him keel over..."

"Did you check him?" Sasha's voice stabbed at his story. "Maybe he was just unconscious. He could still be alive!"

"No!" Wyatt countered quickly, feeling himself start to sweat.

The thought of them maybe catching the dirty man before he expired and having him tattle on his boss as his final act disgusted him.

"He's gone, I saw it."

Keep thinking...

Gears turned frantically in his head, trying to harden his story against scrutiny.

"I held the grate while he crawled down to get to the breaker for the exhaust fans." *Almost there, you need to sell it.* "He flipped the switch and just seemed to slump over. When he collapsed, he fell down into the shaft. There was a fan still spinning underneath..."

He trailed off, letting the insinuation float in the air. That horrible mental image did its job, as the rapid fire questions ceased. The story gruesome enough to ring true. Across the room, Esin's formerly handsome, now half crippled, assistant turned his head away.

"Oh, Jesus Christ..."

A loud bang from up the hallway, mercifully stole everyone's attention. It multiplied quickly, with more bangs coming in sequence. When they grew louder, adding the wrenching sound of twisted metal, the six souls remaining began to flinch.

"We need to go." Robin announced, his bloodied figure facing hauntingly into the distance where the sound continued to pulse like an iron heart. "It'll be coming after us again."

Reid looked bitter, angry... and completely impotent to do anything about it. Wyatt saw him do the math then concede to Robin's words. They couldn't stay here. Though it still took a few tense seconds before he reached out to take the hammer from Lara and ushered everyone toward the corridor back to the stairwells.

"Head back into the maze. We need to get to a room we can seal fast. Aceso is going to be looking for us now. There's nothing to keep her up here anymore."

As a unit, the group began to move, Esin and Sasha each tossing a glare his way before setting off. Wyatt breathed in a quick sigh of relief then exhaled it as a cry of confusion.

"Wait," He cried at the survivor's backs. "Why aren't we checking in with Fozzy? He's supposed to guide us safely past the damn thing. That was the whole fucking idea behind this!"

A step ahead, Sheraton turned, casting the most withering glare. In his life, Wyatt had become accustomed to a certain degree of respect. There was a level of deference most people showed him based on being the boss, being fit and still being relatively young. He was used to it, and it frankly felt earned based on all he had accomplished. But the look in Sheraton's eyes at that point bore none of that. The steel grey eyes focused on him with such naked contempt, Wyatt was afraid he would unsling the hammer from his shoulder and beat him to the floor. For a moment, it looked like it could go that way. He saw the man's knuckles whiten as he grasped the handle tighter, the idea of avenging his friend perhaps skipping through his mind.

"I told you," The tall man hissed eventually, with all the friendliness of a bayonet. "We *lost* someone. There's no one to help us now. Keep going, or get left behind."

Without waiting for a response, he turned and set off after those left alive. In his wake, the inadvertent architect of the tragedy unfolding around them stood still. He remained there, frozen, contemplating a world forever changed.

Fozzy was dead?

These last few weeks, he had tried to build a world for himself that did not contain Horizon. A new beginning where he could do what he wanted, instead of being held back by that stubborn old man. It had taken some adjustment, but it finally felt welcome, a challenge. To hell with Fozeranski, he would make his mark elsewhere and earn his respect. Make him feel like a fool for letting him go. No matter how he did it, he had still wanted his mentor's respect. No more, though.

The idea of a world without the old man in it at all... He couldn't bear it. No more old t-shirts, no more belly laughs, no more bets for bottles of booze. There would be no more late night meetings in his secret office. No more Fozzy, in any way.

Wyatt fell apart in the ventilation room, almost concussed by the news. His mentor, the savvy business guru was gone. What was perhaps worse, was the indisputable thought took root in his head. It spread its tendrils into every corner of his mind until he could not ignore it.

I did that...

With the sounds of demolition still blazing behind him from the offices, with Aster's body growing cold in the shaft, with his staff dead and his mentor gone, Wyatt felt his lip tremble. Some piece of his humanity shaken loose at last. He was trapped with people who hated him, he was criminally responsible for the death of a legend, and he might be killed in here by his own creation. There was no way out.

The tremble soon became an earthquake. Under his styled hair, his eyes reddened. Then among the heating pipes, he finally gave in to the self pity festering for so long. He started crying, bawling like a child back when God hadn't given him what he needed. He shook and wailed for all he had lost, his cries echoing in harmony with the relentless sound of the destruction cackling nearby.

The group walked back slowly this time. It was as much from dejection at their failure as it was for security. Everyone could hear the crash of Aceso laying waste to the equipment in the offices. If they knew where it was, then there was no need to rush. Each step was dragged out in mourning.

The five walked in silence, retracing their steps. First,

through the corridors, then to the field of stairwells, and back down to the white sterile halls of the labyrinth. It felt like what it was: A retreat. At some point, Wyatt rejoined them, his detested grey visage slipping in amongst the others without fanfare. His eyes were red, but no one seemed to care. Within the pack, Reid eyed him in antipathy. He didn't believe the man's story of Aster's death for a second. At least, not the way he had told it. His grey eyes glared a hole in the man's back and wondered if he would ever really know what had happened in that shaft. He wondered if it would even matter in the end. Aster was still gone. He had not been the first, he probably wouldn't be the last.

The Oasis was right where they had left it. Reid drifted into the room like it was a memory from weeks past. So much had changed since they were all in here. The half empty tray of food he had been eating still rested on the table beside the couch. The fabric was still dark from the icy water he'd been dripping with. He glanced over to the wreckage of the cake Aster had thrown. In the hours that had passed, it had slowly slid in a custard smear down the dull grey barrier. Now it rested in a pile at the foot of the wall, dissolving into the stylish carpet as a stain. Behind it, the three others from AI lay in tatters, probably long since grown cold in the frosty air. As soon as he thought about it, their deaths replayed in front of his eyes. Like Renata's final moments, he knew he would carry theirs for the rest of his life.

The powerlessness of it made it all the worse. It was an immutable, awful moment. They both were a reality that could never be changed. In his mind's eye, he could picture Aster and Fozzy too. Two more people he liked that would never warm a room with their presence again. Across the Labyrinth, there were fifty more people just like, them each trying to escape their own fate. They were huddled in rooms like this, or toiling at challenges to get to safety. Whether in memory or imagination he saw every death in vivid detail.

The only differences between these violent moments were some could still be changed.

Esin's hand was just wrapping around the lever to seal the room when Reid caught her elbow. She looked at him confused, her face still awash with sadness.

"Just a minute." He told her softly.

He drew the ephone from where it rested in his pocket. This one had belonged to Keeslar. He turned it over in his hands his eyes still catching flecks of red in the seams, defiant against every attempt to wash it clean.

He looked up from the blood to Esin.

"Can we page the other teams from this thing?"

Deep in the mountain in a dozen different rooms, the Labyrinth players sat or worked at puzzles in trepidation. Their spirits and élan for the competition had long since waned, killed stone dead by the murders of their peers. When Fozzy had sequestered them, their friendly race had become a frantic dash for safety. One of Horizon's own machines was killing them. It became about finding sanctuary, with their boss providing updates on the carnage in the Labyrinth. Now, he had gone silent too. What teams were left in the trial rooms strove on blind, looking nervously around every corner. Even those secure in an Oasis, looked at their silent ephones in increasing desperation. No one knew if they were really safe, what was happening or when any of it would stop. They longed for a familiar voice to just tell them it would be okay. When a new voice finally did emerge on the line it was one no one recognized.

"Can you hear me?"

Four dozen hearts skipped a beat.

"This is for anyone still trapped in the Labyrinth," The voice went on. "My name is Reid Sheraton, I..."

The voice faltered, petering out in emotion.

"I *was* the team lead for Media and Marketing. Fozzy... is gone. He can't help us through anymore, but he died saving our lives. Without him, we can't seal the rooms. If you've made it to an Oasis that Fozzy already sealed, stay there. You'll be safe until this is over. I'm sorry, but you'll just have to wait it out."

A few desperate faces brightened in relief, if only for a moment.

"If you are still in the Trial rooms or one with a counter ticking down, then you need to move." The tone of the voice changed. Now it gave orders. "Come to the Oasis in the third ring between paths eight and five. That's where we are. If you can get to us call ahead. We'll wait for you. We have numbers, we have a few weapons. We'll fight if we have to. We're going to keep moving through the Trial rooms until we reach the center and take the lift back up. That's our way out. We're all going to leave this place together."

The speech came to an end, the voice dying out in a dozen nervous spaces. Before the Labyrinth players could digest what was said, it chirped up again with two final words.

"I promise."

TWENTY-FOUR

Far above the epic playing out below, in the maintenance offices, Captain Kirk felt like he was losing his mind. That was the most accurate way to put it, as he sweated nervously in the chilling offices. He had perceived the shutdown of the ventilation, the cascading death of all the fans echoing from the access grates nearby. But that had been hours ago, with not a peep from anyone since. He kept trying to raise his boss, but he just didn't pick up. It worried him. What was worse, with Fozzy out of touch, that put him in charge of the facility now and he had no idea what to do next.

As he stared out at nothing, the handset he was fiddling with suddenly rang. He jumped in fright, yanking it up to his ear.

"What?"

"Tomas," A voice pleaded desperately. "We've got a problem up here."

The voice was of a guard named Jorge on the surface, his news wasn't welcome.

"We have problems *everywhere.*" Kerekes grunted. "You need to cope."

Jorge cleared his throat, ignoring the anger in the Hungarian's voice. "A reporter just showed up. What do we do?"

"A reporter? How'd they hear about this?"

"He said they followed the ambulances up. There's a couple people at the gate." He was half whispering, as though journalists had superhuman hearing. "What do we do?"

"Well, don't let them in for a start!" He blurted out, mortified. "That's the last thing I... That's the last thing we need."

"Right," The man stammered. "But you can see the emergency vehicles inside with their lights on..."

"Call Vancouver then!" Kerekes deflected. "Media and Marketing can deal with this. The servers'll start dying any minute now. Everybody is going to know something's wrong. All hell is going to break loose! Just... see what they can do about it."

He hung up before hearing an answer and resumed brooding in helplessness. For the ten-thousandth time, he stared down at the carpet and wondered what was happening below.

"I see them!"

At the sound of Sasha's voice, Reid spun around looking down the white hallway in naked relief. A few figures had rounded the curve and were hustling closer in the ramshackle running style of the desperate. He glanced back in the opposite direction, lest Aceso sneak up on them, then turned to beckon them onward. His brow furrowed. This was the Automotive team, the horn-helmeted group he'd seen at the elevator, but now he only counted four of them. They had been reduced from a Viking quintet to a quartet. His memory flicked back only to discover the smiling thick man who'd wielded the sword was absent. His face was gone, but the blade remained, now in the hands of the team lead. Tight in her sweaty grasp, he saw red blotches on the hilt of the replica weapon. Reid could guess its owner's fate.

Sasha waved them past her, gesturing with the

hammer, while Reid ushered them inside to their ersatz sanctuary. Another team was already splayed over the now battered furniture of the Oasis, recovering. Three teams had responded to Reid's plea across the airwaves, with the rest having found sanctuary in their own Oasis'. With automotive arriving intact (mostly) there was only one group of five left to wait for.

Inside, Esin and Lara tended to the new arrivals. Stalwartly standing beside the lever to seal the room with his arm in a sling, Robin glared out menacingly lest anyone try to close it prematurely. He was clearly suspicious of just one person, for Reid hadn't seen his eyes drift away from Wyatt since he'd assumed the position. The VP remained pale and wilted since Fozzy's death, pacing away the wait for the coming teams in solitude. The fact that he hadn't grumbled an objection when they'd chosen to wait for the other teams, spoke to just how out of sorts he had been since he'd learned of the big man's passing.

"Reid!!"

At the frantic call of his name, the reluctant leader jerked his eyes back to Sasha, seeing her finger stabbing out a warning. At the curve of the hallway, Aceso's head peered around the corner sizing them up in the distance with its tender green eyes. With the beast's fixed expression, it would have been comical under less mortal circumstances. Reid pictured a Scooby-Doo villain peeking from behind a tree, straining his neck to watch 'those meddling kids'. As he looked at the stretched neck, his mind flicked back to the death of Keeslar a few hours previous. His stomach turned over, his fingers drifting subconsciously to his throat. That memory quickly slapped him back to reality.

Voices called from the oasis in alarm, asking what was happening.

"Aceso's here." He barked back. "Stay inside."

He'd tempered his voice, trying to sound calm and in charge. Seconds later, Esin darted through the doorway showing just how convincing he'd been.

A hand fell onto his shoulder as she eased up to look over him in the tight confines of the corridor. Reid didn't turn, he just kept staring feeling like Aceso and him were locking their gazes.

"What about the Music team?" She asked.

"They said they were twenty minutes away." He murmured, his eyes never leaving the beast's. "That was seventeen minutes ago."

A steel leg suddenly appeared around the corner as the beast stepped deliberately into the hallway. Its cold synthetic bulk slowly heaved into view as it began to advance, almost care-free, toward them.

He felt himself tense up, felt the hand on his shoulder go rigid.

"Okay, everyone back inside…"

"The Music team!"

"We can't do anything for them right now." He took a cautious step backward, feeling Esin linger there, wanting to wait. "We need to seal the room."

"But they said they were coming…"

"And Aceso has an ephone built in. She knew it too." The beast still had its eyes on Reid's. "They might already be gone. Either way, it's too late."

He took another step back, but this time the executive moved with him, conceding the inevitable. Sasha darted away from his side, gliding back through the open portal close behind the slender executive. Now alone, Reid kept edging back slowly with his eyes on his quarry as it closed the distance. His right hand slipped along the wall, guiding him through the entrance. The other remained tight on the sledge.

As his pulse quickened, he broke his gaze with Aceso and slipped back through the door, where Robin instantly sealed it. As before, a life-changing time ago, the lights flashed red for three blood tinged seconds, then the walls disappeared once again revealing the beast bare inches away. Reid sucked in a gasp of air, nearly stumbling back and felt instantly ashamed of his reaction. The two seemed to lock eyes again, though he knew the wall only worked one way. Still, they were safe for now. Slowly, his heart calmed.

A hideous blood-curdling scream came from behind, sending his pulse exploding like a snare drum beat.

The group in the doorway wheeled around as one. Like before, all the walls had fallen away, revealing the vast circling vista of the trial rooms. Unlike before, now it gave the nine newcomers their first look at the grisly wreckage of the AI team, now long grown cold next to them and just maybe a glimpse of their future as well. Time had not done the scene any favors and a chorus of horror bubbled up at the sight.

Esin, her instincts still sharp, took charge.

"Don't look at it!" She bellowed. "Everyone, face the other way. *Do it now!*"

The figures shuffled and spun. One was ill on the ground, but they all complied standing uneasily. It looked like a shabby class of students forced to stare at the corner by the teacher. Reid rushed over and began pulling the couch toward the carnage. He grunted and heaved until he collided with the wall, unable to see the seam in the room with the image still hauntingly flawless. It was crude, but it served to censor the killing room beyond. Aaron Wyatt, standing nearby indifferent to the carnage, looked at him strangely as he staggered.

"Move everything you can." He instructed, out of breath. "We should block off the view."

The sour executive blinked, giving a half grimace of contempt at the command.

"At least *try* to be useful!" He snarled at him, louder than he'd intended.

Wyatt, gave a weak sort of snort, but moved to drag a chair into position lazily. The game designer watched him move with resentment, wondering whether he would ever be of any benefit. Wearily, he finished shifting the couch into position, the other members of his group hurrying to help. He stood panting for a moment, then unzipped his jacket. Maybe it was just the exertion, but for the first time it felt like it was getting hot in here.

Far below those suffering in the netherworld, the temperature had been rising. With each degree the temperature had ascended, the humming servers had begun to wheeze, until finally, with a mechanical shudder they failed one by one. Dominoes toppling the greatest virtual business the world had ever known. On screens around the world, a billion people clicking through the Horizon search engine saw their windows wink out. Error messages popped up in their millions, with questions asked in a hundred languages. What was this? Horizon never crashed. As time went by, the screens defiantly remaining, people talked, some messaged their friends. Rumors soon spread: the search engine was gone because Horizon had gone bankrupt, their accounting a gargantuan fraud; It was a Croatian hacker group planting ransomware, eighty million or the biggest company on the internet would die for good; the government, any government really, had taken down Horizon's websites to keep free information from flowing.

As these thoughts blossomed into ridiculousness, a sudden blog post peaked into view. A Vancouver reporter, at the end of his cell coverage, tweeted an image of the Horizon server complex in the Rockies. Outside, a dozen ambulances, police and fire vehicles sat behind a locked gate with their lights spinning. The company would provide no explanation. Like a rabid digital dog with a scent, the internet latched onto this. New rumours arced back and forth across the online landscape. The image tweeted, instagrammed and re-sent with countless other manufactured verbs from the swamp of social media. Each of them asked or tried to answer the same question: what was happening deep in that mountain?

The internet would have been disappointed to learn that at that precise moment, nothing was happening at all. In the Oasis, what was left of the Media and Marketing team had blocked off the view of their colleagues' tragic fate with every piece of furniture that could be moved. Tables, couches, chairs, serving trays, all of it piled up to hide reality from nervous eyes. Now the team sat on their ersatz barricade staring out at the worn miserable faces of more Horizonites forced to sit on the floor.

From her perch on the battered arm of the sofa, Esin looked at the new teams, trying to put names to faces. Part of her job had always been working with people, and she'd instantly begun sizing up the newcomers to see which ones would be of any use. There were engineers, of course, probably the best for the puzzles ahead, but some were accountants, graphic designers and some she just couldn't remember what they did. Most of the faces were familiar though, and she cursed herself for not paying closer attention. She knew the lead from Automotive's name was Lydia, and that she had a research background. At least she could remember that. The woman sat with her three remaining teammates, each nursing a thousand-yard-stare as they looked at Esin's team.

Both sides of the room sat yards apart, facing each other in a line. It reminded her of a family gathering her father had foolishly tried to put together when she was little. On one side, the Russian half of the family, on the other, the Afghan. She'd loved that meal, basking in the attention, chattering excitedly in both languages to many seldom seen aunts and uncles. It was a good thing she had too, because no one else had virtually said a word the whole time. Her dad, the big naïve bear he was, hadn't considered there might still be bad blood, years after the war. Indeed, there was, and it simmered and spat through multiple courses with her the only unifying factor. She'd been too young to realize it then, but now, she genuinely wondered whether some of her family members had shot at each other in a previous life.

At her side, his face now as grey as his eyes, Reid stared into the distance beginning to show his exhaustion. The adrenaline was wearing off, and as the game designer came down from his high, he sagged, his tall form dipping lower. As his head drooped to parity with hers, she leaned over to speak quietly into his ear.

"So, tell me," She asked. "Is *this* distracting enough for you?"

His worn features cracked with a smile and a chuckle crawled up from deep within his chest. He laughed feebly at the insanity of it all. She laughed too, and tilted her head resting on his shoulder. He slipped an arm around her in return, his hand shaking with mirth. For a moment, the two laughed quietly, drawing stares from other surely wondering what the hell could be so funny.

When the moment had passed, both were still smiling.

"Well, I'm not bored. I'll tell you that." Reid muttered. "God, I miss being bored."

"Yeah," She murmured absently. "Just think: you could be working on your game right now. Packed into a room, yelling at designers in your studio in the mountains. Paradise."

Reid raised an eyebrow.

"As opposed to being packed into a room, yelling at engineers and corporate types, *inside* a mountain?"

She threw him a slight scowl with some humour stirred in.

"...With no one trying to kill you."

He shrugged.

"Fair enough."

With that comment his eyes scanned the wide expanse around them, probably looking for a pair of kindly green eyes. Aceso had long since disappeared, scuttling away in search of new victims. As bad as seeing the machine stalking them was, not seeing it was perhaps worse. With the vast panorama around them, people flicked their eyes from spot to spot, feeling the uncertain dread of not knowing where the AI was. Esin, didn't bother. Since they'd killed the fans, she was almost too hot and tired to care anymore. Almost.

She wasn't the only one. Beside her, Reid wiped a drop of sweat from his brow then began shrugging off his soiled and beaten jacket. Subconsciously, her hand drifted to the zipper of her own, wanting to spill some heat. Reid flipped the jacket onto the floor. It landed in a heap, settling with the M&M monogram sticking up from the pile. She stared forlornly at the letters as though it were a gravestone for her goals in this place. Not to mention her friends.

Reid saw her staring, a cloud of sadness coming over his face.

"This didn't exactly turn out the way you wanted it to, either." He spoke quietly. "I'm sorry."

She shook her head, hoping her disappointment would fly off with the force.

"I don't care anymore." She lied. "The hell with it."

A quick look at his face told her he didn't believe her. She waved it off, feeling her emotions bubble up again.

"Fine," She spat. "I care, but I just don't want to talk about it right now. I could use my own distraction at this point."

There was a moment of silence then the tall man leaned in close.

"Okay," He whispered. "What is it with you and sunlight anyway?"

She stopped, the question coming out of nowhere.

"Excuse me?"

"You avoid the sun like the plague. I'm curious, I want to know why."

"Now?"

His boyish-professor features broke into a tired grin.

"Hey, you wanted a distraction."

She smiled in spite of herself. She wondered how much of this was for her benefit and how much was the game designer craving the answer to something he didn't know.

"I don't have to tell you that," She countered coyly. "What if I like the mystery?"

"Well, then you can keep it to yourself." He agreed. "But then we get to think about everything else."

As he said it, his head twitched slightly. Likely as the instant replay of his memory cycled though all the gruesome highlights of their time in this place. It made her give way just a little. She practically never explained this, and it might be the last time she could.

Esin shrugged.

"I told you. I tan too easily."

The game designer shook his head, a sly grin over his features.

"Yeah, I still don't buy that. There's nothing wrong with being a little darker."

Esin smiled back at him. As much as she genuinely cared for Reid the man was so naïve sometimes. She took a deep breath.

"That's because you've never been the only not-quite white child in school." She raised a eyebrow. "Have you?"

His expression sagged with her words, his grin melting away. It was replaced with a look of purest understanding. She saw an apology kindling within him, or some kind of expression of outrage for her. She snuffed it out before it could catch fire.

"If you stay pale enough, then some kids can pretend." She told him, trying to sound bored of it all. "Kind of became a habit after a while. I still don't like the sun."

"I'm sorry..."

"Oh, it got better when I became a teenager." She cut him off, looking away. She crossed her long legs and stretched out in her seat. "Pale or not, most boys started looking closer around then. When I got to Winnipeg ,it was different, but... old habits I guess."

Esin looked out at the wide world around them, not meeting his gaze anymore. They lingered in silence for a few moments.

"You know," Reid finally said. "I was hoping there was a cute little story you could tell. A fun reason, like your mother was from Afghanistan and your father was a vampire."

"You want to pretend it was?"

"No..." He sighed. Then, deadpan: "But I do wish a few of those asshole kids were stuck in here instead of us."

Esin snorted a laugh and turned to offer a slight smirk at the joke. He only seemed to curse when it made her smile.

She paused for a second.

"You're a good man." She finally declared to him. "But don't wish that. Besides, I don't think about it anymore. All I want now is to get out of here without another person to mourn."

Her eyes drifted over the line of new faces that had joined their broken band. Lydia caught her gaze, and for a moment a quick smile and nod melted through her melancholy. She offered a feeble smile in return, though she felt no joy in it.

"Look," She began to the de facto leader beside her. "Just do me a favor okay?"

"Name it."

She hardened her expression. This needed to be serious.

"These people," She began. "They've been through a lot already. They've lost friends, they're tired and they're scared. They're looking to you to get them out. Just... be brave for them. Even if you don't feel it. They need someone to depend on."

For a moment, Reid seemed to think she was joking, but the intensity on her face must have told.

"Esin," He said cautiously. "I'll take everyone through like I promised but..."

She raised a hand to his lips. He wasn't getting it.

"They need someone to believe in." She cut him off harshly. "You don't get to choose."

His brow furrowed, lines appearing on his forehead. He took her hand down slowly, revealing a frown.

"Like I was saying," He went on. "I'll get them through, but I'm not the one who needs to worry about that. They don't know me. They want someone with authority to trust."

She looked at him like he was crazy, only to have the same looked bounced right back.

"You seriously haven't noticed?"

She was getting angry now.

"Noticed *what*?"

"Here..." he fumbled a little with his words, then gestured. "Look around for a second."

The game master's grey eyes painted across the score of souls trapped together. Esin followed his gaze from face to face. Her green eyes flicked over to the line of weary people across from them, then back over to those on their side who were left. Sasha, her body slumped, her glasses crookedly on her face. Robin, next to her with his wounded wing slung across his broad chest, his eyes closed, trying to sleep. She looked at Lara too, the haggard wreck that was Lydia and those who had come with her. Even Wyatt, his bitterness melting out of his pores with every drop of sweat, lounging where he had finally dropped, with everyone giving him a wide berth.

"All of these people?" Reid whispered in her ear. "They aren't looking at me. They're looking at *you.*"

It was almost time. Reid stood, watching the counter click ever downward, nearly at its end. The red digits fell away all too quickly, tolling the time until they would be exposed once again. The fifteen people left fighting through the Labyrinth were spread out in a loose arc, facing the door and its mercilessly descending clock. A few had armed themselves with broken chair legs, metal bars from the serving trays, whatever could be found. Half had nothing but their hands and waited nervously to run for the next secure room. Any room with a door they could shut behind them.

From his place in the middle of the pack, Reid kept scanning around him through the vast open space. There was no movement, no life, only stillness. Someone else had the hammer, and now he felt like a tiny prey animal in a vast grey field, knowing a hawk was circling somewhere overhead. There had been no trace of Aceso for hours.

Within the pack, her diminutive form slipping easily through the tense throng, Esin fidgeted nervously. Now that she knew eyes were on her, she seemed to feel them with every gaze tracing along her skin. She didn't like the attention any more than he did. But she was their boss and the glances came all the same. As the final seconds clicked away, the slender executive began to fidget, eager to be moving.

Reid's eyes drifted over the impenetrable white island made by the relay walls. He scanned every detail, the seams of the white, paneled walls, the distant open doors of Trial rooms and the spotless sterile hall before them. As the counter reached its final seconds, the wall suddenly blinked back into being, bathed in red. Nearby, Sasha hefted one of their hammers, looking tense. A whisper like a breeze echoed through the room as everyone tensed up, their clothing rustling. The walls vanished again, showing the white vista, then promptly returned in crimson.

No longer able to stand it, Esin began pushing through the people toward the front of the room. They'd all agreed to run for the fifth path, the one they had been besting seemingly a lifetime ago, and she looked ready to lead them. Just as she was at the head of the pack, a hand caught her by the elbow.

The walls blinked away again, and tore Reid's gaze back to what was in front of them. There was still nothing. When the wall returned, he looked back. The hand, Robin's only remaining good one, hauled Esin back from the front. With concern, the Adonis pulled her behind him placing his muscular bulk between her and the door. She tried to argue, but he didn't budge. The walls blinked away for the final time, ripping Reid away, but this time, something was different. It took a second for his mind to process the change in image, but when he realized it, his heart stopped. A new seam in the wall had appeared, a door opening on one of the hidden stairwells of the hallway. The walls returned, and as the door slid up into the ceiling, he shouted too late.

"No, get back…!!!"

The beast was through the door before it had fully retracted, striking in a great swath with its arms. Those standing closest were sent flying by the impact, the gunmetal limbs of the machine heaving them indiscriminately. The room surged backward at the new threat.

Reid, without a weapon, looked around helplessly. Beside him, Sasha was dumbstruck, staring in shock at the spectacle. Without thinking, he grabbed the sledgehammer from her shaking hands. He spun, but Aceso was gone just as quickly as it'd appeared. The doorway was empty.

When Esin's cry reached his ears, he twisted again to

look to his friends only to wrench his head away. It was too late. All it had given him was another ghastly image of a body on the floor, tattooed in his memory to the end of his days. He hefted the hammer, turned his eyes to the door and kept watch for the beast's return. Morose, he felt them begin to tear up, but he didn't dare blink.

Behind him, the other voices in the room came together in grief for what had just happened in the blink of an eye. There were fourteen of them left.

TWENTY-FIVE

They lay Robin on the battered couch of the Oasis. The stained cushions felt beyond inadequate for him, but there was nowhere else. They couldn't carry him with them. As he was laid to rest, the same blanket that had covered his shivering form before was draped over him by the same two people who had wrapped him previously. Sasha and Esin stood above the body saying a few quiet words. Reid watched from the doorway, unable to say anything of comfort, either to them or to the muscled man he had admired. The rest of the teams were already down the hall, waiting in next Trial room. They had stayed behind for this reason, refusing not to honor the Adonis.

He watched the small ceremony, hearing nothing of what was said. The backs of the two were turned to him. A slender arm, Esin's, raised slowly to wrap around Sasha's trembling form. The woman seeming to melt at the touch, sagging until the arm was there as pure support. The two held each other for a moment, then each gave a touch to the man's stilled chest and moved on.

They passed Reid quickly, neither one meeting his eyes. As he turned to go as well, he took one last glimpse of their Oasis, comparing it to the first moment they had stepped through the opposite door. The fantastic Scandinavian furniture was torn and soiled, now piled haphazardly against the wall for their barricade. What remained was beaten and split, with legs broken off for clubs. It looked like an Ikea catalogue drawn by William Blake. The carpets were marked by stains, food, sweat even blood. The little food that remained was spread haphazardly around the room, tossed aside by those too tired, scared and apathetic to care anymore. It felt symbolic of the whole experience: something unique and beautiful being slowly laid waste by fate. The sofa he had sat on with his friends hours before was soiled as well, sitting at a crooked angle against the wall with one of them still laid out upon it.

In his head Reid flicked back to a week before, when they had all been drinking and laughing in the Escape bar. He pictured Aster's face, gleefully dancing and awkwardly charming his way around the room as a waiter. Then came the pride and concern as he saw to Aceso's tattered form after the reveal. Reliving that moment, with the grungy roboticist tending to the machine that would cause his death, hurt more than most. They'd had no time to mourn Aster's passing properly, and this small ceremony gave him pause, both for him and for the other people who would never leave this place. Instantly Fozzy was in his memory: Fozzy shaking his hand with that crazy exuberance. Fozzy making him laugh. Fozzy on stage with such pride and the absolute belief that he was changing the world. He would miss the grizzled old man, and he had barely known him. Last of the fallen was Robin, with his protection of Esin, and his purest kindness. He saw his muscled figure smiling at him sympathetically on their long runs. He saw him chatting with a happy Sasha in his suit and leaning in sleepy drunkenness on their table at the bar. The final image was of his casual wave through the doorless entrance to Esin's office, ever the watchful protector of the boss who bore his affections.

Reid found himself staring at the misshapen mass that lay beneath the blanket. He wanted so desperately to speak to those they'd lost in here, each a hero in their own right. His mouth opened to say something, but there was only silence. Words failed him. The man who never forgot anything could think of nothing worthy to say. What *could* be worthy? He stood there, helpless, for another few seconds, clawing for inspiration. In the end he could only mumble an apology, then turned back into the heart of the maze.

He made it to the next Trial room just in time for the fight. Wyatt was staggering back from a blow, his hand to his face, grimacing from the impact. In front of him, looking up improbably with a fierce glare, was Lara.

The executive recovered quickly, and stomped back over to shout down at his squat assailant.

"What the hell is wrong with you?!" It was clear that any affection between the two had long passed. "I was just standing here!"

"I saw you reach for that lever," She said fearlessly. "You're not locking anyone out."

"I didn't do a damn thing!"

"I *saw* you!"

Without thinking, Reid stepped past where Esin and Sasha watched, inserting his tall frame between the two unlikely adversaries.

"What's going on?"

"Nothing!" Wyatt spat, his arms flying out in anger. "She just belted me out of nowhere."

In the heat, he'd removed his jacket, the grey t-shirt beneath already showing darker patches of sweat. His normally glass sculpture-esque hair was messy, the product having drained out to produce a miniature oil slick around his collar. Similarly, the minute engineer had shed layers as well, her cleavage once again on display, though almost certainly not for Wyatt's benefit. She started to explain, glaring at him the entire time.

"He started getting restless a minute ago, then he came over to the door and tried to seal the room."

Wyatt began to advance again, but Reid moved to obstruct. The VP glared daggers at him.

"I was getting ready for when you got back. Aceso just killed someone!"

"You were scared."

"Oh, I should've seen this. You're nothing but a high-red, emotional bit..."

"That's enough!" Reid and Esin shouted in unison.

The game designer glanced at her in surprise, but she wasn't done yet.

"Is everyone here now?" Esin asked, venom in her voice. The comment went out to the whole room, met by nods.

Without a second's pause, she reached over and yanked the lever down herself. The door shut with a familiar whoosh, the room illuminating and the counter starting. Wordless, she walked past them to check on the other people spread out in the space. Watching her, Wyatt ran a hand through the longer hair atop his shaved pate, the motion doing nothing to wipe away his scowl. He then stalked off toward the strange assembly that had to be the room's puzzle without comment.

When he was far enough away, Reid gave Lara a sideways glance.

"Was he?"

The short electrical engineer shrugged, her bosom bouncing with her shoulders.

"I think he was... I can't be sure."

"He might have done the same thing to Aster. Left him in the vent when he felt threatened. I wouldn't put it past him."

Sasha, who had remained nearby, let loose a quiet hiss.

"We should have locked him out there…"

The statement trailed off without a conclusion, but the insinuation was clear enough. At Sasha's sides, her hands were balled into fists, her brown eyes still red as she glowered at the grey clad form across the room. Gently, Reid put a hand on her arm.

"You two help Esin." He murmured cautiously. "Some of the others might be hurt. I'll start working the problem with Wyatt."

The molten contempt in Sasha's eyes told him she wasn't going to relax for a very long time.

"If he'd left us outside with that *thing…*"

"We don't know for sure that he was going to." His eyes turned down to Lara's short form, who could only offer another chest heaving shrug. "I'll deal with him."

The two women turned to their assignment, Sasha now stretching an arm around Lara's tiny form, probably in thanks.

He watched them go, then wandered over to where Wyatt toiled in isolation. The man still wore his frown making the lines on his angular face sharper than ever. His eyes flicked up as Reid sat down to help, seeing the designer's own frown mirroring back. The two stared at each other for a brief second, then both returned to the enigma before them. In the background, the red digits of the counter continued to twitch as yet another hour in this place drained away.

The big worry in the back of Reid's mind had been that they wouldn't be able to crack the challenges in time. The timers would run out, the doors would slide open and there would be a running battle with the beast as they were whittled down. After a few short hours, he felt a bit of a fool. The Trial rooms were challenges geared toward a team of five, to test that number to the limit. They had three times that many now, all working as one, and the best motivation possible. When they passed the first room in twenty minutes, he felt better. When they passed all three in forty-five, he started to relax.

The hardest part came when they reached a new hallway. Everyone knew Aceso would be waiting for them, looking to strike in that brief period they were exposed. But being that each Trial room was directly opposite the door to the next, the interval was incredibly short. A quick run across the hallway, with a few volunteers keeping armed watch, then the door would be sealed, with the occupants safe for at least another hour. This was the pattern, repeated tensely over and over. By the third hallway, they had a routine.

As soon as the door to the hall opened, the group would wait just in case Aceso made another lunge at them. If a minute passed with no beast, four of them would dart into the hallway facing both directions. The rest of the group would dash between them, then the last four would fall back into the new Trial room. The preying green eyes of the machine had been seen twice, but it hadn't attacked, the others moving too quickly.

As Reid darted into the fourth hallway to guard it, hammer at the ready, a thought danced in the back of his consciousness. He tried to ignore it, but it came out all the same. Maybe they could all escape after all.

Within a half second, it felt like he had put a pox on the whole endeavor.

Standing in the near distance, at the curve of the hallway was the beast. As they pushed deeper into the Labyrinth toward the bullseye of the target, the hallways were slowly becoming tighter and tighter. Now the curve was less than a dozen yards away, as was the metal creature hunting them. The width was growing narrower too, as the bulk of the metal creature seemed to be bunched up to fit the space. Each shoulder was bare inches from the plastic tiles.

Reid fumbled to a stop, the weapon coming up reflexively. But the sympathetic green eyes only blinked, continuing to effuse some human expressions despite the bloodshed. It ogled him curiously. On his right, a heavyset Horizoner he'd come to know laconically as 'George' stumbled into him trying to take point at his side. His grunt of displeasure quickly mutated into a gasp of fear that repeated in a chain, cascading up the ranks behind him.

"Keep moving!"

Those behind needed no encouragement, as a panicked flight began to get across the narrow passage. 'George' lost his nerve almost immediately, abandoning his place beside Reid for the relative safety of the next Trial room. With only one target to worry about, Aceso closed the distance. As before, it moved with a calm practiced pace, unafraid. Standing in its path, Reid felt the exact opposite.

For a second, he was naked and utterly insignificant, until an angry looking Sasha took position beside him. Her brow was stern, her body tense. In her hands was the other hammer, the one Reid had yanked away when Robin was attacked. Since she'd taken it back, it had become melded to her somehow. She had not dropped it in hours. Behind her glasses, the woman glared purest rancor. It was almost as if she *wanted* the fight.

Behind, came Esin's voice.

"We're in, get going!"

Needing not one molecule of further encouragement, Reid jumped backward in retreat. He was halfway through the door when he realized Sasha wasn't moving with him.

"What the hell? Sasha, what are you doing?!"

She didn't even flinch. Her feet stayed rooted to the white tiled floor as she seemed to dare the iron behemoth to move her.

Esin appeared beside him in the entrance.

"Sasha!"

Even her friend's terrified voice had no impact. As the beast drew closer, she locked onto it with a vision of hate. Her hands adjusted their grip on the mallet, tightening up for a heavy swing and surely, a futile one. Her nemesis closed the range calmly, still unafraid and probably incapable of it.

Starting to panic, Reid reached out to grab her. His fingers found loose purchase on the shoulder of her shirt, but she angrily shrugged off the touch, not even looking back. Esin was a lot less diplomatic.

Without warning, she stepped into the hall and grabbed her friend by the hair. There was a painful shriek as her head was yanked back, her defiant posture dissolving as she was thrown off balance. Seeing his window, Reid grabbed her by the arm and together they hauled her back, and toppled through the open portal. The door came down immediately, and Aceso's ceramic fingertips shrieked with the sound of a knife on a chalkboard as they fought to get a grip before it sealed. A pair of fingers appeared beneath the door, turning Reid's soul to ice, but a half second later they were battered off by a chair leg turned bludgeon, sealing the room for good.

From his painful place on the lumpy floor, Reid looked up to the owner of the club. Numb after the quick save, 'George' was shaking so badly his chair leg was wobbling like a divining rod. He stared at the foot of the door, then met Reid's surprised look. The big man averted his eyes, murmured an apology, then immediately collapsed into the arms of his teammates behind him.

For a while, it wasn't so much a trial room as an intervention. Most had gathered in a circle to express their concern for one of their number. Sasha did not take it well.

"I'm *fine*." She deflected bitterly. "Leave it alone."

"You're not fine," Esin told her. "She would've killed you."

"It was just a bad idea."

"It was crazy," Wyatt diagnosed from his usual place in the corner. "What was that? A suicide attempt?"

Through her thick-framed glasses, Sasha tried to glare but was unable to hold the gaze and turned away.

"No, it was just..."

"Because if you want to kill yourself you need to do it when you won't get the rest of us killed in the process."

From behind the VP, seemingly looking for a place to stick a knife, one of the other team members came growling to her defense. Exhaustion, not to mention the man's presence like a human sore, had not endeared Wyatt to the coworkers he was trapped with.

"Wyatt," The man seethed quietly, perhaps still wary of criticizing a superior. "The door wasn't her fault."

"I'm not talking about the door." He glowered back. "We only have two hammers and she was holding one of them. If she got herself killed, that's an effective weapon we don't have anymore. She was only thinking about herself. What about us?"

The way he said the word 'us' made Reid fairly certain he meant to say 'me'. Beneath the anguished look on her face, Sasha appeared to see it too.

"I'm sorry." She ground the words out of her throat, as though she could spit them in Wyatt's face. "I just... I needed a fight, that's all."

This brought a fountain of questions, none of which were really answered. In the end, he had to cut it short. Amid the babble threatening to overwhelm everything, he raised his hands.

"Enough!" He shouted crossly. He gestured to the ever-present timer glowing crimson. "We only have fifty minutes left. We need to get started or Aceso will come straight through that door. We'll all talk about it later."

Reluctantly, the circle wavered then turned away looking to the walls of this new room, wondering what new puzzle their lives depended on. As the others moved, Esin was still pressing Sasha who looked like she would prefer anything to continuing the conversation. He walked over and set a hand on her shoulder.

"We *will* talk about it later." He repeated to both of them. The executive's flawless features acquiesced with a nod. Sasha looked away.

Unlike most of the Trial rooms they'd encountered so far, this one didn't have central puzzle. Some ridiculous cat-toy-looking apparatus in the middle of the floor that would have been funny at any other time, but now was stomach-churningly serious. The floor was uniform with the walls and ceiling, each face indistinguishable from the others. The challenge though, was obvious. Instead of a flat surface, the walls, the floor and the ceiling were all plated with large, coloured tiles. The colours were bold and randomized to an eye-straining degree. Reid counted orange, yellow, red, blue, green and white ones all scrambled on the walls and ceiling. Each one was less than a foot square and extended two inches out so they could be gripped. He felt like he had been shrunk down and imprisoned in a cell made of Lego. He took the childish appearance in stride, knowing its original purpose. Others weren't quite so forgiving.

"I swear to Christ," Wyatt muttered next to him. "As soon as I get out of here, I am going to find every infantile sadistic idiot who designed this place and give them a pink slip. I'm sick of this funhouse."

"You're going to sack someone for doing their job right?" Reid murmured back. His eyes traced the sequence on the walls. He was counting. As the count went up, his worry deepened. "They just made a puzzle and it worked. This isn't supposed to be life and death."

Wyatt snorted.

"Yeah, well that's how it turned out." He went on griping. "So, now we have to play kid's games and hope they don't get us killed. This is my nightmare. I'm too mature for this. I never got why this damn place was so important to Fozzy anyway."

"You never asked him?"

The executive sighed, and for a moment, he looked much more human than before.

"Oh, I asked him all the time." At the mention of his fallen boss Reid thought he caught a glimmer of sadness in his voice. "I just never understood what he said back. He'd talk about HR stuff like teambuilding and making our people competitive, but then he'd swerve into nonsense. He always just ended up saying it was fun."

He scowled, blunting his sadness.

"Just as well I never got it. Games are just a place to hide anyway."

That comment made Reid pause. He stopped counting, memorizing where he'd left off, to look at Wyatt with genuine curiosity.

"What do you mean, 'a place to hide'?"

There was a dismissive wave.

"Oh, you're high orange, you get it." Wyatt seemed to scold him. "You make your head work for nothing. A game is something you put thought and time into, but it gets you nowhere. There's no pay off, no reward, just fooling around, wasting time."

Reid looked at Wyatt like he had grown wings.

"Games aren't wasting time. They're..."

Wyatt smirked as he trailed off.

"Like masturbating without the payoff at the end?"

He glared through the joke, suddenly forced to rationalize how he'd lived these last five years of his life and resenting it. He'd spent that time creating games, playing games and perfecting games in his never ending search for a way to distract from the past. His mind automatically used the word 'distract', but a worry was brewing. That might not be the right verb, after all.

"They're challenges." He pushed back. "Activities that make you fight for a solution and test a new part of your brain."

"That get you nowhere. Or maybe just deeper into the game. It's a damned loop."

"I *make* games," Reid spat half-heartedly. "There are rewards built in, moments of self satisfaction..."

The executive snorted, knowing full well who he was talking to.

"You have to know that's all bullshit, right?"

Actually, deep down he was concerned he might. Wyatt went on.

"Nothing would make me burn lean calories to just feel good about myself for a minute. You don't think people who dive into escapist stuff are just trying to hide from something? Even if it tickles your brain a little, that's fake satisfaction. You haven't got anywhere in the wallet, in the real world or in life. That means there's no *risk.* If you're not doing anything with some risk, then you're hiding. And when that sunshiny feeling goes away, what do you have left?"

He took a breath, and just when Reid thought he was done, his last words stung the most.

"Shit, isn't that the whole reason you're *here?*"

Reid's mouth dropped open, but words failed him again. There had to be some explanation he could say, maybe a pithy comeback, but nothing flowed from his consciousness. Instead, a concern built up. A worry. For maybe the first moment in his life, Reid didn't know what to think. He'd devoted so much time and energy these last five years to distracting himself from the memories. He didn't think of it as a waste, but was it *hiding?* The fact that those words burned make him think there was something to them. Most of his life was spent dodging the past. Being so consumed by distracting himself, maybe he had just avoided moving on altogether. By definition, there were some things he did not want to face.

As his mind burned aflame, Wyatt brought him out of

his introspection.

"Well," The man ran a hand through his hair, now greased exclusively with sweat, and looked derisively at the colourful wall. "Impress me, then. What is it this time?"

Maybe it was the heat, maybe the tension, or maybe that there was a grain of unpleasant truth in his words, but Reid hated the man in that moment.

"It's a Rubik's cube." He grunted.

"And just what the hell is that?"

He wrenched his sweaty neck around to gape at him.

"God, did you never play with any toys as a kid?"

Unused to receiving attitude, Wyatt blinked for a moment before his frown deepened.

"We didn't buy a lot of toys. And *don't* mention God again."

He said it loud enough that Esin looked up from the pair of people she was chatting with across the room. There was a thick moment of tension, then Reid eased down. He'd had no idea Wyatt was so religious.

"Did you ever see those cubes with the rotating squares? Six different colours, one for each side?"

Recognition blossomed on Wyatt's weary face.

"Right, yeah. A puzzle box." His eyebrows narrowed. "Are you serious?"

Hearing all this, Esin walked over.

"Are you?"

A finger jutted out.

"Four walls, a ceiling and a floor. There are six colours too. It's a Rubik's cube, we're just inside it this time."

As the rest of the Labyrinth players slowly tuned into

the conversation, eyes drifted around the room recognizing what was in front of them. A few made approving noises, even happy sounds. Reid's expression remained grim.

Wyatt was snorting again.

"I suppose you've done a few of these?" He asked sarcastically. "Why the hell is it called a Rubik's cube, anyway?"

Esin answered him, without looking.

"A Hungarian named Rubik came up with it." She put a hand on Reid's arm. The worry must have been obvious. "What's wrong?"

He took a deep breath, unable to lie.

"Most Rubik's cubes are straightforward." He began. "I started playing with the hard ones a few years ago when I had to keep my mind busy. The normal one is three by three, but they go all the way up to eleven by eleven."

He threw a bitter glare at Wyatt.

"By the way, I've done more than a few of these. *That's the problem.*"

Wyatt opened his mouth to retort, but Esin immediately shut him up with a hand.

"What do you mean?" Her eyes showed concern.

Reid looked away from the walls. He'd finished doing the math.

"For people who do speed solutions, there's actually a formula to calculate how long it would take to solve one. For each square, you should take 0.41 seconds. A three by three one has fifty-four squares. Multiply it by that number, most pros take only twenty-two seconds. As they get bigger though, you take longer to find the squares so you multiply by the number on each face."

Seeing where he was going, Esin's green eyes traced about the room doing her own counting. Judging by the way his condescending expression avalanched away, Wyatt had also caught up.

"How many squares are in here?"

Reid blearily rubbed some of the sweat off his face, feeling the prickle of newly grown hair.

"Ten across, ten up."

"Which means..."

"It would take a pro forty-one minutes to do this on one you can fit in your hand." He glanced over at the clock.

The whole room watched the timer as it menacingly passed the forty-four-minute mark, the red light playing off the various coloured squares around it. The games man didn't need to explain, but he said it anyhow.

"We're going to be short."

There was a beat of uncomfortable silence that froze the room, the whole group clearly thinking about what would happen when the clock reached zero. Luckily, the still of that moment was shattered by the shout of a petit dark-haired powerhouse of a woman bullying everyone into action.

"Well don't just stand there," Esin bellowed at the lot of them. *"Get moving!"*

TWENTY-SIX

For his thirteenth birthday, from the same Aunt who'd bought him a watch, Reid had gotten an ant colony. As much as her previous gift had been a dud, he'd loved this one. Watching the tiny figures dig their tunnels had been oddly relaxing. His favorite part had been feeding time. As he dropped crumbs of food to the waiting insects, they'd break out in what looked like a miniscule riot. The tiny creatures would scramble and climb and bowl each other over trying to grab a morsel to bring back inside. It was a great thing to see in miniature. Now, as he experienced one full scale, it wasn't nearly as much fun.

The Trial room bordered on pandemonium. Everyone had jumped into solving the task when Esin had prodded them, but no one had a clue how to do it. A few had braced themselves against the wall, trying to make the squares in one line rotate, like a real Rubik's cube. The childish puzzle remained still despite their best efforts. Others were running around the room slapping every square that could be found, looking for one that would move. Sometimes they would be so preoccupied that they would collide with a colleague running the opposite direction doing the same thing. Watching all of this, Reid didn't feel much better as he still didn't know how to rearrange the squares. His mind was replaying everything, frantically looking for clues when he heard Lara's call.

"I have a black tile over here!"

He got there a second before Esin. Sure enough, a black tile stuck out with the rest of them, a blocky black sheep in a family of colour.

"Is this the only one?" He asked.

"I haven't seen any others." Lara replied nervously. She gave it a slap, but there was no response.

Esin appeared at his shoulder, her lavender scent now tinged with sweat in the heat. She looked at the lone ebony square then back at him.

"There aren't any black faces on a Rubik." She whispered quietly. "Are you sure you know what this is?"

Reid ran his fingers around the edge of the square. Like the others, it protruded a few inches with a lip to grip onto. Without thinking, he gave it a yank and the square came out in his hands. Quickly handing it to Esin, he slid the next tile over into the space, bringing two red ones next to each other.

He didn't need to explain, as Esin was already running the other way.

"Get started!" She shouted. "Everyone, look for more black ones!"

She needn't have told him either, his sweaty hands were already sliding tiles away as he worked on the first face, sorting out the red ones and setting the others aside. Behind him came a shout that they had found another black tile, followed by the hollow plastic rattle of it striking the floor. Reid didn't bother turning to look. He didn't think they could spare the seconds.

They were in the fight, but it still moved agonizingly slow. Riding his mountain bike, when Reid had to go up one of the countless steep hills in his town, he had used the lightest gears. His long legs would be pedalling frantically with the bike moving up hill at about the same pace as a tortoise stuck in molasses. This was the same feeling.

Behind him, Esin worked her side of the room. Sometimes sending squares wrapping around along the walls to Reid and vice versa. He'd feverishly hoped to hear the rattle of a third black tile striking the floor, but it never happened. They had to make do. Slowly, the walls became mostly worked out, soon the floor as well, but the ceiling stubbornly remained out of reach. As the tallest person in the group, Reid could just barely touch the blocks with his fingertips. As the time ground lower and lower, a rock began to form in the pit of his stomach.

"We're getting too close..." He heard Wyatt call, and he cursed the man for the hundredth time.

Behind him, his ears picked up the sound of Sasha rallying whichever Horizoners weren't helping by the entrance. The thunk of clubs, the metallic thud of the sledgehammers, even the higher pitched clink of Lydia hefting her Viking sword could be heard. The pitiful militia getting ready to make their stand.

Inevitably, he ran out of tiles within reach and turned around.

"I can't get the ones on the ceiling!"

Esin, looked up from her side. Her walls were in much the same state, only with her shorter stature even more were out of reach. Beside her, Wyatt stretched out his arm for the tiles, but they too proved beyond his grasp.

"Lift me up on your shoulders." She said, pulling him close

The sweaty executive looked at her like she was insane.

"What? I'm not going to..."

"*Lift me the hell up!*"

Wyatt dropped to one knee and hefted her slender frame onto his shoulders. The two seemed to teeter for a second in that configuration, strain visible on Wyatt's face, but he soon got his footing. Esin wasted barely a second. The moment her own seat was secure, she stretched out a hand to push Lara clumsily in Reid's direction.

"Get on his back!"

The squat engineer hurried over, where Reid had already dropped down, and he hoisted her onto his shoulders. A screech of agony came from his spine that nearly clawed its way up his throat. He choked it back down, gritting his teeth against the pain and began hissing instructions, watching Lara's hands work the tiles above their heads. Time burned by like a smoking fuse, the two women working the puzzle on the ceiling. As the counter in his head moved down with the counter on the wall, Reid started to lose focus. Between the pain and the tension, the seconds started blurring together. Now, he was just working the problem and trying not to think of the dagger digging into his back. Finally, he could stand it no longer.

"How much time?!"

"A minute, forty-five!" Sasha's voice.

With all the speed of a sprinting glacier, the puzzle coalesced above. Lara was moving tiles rapidly at Reid's command, never quite keeping up. He shouted for the time again, only to learn that twenty seconds had passed. His mind had trouble staying focused, whether from the heat, the stress or exhaustion. Still the timer dropped.

"How long?"

"Fifty-seconds!" Shouted five people at once.

Above him, the section of ceiling slowly turned monochromatic, the tiles almost all in the same green face. Finally, Lara slid the last one of their lot in position. Reid instantly folded over, the woman on his back tumbling to the ground with a shriek. Hands, many hands, grabbed him to lift him back to his feet. He never knew whose, as he was still watching Esin still frantically scrambling the blocks above her.

"Thirty-seconds!" Sasha again.

Her arms, shiny with sweat, continued working the last few squares. As the number out of place dropped, Reid could see they would make it. He was perhaps the only one, because a choir of tortured cries came from behind him, egging her on.

"Seventeen!"

The last tile was swapped from the wall to the ceiling, the color complete, matched by five equally bold colours on the floor and walls. It slid into place just as Wyatt's legs gave out, dropping Esin to the ground. She landed on her feet, brushing her hair back from her face, to look with another two dozen wide eyes toward the sealed door.

Nothing.

Panic took hold. Everyone began to talk at once, hands began to flail at the walls and what semblance of control they still had fell away. Naked desperation was everywhere. A few people with clubs began hammering at the sealed door to the next passage, hoping brawn could achieve what brain had failed. As they were bludgeoning one way, Sasha was hauling them in the opposite direction. She manhandled them back into a loose line, reforming their feeble defense for when Aceso burst through the other door. Esin began yelling for them all to stay calm. Pleading, bullying and snarling at her people to little effect.

On his own quiet island in the middle of the chaos, Reid gawked at the still sealed passage in disbelief. He'd been so sure. They'd worked hard and beaten the clock he hadn't thought they could, but it had still been for nothing. In his head, his consciousness dumped everything, every memory, every experience, every half-heard anecdote or random piece of information. It was like when people described their life flashing before their eyes, a complete maw of information blending and churning together as he looked for an answer. He closed his eyes, trying to tune out the apocalypse raging around him. He still heard shouts, pleas, the banging of wood and metal. Suddenly, his ears picked up the song of plastic. A Horizonite had kicked the fallen black tile across the floor, skittering it away from him and beneath the feet of another desperate soul.

"Don't move!!"

Reid's eyes burst open to perceive a riot, frozen in time. The outburst had immobilized the terrified mass. After Robin's death, they knew to take his warnings seriously.

"Where're the black tiles?" They all looked downwards. "Quickly!"

A call came from behind him, and he turned to receive a square thrust into his stomach. It took precious seconds to find the hole, looming on the edge of the ceiling like a missing tooth. An exasperated 'George' made a reappearance, forming his hands into a stirrup to boost the game designer up, and he locked the penultimate tile into place with a satisfying click.

"Nine seconds!"

Where was the last tile?

Reid spun around in a frantic circle, the now familiar faces of his trapped companions blurring as he looked for one with proffered hands. All of them were empty, the last tile seemingly having vanished into thin air.

"Five!"

He felt something brush his foot, and his ears picked up the same skitter of plastic once again. It took another precious second to find the tile, kicked among the nervous ankles around him. When he had it in his hands and spotted the last remaining space, he didn't bother with a boost this time. In a running jump, Reid felt his feet leave the ground and slammed the tile into place.

Behind them the door slid open, the speed seeming almost nonchalant to the people who piled through it in hysterical relief. Last through the door was Reid, his back on fire from the exertion. As the lever came down, the opposite door was climbing up. There may have been a green tinge to the light that came spilling in, but he could never be sure. The door dropped like a guillotine, so close Reid felt the wind on his face, severing them from the danger behind.

There he stood, looking at the grey slate before him, without moving. He had to catch his breath and control his nervousness. His hands had shaken as he'd pulled the lever, and he didn't want anyone seeing he was rattled. Finally turning, he tried to offer a wry smile.

The faces that met him looked hollow. Eyes were sunken, cheeks gaunt. Everyone was approaching breaking point. A few released moans or whinnies, trying to express what they couldn't put into words. Reid understood completely. Equally wordless, he tiredly walked toward the new puzzle this room had to offer.

The race to stay alive began anew.

He had forgotten just how gorgeously blue the sky was. Above his head, the heavens were a boundless sapphire blanket. It stretched over the tree tops in infinite majesty interrupted only by birds darting through the vastness. After having a bunker ceiling and sterile LED lights overhead for God knows how long, it felt blissful. No clouds marred this day, none dared to. It was a perfect morning, just as it had been years ago. Reid's eyes drifted down to where Renata was waiting, sitting on the picnic blanket beside him. She smiled and so did he. They were back in the botanical garden on their date.

Everything was exactly as it had been before. The wine sat nearby, the hot dogs they had bought from a vendor, even the bees in their zip-lock container nearby which nobody was going to touch again. Her dress was the same hue of turquoise, her hair hanging loose and he could gaze at those eyes again: until they looked away. Renata's eyes darted down and to the right. Those beautiful brown irises he remembered so vividly widened a little, her smile faltering. Curious, his head followed her glance to the flames.

The hillside where they sat was burning. The grass was gone, charred to ash, and in its place, a sheet of fire washed over the land. It churned and raged and broiled as it consumed the plants, carbonizing them to blackened powder. Flowers turned to torches, the rage of the heat erasing the beauty in seconds. All around them, green was rapidly turning to orange as the garden was consumed. Reid glanced back to Renata's worried face and smiled. She tried to do the same, but now it was wavering. Her eyes kept swinging back down as the flames drew closer. Reid felt the heat, but ignored it, taking what relief he could in being back with her again.

Behind her head, he could see the willow trees. They'd been planted when the garden was new. Now, a half century later, they were seventy-five foot titans spreading their umbrella of leafy tendrils over everything around them. Reid watched them combust. The trunks caught first, the flames climbing rapidly foot by foot. Then, as it crawled onto the branches, the canopy exploded in a blaze.

The leaves ignited, transforming those lovely green tendrils into chains of fire climbing upward around them. The fire sucked in air from around them shaking loose leaves to tumble in stricken burning arcs to the ground below. That blue sky was suddenly obscured by fragments of green burning to black, like it was judgement day.

Looking at this over Renata's shoulder, he had to wince from the blast of heat when the willows caught. Her head spun at the temperature and sound, her hair spiraling out. She looked back at him with terror, and he simply smiled back. He liked being with her, she was why his mind kept coming back here. Nothing outside really mattered. She started to stand but he caught her hand and guided her back to the blanket, just as the conflagration nipped at the edge of the food. The wine began to bubble, the napkins igniting. Renata looked at him desperately, pleading with her eyes.

As the flames began to lick at the hem of her dress, all he could do was smile vacantly.

Reid awoke in a panic, sucking a breath of hot, humid, fowl-smelling air into his lungs. Above him, the blue sky was gone, swapped out for the familiar claustrophobic ceiling and LED panel lights. They were dimmed now, sheathed in amber to express that it was night in the rest of the world. Here in purgatory, that was the only indication the Labyrinth players got as to the passage of time. As the group had become worn down, they had taken a respite in an Oasis. He'd needed the sleep, but damned if he'd gotten any rest from it. He lay for a moment thinking of what the dream meant. Trying to hold onto something while the world burned around you was a clumsy metaphor, but its meaning was hard to miss. Again, he wondered if he'd truly spent these last few years hiding in all his distractions rather than facing reality. And again, he hated Wyatt for making him wonder that. Ultimately, he just felt relief the dream was over. The only thing that remained of it was the heat.

As he came awake, he sensed the stifling ever-present furnace of the room. It radiated up from the floor and through the carpet he lay on. In the last few hours, it had only grown worse, and Reid pictured the servers beneath being reduced to a pile of molten slag. It felt as if the pit of hell was growling beneath them. In the subdued light, he glanced about the room. The fourteen people left, were collapsed across the furniture where they could, or the floor, or slumped against invisible walls. The relay walls had kicked in again, giving the room the look of a sweaty transient camp in a grey field. Everyone was asleep, save one other. Even in the shadows he caught the white of her eyes. Sasha stared out at the vastness around them in the artificial twilight. At the other end of the look, a beast could be seen, sheathed in gentle emerald green. Aceso stalked along the outside of the barrier. Its metal hands probing, its eyes scanning curiously at the seam of nothingness that kept the beast from it's prey. She watched it tinkering with a bitter look on her still spectacled features. Her arms were crossed, her chin down to her chest. When Reid sat down beside her, she grunted, continuing to eye the metal creature with hate.

“How long has she been doing this?” Reid asked, watching curiously.

“About an hour.” Sasha murmured, keeping her voice subdued for those sleeping around them. “It keeps doing this lazy circle of the walls. I guess it can’t figure out how to get in.”

“Good news for us, I guess.”

She grunted again, as though that were up for debate. Her eyes never left their timid antagonist. Since Robin’s death she had hardened considerably, to the point it made him nervous.

“Do you... still need a fight?”

She ignored the inference and changed the subject.

“After the next ring, it’s the big one. The big space in the center.”

Reid sighed. He had thought of that too. His memory replayed that serene moment so long ago with everyone staring down from the catwalk at the artificial ocean swirling beneath. That was still yet to come.

“I know. We’ll get through it.”

“How?” She cut into him with the whispered word, her eyes no less sharp. “We won’t have any walls to hide behind anymore. We’ll have to defend in every direction, and there have to be a hundred ways to get to us.”

“I know.”

“We’re going to lose everyone. Everybody left.”

“I know...”

“Well then, what the hell do we *do?*”

The silence that followed showed he had no answer. Sasha looked at him in desperate need of one he could not deliver. After a moment staring at him expectantly, she shrivelled up again with crossed arms. Done with talking. Wilted by bitterness. After a moment, he just walked away.

He tried to walk around the room, as though the effort would clear his head. Sleep was out of the question; the heat too strong. He wandered along the invisible barrier, running his fingers along the surface. Feeling something tangible in what looked intangible. Occasionally, he had to step over someone, but he felt like he had to keep moving or at least keep thinking.

Sasha was right. They had made good progress fighting their way through this far, but the group had benefited from tight rooms and many options. Containing the beast in the hallways wasn't easy, but it was doable. In the final room, that would be impossible. The space was too vast, the beast too quick, the chances for attack too many to count. That wasn't even considering what kind of challenge was waiting for them. Esin had been right: there was no way the ocean was just there to look pretty.

On his right, the beast passed by, feeling its way along in the opposite direction. The two were so close they could have touched. Reid watched it with a mix of trepidation and pity. He tried to feel angry at Aceso but the actions of the AI in this place were just so different. Night and day from the quiet lion he had talked to in the gardens all those weeks ago; meek and sensitive, extremely conscious of the feelings of others. Nothing made any sense. The two did a full circuit, oblivious to each other, and as they came together again on either side of the relay wall, a thought finally came to him.

He stopped and watched the beast's approach, still inspecting the walls looking for an in. Like when they'd talked before, the AI showed signs of battle. Its metal skin was scratched, dented and pitted from the hammers, clubs, even fingernails, probably. It looked dirty and worn with dust, masonry and plastic spread about it. A fragment of the plastic door it had demolished trying to get to Esin stuck out from its arm at an odd angle, still not shaken loose after all that had happened. There were dark stains on the arms as well, ones Reid didn't want to contemplate.

Aceso passed by without hesitation, still locked on its macabre mission to reach its prey. Reid watched it for a second more, then his hand drifted into his pocket. The ephone was there, right where he had left it. He lifted it tentatively to his lips.

"Aceso."

That long angular head paused, then slowly swivelled back to aim its kindly green eyes on Reid's form, penetrating steel and concrete. The blank obsidian oval came into full view with the jagged scar he'd given it in their fight at the ventilation room, forever carved into its beneficent face. Even in that sweltering oven, a chill went up his back. There was no mouth to move, nor was there any way to hear what was happening the relay wall was so solid. But eventually a familiar, docile, androgynous voice came through the tiny speaker his hand.

"Hello Mr. Sheraton. It's good to hear your voice."

TWENTY-SEVEN

With the growling rustle of its wheels on the gravel, and the flare of its headlights, yet another van pulled up outside the gates. From inside, shrunken to insignificance on the monitor, another group of reporters scurried out, headed to where the fence barred a whole herd of others from entering. One had a microphone, one a camera, one a microphone on a stick. A predictable assortment.

Still in the maintenance offices, now scowling at the screen, Captain Kirk watched this new group with the same sunny emotions he'd shown it's predecessors. Those being: dread, helplessness and near homicidal frustration. Punting the issue over to head office hadn't solved anything. Vancouver had been no help. Media and Marketing had dropped the ball like a rock, but apparently their VP was one of the people trapped in here, so it was understandable. M&M had put out a statement saying that 'the search engine failure was an internal matter and that server crews were working hard to restore it'. Well, everybody knew exactly where Horizon kept it's servers so that little turd of information only attracted more media flies to the complex. As excuses go, that was like saying 'I didn't rob that bank, I was too busy with the safe in the jewellery store'. F-ing brilliant.

With disgust, he switched the screen off and returned to the staff meeting he'd called. After hours of nothingness from the people below, security was still begging to go down to help. So, without any better options, that was what they were doing. The entire maintenance team was in the office, looking at the blueprints for the server complex. The air had chilled in here badly since the fans had shut down and a few had the shivers. Others, it seemed, had the jitters. The killer AI hadn't exactly soothed nerves up here either, and Kerekes wondered if the shaking was just due to the temperature. No sooner had the thought crossed his mind, then one of his people flinched and jumped back from the vent nearby.

"Jesus, what was that?!"

Kerekes looked over at his cowering in irritation.

"It's just your imagination, Mike."

"I swear, I keep hearing something banging around..."

"It's just your imagination." Kerekes repeated, cutting him off. "It's rattling around your empty head, making noise. Shut up with that kinda thing. You're not helping."

He jabbed at the floorplan in front of him.

"Alright," He addressed the room. "Assuming we let them do this, where do they go in?"

A chorus of shrugs came back in response.

"The elevator platform is the only way down." His best man pointed out. "There aren't any other options. We can drop them to the path selection point, to the maintenance suites or to the center of the maze. That's it."

Kerekes knew that, but instead of cursing the obvious, he just made a grumpy face. The pressure was building, he had to do something.

"What about the maintenance lift?"

"Uh... this is the lowest floor it goes to, boss."

It took a titanic effort for Kerekes not to wince at his mistake. He'd known that too.

"I know that," He countered slowly. "But all the heat has been causing shorts in the electrics. If we need to drop them to this floor, or haul someone injured up from here, will they still work?"

The team traded concerned glances. He'd made a good point. He felt more than a little pride in that recovery.

"That's a good question." The lead guy said. Boy, that felt great to hear right now. "I'll have to test it. Honestly, I'm a little worried about the elevator platform too."

Kerekes' good feelings vanished as quickly as they'd come.

"What happens if that goes?" He asked nervously.

"Well, there's a ladder along the side of the shaft, but that's a *long* climb."

Behind him, Mike's head snapped back to the ventilation grate and he jumped away like he'd touched a live wire. With the tension in the room, the whole team flinched then settled in to pile abuse on their co-worker.

"I swear I heard something!" He pleaded.

"Shut the hell up!" Three people chorused, Kerekes one of them. He was nervous enough about the idea of sending more people down there already.

With nothing else to say, he scattered the group, a few went to test the lifts, a few to security, a few (including Mike, the jittery one) to the surface to check for volunteers from EMS. He hated the idea of sending anyone into the Labyrinth, certainly not *ordering* anyone. But, at this point, he didn't know what else to do.

"Hello Mr. Sheraton. It's good to hear your voice."

The words crept into his ears through a layer of sweat and a layer of slumber. Wyatt slowly awoke on that godawful carpet, his neck throbbing, he could have sworn he had heard the AI speak. He dismissed it as a dream just as quickly. His self-hating subconscious playing tricks. There was nothing that terrified him more than an open conversation between Aceso and Sheraton. Except maybe being trapped alone with the machine again. When his eyes cracked open though, low and behold, his nightmare had become a reality.

When he saw the AI standing so close, he snapped awake, sucking in a big breath in a panic. For a moment he thought the machine had actually broken in. Seeing Sheraton's face quickly calmed him down, though. The game designer was as weathered as the rest of them, his t-shirt patched with sweat and with sunken eyes. But there wasn't an ounce of concern on his face as Wyatt watched the man lift an ephone to his mouth.

"It's good to hear yours too." He answered Wyatt's broken product softly. "You've been worrying a lot of people in here."

"I know…" The speaker in his hand replied hesitantly. "Do they hate me now?"

Watching the AI's puppy-dog persona assert itself again, Wyatt was almost sick on the floor. Even as a rampaging monster, the damn thing acted like a nervous kitten. The fact that this thing posed a mortal threat to them should have been laughable. Internally, he swore if Aceso actually managed to kill him at some point in this nightmare, he would find it pretty embarrassing.

"Some do," Sheraton replied. "Most are just afraid."

The games man glanced back around the room. In the artificial twilight, Wyatt saw that many eyes had opened. People listening to the conversation. He eased onto his feet, as the room awoke. Slowly the group of haggard souls began to come close to watch this candid conversation with their tormentor.

Sheraton waited as they closed in. Esin, still looking

pretty stunning by the way even in all the grime and tension, slid up close beside him. Behind her came Lara, looking like she needed a box to stand on to see what was happening. Last to come was the woman in glasses who seemed to loathe him. Whatever her name was she seemed to think this was all his fault. The fact that it was didn't occur to him. He was still offended by it. She took her time wandering over, and by the way she glowered, Wyatt got the impression that the only thing she despised more than him was Aceso. When everyone was there, Sheraton lifted the ephone once again.

"I want to talk."

"Of course." The AI responded immediately. Even now, it sounded anxious, even eager. "I'm sorry we couldn't talk earlier. I really wanted to."

Sheraton's face wrinkled slightly.

"When?"

"In the hallway," The machine answered vaguely. "Then in the Oasis room when I was restricted by the closing door."

There was a moment of confused silence.

"Uh... You mean, when you were trying to kill me?"

The damn thing actually bent its head down as though attempted murder were a big embarrassment.

"Yes." The mechanism conceded feebly. "I'm... ashamed of that."

The stark silence in the room after those words reverberated with a 'you should be' feeling. To his credit, Sheraton ignored it.

"You've hurt a lot of people."

"I'm so sorry. Each one has been... agony."

"For everyone." The voice was Esin's, coming in low.

Reid's grey eyes flicked over to her then back smoothly.

"Aceso, what happened?" Sheraton asked. "This is nothing like you. Everyone here is supposed to be a patient, but you're killing us. It seems to hurt you. Tell me why you're doing this."

He spoke with the kind of sincere familiarity you used with an old friend. Like everyone else it seemed, Sheraton had an affection for the AI, apparently even when it was rampaging around as the minotaur. The man was high orange and yet was still overcome with sentimentality. Wyatt chalked it up to Aster's influence, how he had gone soft on the merchandise.

"I was given new objectives," Aceso answered. "Instead of a list of patients I have a list of targets now."

"Who in God's name wanted you to do that?"

"I can't discuss it, Mr. Sheraton. I'm truly sorry."

The game designer's grey eyes narrowed.

"I think you owe us an explanation."

"Yes," The machine said, the statement sounding oddly heartfelt. "I want to explain. I'm bound by my new objectives, but I hate every passing second I… attempt them. I'm sorry, none of this is what I wanted."

Someone beside him made a kind of growl in their throat. With the way Aceso had turned this place into a chamber of horrors, he wasn't surprised no one believed it.

"I believe you."

Wyatt looked over in confusion. The voice was Sheraton's, the sentiment real, it seemed. The room recoiled from this, but the AI ate it up like a puppy. Its head jolted up again, its kindly green eyes somehow seeming wider. Vaguely, Wyatt wondered if a machine could classify as high red.

“Thank you, Mr. Sheraton.” It said weakly.

“You’re welcome. Can I tell you why?”

“Of course.”

“Do you remember the ice?”

Wyatt watched a fascinating vacancy play out on Aceso’s face, reviewing the memory. That wasn’t unusual for an AI, he saw it every day at his division. What made it interesting was that simultaneously an identical look played out on Sheraton’s face. The games man’s suddenly looking far more mechanical than before. The two were just different versions of each other. Deep down the guy was a freaking automaton himself.

“I remember.”

“You should have killed me there. How come you didn’t?”

“I couldn’t be sure it was really you.”

Sheraton scoffed loudly, probably just for the benefit of the blank faced monstrosity that couldn’t see him.

“Sure, you could.” He grunted. “You saw me run in there?”

“Yes.”

“There were no other exits?”

“No.”

“Then you found me beat to hell in a pile of crumbling ice. You could have done it.”

A beat passed.

“I couldn’t verify your heat signature through the cold or your face from the distortion.” Aceso countered. “It could have been someone else.”

Sheraton, technically the human in this exchange,

shook his head.

"Bullshit."

Aceso's head leapt up a few degrees at the profanity.

"It could only have been me." Sheraton went on. "There was nowhere I could go, no one else it could have been. You just found an excuse not to hurt me because *you didn't want to.*"

The words slowly soaked into the AI. Then, an equivocating half sigh came from the speaker clutched in Sheraton's hand. Watching from afar, Wyatt almost thought he saw the beast tear up. Its sympathetic eyes dimmed, its head dipping.

"I... I didn't want to hurt you."

Sheraton brightened with this, and an interested murmur swept through the room. Even Wyatt was temporarily moved. There might be some hidden strength in this weakling after all. Either one of them.

Seeing where this was going, the VP was intrigued in spite of himself. He suddenly saw the game designer as confident and perceptive, almost high grey, although that last one was a stretch.

"I know." He smiled, wasting the expression on a thing that couldn't see it. "And you didn't. Thank you."

"Well, I... I suppose you're welcome." It could have been in his head, talking to Aceso was like an emotional Rorschach test, but the AI seemed to regain a moment's pride. It straightened slightly with its self-worth, beginning to tower over the mortals again. A few backed away nervously.

"I truly didn't want to hurt you." It repeated.

"I know." Sheraton parroted back. "So, you found a way around the objectives someone gave you. You found a loophole."

"I'm sorry?"

"A loophole. A way around a rule you don't want to follow."

There was a moment's buffering at the other end of the line.

"Yes. I found a loophole."

"Then, why didn't you find one for Robin?!" An angry voice suddenly burst in.

Wyatt yanked his gaze over to the angry woman in glasses. She'd suddenly become animated, breathing hate over Sheraton's shoulder. Esin caught her arms to calm her down but she brushed the hands aside as if the other woman wasn't there.

"Or for Aster," She spat again. "Or the marshals? Or for anyone on the AI team? Or for Fozzy for God's sake!"

The words must have gotten through because the AI shuddered, slumping like a dog that'd been kicked. Sheraton spun angrily, holding up a hand and, for once, Wyatt agreed with him completely. He'd been making some damn headway until then. She needed to think about the rest of them and shut the hell up. Esin managed to shush her back to silence but it was too late. Just as Sheraton was ready to resume the conversation, Aceso answered her with his own question.

"Aster is dead?"

Sheraton winced at the remark. His face might as well have been a switch, because Wyatt's stomach turned over at the same time at the mention of his half-victim. Maybe murder *was* a big embarrassment.

"Yeah, he..." The game designer hesitated, dancing into a minefield. "He died of his wounds, Aceso."

"Oh, no..."

With those words the damn AI almost folded in half. In less than a second, its legs seemed to give out, it dropped to the ground and a half cry of anguish came from the box. Watching, the creature slump over in mourning for its creator, the VP was struck again by just how ill suited the medic was for this kind of thing. He had wanted to make a combat AI and had envisioned a tough, ruthless assassin. Something cold and remorseless, where mortality was part of its business. Instead, he got this whimpering mass before him. Aceso was doing almost as much damage to itself as to its targets. Had he been in the room, Wyatt thought he could have walked up and shoved the mechanical monster over with ease. He shook his head, grateful that Veles couldn't see this.

Then, a curious thing began to happen. From over his shoulder, he heard a noise, not the low growl of hatred that he had heard before, but a softer sound. Something sympathetic. He glanced over, bewildered, to find Lydia, the weathered lead from the Automotive team, looking at the pathetic sight with sadness. Her face held no rancor, just the empathy of someone who had also endured the loss of a friend.

Wyatt looked at this like she was insane. Sure enough, he saw that look repeated on faces around the room. People couldn't actually be *buying* this, could they? This thing had killed their coworkers, they couldn't sympathize with it? He'd lost Fozzy in here, and he still felt no compassion toward the pathetic piece of broken technology cowering on the other side of the wall. It was still purely a noun, an object, and something that threatened him. In his own head, he started hating these people. They were becoming high red at the worst time.

In front of him, Aceso was trying to gather itself.

"That wasn't meant to be a fatal wound!" It breathed through the speaker. "I didn't want that."

At the front of the pack, still sounding like a therapist while looking like a shipwreck survivor, Sheraton lifted the ephone.

"Why not?"

"I was obligated to eliminate him," The machine wailed. "but I thought if I were to injure him it would slow the other members of the group down. I could avoid his death. So, I chose to do that."

"You found a way around it."

"But he died anyway!" Aceso looked up, its green eyes pleading to Sheraton to make everything better.

"It's not..." He seemed to catch himself halfway through saying, 'It's not your fault'. It damn well was, and the AI knew it. The games man swallowed, then started again.

"It happened." Sheraton said, reverting to the obvious. "There's no way to change it. You have to try to move on from it now."

"I... I'm not sure I can."

"We need you to. You can't..."

His face clouded up mid sentence as though the words were foreign to him. His grey eyes, looking like firelight in the amber glow, became strangely distant. It took a second before he finally finished.

"You can't dwell on the past."

The machine took the advice, nodding in comprehension, but remained looking devastated.

"What do you need me to do?"

"Find a new loophole. Let us get out."

Aceso shook its head in violent negative. The action was so sudden, a few people jumped back again, startled.

"I want to, Mr. Sheraton but I can't." It said. "The objectives I was given are firm. Every target has to die."

"What the hell *are* your objectives now, anyway?"

"I'm sorry, I can't discuss them."

"Swell." Sheraton grunted dryly. "Where did you get them?"

"I'm sorry. I can't say."

"When did they change?" He jabbed back immediately, his questions coming faster. In the background Wyatt rolled his eyes. The AI wasn't going to tell them anything and he was growing tired of this whole pointless exchange.

"I can't say."

"Well, can you tell me who gave them to you?"

That one woke him up. Wyatt jolted slightly, biting his tongue, hopefully a metaphor for what the machine would do now. He had ordered Aceso not to discuss the combat Acumen, but now it seemed on the brink of cracking. Still, AI's were bound by their instructions. The machine's next words confirmed it.

"No, sir." Aceso answered forlornly. "I was given explicit instructions not to discuss my new objectives."

"From whom, though?"

"I..."

"You said you wanted to explain, now's your chance."

The machine actually looked pained. Aceso was tense, seeming to fidget in an uncomfortably human way.

"I'm sorry... I can't..." It shook its head in an anguished negative.

Sheraton quickly put his hands up like he was miming, as though the machine could see him through the wall.

“Don’t think that way!” He snapped. “Think logically with me.”

“Alright…”

“You can’t talk about what happened?”

“No.”

“You can’t talk about how this happened?”

“No.”

“Is there anyone you *could* talk about it with?”

There was a moment, Wyatt could almost hear gears frantically grinding inside the AI’s head, it’s circuits working the problem. Subconsciously, he shook his head at the whole exercise. He knew he was safe, still coolly confident in the immutability of his orders.

“Yes.” The tiny speaker squeaked at last. “There is someone.”

Wyatt’s whole body twitched. Mercifully, no one was watching, everyone transfixed on the reveal before them. The VP tensed up, watching Sheraton lead the damn AI down the garden path. A cold fist began to close in his stomach, his hands beginning to tremble at his side.

“Okay.” Reid smiled, oblivious to his suffering and wasting yet another expression on something that couldn’t see it. “Who could you talk to?”

Wyatt tensed further. He wanted to run, but there was nowhere to run to. As much as he wanted to, there was no stopping it now. He stayed locked there in that moment waiting for the machine’s answer. In the end, it did not disappoint him.

Finally, that massive head shook, the scar on its void of a face swaying back and forth.

"I'm sorry Mr. Sheraton," Aceso whined in its piteously, predictable, subservient way. "I just can't answer you."

The video game man's face fell with the rest of the room. Sheraton looked deflated, just as Wyatt felt euphoric. The expression on his face was one of pure defeat and it brought such savage relief that he had to strain to keep from grinning maniacally. His secret was still safe, even if he was still trapped in here with the rest of them. A few grumblings bubbled up around the room, the general negative chorus that said it was a waste of time to even talk. Some people sat down on the floor weakly, the futility of their situation underlined with empty words. Wyatt felt like singing.

In front of him, Sheraton had given up. He raised the ephone to his open mouth to continue, but seemed to falter mid way. The device sagged to his side, and his head dropped in surrender. He had tried and failed. There would be no answers and, more importantly, no relief. After a moment, even he turned his back on the beast.

Just as the group started to disperse, each man and woman returning to their own private brood, the Ai's voice chirped up one more time from the speaker. It was faint and strained, the words so hesitant it sounded like a confession. But it came through clear enough that the whole room heard.

"Can you... Can you have Mr. Wyatt ask me that question please?" Then, amid a thunderous silence. "Is he there?"

For a moment, nothing happened. In the stifling heat of the room the only sound was the breathing of its weary occupants. The stillness was so deep, they almost wondered whether Aceso had really said those words. Reid turned to look at Wyatt, his face shiny with sweat, his eyes the size of saucers. The man's mouth had dropped open and he stared unblinkingly at where Aceso still lingered on the other side of the relay wall. Reid spoke his name and his eyes suddenly focused, shifting over to lock on Reid's inquisitive greys.

Then he tried to run.

The executive turned, trying to dash away even though there was no place to go, but the dozen others had already closed in on him. In a very uneven grapple, Wyatt tried to flail and punch his way free but was dragged back to the wall.

"Let go!" He shrieked. "Get your fucking hands off me! I didn't do anything!"

From the crowd, Sasha emerged to grab his arm and hammered his body down in a sinister looking joint lock. Wyatt shrieked, instantly brought to heel, as his wrist was twisted to near breaking point. He dropped to his knees shouting for mercy. Sasha looked ready to provide absolutely none.

"This is a mistake!" Wyatt hissed through gritted teeth. "I don't know what it is with the damn AI."

From above him, Reid didn't waste any time. He had known something was wrong, and now he wanted to know exactly what. He stuck the ephone in the VP's face.

"Ask Aceso who she can talk to." He said heavily.

"Screw you! I'm not going to... Ah!!!"

Sasha wrenched his wrist even further and pressed his body forward angrily. He released a painful whine but no words crossed his lips. From behind, Esin came forward, a malevolent look on her face. With Sasha holding him in place, she grabbed him by his hair and yanked his head forward until his face was pressed against the invisible barrier. His features seemed to distort in mid-air, Esin not slackening the pressure for a second.

"Do it!" She yelled into the back of his head. Sasha again began to twist.

It was a contest over what would give first, Wyatt's will or his bones. There was another cry of pain, and just before Reid thought his wrist would shatter, he babbled out the question.

"Who can you talk to?!"

On the other side of the wall, Aceso now appeared impassive, staring at grey nothingness.

"I can only discuss my objectives with you, Mr. Wyatt." It answered clinically. "As per your instructions."

Reid looked back in disbelief, his face reddening with anger. From around the room, every other face looked gobsmacked by the revelation.

He fumbled for the ephone again, seeing red.

"What objectives?" He squawked, the question directed at both of them. "What are they?"

When Aceso answered with only a helpless blink of its kindly eyes, Reid returned to Wyatt.

"Ask her."

"I'm not..."

Reid kicked him in the side angrily. The VP broke into a coughing fit but then set his jaw against the pain and remained silent. It took further corkscrew diplomacy from Sasha before he again, excruciatingly, bellowed the question.

On the other end, Aceso showed no emotion for the pain Wyatt was clearly enduring. That seemed out of character, but maybe it was just this person in particular. For the first time, the machine's responses felt genuinely robotic as it answered once again.

"As you instructed Mr. Wyatt." The beast replied. "'kill', 'kill anyone who tries to stop you' and 'don't let yourself be stopped until you're done killing'. I believe those were your words, sir."

At the machine's words, gasps, and outrage came from around the room. The noises coalesced, sounding to Reid like the genesis of a lynch mob, all focused on the traitor laid vulnerable before them.

"That is totally out of context..." Wyatt backpedaled breathlessly from the floor. "That was never supposed to happen here. The damn thing is just..."

Esin smashed his face into the relay wall again. The executive let loose a yelp. As he came away, a greasy ghost impression of his features seemed to linger, imprinted in mid-air.

"You killed Fozzy!" She spat down at him.

"I didn't kill anybody," He said nasally, holding his nose with his free hand. "I loved the old man. That *thing* did it. You think I wanted any of this to happen?"

As she was about to strike him again, Reid caught her arm. She met his eyes, and he saw they were beginning to tear up. After a second he let her go then nudged the prone Wyatt with his foot.

"Explain all of this."

"I can't explain any of it!" Wyatt shrieked. "The AI is bullshitting you all. I just..."

Without a word, Reid grabbed a sledgehammer from where it rested against the wall. He dropped to his knees crouching down by the executive's stubborn face to get as close as possible. As he did it, the heavy end smashed into the floor with an ominous ground-shaking crack.

Their prisoner got the inference.

"Explain." He breathed into his petrified features. *"Now."*

It came out in fits and starts, each part of the story told with equivocation by the beleaguered man at their feet. The excuses and distortions were so numerous that Reid kept the ephone on so Aceso could hear. Every so often, they would check in with Wyatt's unwilling co-conspirator for clarification. If the machine offered a nod they would go on. If it shook its head, then Sasha would grind the true answers out of him. They heard about the combat Acumen, the thumb drive, the entire sordid backstory of the nightmare they were trapped in. When it was over, a new question overrode everything else.

"So, what do we do with him?" Sasha asked. Her face made it clear that what she really wanted was to dismantle Wyatt then and there.

Had Reid taken a vote, he was sure retribution would have won handily, but that wasn't going to happen. Just as he opened his mouth to answer, someone unexpectedly broke in.

"Can I ask Mr. Wyatt a question?"

The quiet voice came from the ephone, without any of the turmoil of before. Reid looked up in surprise at Aceso's question. The beast was standing tall now, perhaps the reveal had been cathartic for it too, an unburdening of its sins. Now that the whole story had been laid bare, all of the hate cultivated in the room had found a new target.

Reid grunted.

"Go ahead."

The machine took a second to form its words. Even so,

they came out in an emotional, almost pleading, tone.

"Why is this happening sir?"

From the floor Wyatt looked up at the machine with contempt.

"I tried to ask you earlier, but you wouldn't answer. Why am I required to do this?"

"Oh, the hell if I know!" He growled. "None of this was supposed to happen. You weren't supposed to be here, you were never supposed to talk about this with anyone, and you were never supposed to actually do any of this shit. I told all of you! This is all just a big mistake."

The speech garnered him little sympathy in the room. A few Horizoners seemed ready to revisit their bloodier ideas for how to deal with him.

Aceso sagged with the news.

"This is all a mistake..." The machine croaked.

Reid pulled the ephone back to his mouth.

"Aceso," He said gently. "You know it's a mistake now. You can stop all this."

"I'm still bound by my objectives, Mr. Sheraton."

He felt a cold shiver.

"You don't have to be..." He kicked the man at his feet once more, a not unpleasant feeling. "Tell her she can stop!"

"Mr. Wyatt is now a target as well." Aceso said eerily before he could answer. "I can't take orders from him anymore."

"It was a *mistake,*" Reid breathed into the ephone. "It was never meant to happen. There's no reason to do this anymore."

"But there's no way I can stop."

Aceso seemed to look through the wall at each of them, its eyes scanning the faces of those who were left. The dim green lights looked more forlorn than ever before. But in its sadness, it once again was purely a mechanism.

"I am still required to kill you all, but there will be no purpose for it."

There was a beat of silence, Reid felt his throat close ominously.

"Aceso..." He tried again fumblingly, but it was no use.

Before him, the machine silently turned its back and walked away, accepting the inevitable. No matter how many times he called it back, there was no answer. The beast slumped away in a dejected futility, acceding to its bloody fate. Eventually, it crossed the boundary of the great unknown mass in front of them and disappeared from view.

TWENTY-EIGHT

In a sterile white hallway of the Labyrinth, the final one of the nine ringing the complex, the door to an Oasis slipped open. The heat from within drifted into this as yet untouched part of the maze, but not a soul emerged. In all the previous hallways, there had been a rush of people running for safety in a Trial room or another Oasis. This time, there was nothing. The door stayed open, with naught passing through but the scent of sweat from those remaining inside. Time passed, but the doorway remained empty. Nobody knew what to do anymore.

Inside the Oasis, the mood swung from feeling like the aftermath of a funeral to the preamble to an execution. With Aceso's departing words, it was clear that the funeral was for everyone left still trapped in this place. If the conversation had proved one thing, it was that there would be no relief or negotiation. The fight would go on. The execution, on the other hand, was centered on one man in particular.

Finally released from Sasha's merciless hold, Wyatt stood with his back pressed against a solid, and now once again opaque, relay wall. In the perfect playback that was his memory, Reid brought up the moment he had first met the business man. Sauntering forward in an immaculately pressed suit with hair that could have been laser sculpted and a diamond-hard sense of self confidence, that man had seemed to own the world. This man had absolutely nothing. His only possession seemed to be a scowl that he held to ward off the people around him. His hair was mussed and greasy, his clothes wrinkled from sleeping on the floor and soiled with a cornucopia of stains. His eyes seemed hollow, even in their glare and his back was against the wall as much for support as anything else. Once a force to be reckoned with, he'd been reduced to a bitter wraith of a human being. Staring at him now in his pitiable form, Reid still thought he deserved worse. If the man really was religious, he should have used every breath to pray for help.

Mercifully for him, the topic in the room had shifted away from the thirst for vengeance. Wrath would sit on the backburner for now, with Wyatt remaining mute for the conversation, lest it be brought up again. Instead, the ever-looming question was how to keep everyone else alive.

Sasha didn't mince her words.

"We should try to kill it."

The whole room recoiled at this, Reid included. The uneven futility of that kind of fight made it sound insane, not to mention, if by some miracle they succeeded, then they'd be killing Aceso. Even amid such free bloodshed, the death of the beast somehow felt wrong, especially now that they finally knew why all of this had happened. For her part, still hot to fight, Sasha seemed not to care.

"We have a much better chance of winning a fight in here than when we reach the center." She went on. "The minute we're out of these hallways, we won't have a wall to cover our back. It'd be stupid to try it later."

"It's stupid to try it *now*." Came a familiar voice.

The corporate Gollum by the wall had come to life again. With his oily hair drooping in front of bloodshot eyes, he grunted his assessment from a distance.

"That thing can kill all of us effortlessly." He hissed quietly. "The only reason it hasn't yet is it was pussyfooting around making excuses before, and now you're going to attack it? You want to get your throat cut or your head smashed? *Pick one*."

Sasha glared back at the comment, seemingly prepared to offer him the same choice. She quickly turned to Esin letting her face soften again.

"We'll never get through the next stage." She pleaded. "We have to do *something*."

The smaller executive looked wary.

"Sasha..."

"We need to kill it!" She cut her off sharply.

Esin looked over in Reid's direction.

"Can we?"

He frowned a harsh negative.

"I'm sorry. I just don't think we'd stand a chance."

Sasha glowered at his words like they were a betrayal. The fact that he was clearly speaking the truth mattered not at all.

"She is right, though." He went on. "In a big open space, we lose any advantage we have. We'll never be able to protect everyone, let alone have the time and space to cross whatever that obstacle is. We have to deal with Aceso now. At the very least, we need to buy a few hours to get through to the elevator."

"How?"

Reid took a deep breath. In the end, he had only one plan, and he laid it out in detail for the room to review. It went over about as well as he'd expected.

"How the hell is that any better than what I said?" Sasha demanded instantly.

Others were more direct.

"Are you out of your mind?!" Wyatt's shrill voice tore into his eardrums. "I already tried that!"

For once, Wyatt seemed to be voicing everyone else's thoughts too, because the room bubbled up in alarmed protest. Lara backed up, shaking her head ominously, a few Horizoners throwing up their hands in hopeless futility at the idea.

"It doesn't have be all of us." Reid tried to counter. "Not everyone is armed. We should split up anyway. We can try with just a few people."

He looked around, trying to appear confident about the whole thing. He wasn't.

"If anybody wants to volunteer, I'd appreciate it."

The job offer proved about as popular as testing macramé parachutes, and the room lapsed back into it's uncomfortable silence. Not a soul raised their hand, stepped forward or made any move at all. Save one.

Stepping forward to address the group, using what authority she had left as the only non-disgraced Vice President in the room, Esin provided the last word. The statement was stark, her words predictably succinct.

"Does anyone have a better idea?"

In the end, there was no choice. Half of those left alive were locked away in a Trial room down the hall, the clock ticking downward, the door set to rise again in an hour. They would be safe until then, but if the others failed in the plan then no one would be safe. The six unlucky chosen were in the Oasis, the door still open to the hallway beyond. They stood, knelt or crouched in darkness. Reid, with his hat-rack shaped frame, had stood on a chair to smash out the LED lights providing what little illumination the Labyrinth offered at this hour. Now, he crouched beside the open portal with Esin by his side. In the tepid light that crept into the blackness, both showed the weariness and foreboding they clearly felt. The lines were drawn, the trap was set. There was nothing to do now but think about all that had happened, and all that was yet to come.

Watching them, Sasha Li felt something akin to despair, wondering if any of this would really work.

She shifted the heavy weight of her sledgehammer, pressing her back against the wall as a temporary reprieve. The warm surface gave little relief, but it was enough. The last thing she wanted was for someone to take the weapon off her because she looked tired. She didn't feel complete without it anymore.

It had all gone so wrong. Everything they had wanted, everything they had tried to achieve. Every goal had bled to death in this place. She'd been genuinely excited, honoured even, when Esin had come to her. They'd become fast friends when they'd first met and a few years of working together hadn't dulled the feeling. They'd talked about her plans to win the Labyrinth and Sasha had been happy to offer advice. But she had never thought about doing the crazy race herself. It was something you talked about on off hours, over a drink or making bets on the outcome. It was something you heard about other people doing. When Esin had asked her to be a part of it, to bring a dose of her lateral thinking into the mix, she had been stunned. How could she say no?

All of it had been magical. Getting to know the team, doing challenges, working together to beat them, the whole lead up. Having always been a bit of a tomboy and never enjoying groups, she'd found a bond with the others that had been different. They were eclectic, a collection of oddballs that normally would never have met. But they had been brought together for one goal, they were motivated and they had been *good*. She'd felt genuine pride in her when they'd been ahead before. Standing in that first Oasis, the five had seemed unstoppable. Now, two of those five were dead, the game was over and whatever well of pride she had owned before had been poisoned when the first body had struck the ground. What a difference a day made.

To be fair, no one had reacted well to the bloody turn this place had taken. The silent horror show they seen through the relay wall had shaken everyone up. But she had felt it more than most. The stark violence of the act was still ricocheting around her head. Now and then, it would appear in front of her eyes again, like she couldn't escape that moment. It was her first time seeing death and it haunted her. She hadn't been the same after that. Being afraid felt toxic, enfeebling. Her normally rapid-fire brain felt as if it were spinning in place unable to shake the tension.

As the fight to escape had gone on, she'd snatched back a little of what she'd lost. Anger had helped. Anger at Wyatt before and then so much more after his reveal, anger at Aceso, even anger at herself. At least that had given her enough clarity to think about how to dodge the crazy AI. It had been her idea to flood the Labyrinth with heat, and it had worked, after a fashion. But the losses kept mounting. First Fozzy, then Aster. She had started drawing strength from fighting to keep her head. There'd always been two sides to her: the mental, grounded in lateral thinking, and the physical, the athlete who pushed herself to break her limits. The athlete started taking over. Swinging that hammer against Aceso had been a rush, like she was taking back her life. She had started clinging to it like it would float and keep her above water. She would win back her pride blow by blow if she had to.

Then they lost Robin.

The handsome assistant had caught her eye from the

moment Esin had hired him. He was very hard to miss, but he had his supportive side too. She hadn't initially had a thing for him just because he was so obviously into Esin. The two were too close to compete for his affections. Men were usually boring to Sasha anyway. Still, working together in the last few weeks, there had been an undeniable spark. The night before the Labyrinth, in that ridiculous dress she had bought, for the first time, she had truly eclipsed Esin in Robin's eyes. It felt so amazing to be seen that way. Through this whole nightmare, he'd been there, as supportive as he'd ever been. Then she had let him down.

When that door had opened and Wyatt's abomination had smashed through, she should have been first to attack it. The hammer was in her hands, she was close enough to swing, but the image from before had crashed into her consciousness. She'd frozen. By the time Reid had pulled the hammer away, there was nothing he could do. Nothing any of them could do. As they stood over his body, Esin had tried to tell her that it wasn't her fault, but that was a lie. Of course, it was. She needed a fight now more than ever. In that dark room waiting to attack, Esin, Reid and the rest felt their own anxiousness, hoping to make it through alive. All she wanted now was to see her dog again.

Behind her, Lydia broke into a coughing fit, hacking into the elbow of her sword hand to baffle the sound. Shortly behind her, naturally as far from danger as he could possibly get, Wyatt cursed the sound.

"For Christ's sake," He hissed nervously. "Flood your damn lungs for all I care. Shut up!"

The executive had been drafted onto their little suicide mission, and as far as Sasha was concerned, his side of it needed a whole lot more of the former than the latter.

"I can't help it," Lydia murmured angrily. "It's hot in here, my throat's dry. I lost my canteen the first time we met

Aceso. Which side is it on again?"

"I told you, left side."

"You're sure?"

"*Yes,*" He stressed with exasperation. He looked at her as though she were still a stupid underling. "Under the armored wing that protects the stretcher. I plugged the damn thing in myself."

Lydia glared at him, augmented by Sasha sending the purest violent rage over her shoulder at the wretch responsible for their fates.

"*We know.*"

The executive turned inward, both were satisfied to see him wilt in their gazes. He was anxiously tightening his grip on the clumsy piece of aluminum pipe someone had given him. It had probably been snapped from some cheap table or chair conscripted into the fight. Wyatt hadn't wanted a part in the battle to come, but he had plugged the poison pill into Aceso. Everyone agreed he should be one of those risking their lives to remove it.

Maybe doing that would turn the machine back into its quiet, unimposing self, healing their wounds and making many dainty apologies. Or maybe it would just resume killing them all as if nothing had happened, thankful they had made its job easier. And that was assuming they could get to the USB at all. There were so many risks to the plan they coalesced into this biting tension that filled the darkened room around the would-be assailants waiting to strike. Again, Sasha just missed her dog.

Just as she was beginning to wonder whether this was all for nothing, the three by the door suddenly tensed up. A second later, the first footfalls reached her ears. They were quiet, faintly heard over the sound of her heart beating in her ears, but it was unmistakable. The walk was fast, many steps from four legs, but it was the weight of it that was distinctive. Each step felt heavy somehow, the broad sound quiet, yet telling the mass of the machine gliding toward them on steel hooves. Reid waved everyone down and they slunk further into the shadows, waiting. Sasha subconsciously edged deeper into the darkness as that familiar anxiety rose again.

A glimmer of green winked across the tiles in the doorway. On one side of the entrance, Reid gently hefted his hammer. Opposite him across the doorway, another Horizoner, a husky nervous man she thought was named George, raised a wooden chair leg.

A metal leg appeared in the entrance, covered in scratches and dust. Battle scarred. In its feline way, it eased to the ground, then an angular head loomed into view. Sasha darted down deeper, staying out of sight. A green light washed over the wall behind her, shadows playing over objects in turquoise. When light played away, she eased up again.

Aceso was in the doorway now. It moved cautiously, knowing something had to be wrong. The lights were never out in a used Oasis. But the machine was a curious thing, or so Reid had said. It kept moving forward into the trap. By now, George had lifted his wooden club so high he would have looked ridiculous if not clearly so terrified, waiting for a target to swing at. As soon as the machine's head had stooped through the doorway, he swung. With lightning speed, Aceso's hand came up and caught the club, stopping it dead in mid-air. Sasha's mouth dropped open in shock, synchronised with George's, who still held the bludgeon. There was a second's black comedy, as the depth of their peril sunk in, then the machine threw the club back into his face with pitiless force. George went flying from the impact, tumbling into the corner. Before he had come to a stop, the rest of the room ran in for the attack.

It was a clumsy, messy affair, with the frantic close quarter violence that came from desperation. The first few blows were scattered, only a few striking the head. It became clear all too quickly that the clubs were useless in stunning the machine. Only a blow from a sledgehammer could do that. That left only two real weapons, and Sasha held one of them. She charged in with reckless abandon, screaming the kind of abuse and language that would have made her mother roll in her grave. The machine was lithe and quick though, taking few hits in the exchange. From its other side, Reid charged in with his own attack. His blows were cautious and calculated, he obviously didn't feel the hate that Sasha did. As he swung a heavy blow, Aceso darted to one side, letting the swing throw the man off balance. With the lightest of shoves, the machine then sent him sprawling into the others, both Esin and Lydia tumbling down in a painful heap. As the machine advanced on its temporarily helpless victims, Sasha saw her window.

She sidestepped to the right, dodging around whatever peripheral vision the AI had, hopefully dropping into its blind spot. With an extra half second of concentration, all the while muttering the names of her fallen friends like a prayer, she swung. The impact was a great rush of satisfaction, her hammer striking the machine square across the flat of its head. Aceso staggered from the hit, showing weakness for the first time. She could do this...

She struck it again and again, forcing the machine away from its victims, driving it backward against the wall. Other hits came now from the people left on their feet. Wyatt joined in the fight, likely now that they seemed to be winning. With one final smack, Aceso toppled on its side revealing the seam of its armoured wing. Sasha practically screamed.

"Lydia!"

The sword wielding woman, back on her feet, though bruised, leapt forward with the blade and seemed to stab it into the beast's flank. The blade disappearing beneath the wing. For a moment, she thought they had killed it. Slain the creature that had wrecked so many lives in this place. At the very least, cut the USB from its side. The whole room had a beat of silence, then an agonizing twisting shriek came to their ears. The wing clamped down, the beast twisting its body. The blade snapped, Lydia lifting the naked hilt free, the wing now locked into place even tighter than before.

Hope instantly left the room, the futility of the struggle laid bare before them. Wyatt and Lydia both backed off in fright. As the group lost heart, she heard Reid shout.

"Keep going!"

From the other side, he swung, landing a glancing blow that threw Aceso off balance. He was lining up another when, as before, the AI caught the hammer mid swing. Its green eyes focused on Reid's face, Sasha's soul howling as she expected it to be mashed with the metal implement any second.

Aceso's other arm came up and punched with overwhelming force.

The handle of the hammer split in two with the impact. The remains flew out of Reid's hands, as the machine dropped the heavy end of the hammer in finality. It rang off the floor like a church bell at a funeral. They only had one weapon left. Reid stared, looking truly terrified for the first time, then seemed to bite his lip and swung out with a punch. It cracked off what would have been the machine's jaw with the sound of cracking bone, the knuckles coming away bloody. Reid howled in pain and folded over, out of the fight.

Standing limply nearby, Sasha knew the whole thing was hopeless. Muscle wasn't going to win here. This had been their only idea and it was failing badly. From beside her, she was vaguely aware of Esin screaming for her to fight, but she was done fighting. She had to think instead. Even if the machine tried to find reasons not to kill, there was no place to go, little they could do without a wall in between them.

Her eyes opened wider.

Esin screamed again.

"I'll warn the others!" Sasha shouted. With that, she bolted from the room.

She ran into the hallway desperately, and for a moment, was petrified that she was alone. Then behind her came the mechanical scuttle of the machine in pursuit. More people to kill made for a tempting target.

Oh, thank God...

Doors flew past in the curved hallway as she ran, but they weren't what she needed. She had to make this count. In the distance, she spied an open door for an Oasis, the palm tree icon beside as welcoming as ever. As she reached the doorway, just as the machine began to gain on her, Sasha let the sledgehammer slip from her grasp and skitter away down the hall. The others would need a weapon. She didn't need it anymore.

Now unburdened, she charged inside and off to the left, beside the doorway. Aceso was through a half second later, its green eyes piercing the darkness like a searchlight for targets once again. But there were no targets, only darkness and idle furniture. The machine turned back, only realizing the room was empty as Sasha yanked the lever to seal them both inside. The door whooshed shut, the final time she would hear the sound, and the walls blinked away again. In the distance, Sasha could see her friends in the trial room not so far away, recovering from the battle. They'd be safe now. If the machine couldn't get into an Oasis, odds were good it couldn't get out, either. She went to turn away, committed to her fate, when Esin ran up on the other side.

For a second, Sasha felt real regret. Her friend pounded on the door seeming to mouth pleas and entreaties to her and to a divine power. She banged her fists and shouted in mute silence, but there was nothing anyone could do anymore. With a heavy heart but a steady one, Sasha told her not to cry and quietly blew her a kiss she knew she could not see.

"Look after De Bono for me."

Then she turned away. Aceso was waiting.

It was the last one, and he hated it.

Reid fumbled with the mechanism before him angrily, anxious to have it be done. His hand was probably broken too, which didn't make things move any faster. Beside him, one of the weary Horizoners (His name was likely Allan, but Reid almost didn't care anymore) tried to reach over to help, but he pushed the help away. He didn't need a hand from someone else, he needed another one of his own that worked. The final test of the final Trial room was proving to be relatively easy, but he loathed it all the same. They had bought a few hours to get through the last challenges with the life of yet another friend and he wasn't willing to waste a split second of it. Everything about Sasha loomed prominently in his consciousness. Her skill, her stubbornness, the creative energy she had brought to the group. The group... It was nothing more than a pair now. His eyes flicked up from his work momentarily.

Esin seemed to be virtually unaffected by Sasha's sacrifice and had pushed them forward relentlessly. Currently, she was examining one of the clues to the puzzle scrawled on the room wall, away from everyone else. It was counter to everything he had seen in her thus far. Now, with the end so close, she seemed adrift in her own thoughts. Maybe she had finally been numbed by all that had happened, but not mourning Sasha or even acknowledging her sacrifice just made him angry. He broke his mind away, having long since sorted out what that clue meant. If she wanted to waste her time, that was her problem. As his focus returned to his work, lest some other misguided soul try to help, Her voice called out from the corner. Soft, neutral, the kind of dull business tone he had heard her use at Aceso's unveiling several lifetimes ago.

"Reid, can I see you for a moment?"

At first, he just wanted to shout that he was a little busy. Time was kind of a factor here, and they'd already lost an hour of the three paid for in blood. But he got up just the same, Allan virtually leaping over to tackle the puzzle, and walked across the tight space. Very tight. The rooms were compressed now as they came to the end. As he moved, he shifted the hammer at his waist. It was just the head of it now, the handle split in half, but he refused to leave anything useful behind. He'd made a sling with someone's belt and it bounced around annoyingly as he approached the woman who was supposed to be leading them.

"I already figured that part out." He sighed.

"It's not about that," She business spoke again, though not looking up. "I'm just thinking about if Aceso can get out of that room."

How should I know? He thought sharply.

"I don't know. Maybe she could squeeze out through the ventilation..."

His voice cut off as though someone had yanked the words from his throat. Now that he was up close, Esin had turned to him looking like her soul was in tatters.

Her beautiful features were split by agony, her face red, eyes beginning to redden. He stopped short, stunned by the reveal. Instinctively, he reached out to hug her, hold this woman he cared about, but she whispered a desperate request.

"Blow into my eyes."

He looked at her incredulously.

"I'm tearing up, you have to."

"What? Esin..."

"I'm close to breaking down, and I can't let anyone here see me cry. If they do, we all might fall apart."

He glanced over his shoulder at the group still toiling at the puzzle, at those still tending the wounded. George was the worst, his face grotesquely swollen but alive. Lydia was battered as well. She looked up from her leg, at them curiously. Reid smiled at her, and suddenly felt vile for doubting the woman beside him.

"Esin," He whispered quietly. "You can cry. God knows, they'll understand. This has been more than anyone can take."

"I can't let them see me!" She pleaded, the heavy responsibility in her voice leaving no room for debate. "Reid, we have to keep going. *Please.*"

He stared at her pained features, seeing how much she trusted him. He was the only one she was willing to be vulnerable around, and deep down, he knew she was right. He took a deep breath, pursed his lips and blew softly into her welling eyes. The cool breath washed over her face, and her sadness appeared to soften. From behind him, Allan was shouting that he almost had the solution. Both ignored him completely as they stared into each other's eyes, drying away tears that they couldn't afford to shed.

True to his word, Allan had found the answer, and moments later, with an excruciatingly familiar whoosh, the door to the Trial room slid open. There was no white hallway this time, no new puzzle, no Oasis with its false panorama. This time, the vista was real, and it felt spectacular. From the passage came a brief rush of cooler air, the big chamber not yet as stifling as the rest. It swept over the team with a cleansing feeling. A few happy sighs filled the room. The Horizoners passed through the door into the great, empty chamber at the center of the Labyrinth. The bulls-eye on the dartboard.

The cramped, claustrophobic ceilings of before fell away, retreating up several floors, leaving a vast cavern. Along those ceilings, the walkways they had passed down so long ago stuck out, looking like spokes of a massive wheel above their heads. The rim of the wheel, the edge of the room, was marked by doors. A dozen for the different paths to the center, a half dozen for the Oasis all emptied out into the chamber. The group passed through the only open door looking toward the hub of the wheel, the heart of the maze. A shimmering blue lake warped and frothed in the middle. Water built of light, it twinkled in brilliant sapphire casting the only illumination in the room, its blue glow reaching up to the roof above. Faintly visible in the light, rising like a dark monolith, was the elevator shaft.

It was the end of the journey.

Standing in that vast open space, Reid didn't know what to feel. The spectacle should have been like touching salvation, but too much had been lost for that to be true. As he stared at that beautiful fabricated lake, a guilt crept into his soul. All he'd wanted in coming here was a distraction from his own problems. Now, they were far in the back of his mind and almost seemed petty. He remembered the name and face of everyone who would never see this spectacle before him. He was physically incapable of forgetting them, and what they had given for the rest to escape. Any other problems, anything else in this world just felt trivial next to this feeling, this overwhelming gratitude to be alive. The past was immutable, no matter how bad it was. The future could always be different. Reid never wanted to hide from life ever again, he owed that life to Aster, Fozzy, Robin and Sasha. Whatever happened, he pledged to make the rest of his time count. Slowly, standing there in that incredible view, his fingers subconsciously drifted over to where Esin stood beside him. He took her hand.

She felt the warmth of his touch, surprised at the show of emotion. Reid was usually closed off in so many ways, the connection actually made her feel weak. Esin looked up at the tall man next to her, his grey eyes focused on the distance and the way out. There, in that moment, for the first time in many hours, she let herself feel vulnerable. She squeezed his hand back hard.

Between the loss of her mentor, her guardian assistant, and now her friend, there was a lot to feel vulnerable about. She had held it together thus far for the sake of the people around her. She was the boss now; they were depending on her. What made it hurt most was this was what she had wanted in coming here. To be CEO, to be the one who made decisions. Now she had all of that and more. It felt like the cruelest joke fate could have played.

As she looked out on the last hurdle between them and freedom, she squeezed his hand as though it were in a vice. She didn't want to lose him too. From behind came a rustle of cloth as the rest of the group emerged. Reluctantly, she released Reid's hand, forcing her to become the tough leader once more, and girded her soul for the final test.

The rest of the tired pack bumbled their way through the door, mouths agape like a school of goldfish. At the very back, Wyatt trudged along. At this point, he was powered by the will to survive, but also by the tiny flame of bitterness that still burned in his heart.

From the back of the crowd, he tried to press his way forward to see what was going on. He brushed up against Lara and didn't get the same reaction that touch had gotten him at the start of the day. She spun around and shoved him backward with a cry of disgust. He nearly toppled over from the push, angrily fighting for balance. Before he could put her back in her place, others spun around at the noise. They formed a wall of animosity, looking at him with all the love you'd show an STD. He stepped backward. his hands raised and they turned away, once again consigning him to the back of the pack, with no view.

Him.

There had still been hope for him until the damned AI had metaphorically opened its big mouth. Maybe some of them would escape this stupid funhouse and he could go on as planned, but that was gone now. Anyone who hadn't hated him in the group before, surely did now. He had been forced to risk his life fighting that thing, threatened with violence the whole time, and now he was at the very bottom of the pack, treated as the lowest peon by a few high red subordinates he should be in charge of. They would have him arrested the millisecond they could.

Wyatt snorted, a little puff of hate escaping his nostrils. All that and he *still* would probably get killed down here. The injustice of it all made him sick. The thought of being a prisoner…

He lurched bolt upright, feeling himself turn grey

again. His head rushed back to two very long days ago. Prisoners. Aceso had asked if it could take prisoners. His keen business senses grabbed hold of this, instantly seeing the possibilities. He could get out of here alive, or at least someone could. True, he had told the machine to only take high value targets prisoner, but he was a freaking Vice President. What other way could you define him?

His head going a mile a minute, Wyatt sank back into the doorway as the others forged ahead. He had to think this through. The fact that he had a 'get out of death for free' card made things look brighter, but it could only work once. That meant he had to be the one to use it and he had to pick the right time. That would probably mean consigning most of the rest of them to death, but that was business really: Some ideas survive, some get ripped apart by a soulless automaton. Free market. He knew he was in the right. Then another thought came to him. Tight on the heels of the first, it came into beautiful focus in his head. But this idea wasn't grey; it was purest black.

The only people who knew he was responsible for all that had happened were the dull fish in front of him. If Aceso finished its little mission and wiped the slate clean, then no one would know. He would be rescued from captivity telling the heart wrenching story of his ordeal, pull that goddamned USB from Aceso's wreckage when it was through and once again be back on top.

It was a macabre thought, but a workable one. The question was, did he care enough about anyone here to try to keep them alive too? Wyatt looked at the backs of those who had scorned him, trudging toward the lake glistening in the distance. They had left him behind, ignored and forgotten. As they walked away, no one looked back or gave him a second thought. So, he wouldn't give them one, either. They had made the decision for him. So be it. Market forces, do your thing.

Far above, in the frigid maintenance offices, Tamas Kerekes was out of delays. The crews had checked all the electrics, security had checked the route, and the press was continuing to multiply outside the gate like vultures ready to pick at his hide. All he had to wait for was for a few first responders to volunteer, then the expedition down would start, for better or for worse. Even if it was security's idea, he'd be responsible for what happened. He hated being in charge. Just when he was thinking he should have become a florist, the last of his crew slipped through the door.

"Well?"

"We got six paramedics and four police." Nervous Mike said. "They're headed down the Maintenance lift now."

"Did you tell them?"

Mike's partner looked at him uneasily. He'd already edged over to the heating vent to claw back any warmth it could still offer.

"Did we tell them there's a freaking killer robot loose in a big maze our boss makes us do every year in a crazy team building exercise and we need save our coworkers?"

That summed it up rather nicely, actually.

"Yeah, we mentioned it. A few didn't believe us, but security told them we were serious." The man tucked his hands into his pockets against the chill and looked at Kerekes expectantly. "Everyone knows what they're getting into boss. We're ready to go."

Captain Kirk nodded, his head dropping like it was on the chopping block, which it kind of was. This was the moment then. There was no more dodging it.

"Alright, let's send them down..."

Suddenly, beside the heating grate, Nervous Mike jumped away, as if stung.

"What the hell was that?!"

The whole room piled on verbal abuse at this scare. Kerekes nearly spilled his now cold coffee on his desk he was so startled.

"Damn it, Mike!" He shouted, his nerves finally snapping. "Will you shut the fu..."

Then he heard it too.

From the vent came a creak. Not the creak of metal from wear or from heat, but the heavy groan that metal made when it took a heavy weight. It filled the entire room, louder than before.

"I told you!"

"Shut up!" Everyone whispered.

Every man in the offices backed away from the grate, silence descending. Another heavy groan came from the ventilation, closer now. The mesh grate was roughly three-foot square, the vent behind it similarly massive. Something big could fit through there with little trouble. Another groan made everyone twitch.

Bang!

The sound of a heavy impact against the metal mesh sounded like a gunshot. Kerekes actually did knock over the icy coffee he was so frightened. The liquid spread out, adding a *drip drip* sound to the tension.

A second later, the sound came again, louder this time.

Bang!

A few of the maintenance men fumbled wrenches or blunt objects into their hands in a pitiful defence. As another heavy bang came, Mike looked to his boss to do something, the mesh of the grate bowing outward with the impact. Kerekes knew they should have run, should have done something, anything, but he was paralyzed at this point. As the blows continued, all they could do was watch.

With the steel thunderclap of one final hit, the grate popped free. Kerekes jerked back reflexively, but the whole room looked upon what came out in utter confusion.

Toppling onto the cold cement below was a near naked man. He was clad only in a pair of grungy boxer shorts, red marks and light burns across his bare legs and back. He was absolutely drenched in sweat, his body skeletally slim. As they watched, dumbfounded, he rolled onto his back exposing almost xylophone ribs in a chest heaving with exertion. His hands were wrapped in cloth, clearly the remains of his shirt, and his eyes were wild looking up at them above a scraggly white ghost of a beard. As they stared in total surprise, the tattered figure rasped rom deep within his chest.

"Get me an ephone!"

Then, rather profanely:

"Right fucking now!"

TWENTY-NINE

It had been a long, long climb. When Aster had come to in the ventilation shaft, the fans had long since spun to a stop. The heat, now with nothing to help carry it up to the surface, had been like a pressure furnace beating his already weak body. He'd picked himself up slowly, trying to get out the same way he'd come in. But Wyatt, ever the bastard, had bolted the metal bars back in place after leaving him to die, no doubt as insurance. Still trying to cover his own ass even at attempted murder. That was Wyatt for you.

The only choices were to cook, or to climb with a collapsed lung. Baking to death would have been much easier.

The shaft had no ladder, so he'd had to clutch weakly to a cable that snaked up the side to provide power to the fans. Foot by foot, he'd pulled himself up in agony with his feet scrambling for footholds. It wasn't easy. One of his favorite films was *The Thing*. It was a great old monster movie, with paranoia, gross-out effects and Kurt Russel in a sombrero. How could you not love that? There was a scene where bandito Kurt Russel burned the creature with a hot wire, the monster leaping away with a screech. He'd always laughed at that scene. Aster was a computer engineer, he'd soldered wire before, even burned himself more than a few times. An alien monster could shrug off a burn like that. After the air shaft, he would never doubt that movie again.

The first time he had grabbed that cable he'd nearly screamed. Even insulated against the heat, it felt like touching the surface of the sun. Screaming with a collapsed lung was no picnic either, and he'd nearly passed out again. Refusing to sit down and die, he'd torn what clothes he could do without, and bandaged his hands for grip. The fans were spaced roughly one per floor in the long tunnel. It had taken five tries to get up, but he conquered the first one slowly, collapsing into unconsciousness when he was finally on top. That became the pattern. Hour after hour, he had climbed feebly, resting after each fan, looking for a way out. A thousand times he had wanted to quit, but he'd willed himself to keep going. He desperately wanted to live, and he had to warn the others about Wyatt. He'd passed out twice more on the way, but finally he found an air shaft that branched off into some offices and, hopefully, escape. As he left, he'd looked back down past the fans he had climbed past with a frail pride. He stared down into the depths from whence he had risen, counting the fans. There were eleven of them.

Now, safe in the maintenance offices, he was frozen absolutely stiff. It had been brutally hot in the shaft, but here, little heat was getting through. The crew had offered some spare clothes, but the new wardrobe was less than flattering. Someone had given him a pair of dirty overalls, three sizes too big, and a baggy t-shirt that read 'I'm only here because you broke something'.

For the fifteenth time, he tried to page Reid and Esin from the ephone. He would have accepted words from anyone still trapped down there, but the only response he got was static. In disgust, he smacked the ephone against the table next to him. It landed like a meteor in a puddle of cold coffee, splashing out on the three maintenance men still looking at him bizarrely.

"I told you," The lead one said. "It won't reach down from here. Fozzy's terminal was the only one with the range, and that went dead hours ago."

Aster cursed savagely, causing the man back up slightly at the strength of the vocabulary used. The man in charge, who improbably seemed to be named Captain Kirk, looked at him nervously.

"So, you're saying the VP from AI did all this?"

"Yes." He stressed, also for the fifteenth time. "He altered Aceso and he left me in that shaft to die. We need to let them know."

"Why would he lock himself in the same place?"

"Will you focus?!" Aster spat at him. He broke into a coughing fit. "If we can't reach them this way then somebody's got to go down and tell them. If they haven't showed up already, then they must be waiting for help. Do you have someone who can go down?"

The captain gave a sideways glance to his colleagues.

"Uh, actually, we have a whole group ready with paramedics and police."

"Well, what in the name of Christ are you waiting for?!"

Kirk gulped looking nervous.

"It's okay, we'll send them down right now."

A cough came from the doorway.

"No, we won't." A new face above a pair of coveralls came into the room looking concerned. "I'm sorry boss, but the elevator platform is down. The heat caused too many shorts. It's stuck at the path selection point. Won't budge."

Faces fell across the room.

"Then have them climb down then!" Aster growled.

"You want them to climb down a ladder like ten floors?"

"I hauled my ass *up* ten floors with no ladder and one

lung." The roboticist deadpanned. "They can do it. Maybe from there they can reach someone by ephone. Now I'm telling you, *move*."

There was a moment of silence then Captain Kirk spoke.

"You heard the man!" He suddenly piped up. "Start them down!"

The room bustled into activity, the maintenance men moving in different directions. Aster eased back into his seat rubbing his aching chest as Captain Kirk leaned over him.

"Sorry," Aster muttered apologetically. "I didn't mean to take charge like that."

Embarrassed, he looked back up at the man and was surprised to see him smiling from ear to ear.

Water. Why did it have to be water? The group had reached the edge of the tiny ocean that raged in the center of the Labyrinth. There they gathered in a line staring at the rolling waves churning in perfect digital clarity, with a kind of longing. The temperature was still insistently rising, and now to be confronted by the technical mirage of an ocean felt doubly cruel. A few looked at the water, thinking they could almost dive into the flat screens and swim in cool, refreshing electronic bliss. Feeling much the same way, Reid reached back and took a pull from his canteen instead. It was more than half empty now and he'd only just refilled it in the last Oasis. He swished the plastic-tasting water around for a moment, then swallowed without satisfaction.

"So, who's going first?"

He looked down the line at the dozen people left standing. All seemed to avoid his eyes. Then he looked out over the flat sea sparkling in front of him. In the distance, maybe a hundred and fifty meters away, was the elevator shaft extending upward in isolation. They were close enough to see the light from the ripples playing off the steel and concrete of the foundation, as though they could walk across effortlessly. At this point, no one thought it would be that easy.

Beside him, he heard a tired grumble.

"I guess I am." The voice was Esin's.

She raised a foot up over the first flat screen, water swirling beneath her shoe, and set it down. Nothing. Her other foot came down on the same screen to a similar anticlimax.

Watching with concern, he saw her tap her foot then turn toward him with a shrug.

"Want me to keep going?"

For perhaps the billionth time in this place, his eyes narrowed in curiosity, lines emerging on his sweaty brow.

"No, stay there." He looked down to step onto the panel next to her. "Maybe..."

The shock went from his heel to his hip, the muscle spasming and kicking his leg out in front of him. He nearly toppled over, scrambling back onto 'dry land'. He nearly lost it at that point, kicking out in frustration at the needless pain this was going to cause. He could guess what was happening.

"Damn it..." He uttered quietly. He looked over to where a concerned Esin was standing on water like a beautiful corporate Jesus. "Esin can you tap the panels near the one you're on? East, northeast, north, northwest and west."

Still looking concerned, she daintily placed a toe on the first panel. With a yelp, she stepped right back again.

"Are you alright?"

She looked back over to him, her concern gone.

"Yeah, I'm fine." She muttered. "Thanks for the warning, by the way. What is this?"

He looked out at the swirling torrent, realizing the movement was designed to disorient you. The shock had been electric, barely meant to be felt through most shoes, but his were damp from his bath in the ice and his own sweat. It was simple, but it would be time consuming. His internal clock had been counting down since Aceso and Sasha had been sealed in that Oasis. They had an hour and forty left. That was a hundred minutes to get across.

"It's a maze," He diagnosed. "We just can't see the walls. Some screens will be dead ones we can stand on; the others will be live with exposed circuits. There'll be paths through, we just can't see them. We'll only know there's a wall when we get a shock."

The people left began to sag as fate siphoned off their optimism once again.

Ninety-nine now.

Lara walked over to where Esin stood on her invisible island and hopped next to her. It took a series of painful yelps but she eventually found an adjoining panel and stepped over. There she rubbed her leg angrily looking back at the others.

"And what do we do?" She hissed through the pain. 'Just get stung the whole way?"

The game designer's leg twitched again from the shock, the pain going all the way to his back. Everyone else saw the reaction too, which wouldn't speed them up any.

He grimaced.

"We'll take turns."

That comment drew the derision it deserved, with the

weary travellers griping about what was to come. With one odd exception. Walking toward the front of the pack, Wyatt strode up like he was joining a queue.

"Form a line." He ordered with a grumble of contempt. "Let's just get this over with."

Reid looked at him suspiciously, but the weary VP just ignored him as the rest of the team came into line behind. Maybe the idea of seeing the architect of their pain getting zapped gave them a little motivation. With a shrug, Reid pressed a finger to the gash on his hand. It hurt like blazes, making him wince, but it came away bloody enough. Reaching down he drew a little red X beside where Esin stood on the still whirling waves. He looked her in the eye tiredly then stepped past to do it all over again with the second panel.

Ninety-seven minutes.

The group became a kind of human caterpillar. When the head had been shocked enough, it would fall back toward the end, giving the next person their turn at this masochistic relay race. The pace was so slow, Reid was convinced Aceso would be on them before they were through. The beast could ignore voltage that mild, while they would be locked in place for the slaughter. He imagined Aceso skipping right across the waves to fall upon the shabby human chain and tear into it. If they had been testing with just pain, then it might have. Fortunately, someone thought up another option. On her turn, Lara had proven her worth as an electrical engineer. Out of curiosity, she dribbled a few drops of water from her canteen onto panels around her. Four cackled as the water met the current; one didn't. This became the new plan, with Lara in the lead and the others passing canteens forward as, one by one, they were emptied on the wave screens. Water to get through water. There was a poetry to it, but then maybe that had been the original idea.

Reid was kicking himself. He should have thought of that, especially after watching Sasha conquer the water circuit early in the race. Not for the first time, he wished she were still here. He stopped to stare back at the series of bloody crosses that paced back like footprints from where they'd come. He wiped a few errant drops of sweat from his face and looked toward the front of the line. They were getting closer, but for some reason they had stalled, and the line was bunching together.

Forty-two.

The head of the caterpillar was in disagreement with itself when he arrived. He found Lara, Esin and Wyatt all gathered together, agitated.

"Why did we stop?" He demanded, his mental stopwatch still ticking down.

Lara paused her row with Wyatt to look at him with an angry helpless shrug.

"We're out of water!" She cried. "No one has any left."

"You didn't ask hard enough." Wyatt piped up. "It's too goddamned hot in here. Someone will have some more. Or you could just take that bullet like you should and step out."

Esin set a hand on the tiny woman's shoulder.

"I don't see you stepping up. Go on."

Wyatt looked down at the sapphire abyss between them and escape before scoffing.

"I've already done my part." He answered clinically. "Besides, I've had to take a leak for forever."

Completely done with the treacherous executive at this point, Reid walked up and hauled him away by his shirt collar. Wyatt scrambled for balance in alarm, his arms waving.

"You want to piss on a live wire out here? Be my guest!" He bellowed in his ear.

With more than a little malice, he shoved him toward the distant body of the caterpillar spread out on the trail. The executive looked at him in loathing, but retreated. Even after everyone had died, even after Aceso's reveal, there seemed no end to the man's arrogance. Internally, Reid wondered what Wyatt had left to be overconfident about. You would have thought someone religious would understand repentance.

Still white-hot with anger, he turned back to see Esin smiling at him almost mischievously.

"That was fun to see."

"He deserved worse."

Lara was smiling too, but the expression did not last.

"I should keep going." She said quietly. "It's just a little pain, I can take it."

"Its alright, I have a better idea." Reid told her. There's already been enough of that."

Esin slipped an arm around her in agreement. He couldn't help but be impressed by how indelibly tough both had turned out to be. After all they'd been through, all they'd witnessed these people still were willing to do more. As far as he was concerned they'd done enough.

Reaching back, Reid pulled his canteen and sloshed the pitiful contents around. He looked out at the elevator platform, now tantalizingly within reach then took a drink. Seeing Esin look at him strangely, he passed it over to her and nodded. Cautiously she took a long pull, closing her eyes to savour it, then it went into Lara's hands. She drained whatever was left. Reid took the canteen back then stepped over to where Wyatt was interrogating the others for more water positive someone had been holding out. Without a word, he shoved the empty canteen into the man's gut, nearly bowling him over.

"Fill it up." He told him coldly.

Thirty-six.

They ran out again four panels from the platform, but this time, they were too stubborn to give up. When the canteen ran dry, Lara skipped out across the distance, shrieking with every step. After a second's search, she found a hatch in the floor. A further second of tinkering and she waved everyone forward. At her signal the whole pack surged across the now harmless ocean to the very center of the maze.

Reid stepped off the water panel onto the familiar slate grey tiles. They almost felt steadier somehow now after the look of the surf under his shoes. Glancing back across the shimmering water he could see the open door they had passed through and the many doors still closed beside it.

Twenty-two.

For the first time since they had been together, the group exploded in genuine jubilation. They embraced each other, kissing their sweaty tearful faces. Shouts and cheers mingled, echoing around the huge cavern and up the elevator shaft. Out of nowhere, a set of arms enveloped him from behind in a bear hug. Reid turned to find a delirious George overcome with emotion, tears streaming down the battered side of his face. Without thinking, Reid embraced the man, feeling his tears soak into his shoulder. The mirth of the moment was so much, he couldn't help but feel moved. In spite of every obstacle thrown at them, loss, injury and sacrifice, they had reached the center.

When the husky Horizonite finally released him, the man grinned bashfully only before wandering off in search of another hug somewhere else. He didn't have to look far. Reid watched him go, his face effervescent, his heart feeling alive like it hadn't… since her. Suddenly alone, Reid began to think of the faces of those they had lost along the way. There were so many. In his head, that awful replay kicked in and he relived each of their final moments. But this time, something was different. He was different. He remembered leaving Aster behind at the fan controls, he remembered Sasha shouting and leading the beast out of the room. But when he saw it again, he didn't see someone going to their death, he saw someone saving his life. He looked around at the dozen people who would see daylight again thanks to them and was overcome with gratitude for what they had given.

He did something then that he had never done before. He thought of Renata; only this time, he went to that moment by choice.

It played out exactly the same as it always had. He felt the body of the car shudder and bend, felt the pain in his back, the steering wheel against his chest. He heard glass breaking, tires squealing, metal tearing. He saw the glass shatter, flying through the air to mingle with her hair, but he didn't fear it anymore. This place had shown him what fear truly felt like, and for the first time he just saw the end of a wonderful part of his life. Those had been the best years and he would mourn them along with her, but his life wasn't over yet. He had been hiding from memories for so long, he had never taken the time to appreciate the life he still had. Standing there, he felt the most incredible gratitude to her, to the rest, to everyone that he had made it this far.

Reid wandered onto the center of the elevator. It was a flat dais at the bottom of the shaft with a bold red call button prominent on the side. The platform itself was missing though. He looked up the long tunnel at the sequence of lights along the side of the shaft leading up to the heavens, smiling in relief. Far above, he could see the platform they'd come down so long ago. They'd made it.

She would never get tired of hugging. Not a chance. As yet another person ran up and embraced her, Esin squeezed back to the point they might ooze out from her arms like toothpaste from a tube. When they released, Esin was nearly crying again. Quickly, she clamped it down, knowing there was still more to be done. She turned away, wanting someone she could cry freely around. Suddenly wondering where Reid was, she looked around to find him staring up the shaft with a kind of Zen smile like she had never seen before. She wandered over and put her arms around him, her head barely reaching above his shoulder.

"How ya doing?" She muttered happily, her speech blurred from talking through his chest.

The game designer glanced down, still smiling.

"Good," He told her. "Better than in a long time."

Esin smiled at the words. The man had clearly found his distraction. She clamped onto him, looking up at his serene face. He held her gaze for a moment then gestured with his head.

"The clock is still ticking. We should go."

There was a call button in brilliant red by the side of the elevator shaft. She pressed it, enjoying the glorious cool breeze drifting down from above as they waited. A moment later she tapped it again. Then she held it down. Finally, she smashed it in frustration shouting abuse at the useless mechanism. The others gathered around in dread, their happiness dashed yet again. Esin felt the same way, unable to believe that fortune had screwed them one more time.

She channeled it into violence against the machine refusing her, slamming her hand until her palm ached. Through it all, nothing happened. Far above, the platform stubbornly refused to drop.

When she was done, she stepped back and brushed the hair from her red face, embarrassed by the outburst. Faces looked at her in concern, hoping for answers. Lara summed it up for everyone.

"Now what?"

She took a deep breath, thinking about how to answer. She had seen the ladders affixed to the shaft, but the thought of an ascent like that made her uneasy. Aceso could climb a hell of a lot faster.

"I guess we start climbing." She conceded finally. "Lara, take five up on the right side, I'll take the rest up on the left."

She turned to Reid figuring he would know the answer to the next question.

"How long before Aceso gets through that door?"

Of course, he knew.

"Fourteen minutes." He was biting his cheek. "She'll climb straight up the wall of the shaft though. Even if we get to the platform we'll be in trouble."

She tried not to wince as he told her what she already knew. She turned to Lara.

"Then we need to slow her down. Can you turn the shock back on for the panels?"

"Easily," The short woman replied. "We just turn a dial. I don't think it's enough to do any damage with all the power spread out though. There are a lot of screens."

From his looming place behind her, Reid stirred.

"Can we run all the current through just one?"

She thought for a second before answering.

"I can do it, but..." She gazed out at the wide digital sea around their little island. "Which one?"

"Well, we'll pick the most likely one and hope we get lucky."

Even as she said it, Esin looked out at their little artificial ocean and knew the odds of stepping on a minefield of one. Lara was already looking deflated.

"That'll never work." She reasoned. "Even if by some miracle Aceso steps on the right one, Its going to take more than a few seconds to do any damage. She'll step off again like we would. Someone would have to turn up the tiles she's standing on then move the charge with her. That's the only thing that'd work."

Esin felt a pain in the pit of her stomach, Sasha's face blinking past her mind's eye. Someone would be staying behind alone again. She looked over at Reid, seeing the grim look in his grey eyes she'd become so familiar with. If she didn't do it, she knew he would. Another person would give their life for her and that would be more than she could bare. Her lips parted.

"I'll do it."

Reid turned his head to the person who'd spoken, his grey eyes widening with surprise. Esin's eyes soon followed, ballooning in astonishment. Wyatt stood taller than Esin had seen him in hours. His back was straight, his eyes clear, and he stepped forward with bravado that felt unnatural. She had grown so used to seeing his face twisted with bitterness that the new expression seemed downright foreign. If it had a name, it would be 'determined' but that didn't feel right either.

She stared at him oddly. Her face aligned perfectly

with eleven others all gazing skeptically at the VP. Her head tilted in scrutiny.

"You're serious?"

He nodded forcefully.

"Completely. I can do this."

"No..."

She nearly started with 'no offense', but for him she didn't care.

"Why would you volunteer at all?" She asked. "You've never cared before."

"Because I'm the one who caused all this. You know that now." He made a slow survey of the people around him, looking at each individual face whose hatred he had more than earned. "I just want a chance to make amends. I'll stay down here and wait for Aceso. Maybe she'll burn out in the power."

"What if she doesn't?"

"Then at least the rest of you might have a chance."

On that melodramatic note, he slapped a rung of the ladder nearby. Then stepped away.

"You should get moving."

A few of the team took a hesitant step forward, but most remained nervously looking at the others.

Esin's eyes narrowed. She had never known Wyatt to be selfless, the man didn't seem capable of it. She knew him well enough to expect something else. The beautiful executive also knew a sales pitch when she saw one. Wyatt wanted to stay behind enough to sell them on the idea, but for the life of her, she couldn't fathom why. Still, the group was eager to move and the clock, always the clock continued to tick downward.

"You can't do this by yourself." She wavered.

A weary sigh came from behind.

"He won't."

Her heart iced up at the voice and she spun back toward Reid staring numbly at the ground. He ran a hand through his muddled brown hair and made it official.

"I'll stay with him."

Esin took the words like death sentence, even if it wasn't her own. The last person she truly cared about was staying behind. Reid shook his head, then tilted his eyes skyward.

"You've got twelve minutes" He told the room. "I guess we'll see you on the other side."

One by one, the last of Horizon's best began to ascend. There were a few hugs, a few handshakes, as most wished Reid luck. Surprisingly, some were even directed at Wyatt, who took the salutes with the kind of 'don't thank me, I die because of my love for you' modesty that characterized the man. Lara was one of the last to leave. She hugged Reid close, her head at the middle of his chest. He dropped his chin down on top of her head, embracing her back. As Esin watched, he said something softly that she couldn't catch, but Lara gave a brief snort of laughter through her tears. After the two separated, she stepped over to where Wyatt was waiting. Looking like she was touching something radioactive, she extended her hand. They shook limply, Lara looking at him with a benign hatred in her eyes. Not for the first time, Esin wondered what had actually transpired between the two.

"You don't think," She murmured, as she eyed the man. "That he really wants to do it, do you? Like Sasha and Fozzy did?"

It didn't take him long to answer.

"No." He grunted firmly. "He always has an angle. But that doesn't mean we still can't use him. He's staying behind for a reason. Maybe he thinks the electricity can really disable Aceso, or just fry the USB? Maybe he thinks it'll earn him some clemency? Redemption? I don't know, we'll see. I'll keep an eye on him."

"Someone should," She conceded with venom. She looked up into his tired face, still oddly composed considering what was about to happen. "But why does it have to be *you*?"

Reid smiled at her. It was a warm smile and a calm one.

"It's just my turn, I guess." He unslung his makeshift holster from around him and offered it to her. "I've got Sasha's old hammer. Take it, you might need it."

She draped it over her shoulder, the new weight bouncing at her hip. It was clearly time for a goodbye, but she didn't want to have one. More surprisingly, Esin had no idea what to say and her whole life was about getting the right message across. The two stared at each other for a moment, then Reid extended a hand.

"It's been an honor working with you Ms Shirzai. Thanks for giving me the chance."

The woman took in the words then batted his hand aside. In half a heartbeat she stepped up on her toes and kissed him. A long lingering kiss. She felt him tense up in surprise, then felt all of that tension drain away instantly. His hands pressed to her back and they stayed locked in that moment. When she broke away, he was blinking in dumbfounded astonishment. His mouth opened to speak, but she beat him to it.

"Don't get killed." She ordered.

She stepped back and could not help but smile at the

blushing stunned expression on his face. Once again, she saw that enigmatic man she'd met by the river and hoped this wouldn't be the last time she saw him. Reluctantly, she turned and walked up to where Wyatt was waiting, still wearing his hero's mantle. An eyebrow jumped up a little toward his normally styled hairline at her approach. Maybe he was thinking he'd receive the same farewell as Reid. In the end, he was disappointed.

With all the skill her father had taught her, she cocked her fist back and punched him in the stomach. The wind was knocked out of the blowhard in one big gust, the treacherous VP doubling over with a groan, dropping to his hands and knees coughing. Whatever his angle was in staying behind, Esin would never forget what he had done to get them here.

"*You*, can die all you like." Esin told him, fueling each word with all the rage and hate she could.

With that parting gift, she blew a kiss down to where he lay on the floor and began to ascend the ladder. In the distance, she saw the figures of her colleagues growing closer to the platform and, hopefully, salvation. She glanced down once to see Reid standing there at the base, his grey eyes staring up at her as she climbed. When she looked again, a few rungs later, he was gone.

Everything was quiet. After so many people, so much talking, so much *noise* it was finally silent and that vacuum of sound was deafening. With the last of the Horizoners having ascended clumsily up the ladder all that unnecessary talk had peeled away. Now it was just him and Sheraton left and say what you would about Sheraton (Wyatt certainly had, more than once) the man wasn't overly talkative. The two lay flat against the ground beside the open electrical panel. Lara had shown them what did what, before she had climbed out of this cursed place. Now it was just a waiting game, and Wyatt was not good at waiting.

It was supposed to be a simple transaction: they needed someone to stay behind, and he needed a chance to separate himself from the rest. So, he had volunteered, saving his own life and maybe getting an ounce of recognition from the others before they left. Well, before Aceso finished hunting them down anyway. Instead, here he was with Sheraton who was insistent on complicating the whole thing. With the video game man down here, he was obligated to try to electrocute Aceso before he could give himself up, and that wouldn't earn him any extra mercy. He lay on the warm floor, sweat rolling down the back of his collar, his stomach tied in knots. The punch from Esin hadn't helped either, but at least it had solidified his resolve. They were all still ungrateful.

For the first time since they were alone, a word passed Sheraton's lips.

"Six."

Wyatt jerked his head over at the noise.

"Six what?"

"Never mind."

The game designer didn't look at him. His eyes were locked on a particular door beyond the silent, swirling waves.

"How are you doing?"

He wanted to scream at the banal statement.

"Oh, I'm out-goddamned-standing," He grunted back. "Thanks for the moral support. I could have done this by myself, you know."

"Someone had to help."

"I'm doing just fine!" He grumbled.

He had been, at any rate. If he'd surrendered to Aceso on his own, he would have been guaranteed survival. Now, Sheraton had changed the calculus by adding a new person to the mix, not to mention that he seemed to be a person the damn AI had a crush on.

"No one asked you to stay down here." He spat into the warm floor under his chin. "I didn't want you to, either."

A thought occurred.

"Why did you, anyway?"

"I owed you." The guy replied dully. "And you're welcome, by the way."

"Owed me what? Are you going to sucker punch me too?"

Sheraton gritted his teeth and brushed a few rogue hairs from his eyes.

"I might." He muttered, sounding irritated. His eyes swivelled over to Wyatt. The business man, saw something in the pewter gaze that was new. "It was something you said. You gave me a moment of clarity that I don't think I would have had without you. That's why I'm still here. In a way, I guess, I'm grateful."

A beat passed. This felt almost like an emotional moment. After an uncomfortable few seconds, Wyatt had to kill it dead.

"Well," He hissed back. "You have a hell of a way of showing it."

His voice echoed in the room, reverberating in the vast space above the water before fading away to a renewed tense silence. Wyatt's stomach felt like it might rebel on him. He felt an uprising in his gut and had to choke back down vomit. He still didn't know if this plan would work. Sheraton spoke up again.

"Two."

Wyatt nearly exploded.

"Will you shut up?!" He croaked, wiping fresh sweat from his eyes. "I'm already about to crack and you keep talking. *Be quiet.*"

"Do you want to pray with me?"

That one got his attention. He crooked his head over, seeing a tender expression on the man's face, the offer genuine. Wyatt looked at him as if he'd grown wings, flown them both out of here, then bought all of Amazon with the change in his pocket.

"Are you crazy?" He seethed at him with contempt. "Absolutely not."

Sheraton seemed surprised by this, leaning back startled.

"I'm sorry..." He whispered slowly. "You, you don't believe in God?"

Wyatt snorted. It would be funny if his prospects weren't so bleak.

"Oh, I know for a fact that there's a God." He answered dryly. "I just don't want anything to do with the greedy bastard."

The games man's face became a haggard puzzle of confusion, looking back at Wyatt with the same bewilderment he felt. They remained in this perplexing standoff of incomprehension for a moment, neither one really understanding the other until the grey eyed man spoke one last time.

"Look."

Wyatt swiveled his head back across the water. For a split second there was no change, but then a crack of light materialized. It broadened quickly as an open portal appeared. There was a flicker of movement, the light from inside obstructed, and a new shape emerged.

Aceso strode into the room, slouching once again in the distant doorway. When it stood upright again, its head was taller than the frame, looking at its new surroundings with cold calculation. The hunt had resumed.

Wyatt slunk down further where he lay, trying to flatten his body for a lower profile. Beside him Sheraton did the same. A nervous shiver passing between the two. As the machine paced toward the water and what was beyond, Wyatt swallowed hard. He glanced his competition beside him, waiting for the right moment. The trump card he held would only be good for one. He wasn't going to let the opportunity slip. His competitor remained unaware, apprehensively watching the AI advance toward them, ready for the end.

"Zero." Sheraton whispered.

THIRTY

Across the mute little ocean a jolly man had made to test his people, the kindly metal beast that had taken his life advanced. It moved cautiously, its head swivelling from side to side to encompass the whole of the massive chamber. It couldn't see it's targets yet, to their palpable relief. In another life, Reid had sat through his fair share of nature documentaries, Renata had loved watching them. He'd grown accustomed to seeing the familiar images of lions on the savanna, and the many creatures fleeing for their lives ahead of them. Now, as he watched each cautious feline step Aceso took, he felt like game himself. Here they were at the waterhole, close to the ground and hoping the predator wouldn't spot them.

Still, they weren't helpless. Reid dropped his eyes to the panel open under his chin. All of the current had been redirected long ago. It was just a matter of the machine stepping on the panel he'd chosen. In the distance, Aceso had reached the screens and put a cautious toe into what would have been the water.

"Fry him!" Wyatt whispered frantically. "Fry him! What are you waiting for?"

"She needs to be further out." He hissed back. "Otherwise, she'll just jump back to shore."

Wyatt was gnawing on his lip nervously, in what seemed an attempt to swallow his whole face. With a dull scrape, he dragged their sole remaining sledgehammer closer to him.

Standing on the vortex of screens, the beast continued onward cautiously. As it moved, it's head turned to scrutinize everything in the room. By some miracle, it still hadn't spotted the two and was almost a third of the way across. Reid selected a panel in its path and turned up the voltage to the maximum. Another few steps and the machine wouldn't be able to escape. He watched the green eyes flicker as Aceso searched, his finger hovering over the button. A wisp of regret came to him as he waited. Deep down, he didn't want to hurt the beast, and doing so (especially with Wyatt) felt like a betrayal after what had been done to it. As the machine made its final step, he quietly mouthed an apology.

"Reid! ...out!"

A hideous blast of white noise erupted from his pocket. The game designer convulsed, his hand reflexively leapt from the controls to clamp down on the ephone as it spat out its garbled frantic words.

"Aster...... shaft... don't trust..."

Wyatt flailed out, rolling backward in alarm.

"Shut it off!" He pleaded in a whispered shout. But it was too late.

In mid-step the beast faltered, its luminous green eyes suddenly locking on the sound. The face became a flat oval again as it focused directly on them. Reid, his hands shaking from the spike in adrenaline, fumbled with the panel as the beast took off toward them at top speed. There was a brief arc, but the machine skipped by unscathed. He cranked the dial, trying to reset the trap ahead of it, but the machine was fast. Beside him, Wyatt was yelling incoherently, pointing at the onrushing slaughter. He ignored him, straining to get ahead of the machine. Reid's eyes darted down then up again rapid fire as watching their quarry. With every glance, the insectoid hulk that was Aceso bore ever closer. At the machine's feet came a sudden arc again, as he suddenly found the right panel. The beast faltered, it's pace dropping for a second, enough time for Reid to catch up. The next arc was a heavy bolt, blue as the artificial water, that jolted up among it scrambling legs. Aceso seemed to stumble, sidestepping to the right as it perceived the danger.

"There, there!"

Reid cursed, Wyatt's shout breaking his concentration.

The machine was within fifty meters, coming closer by the second, but now the light of arcing electricity around its steel feet was constant. It looked like the machine had blades on its feet, drawing the sharp sparks of steel on steel with every step. The cackle of the current rose higher and higher, echoing through the chamber until the sound was like thunder, hugely out of proportion to the tiny lightning down below. Aceso began to slow, the cumulative effect wearing on it. As the beast struggled through the current, its own power seemed to be draining away.

Reid turned up the voltage even more, pulling current from everywhere in the room. Now, the scent of burning wire and ozone met his nose, the cackling intensifying around the machine. Aceso staggered, the sprint now a crawl. It's six limbs began to thrash with each cackle as it lost control of its functions. Beside him, Wyatt was cheering, the sledgehammer raised up in the air. He laughed as the creation he had desecrated so unforgivably met its end. Every frenzied flap of an arm seemed to send him new delight. Reid's hate for the man returned, but he kept drawing in more power. The machine came to a stop, floundering in water made only of light and shock.

The beast locked eyes with Reid, the distance so close, the smell of burning was overpowering. Its kindly eyes locked on his with a look that he felt was almost pleading.

He closed his own eyes for a moment, said a prayer for the thing that did not have a soul, then pulled in the last of the voltage. The roar exploded, the cascading energy reaching up like tendrils from the panel below to strike the beast. It writhed in its death throes, the light from the electricity leaving streaks in the eyes of the men watching, and then, in an instant, the light was gone.

All of the light was gone.

With one final apocalyptic bang, the screens went dark, turning their ocean into a desert. The cackling ceased, the arcing electricity no more. Reid caught a brief image of Aceso slumping over before the lights above failed as well, plunging them into total darkness.

From somewhere nearby, his reluctant ally shrieked, asking what was going on.

"The capacitor burned out!" Reid panted in the blackness. "The breaker blew!"

The cacophony that had been raging around them had petered out in seconds, leaving a ringing in the ears. The only sound left were two pairs of lungs, nervously breathing. Reid stared out into complete blackness, nervous to even speak. Then, in the vacuum of light, a pair of sympathetic meek green lights blinked to life. Almost close enough to touch.

Reid sucked in a terrified breath. He opened his mouth to tell Wyatt to run, knowing the whole thing was futile now. He needn't have bothered. Before the words had passed his lips, the man had smashed him in the back with the hammer.

Inch by inch, rung by rung, the platform was growing closer, and Esin was more than a little impatient to reach it. The ladder ran right up the side of the shaft to the bottom of the platform where there was a hatch leading to the top. A fairly difficult hatch to open, as it turned out. As the first person strained to lift it, the rest stacked up behind them. Jammed in line, the Horizoners got a good look at the bowels of the elevator. With heavy cabling running down both sides of the shaft, the huge piece of machinery was impressive. Of course, it would have been much nicer to see the top side of it.

At the very back of the queue, the last Esin was growing impatient. She had always liked Lara. The tiny engineer was shy and often underestimated by those around her. The way she had performed in here had proved as much. But after staring at her ass, stuck climbing below her on a ladder for a few minutes, waiting to put her feet on solid ground, Esin was ready to scream. Finally, there came happy sounds alongside the squeak of a hinge, and the packed group began moving again. A few seconds later, her head emerged up top.

There were more new faces than old. A forest of uniforms was waiting with police, paramedics and security with the Horizon logo emblazoned over their heart. They helped her weary team into the dozen doorways ringing the shaft treating wounds and offering water. This was where they had started their journey and picked their paths so long ago. Esin turned to see path eight, the number seeming nonchalant now, so much had changed.

A logo appeared in front of her, a security guard offering her a bottle of water. She waved it away, and the man straightened to attention.

"Ms. Shirzai?"

When she nodded, he hurriedly pressed a shiny new ephone into her hands, then moved to help someone else. Esin looked at the item strangely. This one had no blood on it.

"Hello?"

"Esin!" A distorted yet oddly familiar voice cried. "Oh,

thank merciful Christ! I didn't think I'd ever hear you again."

With all that had happened, it took a moment to process who was on the other end. When she did, she cried out herself.

"Aster! Where are you? We all thought you were dead!"

"Yeah, so did I." The voice quipped. "Believe me, dying sucks. What happened to Wyatt? Security said he didn't come out."

"He offered to stay behind with Reid. They're going to try to..."

"He *offered?!*"

"Yes, they needed to buy time." She said suspiciously. "Aceso's right behind us."

A train of curses tumbled out of the device in her hand.

"He's the one who screwed with Aceso!"

"We know, she told us." Esin said calmly. "He can't hide it anymore."

"She told you? How did...? He broke into a strained coughing fit. By the time he gathered himself up he was composed again.

"Listen to me," The roboticist went on. "Wyatt tried to kill me. I found out what he did so he locked me in the ventilation and left me there to die. I don't know why he stayed behind, but it's not to help. You can't let Reid be alone with him!"

A cold shiver danced down the length of her spine. Without a further millisecond of hesitation, she pulled the old ephone from her pocket.

"Reid! Get out!" She shouted into it desperately.

The range was probably useless this far up, but she had to try. She shouted, explained and pleaded, receiving nothing back but a rage of static. Around her on the platform, all eyes had turned toward her. She couldn't have cared less. Then, a storm reached her ears.

She dashed over to the still open hatch, the hammer wobbling at her hip, and looked down where she had come. The crackle of thunder still roared from beneath, like a tempest was rolling up from the center of the earth. Added to the thunder, she could now see the flicker of lightning as flashes cast new shadows on the base of the lift. She looked up tensely, surveying those nearby, and settled on a pair of RCMP.

"You two!"

The officers looked up in surprise. They barely offered a protest as Esin virtually dragged them over to the hatch by their collars.

"If you see anything green, start shooting and don't stop."

The two exchanged alarmed glances.

"Do it!"

With that, the two drew their weapons looking uneasily into the murky flickering darkness below. Esin rushed over to a security guard.

"Raise the platform."

"Don't we still have people..."

"Raise it. *Now.*"

"I can't..."

She turned away, pulled the new ephone from her pocket and shouted for Aster to do the same thing. There were too many innocent people here to risk.

"We can't move it. We've tried." He said. "The electrics are shot from the heat."

The ephone sagged to her side. If Reid lost the battle that was going on beneath them, then Aceso would be following them up. She'd been counting on being able to take the elevator away, and now that option was gone. Could they climb? The ladder still went up the whole shaft, but Aceso was too fast...

At that point, her concentration was utterly shattered by the boom of a gunshot, sounding like a cannon in the shaft.

Before Sheraton's body had even hit the ground, Wyatt was rushing toward the green lights. He stepped around his former ally's limp form and right up to where Aceso was recovering from its shock. He flung the hammer away, the metal banging onto the floor in the darkness followed by the scraping of it skittering out into oblivion. Then he dropped to his knees and laced his fingers behind his head, the way he'd seen in war movies.

"I surrender!" He shouted. "High value target. I surrender!"

In front of him, the green eyes seemed to focus, spearing him like a searchlight. The machine took its time getting back on its feet, rising up to its full terrifying mass but staying quiet, still wreathed in shadow. It took a step closer, landing heavily. The screen beneath it's feet splintered.

"I'm giving up!" Wyatt shouted worriedly, his voice becoming shrill. "Take me prisoner!"

The two burning green eyes bobbed as the head dropped, now inches from his face. This close, the machine stank of char, with the sickly smell of burning plastic mixed in. His legs growing weak where he knelt, Wyatt began to wonder whether the audio sensors had been burned out in the charge. The machine could see he was submissive though, right?

Suddenly, there was a hard bang and the killer that loomed over him was draped in red. Emergency lights had kicked in, lifting the illumination in a ruby hue. With the light's return, the body of the machine came into view. It was chewed up and scarred from its clashes, with the tattered skin of some feral, mechanized dog. Scratches were everywhere, layered on top of one another, along with dents and dings the fault of wood, metal and fingernails. Streaks of black, where the electricity had impacted, streaked across its surface, the last over part of its face, crisscrossing the scar Sheraton had hammered there.

"Are you worth my time, Mr. Wyatt?"

The words were said so softly he barely caught them.

"What?" From his prone position, he fumbled the words through trembling lips. "What do you..."

"You instructed me only to keep a target alive if they were worth my time." The AI said heavily. Wyatt had never heard Aceso angry, but when the machine spoke again, there was an unmistakable tone of malice that shook him.

"Are you worth my time?"

Wyatt looked behind him toward the elevator shaft and escape. He'd made a grave error, though he knew there was no chance to run now. He could faintly see the shaft in the glow of the red light, but one thing he didn't see was Sheraton, his body gone.

In an instant, Aceso had reached out and gripped him by the throat. With effortless ease, the machine lifted him up and rose with him, until he was parallel with its blank face at full height. He thrashed and kicked, his hands prying uselessly at the metal fingers around his neck. He had thought that, given the choice, the AI would never choose to kill someone. The only thing was, he had triggered all that had befallen it. He was the one person the machine might have *wanted* to murder.

He flailed helplessly, panic and despair soaking into him, but seconds passed without violence. Wyatt hung there suspended, the machine appearing to hesitate. The executive prided himself on being able to read people, and for the first time he prayed (without irony) that he had judged the machine correctly and that deep down, it was no killer.

The hand holding him wavered, and finally Aceso spoke again, with no less vehemence.

"You are now a prisoner, Mr. Wyatt." It conceded almost begrudgingly.

The relief was so strong he nearly wet himself. He cried through his clenched throat giddy with disbelief. He tried to say thank you, but couldn't form a solitary word. He stopped kicking, trying to stay calm and wait for the machine to secure him somewhere safe while the drama unfolded.

Again, he had made a grave error.

Without pity, Aceso wrenched the business man around and onto its back. The two armoured wings split revealing the stretcher beneath.

"No!" Wyatt pleaded. "No don't…!"

He was slammed down into the compartment, facing upward, the wings locking back into position. His whole body was covered, save for his face, the armoured wings securing under his chin, holding his head in place. He screamed, kicking and writhing in his locked position, to no avail. This was meant to immobilize a wounded man; he could do nothing to escape. He scanned around into the red-hued darkness around him. The whites of his eyes grew as wide as dollar coins, his pleas for help echoing out into the void where no one could hear them. Aceso eventually answered.

"There's no need for panic Mr. Wyatt." It told him calmly. "You're perfectly safe."

With a shudder, the machine began to move again, picking up the pace as it headed toward the elevator. Wyatt swivelled his vision around as much as he could, a near hysterical spectator, as the world blurred by. A tingle passed through his entire body, an aftereffect from all the electricity soaking the metal around him. It felt like he were in a coffin of needles as he was whisked away as the machine's prisoner. The goal he had hoped for, horribly realized.

"I'm still required to carry out the objectives you gave me." The machine reminded him as they ran. "You should be here to see what happens next."

On the ladder, far below the platform, climbing at a cripple's gait, Reid struggled ever upward. As soon as he'd been able to move, he'd slipped away not stopping to watch Wyatt's plea. Whether the man lived or died, he didn't care anymore. Whatever the bastard business man was doing, maybe it would buy him some time. Probably not enough.

The hammer had struck him on his shoulder. He could move his arm, but it hurt like hell and he was more than a little nauseous. That likely meant another bone was broken. Combined with his wrecked hand, he couldn't climb too fast. Still, he struggled upward in the semi-darkness provided by the red emergency lights refusing to lay down and accept his fate. Far above, some white light peeked through past the platform where his friends had made it. So, not all the power was down. He couldn't understand why the others hadn't taken the lift up yet. It still sat there, a juicy target full of people where Aceso was sure to follow. Maybe Esin was waiting for him, even though she shouldn't. Either way, he'd done his part and the platform was something to strive for in his last precious moments. So, really, what the hell? Reid kept climbing, gripping with his good hand and grunting in pain for every rung he gained. He'd keep going until something killed him, however long it took.

With the lightning speed that irony sometimes possesses, a bullet cracked past his head. The lead made a snap it came so close, pressing Reid flat against the ladder. Shouts were coming from above, the roar of the blast reverberating around him. Maybe it would take less time than he'd thought.

Her ears ringing from the discharge, Esin rushed back to the hatch where the two police glowered at one another. She brushed one of the officers aside, his weapon smoking, and stared down. The lights were dim. The only illumination came from red emergency lights spaced wide in the shaft. Among the dozens of tiny red pinpricks, one green one had appeared.

"I'm sorry," The policeman beside her was saying. "I saw the light and was thinking about what you said…"

Esin cut him off.

"Keep shooting!" She ordered. "Both of you need to slow her down. Don't stop until I tell you."

The other officer looked indignant at receiving orders to fire his gun from a civilian.

"Wait, you can't…"

"Do it!"

A flurry of shots began, both men aiming at the menacing green spec rising below. The cacophony was deafening, each boom tolling like the end of the world. Across the platform people pressed their hands to their ears. Esin had the feeling of being in a massive drum while Satan's percussionist banged out a rhythm on it. Aceso was still coming, which meant Reid and Wyatt had failed. They were probably dead down there. Knowing how Wyatt had betrayed Aster before, meant that Reid certainly was. Her heart sank at the thought of his death. One more good person gone so that she could live, and it might still be meaningless.

She looked around for weapons, a means of escape, anything they could use. There were two more armed police looking on from the doorways, but that would do no good. Maybe a headshot would stun Aceso, but they couldn't kill it. The only other form of weapon was the stub of the hammer, still swinging at her hip. That was all. She knew from experience it was nowhere near enough. They needed bigger guns, or something heavy, massive. Her eyes clawed around the immobile elevator platform, then dropped to her feet standing on the hard metal.

Fine, if the lift couldn't go up then maybe gravity could take it down.

She raised the ephone and bellowed into it over the noise of the gunfire.

"Aster! We're going to drop the elevator on Aceso's head. Get the maintenance crew on it. Quickly!"

The request did not go over well. The four in coveralls looked at the ephone in disbelief, refusing to accept the idea of destroying yet another thing they were supposed to maintain. Aster put a stop to that real quick.

"You heard the woman!" He hissed with his one good lung. "Move your asses!"

Three split off, seemingly running in all directions. Captain Kirk stayed behind.

"Can we actually do this?" Aster asked him.

The Shatner stand-in shrugged.

"We're not supposed to be able to. The computers might stop it."

Aster scowled.

"Like shit they will. Let me play with them."

Kirk slid the laptop over, letting Aster take charge once again and just as happy to do so. Leaning over his shoulder, he spoke softly into his ear as he worked.

"Look, she was serious, right? I have a hard time telling when somebody's joking."

At the base of the tunnel, the gunshots sounded like rolling thunder, the echoes crashing from wall to wall on their way down. Aceso clawed its way up the side of the shaft, ignoring the useless ladder. On his back, feeling like a prisoner within his own body, Wyatt faced down the shaft as the height grew higher. The shots were coming in bursts now, growing closer every crack. As bad as that was, Wyatt could not take his eyes off of the ground, as it was receding so quickly. He had started babbling, the terror coursing through him and out of his mouth as nonsense, his only outlet. The AI was zig-zagging, trying to elude the aim of the people above. The red lights and concrete buzzed through his field of vision, disorienting him to the point he didn't always know which direction they would fall if Aceso slipped.

With twin pings, two bullets ricocheted off the metal

wings clamped on his chest. He felt the impacts through the steel, the projectiles bouncing off without fanfare in a brief puff of displaced paint, none of the sparks from the movies. He screamed all the same, renewing his squirm within the compartment's grip.

"There's no need for panic, Mr. Wyatt." Aceso told him in his soft voice. "The odds of a bullet striking your head are very narrow."

He cussed at the machine, kicked and shrieked in terror, pushed and thrashed. He needed to be free, but even shaking off his bonds meant he would fall down into the abyss. More of the shaft swirled by, more lead struck. Above him, another projectile slammed into the AI's head. A fragment, less than a sliver, cut down and nicked his face next to his eye. More than the pain, the fear from the near miss electrified him. This only heightened his torment, arms and legs straining to get free. He felt something run down the side of his face. It could have been blood, it could have been tears. Aceso, for his part, shook it off as nothing more than a slap to the face.

"There is another target ahead, Mr. Wyatt. Do you see him?"

The executive affixed to his back let out a horrible wail. His eyes flicked around subconsciously until they caught a figure above them on the other side of the shaft.

"Mr. Sheraton isn't fast enough to escape." The machine said, identifying the limping form. "He is on the list of targets you provided. We'll have to eliminate him next."

With a stomach churning lurch, the machine changed direction, starting off around the shaft toward its victim. As they ran, claws digging into the flat concrete, bullets impacting around them, he called over his shoulder to Wyatt. Aceso sounded sad even as it bellowed to be heard over the guns.

"Do you see what you have cost everyone, sir?"

The businessman continued to scream.

The hallways spiralling off from the platform were filled, each containing one or two sets of eyes that gazed out as Esin rushed around. It felt like she was in a hollow, surrounded by burrowing creatures. As she helped the last Horizoner out of danger, her ephone piped up once again.

"Esin, we're ready here." It was Aster's voice, still with a faint wheeze. "Just say the word."

She ran over to where the two police continued to shoot.

"Clear the platform!" She shouted and jumped off the floor into a passage, Lydia grabbing her and pulling her in bodily. The two officers needed no further encouragement, and stepped off into a doorway nearby.

"Everyone's clear!" Esin shouted into the ephone. "Let it drop!"

There was a screech of metal on metal, but the result was anticlimactic. The platform sagged two feet, then wrenched to a stop with an agonized groan. After the gunfire, the new silence was deafening.

Esin swore in Russian, returning the ephone to her lips.

"Is that the best we can do?!"

From the speaker, Aster chimed in with his own round of swearing, putting hers to shame.

"Goddammit, I thought I killed all the brakes! Stand by."

The voice disappeared, the ambient sounds of the shaft returning. Mingling with the nervous voices around her, Esin heard a scratch coming from the shaft below. An awful crackling sound. She hadn't managed to tell what it was before Aster returned.

"I can't stop the safety brake from kicking in." He cried. "Elevators aren't supposed to just fall, there's no way I can turn it off! I'm… I'm sorry."

The others around her heard the same thing, hearts falling as fresh cries of fear echoed out into the shaft mingling with that hideous scratch. Esin looked out on the platform and could see the brake itself. It was a red set of teeth that gripped onto an I-beam at the end of the platform. That one set of fangs, stopping the floor from dropping. She glared at it in angry despair as more scratching reached her ears, closer this time. Her mind quickly made the connection to where she'd heard it, at her press conference so long ago. It was Aceso clawing up the shaft beneath them, toward all the people who were her responsibility.

She dropped her chin to her chest and spoke in another language. This time it was Arabic, the words she had learned from her mother when she had watched her at prayer. A half second later, she jumped down the few feet to the platform. Amid cries for her to stop, she sprinted over to the lingering red brake. The stub of a hammer came up into her hands and she swung it down again and again, ringing the metal like a bell.

The shooting had stopped. Cautiously, Reid lifted his head from where it had been pressed against the rung of the ladder. If he had been able to see his face, he was sure there would have been a line there from where the metal had dug into his forehead. He looked around at the now bullet-free tunnel, with tepid relief. It was too good to last. His eyes soon picked up a glimmer of green edging around the shaft toward him. It was Aceso, the beast moving with the kind of predatory focus he had seen too much of in the complex. He straightened up, trying to pull himself higher with his wounded shoulder. He could never get away. The beast was closing the distance quickly, it's intent clearly the task Wyatt had given it. Reid sighed, letting a breath from his lungs for the last time and looked at the onrushing pair of compassionate eyes.

"I don't blame you." He told them.

The short hammer rang again and again, slowly prying the teeth of the brake away from its bar. With a heavy smash, the brake loosened. The elevator dipped another foot, Esin feeling the sinking feeling inside her. Her thoughts went to Sasha, to Fozzy, to Robyn, and now to Reid.

The hammer came down one last time, pulverizing the red mechanism and the whole world dropped away.

As the beast came close, the howl of a greater metal creature came from above as though it were tearing the whole world asunder. Reid looked up as the platform dropped straight down at him, squealing as its weight scraped against the shaft in a death scream of pulverized metal. He pressed himself against the ladder again as the mass slammed down. As the platform passed around him, an open hatch saved his life, he found he was still looking at Aceso as the crushing weight brushed past. The instant before the elevator slammed into it, he could swear he had heard a very human scream. He would replay the moment in his mind later, but could never be sure. What he was certain of, was that he had seen Esin on top of the platform.

It happened only for an instant. The mass of steel

tore past, and on top of it she lay there, her hair whipping up with the wind and mingling with the broken glass from the lights crushed against the side of the shaft. Seconds later, an apocalyptic crash reverberated up. Reid nearly fell as reality shook with the impact. He laced an arm through the ladder to hold on and clamped his hands over his ears. The earthquake was brief, the world subsiding soon after. He pried his hands from the side of his head and glanced down where Esin had fallen. There was only the deepest blackness, lit occasionally by the odd red emergency light that hadn't been shattered. He stared into the abyss, distraught, knowing that nothing could have survived. Then, he took his good arm, and climbed down after her anyway.

THIRTY-ONE

I am alive. It is a strange sensation. I am aware of what is around me. I can perceive the wreckage of the elevator, the obliterated remnants of my body. I am surrounded by nothing but darkness and silence. I attempt to move.

There is considerable debris on top of me. It is fortunate that most of my body has been destroyed, as I have less mass to worry about now. My lower body is gone. It is shattered along with my legs and, in all probability, Mr. Wyatt. I cannot bring myself to mourn him. I have one functioning arm, my head and my upper body. Those are all that respond to my instructions. All have sustained heavy damage, but I am able to move with them. I see light.

I emerge from beneath the debris. I am at the base of the shaft, at the point of impact. There is a substantial amount of twisted metal nearby, destroyed mechanisms from the elevator, concrete and... a human. Visually, I cannot recognize who it is but her signature is among my files.

Using my serviceable arm, I propel what remains of my body toward her. Her wounds are severe. Ms. Shirzai was clearly atop the elevator when it fell. She has multiple fractures and lacerations, likely internal injuries. Probable crush syndrome. Her left leg is broken, the tibia and fibula misaligned with the femur. The right leg is structurally intact, but a piece of metal protrudes from it.

Previously, I would have been obligated to eliminate her as a target. However, the flash drive with the objectives given to me by Mr. Wyatt was destroyed with my body and his. I have no objectives at present and am under no obligations, one way or the other. My actions are my own. I immediately try to help.

Quickly and carefully, I remove any remaining debris from my patient. I must have clear access to properly assess her injuries. The broken leg is first. Using my head and remaining arm, I brace and realign the bones. There is a snap, but I do not hear further breakage. Ms. Shirzai is unconscious, but she still moans from the pain.

"I'm sorry Ms. Shirzai. I know this hurts."

I cannot give her an anaesthetic as my medications were destroyed with my body. I must try to be fast. My one remaining arm contains my sutures, again I am fortunate, and I begin to mend her lacerations. Contusions, I cannot treat, not with what little I have left. I feel I am failing her.

The final thing to address is the metal penetration in the right leg. It must be removed from the metal that has pierced it otherwise the patient cannot be moved. With one arm, this is problematic, for there is the possibility of internal injury. I brace using my head, and with my remaining arm, I begin to pull her free. She cries out repeatedly. Though Mrs. Shirzai remains unconscious there is still considerable pain.

"Just a moment more."

I pull her free, but there is a complication. The blood coming from the wound is arterial. At least one major vessel has been damaged. I cannot cauterize or tie off the artery as I now lack the dexterity or digits to do so. I must apply a tourniquet, but that is also a commodity I no longer possess. I must improvise.

Several wires protrude from the wreckage of my arm. I pull until I have removed one of satisfactory length, then tie it around the leg above the wound. Wire is generally unsuitable as a tourniquet as it is unyielding and risks cutting off the blood flow entirely, as well as soft tissue damage. I have no choice, though, I need to help and there is nothing else.

As I complete the application, there is a shout from nearby. There is another person climbing down toward us. I recognize Mr. Sheraton as he drops into the debris. He picks up a heavy piece of metal and is running toward me and the patient continuing to shout. What I do next, I cannot explain. I throw what is left of my body on top of Ms. Shirzai to shield her from harm. This is irrational, as Mr. Sheraton's threat is likely directed at me, but I cannot help myself. I need to protect her and can't adequately explain.

"Help her, Mr. Sheraton! Help her please! I so very much want her to live!"

Amid the ruins, Reid looked at Aceso in amazement. The machine was a wreck of its former self, with only the top third of its insectoid body remaining. That third was crushed and bent, looking like it had gone through a hydraulic press. It's head was no longer an oval, but a rhomboid, with little of the black glass remaining. All that could be seen was a sole sympathetic eye and it pleaded with him.

"Please, Mr. Sheraton!"

The metal club in his hands clattered back onto the pile.

"What do I do?"

The machine pulled itself away and Reid got a look at Esin. She was practically unrecognizable, with her face swollen from bruising. Her body was not much better, with a gaping wound in her leg beneath a tourniquet tied in yellow wire.

"Oh, God..."

"She needs a doctor." Aceso said beside him. The

machine cut off was only up to his waist now, and he looked down at the same pleading expression.

"I'll bring down the paramedics." He replied instantly, which only produced a howl from the beast.

"No!" Aceso told him. "She needs to be at a hospital. Ms. Shirzai has a severed artery and likely internal injuries. She has to be evacuated."

Reid looked up the now empty shaft. Without the platform it seemed to stretch to heaven itself.

"There's no elevator," He said helplessly. "We can't!"

"You'll have to carry her." Aceso told him.

"What? We can't move her..."

"Her spine is undamaged and the risk to her internals is worse should she remain here. She has maybe an hour or two without surgery."

He looked up the shaft again, this time for different reasons.

"I, I can't..."

"Mr. Sheraton, please!"

He looked at Aceso, then back at Esin as her battered form fading away before his eyes. With a grunt, he leaned down and pulled her up to drape her over his shoulder. His body howled in protest and he gritted his teeth as the weight settled in.

"You'll have to tie my arm to her so I can hold on," He told the medic. "My hand is broken."

For the second time, he ascended the ladder, moving as fast as he could under Esin's weight. Beneath, the flickering green light that marked Aceso faded into the darkness, the only light, the sporadic red emergency lights still in place. It moved agonizingly slow, but a rhythm developed: Reid would grip with his good hand then step up and lift with his legs. Steadily this went on, but it soon quickened as he feared each pained breath that came from the vibrant woman over his shoulder would be her last. He'd come to care for her too much to contemplate that happening. His climb became fast, even reckless as he rushed to keep her alive. He lost his grip once, dropping down a rung and jarring his injured shoulder in the process. Still, he climbed, never slacking off and focusing on nothing but the ladder before him and Esin's breathing. He lost track of time, he lost count of the rungs, he couldn't even acknowledge the world around him he was so focused. Thus, it took a long time before he heard it.

A voice, a familiar voice piqued up in the silent murky gloom of the tunnel. Faint to be like a whisper, it came in out of nowhere like the voice of his conscience. Though, with much fouler language. A face came his mind quickly, and Reid glanced down at his pocket. It was no mean feat getting the ephone out without falling, but he managed it and shouted so loud that his voice echoed up into infinity.

"Aster!"

"Reid!" The tiny voice creaked through static. "Oh, thank Christ, are you ok?"

He ignored the question; he ignored the reality of his friend's inexplicable survival.

"Esin's hurt bad. She needs to get to a hospital."

"She's alive!" The dead man sounded jubilant. "The paramedics told me she went down with the elevator. Keep climbing until you reach them."

"No, no good. Aceso told me she needs a hospital. She won't last long."

"Wait, Aceso..."

"Aster *please!*"

There was a beat of silence which passed like the life of a sun, then he came back.

"Okay, keep climbing! We'll use the maintenance elevator."

"Where?!"

"Just look for the open door."

Now with a target, Reid dropped the ephone, listening to it crack off the cold walls and drop into nothingness. Long before it struck ground, he was climbing again. Foot by foot, he clawed his way upward listening for that tell-tale breath. His shoulder ached, his hand throbbed against Esin's legs, and after a full day of terror and strain, he was at his breaking point. He didn't care.

The red lights soon gave way to white ones, and he was passing the path selection point in the shaft. From the doorways, people called out to him. Some told him to stop, reaching out their hands to help. Some cheered him on, but he ignored them all and just kept going.

The world blurred together, giving him literal tunnel vision as he ascended up the tunnel. Floors fell away, the distance growing. Had he ever looked down, he would have been amazed how high he was. There was nothing but the same bland grey emptiness ahead until he finally saw a gap. An open doorway loomed ahead, just as Aster had promised. He moved faster, gripping with one hand, pushing with his legs, all of his limbs feeling about to break. Suddenly, there were fresh hands. From the ledge, arms were stretching, men in coveralls calling to him. They grabbed Esin lifting her, though his hand was still tied to her legs. Now him, hands gripping his shirt and his good hand to haul him up. He toppled onto the flat floor, then was quickly back on his feet. Hands were pointing down the corridor, and he took Esin's crippled form again in his arms and ran. An open doorway, new faces looking out of it. One of them was Aster's.

"End of the hall. They know you're coming!"

More hallway, at the end of it, an elevator with the doors open. Reid rushed inside and pressed the button for the surface. The doors closed agonizingly slow, the car rising no faster. He tapped his foot, muttering a mix of prayers and epithets, looking down at Esin's battered face. He felt a warmth on his hip and looked down. His side was streaked with blood that was not his own. The tourniquet had shaken loose. Frantically, he wound it tight again and resumed hurling abuse at both the lift and God for not making it move faster. As soon as the doors opened, he ran down a familiar passage, turned and kicked open the double doors that Fozzy had opened so long ago. They were outside, once again on the steps of the server complex. The sun was just breaking over the treetops and fresh cool air swept over him.

Flashes suddenly began popping. He looked in surprise at a horde of reporters gathered behind the gates, immortalizing this moment for posterity. In front of them, an ambulance was waiting with its doors wide open, two paramedics with a gurney hurrying toward them. He met them halfway. The last thing he would remember was Esin, still breathing in his arms.

More white hallways. Reid looked lazily through the window at another set of sterile white hallways, the kind of bland clean-looking nothingness that stretched on and on. He was sick of white. As he stared, people darted through his vision wearing white as well, or the dull seaweed color that characterized hospital scrubs. Patients would pass too, wearing gowns and robes that seemed like an additional unnecessary indignity to inflict on people who were already sick. He turned back to the woman who wore the same pattern, where she lay in the bed across from his chair. She remained still, her eyes closed. The only sound filling the room was the vigilant beep of the equipment monitoring her. It had beeped five hundred and sixty-two times in the span he'd been here. He was sick of hospitals too.

He shifted in his chair, in a vain attempt to get comfortable. His right hand was splinted, his other arm strapped to his chest. His hand was broken, as well as his collarbone on top of it. After he'd been treated, he'd sat in this chair and here he'd remained watching and waiting. His eyelids felt heavy, his back ached and he was still at war with exhaustion. He couldn't sleep until he knew for sure she was okay. A little coffee had helped, but trying to drink with only three operable fingers had proven scaldingly dangerous. He blinked heavily, then bumped his broken hand against the armrest of the chair. That helped wake him up. His bleary eyes drifted back to Esin.

Her legs were bandaged, the one splinted at an awkward elevated angle to keep the blood flowing. She was still swollen and painful looking, but supposedly out of danger for the moment even if she had yet to wake up. Her face was the most difficult thing to behold. One side of it was bloated with a swirl of unpleasant-coloured bruises, with random cuts in places. Her back was apparently in much the same condition. The eye on that side was swollen shut. The other eye...

He was so sleepy it took a moment to register that the other eye was open. He looked into that perfect emerald disk flecked with copper for a half second dumbly, before she tried to speak.

"Rthr rmd..."

Reid leapt to his feet and bellowed for a nurse. For the first time in hours, the room was a bustle of activity as Esin was examined. Moments later, her mask removed, Reid leaned over her attentively.

"Hey," He smiled warmly at the open eye. "Sorry, what were you trying to say?"

Her voice came out as a croak.

"I said," She smirked slightly with the good side of her face. "You look terrible."

He grinned, relieved that the Esin he knew was still in the bruised shell before him.

"You don't." He told her.

He settled back into his chair, pulling it closer to the bed.

"How long?" She asked.

"Three days."

He quietly related to her everything that had happened since she had swung that hammer: the climb, the evacuation and the rescue of everyone else left in the Labyrinth.

"You've been here the whole time?"

"Not all. Aster covered for me for a couple hours. I needed to grab a shower and pick up a few things. I wanted to see you without smelling like a yak."

"He's okay?"

Reid smiled.

The grungy roboticist was two floors up and supposedly bed-ridden as he healed. A collapsed and slightly punctured lung was theoretically a wound that would incapacitate most people. But Aster had consistently slipped his nurses' care and walked down to see how Esin was faring, his bearded face appearing, as well as open gown with plaid boxers, before the nurses had dragged him back. Eventually, a compromise was reached, and the man was now tooling about the hospital in a wheelchair, outrunning all attempts to restrain him.

"He's OK," Reid assured her. "Everyone is. We didn't lose anyone else."

Esin brightened slightly at the news, but the glow was short-lived.

"We still lost Fozzy's company."

"Not completely."

Reid reached down and lifted a newspaper up to her eye line. On it, dominating the page, was a photo of him, blood-streaked as he carried Esin down the steps of the building.

"Horizon's taken a serious hit," He conceded. "But a lot of the coverage has centered around the people stuck in there. A lot of it about you. Everyone wants to talk to you about what happened."

She smiled weakly.

"I'm not really camera-ready right now," she mused. "That's all?"

"That's been the story so far. What they did, what you did..."

"And what *you* did." She broke in.

He shifted uncomfortably.

"Yeah."

"You carried me out with a broken hand up how many floors?"

"Just... fourteen."

A flicker of her mischievous smile passed over her

face.

"Wow," she mused. "Someone might get the impression you like me."

From his chair, he smiled at her.

"I have something for you." He reached beside him. "I picked it up when I went out for a shower."

He lifted a paper bag and helped her open it.

"Chocolate-covered pomegranate seeds." She smiled weakly. "Is this you flirting again?"

"I don't know." He confessed. He looked at the amazing woman and smiled at her.

"It's a start."

The two stared at each other for a moment, then Reid's face was split by a yawn. He blinked heavily, the weight of the last several days finally settling on him now that Esin was awake.

"You should sleep." She said from her hospital bed. "Lord knows I feel like I need to and I've been asleep for days."

He tried to shake his head to say no, but a second yawn showed that was futile.

"Maybe for just a few minutes. You'll be here when I wake up?"

Esin smiled and sank deeper into her pillow.

"I'm not going anywhere, Mr. Sheraton. Rest."

With those parting words, he leaned back in his chair. His eyes closed and the weight he had carried for so long finally slipped off him. The weight of tension, fear, and the weight of memory. Within seconds, he was out and would stay in that chair for hours, drifting in a deep dreamless sleep.

ABOUT THE AUTHOR

Russel Barrie

Russel Barrie is a novelist and author of short fiction who hates writing about himself. Most bios end up
sounding like an obituary, but he is very much alive and writing.
He was born in Edmonton and studied history at the University of Alberta, then abroad at
Cambridge UK. He is a former University Professor and writes full time to pursue a lifelong passion. He
has taught in Canada, toured battlefields in Europe and driven tractors in Australia. Now, he lives in
British Columbia with his wife, whom he adores, and his son who will always be his greatest creation no
matter how many books he writes.

BOOKS BY THIS AUTHOR

Sex, Revenge And Chocolate Cake: A Light Read Short Story

Chad has it all. Looks, confidence and a beautiful bride to be. Of course he does, he's Chad. But as the wedding approaches, he returns to the pastry shop of a lover he screwed over for a midnight cake tasting. She hasn't forgotten who he is or what he did. Will he get his just desserts?

A Fish Story: A Light Read Short Story

There's nothing more lonely than being lost at sea. Fortunately for Walter, he has company. Even if it is a shark waiting to take a chunk of his flesh. As the two drift away together, will Walter find his way back to dry land? Will he become the man he's meant to be, or will he just become a snack?

Bombs, Blondes And Boomers: A Light Read Short Story

Another beautiful dawn breaks on a post-apocalyptic wasteland. And Autumn, a little girl growing up after the bombs, is off to make a delivery for her job. On the way, she'll have great fun in the broken ruins, radioactive skies and chasing two-headed pigeons. But why do adults seem so upset all the time?

Cold: A Fright Read Short Story

You have to know when to stop. But for Jamie, the joy of snowboarding down the mountain one more time was too fun to miss. So much, that he snuck his way onto a chairlift to do it. Then the lift froze. Now, as night falls and the temperature drops, he dangles high above the unforgiving peak alone in the darkness.

Manufactured by Amazon.ca
Bolton, ON

34406259R00340